SECOND SIGHT

Meg Henderson was born in Glasgow. She is a journalist and the author of the bestselling memoir *Finding Peggy*, and the highly acclaimed novels *The Holy City*, *Bloody Mary*, *Chasing Angels* and *The Last Wanderer*.

D0522503

SECOND SIGHT

Meg Henderson

HarperCollins*Publishers*

HarperCollins*Publishers*
77–85 Fulham Palace Road,
Hammersmith, London W6 8JB

www.harpercollins.co.uk

This paperback edition 2004

1

First published in Great Britain by Flamingo,
an imprint of HarperCollins*Publishers* 2004

Copyright © Meg Henderson 2004

Photograph of airman on inside back cover © George Blakeman

The Author asserts the moral right to
be identified as the author of this work

ISBN 0 00 655245 5

Set in Bembo

Printed and bound in Great Britain by
Clays Limited, St Ives plc

For our son, Euan, who brought us so much love and happiness,
and his wife, Suzanne, who has done the same for him.
13 November 2003

I

For a long time Nancy had been slightly embarrassed by her mother. All children are, of course, when they reach a certain age. It's part of growing up, of loosening the ties that bind, and it would be a strange world if it were otherwise, but Nancy had slightly more reason, or she thought she had until that summer when she was fifteen. For as long as Nancy could remember, her mother, Martha, claimed, on a few occasions, to have seen people no one else could see and, on more occasions, that she could see the future, and as far as twentieth-century Canada was concerned, there was a hint of madness about claims like that.

Martha had been born in Mull River, Mabou, in Cape Breton in 1865, twenty years after her grandparents, Donald and Morag MacKenzie, had arrived there from the Isle of Raasay, a streak of mainly rock between the mainland and the more famous Isle of Skye off the Scottish west coast. When they got off the ship that had brought them to Canada, Donald and Morag already had three sons, the fourth, Ruairidh Beag, Martha's father, had been born within weeks of their arrival in the home of Donald's uncle and aunt in Mull River. Ruairidh Beag was the only one not to have been born in Scotland, but he had been conceived there and so grew up just like the others, attached to the old country of his forefathers, speaking Gaelic and talking of the 'home' he would never see. Well, not physically see, anyway.

In their new home, the MacKenzies, as all migrant families tend to do, still lived as they had in their native country. For the Cape Breton Scots the fact that the landscape so closely resembled 'home', made it that much easier to keep their culture not only alive but intact. It was a God-fearing culture in the main, the lives of the people as dominated by the clergy as they had been and would continue to be in Scotland, and it was also one where music and storytelling were part of life, instead of being part of leisure. In those earlier decades Christmas wasn't celebrated in their new home, it had never been a Scottish custom and only became one in Nova Scotia in the early 1900s, the influences coming from the USA, from Scots who had intermarried with English immigrants. They had their own celebrations with the First Footing of New Year, when groups would go around beating the outsides of houses with sticks to drive out the old year, and were then invited in for a drink, a song and some storytelling. It was a simpler, more innocent time, when no one, for instance, thought those with *taibhsearachd*, or the Gift, were mad, or that the Second Sight was something to be mocked.

With each generation that passed it was inevitable that the blood and the old ways would weaken despite their best efforts; it was progress, the way of the world and Nancy was fairly typical of her time in that she no longer considered herself to be a Scot, even if she never said this to her mother. She was, after all, third-generation Canadian and, even if she didn't count her grandfather, she was certainly second-generation Canadian. She had the Gaelic and spoke it within her own family and community, but deep down she thought it old-fashioned and would have been embarrassed if anyone outside Cape Breton knew she could. She was born in Cape Breton in 1900, so she was a modern Canadian. When she was a child she had believed everything her mother had said, but as the years had passed she had come to regard her as odd. Even then she had turned a blind eye to her claims, never exactly saying she didn't believe a word, but never exactly saying that she did either. Naturally, as Nancy had grown up, she had progressed to contesting everything about her mother's beliefs, as we all have to do. All her life she had heard the tales those first arrivals had told, and she had great affection for the stories and the people who handed them down, even those she had never actually known. No one could help admiring how they had taken their futures in their hands and left their lives and families behind in the hope of finding better for their children and grandchildren. And you couldn't help feeling for them, too, as you listened to the stories of how they had embarked on those long sea journeys, knowing, as they certainly did, that not all would survive, but deep down Nancy had never regarded their tales as anything more than tales.

She knew them off by heart, of course, knew them so well that they played out in her mind like a film her ancestors had made purposely to be handed down to each generation. She had heard many times of the spring day in 1844 when her great-great-grandfather, Ruairidh Iain MacKenzie, had buried his wife, Annie MacLeod, on the Isle of Raasay, knowing as he did so that he would face other partings in the very near future; knowing this because he had decided upon it. From 1830 onwards the harsh lives of the Highland and Island people had become harsher, with crop failures, economic collapse and famine. Though they weren't aware of it, they were living near the end of the Little Ice Age, a three-hundred-year span when the world had grown colder. In Raasay, as everywhere else, every winter was bad and there was no way of knowing when the climate would improve, or, indeed, if it ever would. Between 1837 and 1839 newspaper adverts had encouraged people to leave a land where little grew and potatoes rotted. There was a place on the other side of the world where they would feel no cold, a land of promise, the Land of Gold, no less, and so *na h-eilthirich*, the emigrants, had set sail from Skye, Cromarty, Oban, Leith and Greenock for Australia. During those years Annie's health had gradually been declining and the winter of 1843 to 1844 had seen the start of the final phase of her life. She had always had a weakness about her lungs, a weakness that had been passed on to two sons who had died before reaching the age of five, but the good Lord had mercifully left the couple with one healthy child, their son, Donald. Every year Annie wheezed and fought for breath, but there was usually a break somewhere, a rest when she built up her strength again before winter brought a different kind of wheezing. Very gradually over the years, though, it seemed that there was less and less time between the different kinds of wheezing till one winter she was so bad that Old Ruaridh thought she might die before her time. And even though she had struggled through, her husband could see she hadn't fully recovered. In his mind he carried a picture of a tree with limbs and branches growing and reaching up and out, but when he thought of Annie he could see one branch dimming and wilting as though the life was slowly but certainly draining from it. At the same time he was aware of a dark shadow and a relentless feeling of cold keeping pace with Annie's growing weakness. With every bout of illness it took less to pull her down again, down deeper and for longer, and though that last winter was no worse than those gone before, Annie never recovered. By the following May her lungs had struggled for breath long enough and simply gave up. Old Ruairidh had sat by her bed, watching her chest heave and gasp, her eyes unseeing, not, he felt, in the battle to live but in the hope that each one would release her. Looking at her when the silence finally came he could see only peace and feel only relief; they had known each other all their lives and been together as man and wife too long for him to selfishly wish more suffering on her for his sake. Besides, he had known this long while by the picture of the tree branch in his mind's eye that it was her time; it couldn't be changed by man nor God.

Raasay was a long island of rock and scrub, a place with tracks but no roads, and next day the family carried Annie's body on the difficult journey by foot to Torran, then they were taken by boat down the west coast to Clachan Cemetery in the south, where her own parents lay in the shadow of the Laird's home, Raasay House. It was on the way home that Old Ruairidh finally decided to persuade his son to take his wife and family away from Raasay to a new life in Cape Breton. It had been in Ruairidh's mind for a very long time before that, of course, ever since his own brother, Sandy, had gone out to Nova Scotia twenty years before, when the Laird, MacLeod of Raasay, had turned them off their land in Hallaig, one of the few fertile areas of the island. The MacLeods liked to live high, and that took more money than the islanders could afford, so families that had worked the land for generations, were turned off it, so that it could be let instead to incomers who would pay more. Ruairidh and Annie had headed for her family home in Arnish, but Sandy had had enough of living at the whim of the greedy MacLeods and had left for Canada rather than Australia, because relatives of his wife were already settled in Cape Breton. Sandy had always been the adventurous one, even when they were boys, though Ruairidh often wondered if all younger brothers thought this of older brothers. It was Sandy who always spoke out against the MacLeods when others thought better of it, and Sandy who had gone to the fishing in the northeast as a young man, returning with more English words in his conversation than Gaelic, and also with a bride, Sarah MacFarlane, from the Isle of Mull, when no one on Raasay knew he had married. That was Sandy, if he decided on a thing then he did it. From Cape Breton he wrote regularly, describing the landscape as not unlike Scotland, but the Scotland of their dreams rather than the reality he and Sarah had left behind, where it was possible to own your own land, to be your own master. They had worked hard in the Mabou Highlands, clearing vast woods to make fields to start growing crops and keep beasts, but the hard work provided a good life instead of hand-to-mouth survival and fear of the future. Over the years he repeatedly asked Ruairidh to join him, but Annie wouldn't leave her elderly parents, just as her own son wouldn't go while his mother lived, and Ruairidh knew that no amount of persuasion would have changed that. It hadn't been in the future, till now.

'It's time,' he told Donald on the day of his mother's funeral. 'You have to leave this place.'

Donald looked at him with his father's brown eyes but his mother's expression, shocked at the suggestion, and on this day of all days. 'You're asking me to leave you?' he demanded. 'With my mother just dead?'

'I knew you wouldn't go while your mother was alive,' Ruairidh smiled sadly.

'And you think I'm the kind of man who'd leave now? Now that my father's on his own? That's truly what you think of me?'

'Boy,' Ruairidh sighed, 'I've survived here all these years, I'll survive when you're gone.'

'If you've survived then so will I,' Donald replied defiantly.

'No, Donald,' his father told him sternly. 'You are not listening, boy. Survival isn't enough. You have my three grandsons to consider and another on the way.' He smiled. 'There has been no lassie born in this family for many years. It will happen one day, but not for some time yet and not on Raasay. The one Morag carries will also be a son, Donald, he will be different from the others and have abilities you won't understand, and he it is who will be the father of the first MacKenzie lassie for generations. There will be another child you and Morag will be parents to,' he laughed quietly. 'You will love him as much as the others, but it's too complicated to explain now. When it happens you will remember my words and understand why I smiled. I want better for him, for all of them, and so do you. Life here will not improve, we've spent generations thinking it would, hoping that next year, or the next, we could live like human beings instead of slaves. It is time to leave here, it's the right thing to do, the only thing to do. Your uncle wants you out there, he has his own land, beholden to no man, and he and Sarah have no children to hand it down to. You know this, you have read his letters, he has written of it often. What is there to think about when I'm telling you to go?'

'Then you come too,' Donald replied. 'You're little more than sixty, men older than you have made the journey.'

'I was born here, I'll die here, Donald, that's the way of it.'

'I was born here too,' Donald persisted. 'Why is it different for me?'

'For the reasons I've given you, Donald, that you must do better for your family than I did for mine,' Ruairidh repeated quietly.

'There isn't a better father anywhere,' Donald said, looking up at him.

'I could've done better by you,' Ruairidh smiled. 'In truth, you would be doing me a kindness because all these years I have carried the guilt of providing less for you than you had a right to expect, but I gave in to your mother's tender heart when I could've forced her to join Sandy and Sarah in Canada. You are the same age now as I was when Sandy left here, I don't want you to have the regrets that I have. I gave in to your mother against my own judgement because she was the only woman in my life and I could refuse her nothing. Do you think I could leave her now?'

Donald looked away.

'When my time comes I'll take the same boat trip and be buried with her in Clachan because that's where I belong,' Ruairidh said. 'But you will take your family and go, Donald. I can see it, it is there, and I'm telling you to go with my blessing and no guilt on my account. You are my son, but that is no more than an accident of blood. Your mother was my chosen wife, I couldn't have left her in life and I won't in death, my place is with her. You are a husband yourself, you know the truth of what I'm saying to you.'

When Ruairidh MacKenzie stood on the shore a few weeks later he not only knew that he would never see his son again, but that he was losing all his remaining relatives. Yet watching the boat taking Donald, his pregnant wife, Morag, and their three sons away from Raasay, the old man felt optimism amidst the inevitable grief, because he knew the family would fare well in Nova Scotia. Donald was going because his father had told him he must, but despite the old man's absolution he carried with him his own guilt at leaving his father alone on the shore. It would remain with him till the end of his days, and he would tell the tale so often that it would become ingrained in the memories of generations of MacKenzies who would never see Raasay except in their mind's eye. Donald's emotional scar would run through them as though they themselves had betrayed Old Ruairidh, and they would carry a mental snapshot of him on that lonely shore as though they had known him all their lives, even the ones born without Old Ruairidh's gift of second sight. It was because of this that Old Ruairidh knew Donald and his family would prosper in the new land, it would take hard work and perseverance, but the MacKenzies were used to that and he had no fears that their future lay in Canada; the branch was strong.

'The branch was strong.' Nancy gritted her teeth. How many times had she heard that phrase? How long, in fact, had every family member been hearing it over the years and, like the rest of the legend, always said in that odd language? Once it would have been understandable, given that the story had to be translated from the Gaelic, but years and years later it was still told in that stilted, tight pattern, making it sound like an announcement of some great truth. The story of the MacKenzies in Cape Breton had been passed on and re-told in exactly that way down through the decades, from those who still translated English back into Gaelic, the next generation who spoke English but still thought in Gaelic, then the ones who only had it in a complementary way, as Nancy herself did. She knew it all word for word and found herself repeating it mentally as it was declaimed yet again. Even when she realised she was doing it and tried to stop she found she couldn't; it was as though it had been brainwashed into her.

'Why have we always got to speak like that?' she would demand tetchily of her mother. 'No one speaks like that any more. Why can't we just say they left this little island –'

'Raasay,' Martha interjected, 'their home. Where we all come from.'

'*This little island*,' Nancy repeated deliberately, 'because life was hard, and just as the old man hoped –'

'As old Ruairidh *predicted*.'

Nancy rolled her eyes. '– they settled down and did well. Why does it have to be this great theatrical production every time?'

Martha smiled. 'You'll tell it to your own children in exactly those words, wait and see.'

'I can promise you now that I won't!' Nancy scoffed. 'All that nonsense about him seeing the birth of the first daughter in the family for generations!'

'And that was me,' Martha said calmly.

'But it was bound to happen sometime, wasn't it? It wasn't as if he gave a date, not even a vague guess. How can you believe things like that in the twentieth century?'

'You'll see,' Martha smiled. 'Just you wait. You'll see.'

'Oh well, that's it all explained, isn't it?' her daughter replied dismissively. 'If it can't be proved we just rely on mystery again.'

2

It was the first week of June when Donald and Morag left reluctantly and tearfully. Morag, now in her fortieth year, had given birth to her third son nearly twelve years before, so this pregnancy had been a hard one, and she had been so sick during the five-week voyage that they often wondered if she and the child she was carrying would ever breathe the air of the New World. What an omen that would be, the death of a mother and child before they had arrived. Not that she was the only pregnant woman aboard, there was Mairead MacDonald and her husband, Alasdair, from Sleat, on the southern tip of Skye, a girl in her late teens who expected their first child around the same time as Morag was due. They were bound for relatives in Margeree Forks, a little farther north from the MacKenzies' destination, and seeing how scared Mairead was, so young and apprehensive about the birth and whatever lay before her in the new land, Morag had befriended her during the long journey and it was a wrench for both of them when they reached Nova Scotia in the middle of July. Sandy MacKenzie had been waiting as the ship arrived and he made straight for his nephew and his exhausted family as they struggled onto dry land and tried to find their balance after so long at sea.

'Donald MacKenzie,' he smiled, putting a hand out towards his nephew. 'I would know you anywhere, boy, you are the image of my father and of yours.'

Looking at him, Donald felt tears spring to his eyes. Part of it was relief that his family had at last arrived safely after the long, difficult journey, when all he had had to hold on to was his father's conviction that all would be well, but also because Sandy

MacKenzie looked so like the past generations of MacKenzie men on Raasay, so like Old Ruairidh, so like the man he himself would become in later years.

'You look a bit like my father yourself,' Donald managed to reply, then couldn't go on.

'Take it easy, boy,' Sandy said kindly, patting his nephew's shoulder. 'No one ever feels on top of the world after a journey like that. But you're here now, everything will look better once you've rested up.'

Sandy, at just over seventy, was ten years older than Ruairidh, but to Donald he didn't look it, he looked younger. He stood somewhere around five feet nine inches tall, but he stood straight, still with dark strands among his greying, curly hair, friendly brown eyes in a tanned face, and he had a look of health and fitness about him that his younger brother never had. Looking at him Donald saw both his father and how his father could have looked had he lived Sandy's life, as Sandy had so often urged him to do. And his uncle looked the world in the eye, Donald noticed that too, there was no hint of the fear and anxiety Ruairidh had absorbed as a way of life, because Sandy MacKenzie was a free man, living in his own house, built on his own land. It was the kind of house Donald MacKenzie could never have imagined. He had grown up in one built from stones, with earthen floors, where there was no heating save for the fire they used to cook their food, and to keep the fire lit wood had to be collected, and peats cut and carried home in baskets. Sandy and Sarah's house was a mansion compared with what he had known. The low-ceilinged house was built of wood with wooden floors and had a large central chimney and four fireplaces. It had separate rooms, a kitchen, a sitting-room and four bedrooms with the first bedsteads he had ever seen, all with their own clean linen and blankets. Even before setting eyes on the house, and tired as he was, the scenery was like an assault on Donald's senses. The Mabou Highlands lay to the north of the Bras d'Or Lakes, nestled among ancient, rolling coastal hills that led inland to the freshwater Lake Ainslie, and everywhere there were fresh meadows like blankets of green velvet. It was so like and yet unlike the landscape of Raasay that Donald could hardly stop looking around him though his eyes ached for sleep.

In the early years of the 1800s, Sarah's relatives, the MacFarlanes, had first cleared the forests to establish their six-hundred-acre farm, calling their community Mull River, in honour of the island home they had left behind, and in the following years the family had grown and the community had expanded with houses dotted here and there. Sandy and Sarah had been absorbed into the community, with the MacKenzies and the MacFarlanes forming an alliance that future generations would strengthen. The MacKenzies' house overlooked green meadows and fields, with the MacFarlane Brook meandering past on its way to the Mull River that fed into the Mabou River system. Donald, brought up on the scrub and rock of Raasay, had no means of imagining the shades of green that now assaulted his senses, the abundant fertility of the place was overwhelming; it was indeed, as his uncle had written in his letters over the years, like the Scotland of his dreams.

Within two weeks Morag had given birth to her fourth son, just as his grandfather had predicted, in the Mull River farmhouse of his great-uncle and aunt in the Mabou Highlands. He was a big, healthy child, an omen of a different sort, and he was immediately given the name of his grandfather, becoming Ruairidh Beag – Wee Rory, a tag he was to carry all his life, despite the fact that no one in Canada would ever set eyes on the original. Back on Raasay, Old Ruairidh would sit in his chair at night, sending his thoughts out, checking his family, testing the pictures he saw of them in his mind for strength and health, and he smiled contentedly as his new grandson arrived in Nova Scotia. On one of the last days of July, Donald MacKenzie and his uncle sat talking. Sandy was sitting back in his favourite chair, pipe in hand, while Donald sat forward on his, head bowed, his arms on his knees and his hands clasped in front of him. He was feeling more relaxed now that the child had been born and he and Morag were both healthy, but somehow the new arrival made him yearn for home and the people he had left behind, and, understanding his nephew's confusion, Sandy was telling him his own story of arriving in Cape Breton.

The French had come first, he explained, joining the Indians, then in 1784, a year after the British had signed a peace treaty with the Americans to end the Revolution, it had become a British Colony. What the British wanted then was to stop the French from taking over and gaining the rich fishing, so they encouraged those who had settled in America and fought on the side of the crown during the Revolution to re-settle in Nova Scotia.

'When we came here in 1825 there were English, French and even Irish people already here, folk from the Channel Islands as well, they had brought the Irish with them for the fishing, but a lot more came out after the Irish Rebellion. So life was already well set up, we didn't have the hard times those settlers did, we lived with Sarah's cousins from Mull, the MacFarlanes. Then I built a log cabin of our own with the help of the family,' Sandy told Donald. 'There were so many trees here, so much wood – still is,' he said, waving an arm towards the outdoors, his other hand still holding his pipe to his mouth. 'And we made use of it, though we have never touched the hardwoods in MacFarlane's Woods. It's about two hundred acres at the far edge of the river there. We still have more than enough for our needs, to burn – you won't be cutting peat here – and build houses and wagons. The Micmac Indians taught us how to work with the wood and how to cut the notches so that the logs would fit tightly against each other, even though they thought we were crazy for wanting to live in cabins. They live in those wickawam things. They've been good to us, probably better than we would have been to them in similar circumstances, if the truth were told. They're a gentle people, don't carry weapons, walk everywhere, too, and they know more about this land than we do. Always give them respect, Donald, that's my tip.' He puffed on his pipe thoughtfully. 'There are some who were scared of them back then, some who still treat them with suspicion now, but there was never any reason for it, they showed us nothing but kindness. Showed us how to hunt, what native plants to eat, and taught us how to survive the winters.' He looked up and smiled. 'There was no snow on Raasay that I can remember, the odd flake, but not real snow like here. Your boys will love it, feet deep it is, lasts from Christmas till the end of March, into April sometimes, and you have to wear special snow shoes to get around.' He looked at his nephew's troubled expression, knowing that he was only half-listening and why. 'Don't worry so much boy, homesickness is normal, it will pass,' he said quietly. 'Many times I've sat here and thought to myself that I'd give anything to walk on that shore where you last saw my brother, or to smell the peat smoke again, then I've thought that if I had been given the right to choose anywhere in the world to live, it would be here in Mull River. I mean that, truly. Home is what and where you make it, Donald. You'll never forget Raasay, it was the place you were born, and it wasn't the land treated us badly there, it was the lairds. This is the place your children will call home, though, and there are no lairds. You've made a good decision bringing them here.'

'It was my father who forced me,' Donald said ruefully. 'I made no decision except to obey him. As I stood on the boat looking back at him it was as if he was becoming one with the hills around him and it became harder to make him out the farther the boat got from the shore. I knew I would never see him again and the last memory I would have of him would be of not being able to see him clearly. I had this feeling in my throat and had to fight the urge to dive overboard and swim back to him, even though I can't swim.' He laughed wryly.

'It does you credit, Donald,' his uncle said, leaning forward in his chair and tapping Donald's knee sympathetically. 'Ruairidh always said you had your mother's tender heart and you did your duty by her to the end, but now you've done your father's bidding and the right thing for your family. What more can you ask?'

'That he had come with us,' Donald replied miserably.

'You must allow a man his own mind, your father most of all,

Donald,' his uncle replied. 'He had his reasons for staying and you must do him the honour of accepting that he knew his own mind and had made his own decision. I have never had sons, but I was one myself, so I'm telling you now that you have no reason to feel guilt on Ruairidh's acount.'

'Yes,' said Donald, uncertainly. 'Yes.'

He knew it to be true, he only wished he could believe it, but, as his descendants knew, in the deepest recesses of his mind, he resolved one day to bring his father here. Holding on to that thought was how he survived those first weeks and months in the New Land, and in the years to come it became Donald's passion to keep alive the stories of home, almost as though he were keeping his father alive with words until he could bring him to Cape Breton. He became known for his stories, it was his gift, people said, but it hadn't been a gift he possessed until he had left Raasay. As he worked through the seasons to come he would think of Ruairidh alone on the island and the thought would spur him on, making him determined another wouldn't pass without his father there to share it all.

3

A few weeks after Ruairidh Beag's arrival, news came from Alasdair MacDonald in Margeree Forks that he too was the father of a son, but he had become a widower at the same time; not every emigrant story was a happy one. Reading the letter, Donald remembered his father's words back on Raasay: 'There will be another child you and Morag will be parents to,' the old man had said, and he had laughed, 'you will love him as much as the others, but it's too complicated to explain now. When it happens you will remember my words and understand why I smiled.' Alasdair had named the child Padraig for his wife's father on Skye. 'I have taken his daughter, it was little enough to do in return,' he wrote. Morag was upset, Mairead had been young enough to be her daughter, and an invitation was immediately sent for Alasdair to visit Mull River as soon as he could, an invitation he immediately took up. He arrived on the doorstep with Padraig wrapped in a blanket, and Morag was overcome with sadness at the sight of them, the unsuspecting child and his young father not yet twenty, looking lost and distraught. Back on Skye he had been a fisherman and he had planned to go off with the whaling fleet in the new land, but his plans had been thrown by the death of his wife, leaving their son motherless. Even though he had relatives in Margeree Forks, he felt uneasy about leaving the child with them; neither he nor the child knew them, even if they did share the same blood. Later, with the visitors asleep, Morag had talked to Donald as she cooked in the kitchen.

'The boy can't look after himself let alone a newborn,' she said briskly. 'There's only one thing to do.'

'I was waiting for this,' Donald sighed.

'Waiting for what?' she demanded, stirring a pot so vigorously that he thought the ladle might come out of the bottom.

'I know what you're going to say, Morag, and I think you might be letting your heart talk instead of your head.'

Morag glared at him, stirring even more viciously.

'And pots are meant to have bottoms,' he smiled, 'and further-more, it's Sarah's pot.'

Morag kept stirring but turned her face away from him. 'If someone had told me you would hesitate over something like this, Donald MacKenzie, I would have hit him,' she said. A long moment passed. 'That you would refuse to help that boy and that motherless child.' She sniffed loudly. 'Refuse out of hand, too, I may say!' She stopped stirring and searched her pinny pocket for a hankie. 'Something's happened to you, Donald MacKenzie,' she said tearfully. 'Since we came here you're not the man I married.'

Donald laughed. 'Morag MacKenzie,' he said softly, 'you've been using those tricks on me since the day I met you.' He put out his arms and hugged her, laughing again at Morag's next move, a half-shrug of protest that was intended to imply that she had no intention of being hugged by an enemy, but, being but a woman, she had no choice. 'What if Alasdair doesn't want to hand over his son?' he asked.

'Don't be silly, the boy's lost,' Morag retorted. 'He's come here for help and you're refusing him,' she said again. 'Think if you were in his position.'

Donald sighed. 'I'm thinking of you,' he said. 'You're not a young woman yourself.' She glared up at him. 'I mean, you're getting used to this new life, you have three big lads to care for and now a new baby of your own and you're saying you should take on another one?'

'Are you saying,' Morag demanded in a cold voice as she pulled away from him, 'that I can't manage?'

'I'm saying, Morag, that it will help no one, the baby and Alasdair least of all, or our own lads, if you find you can't.'

'Why are men so . . . so stupid?' she demanded angrily, then she smoothed her pinny down and took a deep breath. 'There's Sarah,' she said calmly, 'and this house is less work than the one we came from.' She picked up the ladle again then put it back down, turning around to face him again. 'Besides,' she said defiantly, 'being a man you wouldn't know this, but once you've got three children you can add however many and it doesn't matter. It's like cooking for ten people and cooking for two, you use the same number of pots.'

Donald shook his head; he was beaten and he knew it. He had been beaten before he had opened his mouth, beaten, he now realised, the minute Morag had heard of Mairead's death. No wonder his father had laughed. 'It's not our house, Morag,' he said. 'I'll have to ask Sandy and Sarah before we say anything to Alasdair.'

Sandy and Sarah had been without children or grandchildren all of their married life; it had just not happened and there had been no way to change that. They had missed all the usual family joys and crises, only experiencing them at secondhand through Sarah's relatives, but it wasn't the same as having children about the house, living with them, taking over their lives as though they had always been there. They could take no real part in discussions about the ages, stages and dilemmas and would miss out on the next generation, by not being grandparents. Though they had adjusted to the situation over the years and were content with their lot, they both acknowledged the void that was in their lives. Sarah blamed herself; in those long-ago days childlessness was always blamed on the woman and the man received sympathy for being trapped into marriage by a barren wife, in the same way as if he had been trapped by a pregnant one. And it was such a shame, Sarah had told Morag, because Sandy loved children so much and had looked forward to having his own family, that was why he had built this big house, but the rooms had remained empty as she failed him year by year until time ran out. The arrival of the MacKenzie brood had brought all sorts of benefits to the old couple, Sarah now had another female to discuss family and other matters with, and they had the children, their own children. It was like an Indian summer, they were both blossoming, she said, having so much life about the place, it was as if the children were giving them their energy, so why would another one, another six – she looked at Morag, who shook her head vigorously – do anything but bring more happiness to them?

Next morning they raised the subject with Alasdair. They put it to him as though he would be doing them a favour. If he was agreeable, the wee one could stay with them while he was at sea. He would be brought up with Ruairidh Beag as though he was their own, but he would, of course, always be Padraig MacDonald, he would know who his father was and who his mother had been, and Morag was in a better position to do that than the relatives in Margeree Forks who had hardly known the girl. When he was on leave he would be welcome to stay at Mull River with them and they would look after Padraig until Alasdair's circumstances changed. What they meant was until he married again, as surely he would, but they didn't put it into words out of respect for his grief. The boy burst into tears as he tried to thank them and soon everyone was in tears. He was doing them a kindness, he was assured, there was such a big gap between Ruairidh Beag and his brothers that he'd be like an only child and they didn't want him to be spoiled. Donald glanced sideways at Sandy and Sarah as they nodded in solemn agreement and he smiled to himself; now there would be two babies for them to spoil.

As the summer hot spell of their arrival in Mull River gave way to fall, people would look at the sky and talk of 'smelling snow in the air'. The first frost arrived in September, then, as Sandy had predicted, the snow started falling at the end of December and, though they had been warned of how heavy it would be, like all newcomers the MacKenzies were awed by how much fell and lay on everything around. It covered roads and tracks, hung on trees, the great boughs sagging with the weight, the branches creaking and moaning in the wind. The snow lay on roofs in unmoving depths, then suddenly it stopped, but not a flake disappeared, it simply lay where it had fallen, a great white blanket feet thick that looked as though it would be there forever. At first it was frightening, and the newcomers found it hard to believe so much snow could be normal or could ever disappear, but there was a beauty about it too, especially at night, when the moon bathed the landscape in crisp black and white, so clear that it almost hurt the eyes, and the snow and ice sparkled and shone. It was the cold that assaulted the senses, though, a harder cold than anyone could ever imagine, the kind of cold that froze moisture within seconds, even moisture on a human body. Donald and his family were indeed lucky that they had come to an established farm and people who had been there for many years, who knew how to cope with the freezing conditions. They knew that wood had to be chopped and stored well in advance, for instance, because anyone thinking of doing so during winter would find the sweat freezing on their brow, and their hair turning stiff and white as they worked; it was easy to die in those conditions, especially when you didn't know it was happening till it had. At first it was confusing, as though the land had died, but it had only gone into hibernation in those months, as the human beings tried to wait it out and survive till spring. Many couldn't adapt, the older ones usually, and headed for warmer climes, for Australia mainly, where those earlier *na h-eilthirich* had gone earlier. Those who didn't want to or couldn't venture that far, took the easiest route out of Cape Breton on the regular boats carrying timber to Boston, while others moved south to Ontario.

'How long does it take to get used to it?' Donald asked, looking out at the alien landscape.

'Oh, that's hard to answer,' his uncle smiled, puffing on his pipe. 'It can take years for some folk, others never do, but if you stick it out you'll be singing its praises one day. Take Iain MacAilean, Bard MacLean as he is now. He went from Tiree to Pictou County in 1819 when he was thirty-two years old and was so disappointed in what he found that he sent his songs and poems back to his family as warnings not to follow him here. The work of clearing trees for the plough was too hard and exhausting and the winters were hell, he was so bitter that they say he actually put people off coming out. Ten years later he was writing a different kind of poetry altogether, verses in praise of his new home, he had so much love for the place that there was nowhere else on earth he would rather be. I dare say you'll be the same one day.'

Donald looked around at him and grimaced doubtfully. Sandy laughed. 'The sea freezes, too, you know,' he said. 'It's so thick that people drive horses and carriages over it, on the lake there, too, though it took me a long time to trust it, I have to say. The young ones have no bother,' he smiled, 'the ones born to it especially. To Ruairidh Beag and Padraig there it will be all they have ever known, it will be home to them. And the other lads will settle down to it soon enough, there's not a lad I know who doesn't like snow, and they'll pick up the new ways without thinking about it. For you and Morag, though,' he grinned, 'it will take a little longer, but when you see what this new land has to offer, you won't mind the winters.'

And just as Sandy had predicted, the MacKenzie brothers loved the frozen winters of their new home. Ruairidh Beag, who had never *not* seen snow before, took the whole thing in his stride, while Padraig looked a little apprehensive, watching Iain, Calum and Colin dashing about in the white stuff, or trying to, before the weight of it dragged them down and left them lying there, caked in it, gasping and laughing. Ruairidh Beag was held in Granny Sarah's arms, a smile on his gummy mouth, his dark eyes bright, watching his brothers play and occasionally he would clap his hands in delight, while the fair-haired, blue-eyed Padraig looked on quietly. Donald felt differently about this son, he realised, watching Ruairidh Beag as he watched his older brothers, though he wasn't sure why this was. It was partly because of the long gap between the other three and him, he knew, he had time to enjoy him, free from the survival anxieties he had felt on Raasay with the others, and Ruairidh Beag was the bridge between the old home and the new one, conceived in the old, carried across the ocean and born in the new, maybe that was it. And there was his father's blessing on the boy before he was born, that he would be different from the others and have abilities Donald wouldn't understand, the old man had probably known the child would be named for him, too. Donald smiled, watching him.

'He has it, that one,' Sandy nodded towards the child, adding his own smile. 'He has, has he not, Sarah?'

'Oh, he has, he has,' Sarah nodded, smiling down at Ruairidh Beag as she rocked to and fro with him in her arms. 'He has that faraway look sometimes. We say it often, don't we Sandy? "That one's seeing more than we can." Don't we say just that, Sandy?'

'You mean you think he has the Second Sight?' Donald asked. Sandy and Sarah laughed aloud and the baby in Sarah's arms turned to look at them, then at his father, and he laughed too.

'Of course he has,' Sandy said. 'Look at that wise wee face there.'

'Look at him,' Donald laughed to his wife, drawing Morag's attention reluctantly away from her three older sons. This snow might well be as normal here as everyone said it was, but it was new to Morag and she wasn't at all sure no harm would come to her boys.

'What, Donald?' she asked, quietly. 'What is it you're saying?'

'They're saying this new boy of yours has the Second Sight.'

'Well of course he has,' Morag replied impatiently, her attention returning once more to the joyful scenes outside.

'You think so, too?' Donald asked.

'Donald, I've never understood how the son of a man with the Gift can be so dense,' Morag replied, and at her side Sandy and Sarah laughed aloud again.

'I must say,' Donald complained sheepishly, 'you two seem to be getting a lot of fun out of me today.'

'Aye, well,' Sandy grinned, 'my own blood you are, but I have to admit there are times when you're not very bright right enough, as Morag says.'

Morag nodded. 'Haven't I told you more times than I can

remember, Donald, that he will look into the distance sometimes and you know he's seeing something? And the times when I've heard his voice in the night and got up to look in on the two of them, and Padraig is always asleep, but there's this one, for all the world as though he's holding a conversation with someone. Haven't I always said that?'

'Aye, but all mothers think their babies are doing something no other baby ever did,' Donald said defensively.

'And I'd pick this one to be daft about, would I,' Morag demanded, 'when I have three before him? You don't think I'd know if one was different from the others?'

Standing at the window Sandy leaned towards his nephew. 'I think you've lost this one,' he said in a stage whisper. 'I've had a wife longer than you have, Donald, it's my opinion you should just surrender now.'

It wasn't that Donald was rejecting the idea of his son having the Gift, he didn't think in those terms. He had grown up witnessing his father's ability to see things in his mind that others couldn't; there was nothing mystical about it, it was part of who his father was and his father was far from being a fanciful man. The Second Sight and those who had it were not regarded as strange or deranged, it was a perfectly natural trait that ran through families as surely as hair colour, or an ability to play the fiddle, and it was deeply respected by those it had missed. He was trying not to jump to conclusions about his son, though. He knew his father's gift was a burden as well as a blessing, he had watched him in distress about the knowledge he had so many times and, though he dearly wanted this child to have a connection with the old man back at home beyond carrying his name, he also had a father's natural wish for his son to have a free, happy life. He didn't possess the Gift himself and had always felt glad to be released from the responsibilities it imposed, assuming that one of his brothers who had died in childhood might have been the one intended to carry them. What he was also trying to do, though, as the father of four, no, five sons, was not to feel favour for one in particular, in case that feeling should transmit itself to the others, Padraig in particular. He loved his children, all his children, there would always be equality in his affections and actions towards them, but inside his heart he knew Ruairidh Beag would always be special.

4

After the hard-packed snow had melted there was still frost the following April, though Sandy had said it could still come back right up to the full moon in June, when the flies arrived. It was like being hit by a different kind of blizzard: black flies, deer flies, mosquitoes, anything with wings and biting parts flew in to Mull River and attacked every living creature. 'They'll be gone by August,' everyone said, like a mantra. In May and June the air was filled with yet another snowfall, the flying blossoms of apple, lilac, cherry and maple trees, with strawberry, raspberry and blueberry flowers adding to the glorious storm; just seeing it and smelling the air lifted the heart, before the dry, hot spell set in again. For Donald and his family this marked their first year in their new home and, to Ruairidh, his first birthday in the house where he had been born. His older brothers were gradually joining Donald in working the farm, and just as gradually Sandy was taking a back seat. He was still there to make suggestions and guide Donald and his sons till they knew the land as well as he did himself. He hadn't brought them all this way to rule them, he wanted to hand everything to the next generation of MacKenzies, and the next, and, as the years passed, there was an air of contentment and satisfaction about him as he watched it happen. Working less meant he had more time to spend with Ruairidh Beag and Padraig as they grew from babies to toddlers and then became small boys, and the man who had never had children became a devoted grandfather. Sandy and the two boys would wander around chatting to each other, taking delight in anything that interested the other. The closeness to the boys was, after all, an experience Sandy had never had before and never thought he would have, so he felt blessed to have it now, in his twilight years, and when he wasn't talking to them he was talking about them.

'He's such a quiet wee lad, Padraig,' he told Sarah, as they sat together at the end of the day. 'He has such a gentle nature, and they're good together, aren't they?'

Sarah looked up from her needlework and nodded. 'There's no jealousy between them,' she smiled. 'If you give one some maple toffee he'll make sure there's some for the other one.'

'They have a deep attachment,' Sandy agreed. 'I suppose one day Padraig's father will come here and say he wants to take him away for good.'

'I suppose so,' Sarah replied.

'It'll be like losing a bit of myself when he does,' he sighed, and puffed at his pipe.

'But it's his right,' Sarah said quietly.

'Aye, I know that, and who would deny young Alasdair some happiness after all he's been through? Every time he comes back from a trip and sees the boy you can tell how much he misses him, and the sadness as he leaves again, well, I have to confess, I have to look away.'

'I sometimes wonder how the two of them will do being separated. They've been together almost since birth, it's harder to think of Ruairidh Beag without Padraig than without Iain, Calum and Colin. I think it's Padraig I would worry about most, I think Ruairidh Beag is the strong one.' Sarah mused. 'I think that one could withstand a lot more than most grown-ups.'

'I know what you mean, he has a way with him,' Sandy said affectionately. 'I don't rightly know how to describe it. He's always talking while Padraig says very little, yet he has a kind of stillness about him, too, for all the talking, a strong stillness, if you see what I mean. Yet Padraig is the one for animals, they just come up to him and he talks to them as natural as he would to you and me. He doesn't have to coax them, they just follow him about.'

'Maybe it's because he doesn't make a fuss,' Sarah smiled proudly, as she struggled to thread a needle. 'Neither does Ruairidh Beag, they're not loud, they don't run about wild, shouting and yelling and causing nothing but trouble like other lads, they have no need of that nonsense. Mind you, when Ruairidh Beag does talk, he speaks his mind. I fancy that will bring him trouble one day, but he'll handle it, he's a clever one, all right.'

'That's true,' Sandy mused. 'It's that . . . that . . . stillness he has about him,' he repeated as though lost for words. He sucked thoughtfully on his pipe. 'Has he told you about the *cailleach*?' he asked.

Sarah shook her head without looking up from her work.

'We were down by the brook today. I was showing Padraig how to cut wood with the grain rather than against it. You know how he likes wood, always trying to carve birds and things, and there was a blue jay sitting on a branch only inches away from him, and he's talking to it softly and it's looking at him, turning its head this way and that, almost like it knew what he was trying to do. Anyway, Ruairidh Beag was a little way from us and I could hear him laughing as though there was someone with him. I asked who he was talking to and he said it was the old woman. Padraig and I looked at each other and shrugged. "We can't see anyone, Ruairidh Beag," I said, and he laughed like I was having a joke with him. "What does she look like?" I asked. "Like Granny Sarah," he says, "only different." She's his other granny, he says, and she comes and talks to him all the time. "Look," he says, "she's just *there*. We'll have to wait for her a minute, she's old and she gets out of breath." And he stands there waiting and looking from me to Padraig to where the *cailleach* is, or isn't, and can I really not see her, he asks. Padraig never sees her, he says, as if that's perfectly all right for Padraig, but is there maybe something bad about my old eyes or what? And he looks at me with those big, solemn eyes, really worried that mine aren't working.'

Sarah laughed. 'Does he know who it is?'

'He's on the right track. He described Annie to perfection,

though he doesn't know that. I asked him if he had seen her before and he said she had always been there, when he was in his cot she sang songs to him, though she had to stop sometimes to catch her breath.'

Sarah looked up. 'Morag told me that he sings songs in his bed, songs from home that she doesn't know all the words to, but he does.'

Sandy nodded. 'He remembers seeing the *cailleach* on Raasay, too, describes the house in Hallaig though he never actually saw it, and the one in Arnish, though he never lived there, never lived on Raasay, come to that. He was telling me about cutting the peats and about the rain and the cold, and him not four years old and never set foot on the place, yet you would swear, listening to him, that he had lived there himself.' He puffed on his pipe. 'My own father used to talk of his grandmother who saw people, but I never heard of anyone else who did.'

'Maybe it's just Donald's stories he's heard, you know how Donald likes to talk about the old place. Maybe that's all it is. If it's what you're suggesting it's a terrible thing to lay on a child, a heavy burden to carry, Sandy.'

'But if it's there, it's there,' Sandy replied quietly. 'I think he's a special one, our Ruairidh Beag.'

When they were five years old, Ruairidh Beag and Padraig were walking in the fields with Donald and Grandpa Sandy, inspecting the beasts, keeping an eye on the ones due to calve soon, as all good cattlemen do. Suddenly Ruairidh Beag turned around as though someone had called his name, and stared back at the house up on the hill.

'Look,' he said, pulling his father's sleeve with one hand and pointing with the other. 'Look.'

The others looked where he was pointing but saw nothing.

'What do you see, wee one?' Sandy asked, stepping near to the boy and laying a hand on his shoulder.

'It's the *cailleach*,' he smiled, 'the other granny. Can you not see her?' He waved happily. 'The *bodach*'s with her, the old man, look,

he's waving.' The boy tugged even harder on his father's sleeve.
'It's you they're waving to,' he said excitedly. 'Wave back!'

Donald found himself waving though he could see no one.

'What is the *bodach* like?' Sandy asked.

'Like you, Grandpa Sandy, a lot like you. Look,' he said,
dancing with delight, 'they're smiling to us. They're going away,
they've just come to say goodbye. Wave then, they're waiting
for you to wave back!' At that he grasped Sandy's hand too and
made him and Donald wave to the figures they couldn't see up
by the house.

'You know what I think?' Sandy said quietly to Donald.

Donald nodded. 'It's my father,' he said. 'My father's died on
Raasay.'

And so the tale continued, many weeks passed before news came
that Old Ruairidh had died on Raasay at just the time his special
grandson saw him with his other granny, waving goodbye to their
family. When he was asked some time later if he ever again saw
the old woman who sang Gaelic songs to him in his cot, Ruairidh
Beag had replied logically, 'No, of course not. She was just waiting
for the *bodach*, then they went away together.'

And when she was a child Nancy knew it and believed it word
for word, of course she did; why would anyone make up stories
like that? Besides, Ruairidh Beag was her grandfather, he was
a good and honest man and when he saw things he presented
them without any fuss, it was just how it was. It didn't happen
regularly, in fact he had only seen people a few times in his long
life and there was no saying when it would happen or when he
would have some pre-knowledge. It was how the Gift was, he
said, he had no control over it and sometimes wished he didn't
have it, but there was nothing he could do about it, and often
he would wonder aloud why he would know one thing and not
another. Sometimes he would look at a stranger and know what
had happened in his past life and what would happen in his future,
yet there were events within his own family affecting his nearest
and dearest that took him completely by surprise. Nancy would

sit by his side and question him about it in a way she would never question her mother.

'Do you never feel afraid when you see someone?'

'No,' her grandfather replied. 'You see, Nancy, when I see them I have no reason to think it's odd. They're just like you or me, you can't see through them or anything like that, they're solid people.'

'But when you were small,' Nancy persisted. 'Weren't you scared then?'

'And why would I be?' he asked. 'They didn't mean me any harm, they came to me because they knew I could pass on some message, that was all. It's just a thing I have. I often think it must be a thing everyone once had, but over the centuries they've cluttered up their minds with other things and now they don't even know that it exists, never mind that they once had it. For some reason there are people like me who have kept it, maybe it was stronger in us, I don't know. My brother, Padraig, now he was a fine musician, voice like an angel, and he could carve wood like one too, you only have to look around the house where you were born to see that. Made fiddles so beautiful it was a shame to let a hand touch them to get music out of them.'

'He played them, though, didn't he?' Nancy asked. 'People still talk about Padraig's fiddles and Padraig's music, don't they?'

'They do indeed,' Ruairidh Beag said with pride. 'He made this big fireplace as a wedding present for your grandmother and me, and have you ever seen anything more beautiful?' He pointed to the fireplace with his pipe. 'Look at the birds and animals, and the flowers, you can see every petal of the blossoms, and the trees are so real you feel you could take a walk and recognise each one, in fact you probably could. He couldn't teach it to me, though,' he laughed at the memory. 'He tried, but it just made him angry. "You're being cruel to the wood, Ruairidh Beag," he used to say. "Put it down, put it down!" and he'd look at me as if he was in pain himself. I only had the one gift but he had two and that was one of them. We grew up together, did everything together, yet he couldn't even teach me the simplest thing, and

I envied him, because his gifts were of far more use than mine ever was.'

'But what about Padraig's father? He was at sea when he died, you must've known he couldn't have been in your bedroom?'

'No, I knew where he was. By that time I knew the people I was seeing had passed on, but it made no difference, they had done me no harm in life, why would they in death? I can't explain it very well, it was always with me, a natural thing if you like, you can't avoid having it if it comes to you.'

5

The story of Padraig's father had always fascinated Nancy, probably because it was nearer in time to her own life, her mother, after all, had known Padraig and had her own tale to tell about him, and Nancy knew it was true because so many people witnessed it and, besides, if it hadn't happened then it was a lie, a deliberate fabrication, and that was unthinkable. Padraig had never doubted her grandfather. Having grown up with stories of Ruairidh Beag's occasional visions and conversations with people no one else could see or hear made no difference, it was how his brother was and Padraig never questioned it. One night, when they were six years old, Ruairidh Beag wakened Padraig and said his father was there, but not downstairs, he was standing by the window of their bedroom. He wanted Padraig to know he loved him and would always be looking out for him, but he wouldn't be seeing him again.

'What does he mean?' Padraig asked, sitting up in his bed and staring at the window. He could see nothing there, but he knew his brother did.

'That's all he's saying. He's holding up a letter and he's saying he's with your mother and she watches you too.'

'I think,' Padraig said quietly, 'it means he's dead.' He got up and went over to the window. 'Can I touch him, Ruairidh Beag?' he asked, putting his hand out.

Ruairidh Beag nodded, smiling. 'He's taking your hand,' he said. 'Can you really not feel it?' Padraig shook his head but kept his hand outstretched. 'Now there's a woman with him, she's kissing your head.' After a moment he said, 'They've gone.'

★　　★　　★

'He was all wet, the floor was full of water that had dripped off him. He was holding out a letter, but he was showing it to me, he didn't want me to take it,' Ruairidh Beag later told his parents and grandparents calmly. 'The woman was only there for a moment, but she was young and pretty.'

Donald got up and crossed to the desk where he did the farm paperwork, slid open a drawer and removed a letter. 'The last time he was here Alasdair left this, to be opened if something befell him at sea,' he said.

'Then I think you'd better open it,' Sandy suggested.

Donald slit the envelope and withdrew a piece of paper wrapped around something bulky. He undid the small parcel and found a gold signet ring bearing the crest of the MacDonalds of Sleat, a crown with a gauntleted fist above it, holding a cross, and the words *Per mare, per terras*: by sea and land. He smoothed the letter with his hand on the desk in front of him.

'Alasdair writes that this ring is the only thing of any worth that he has, and if anything should happen to him at sea, it should pass to his son in due course, and, if we are agreeable, that if the worst should happen, he would like Padraig to remain here rather than go back to Margeree Forks or anywhere else.'

'There was never any doubt about that,' Morag murmured, putting her arms protectively around both her boys.

'And he goes on about being grateful to us for everything.'

'And no need for that,' Morag said.

Nancy knew the story was roughly true, but still, she thought, feeling a guilty blush creep over her cheeks, you wouldn't want to tell anyone outside Cape Breton, they might not understand. Until, that was, she was fifteen. By that time the town of Mabou was a thriving community, with general merchants, traders, blacksmiths, carriage-makers, banks and hotels. There were three schools, one for Baptists and one for Presbyterians, plus a Roman Catholic school all children attended after grade 9. The town boasted two doctors and three churches, and it had also had its own County Council with elected wardens, or leaders, since 1888. When Nancy was growing up in the early 1900s, it was a busy, expanding town, but not one that would hold her, she had long decided – not if she had any say in it.

As the years passed in Mull River so did the generations. Sandy died in due course, then Sarah, leaving the farm to Donald, who had been running it for years anyway with his sons. In time the three elder MacKenzie boys moved on, married and built up their own farms nearby with land from Sandy's original hundreds of acres; there was more than enough to provide a very good living for three more families. The two younger ones continued to run Mull River with their father, just as Donald had taken over from Sandy and in just the same way the Mull River farmhouse and land would pass in time to following generations. They were prospering, keeping sheep and raising milk beasts for the lucrative butter trade that exported to all over America. The fertile fields of Mull River grew potatoes, oats, turnips and grain and, through hard work and commitment to the land, the family was gradually leaving comfortable behind to become wealthy. The older ones, who had worked the land 'at home' just as devotedly, would shake their heads in wonder at what was possible in this new land, while the younger ones, as was the way of things, knew nothing of that time and simply accepted what they had. Over the years Alasdair MacDonald had been a frequent and welcome visitor who was as fond of all the family as they were of him and, though Padraig knew who he was and about his background, it was natural that he should consider his father to be just what he was, an affectionate but mostly absent relative. He was eighteen years old when he was given Alasdair's last gift, the gold ring left in safe-keeping at Mull River, and he wore it with pride, but he had always called Donald 'Father' and Morag 'Mother' and regarded Sandy and Sarah as just as much his grandparents as Ruairidh Beag's. The two youngsters complemented each other in personality as much as in appearance, the strong character of Ruairidh Beag, who had the characteristic MacKenzie colouring, dark, curly hair and brown eyes, and his brother, the quieter, more reticent Padraig, blue-eyed, fairer and smaller in height and width, and they were always together. By the time he was an adult Ruairidh Beag had grown taller than his own father and broader, but the resemblance was only too apparent. 'My word,' the old ones would say, looking at him, 'you wouldn't be able to get away with anything, Ruairidh Beag, you have such a strong look of your father that everyone would know who you were,' and Ruairidh Beag would smile wisely, as he did at everything. Dependable, a fine man, good company and wise beyond his years, that's what people said of him. Some thought he was shy, but he had no need for noise and fuss, as Granny Sarah had always proudly maintained; he had a presence, an assurance and a stillness about him too, as Grandpa Sandy noted. Padraig was a handsomer man in many ways than his brother, with finer features and a gentleness where Ruairidh Beag had strength. From early on he liked working with wood and he began making furniture and fiddles as a hobby that gradually became his business, making not just functional objects, but carving fine details into his pieces. As the earlier Nova Scotia immigrants flourished and prospered they looked for some means of advertising their success, and Padraig's furniture and fiddles became status symbols. He loved to sing, too, in his fine tenor voice, and any instrument he came across he could play without being taught, so despite his quiet nature, he was in great demand at ceilidhs.

Ruairidh Beag was, first and foremost, a man of the soil. He loved the farm and the countryside around the house where he had been born, though the attachment to Raasay and Scotland remained strong. He was twenty-one years old when, with Padraig by his side, he married Jess MacFarlane, a descendant of the first MacFarlanes who had arrived from Mull and therefore related in some way to Sandy's wife, Sarah, prompting one wag to remark that they didn't spread themselves about very far, the MacKenzies and the MacFarlanes. Ruairidh Beag had been hearing his father's stories all of his life, of the aftermath of the '45 and how the religious leaders had backed the lairds when people were being evicted from their homes and transported to places all over the world against their will, but Jess's father was a religious man and, out of respect for him, the marriage was conducted by the local Presbyterian minister, not that there was any alternative.

In honour of the marriage it was decided to rebuild the Mull River farmhouse, to raise the low ceilings and replace the centre-chimney arrangement with a more modern central hallway and an impressive staircase. A new heating system was installed using stoves instead of open fires and the number of bedrooms was increased, but the ultimate sign that the family had prospered was the building of a fine Gothic peak with leaded windows in front to allow light into the upstairs rooms.

Padraig's wedding present to his brother was a carved fireplace for the new parlour, with all the wildlife of Cape Breton represented, together with a thistle and a saltire and the date of the marriage. When the new building had been completed, a ceilidh was held in the yard to celebrate and people came from miles around to dance, play the fiddle and sing. The design of the house would be copied by other locals, but the fireplace was a one-off, created by a true craftsman and, though no one had any reason to think of such things at the time, Padraig's present and the house would still be lived in and admired over a hundred years later.

After a year of marriage, Jess had given birth to the first daughter in the MacKenzie family for many generations, just as Old Ruairidh had predicted all those years ago, and Ruairidh Beag was glad his father had lived to see her. So it was that Martha MacKenzie grew up hearing the family tales at Grandpa Donald's knee, and, when he had gone, at her father, Ruairidh Beag's knee. It didn't matter to Martha or to her father that neither of them had any memory of the land left behind, or of the voyage to Cape Breton, because they could recall it in detail through those oft-told stories and also because Martha, too, had the Second Sight, the Gift handed down by generations of MacKenzies. Martha didn't need to witness the weeping of Morag's family, the MacLeods, as Donald and Morag left Raasay, to be hearing it decades later, nor did she have to hear the earnest words of encouragement of the elder, widowed MacKenzie, bidding goodbye to his son and his family, knowing that they would never meet again, to feel the pain he and they felt. The link with the old country stayed strong and future generations would proclaim themselves Scots first, Canadians second, and for generations more they would still believe it in their hearts. It was partly because Cape Breton was so similar in many ways to the 'home' most of those Canadian-born generations would never see, that it was easy for the old ones to keep their values and culture alive, more alive, sometimes, than they were at 'home'. Indeed, Gaelic would continue to be their first language long after it had faded or been forced out of the land they had come from and still considered to be their own. In Nova Scotia, even in Martha's lifetime, they lived as they had on Raasay, only better, as Sandy MacKenzie had said so often over the years, and it still held true as the nineteenth century moved towards the twentieth.

Less than a year after Ruairidh Beag and Jess had married, her plain older sister, Catherine, had caused eyebrows to be raised by marrying John MacVicar, who was twenty years older than her but, far worse, whose people came from Uist. All the inhabitants of Cape Breton tried to keep to their own, the English to the English, the French to the French and the Scots, who were by that time the dominant group, to the Scots, but a Scot marrying a Scot wasn't necessarily good enough, the old clan rivalries and animosities still held true. John MacVicar was from Uist people, and Uist people did not get on with Mull people and, as the bride came from a Mull family, the match drew some disapproval, and it wasn't always silent. Ruairidh Beag disliked John MacVicar, and not just because the man came from North Uist, his feelings were well founded and ran deeper. John MacVicar was a man on the make, that is to say a man who would use any means, and hard work was not necessarily one of them, to advance and enrich himself. Even changing his name from the Gaelic Iain was, said Ruairidh Beag, to make him more acceptable to those further afield who did not have the Gaelic – he would deny his own people for profit. If someone's business was in trouble, John MacVicar was on their doorstep offering to 'help' by buying them up, and no matter how many houses he acquired by similar means, he always had room for another. Ruairidh Beag despised everything about him, including his ever present smile, and the subtle way it changed from ingratiating to smug as his wealth increased over the years. And, furthermore, he even suspected that John's marriage to Catherine, who was as boring as she was plain, though he softened this to 'not anything like you are yourself, Jess' when talking to his wife, was a means of connecting himself to the MacKenzies.

'That's nonsense!' Jess replied.

'Are you saying we don't have some standing in Mabou?' Ruairidh Beag asked quietly, raising his eyebrows without looking at his wife.

'Well of course that's true,' Jess replied.

'And can you deny that the one thing he lacks is standing?' Jess opened her mouth to protest. 'He's made money, and he'll never stop making it, there's nothing surer than that, Jess, but mark my words, deep down he knows he'll never have respect from anyone, and part of Catherine's attraction is that he thinks he can call me and Padraig brothers-in-law, when in fact he's only *your* in-law, that's all I'm saying.'

'Ruairidh Beag,' Jess pleaded, 'you're not going to cause ill-feeling, are you?'

'Not at all,' he replied pleasantly. 'I've always had ill-feeling towards the wee man.'

Jess glowered at him. 'You see?' she demanded. 'You called him "the wee man", I know what that means.'

'It means,' said Ruairidh Beag, settling down behind his desk, 'that he's a wee man. Are you saying that he's a big man, Jess?'

Padraig, who was sitting by the fire lovingly oiling the wood of a violin he was making, laughed softly, knowing from experience that Jess couldn't win this argument.

'There you go!' Jess said accusingly. 'Padraig laughed.'

'Och, he does that sometimes,' her husband replied kindly,

beaming an affectionate smile in Padraig's direction. 'I don't mind it, he's my brother after all, he can have a laugh if he feels like it.'

'Ruairidh Beag!' Jess protested.

'Is it not so, Padraig,' he said, looking up at his brother, 'that the wee man always tried to make himself welcome in our company when we were younger?'

'It is,' replied Padraig.

'And uninvited?'

'And uninvited at that,' Padraig agreed.

'And us with Mull family and him with just Uist family?'

'All true, Ruairidh Beag,' Padraig grinned. 'All true, to be sure.'

'And wouldn't you say, Padraig, that he didn't have any real liking for either of us, and it was because we had land and he knew we must have a penny or two?'

'That was always my understanding,' Padraig nodded, his eyes still on the violin.

'Padraig!' Jess said. 'Don't you go agreeing with him, you know what he's up to.'

'And,' continued Ruairidh Beag in a casual voice that belied what he was saying, 'if you or I had been in his position, Padraig, do you think we would have sought his company when it plainly wasn't wanted?'

'We would not,' Padraig replied firmly.

Ruairidh Beag looked up at Jess as though a great truth had been revealed. 'There you have it,' he said innocently. 'And from Padraig himself, the only man I know who bears no animosity to another, even one as ugly as Iain MacVicar, even though he calls himself John.'

What Ruairidh Beag didn't say, for fear of really upsetting his wife, was that her widower father, James MacFarlane, only approved of the match because he could see that John MacVicar was not only a man on the make, but a man on the move – James confused ambition and application with greed. It was something Ruairidh Beag often noticed about the seriously religious, that they were somehow open to bestowing virtue on those who zealously sought money and position, and as John MacVicar continued in his quest for both, so James MacFarlane deferred to him more and more. Still, it wasn't his business, it was MacFarlane family business, he would simply evade all attempts by MacVicar to ally himself to the MacKenzies, and though he couldn't help feeling disappointed in his father-in-law, for Jess's sake, and that of the child she was carrying, he coolly kept his distance but said nothing outside his own four walls.

Martha MacKenzie was like her MacFarlane mother, small and birdlike, and unlike her father's family, she was fair-haired and grey-eyed, characteristics that brought a few chuckles from the locals, who wisecracked that she resembled her godfather, her Uncle Padraig, more than her father. Strangely enough she loved wildlife and could mimic the birds and animals around her, and she, too, sang like an angel. Padraig adored her, he was delighted that there was someone else in the family who was musical and he taught her songs and how to play all the instruments he had mastered. She was a child of nature in every way. She grew up knowing the Micmac Indians, and she was fascinated by their culture. Some, as Sandy had told his nephew many years before, had been and still were afraid of the native people, though the MacKenzies gave them nothing but respect and gratitude, but it was Martha, born among them, who saw them as friends and equals. She loved their steep-sided 'wickawams' made of animal hides, the long poles held together at the opening on top with leather strands. Inside, a small circle of stones formed the fireplace that gave them warmth and somewhere to cook, with the smoke drifting through the hole at the apex of the long poles. The inner walls were decorated with drawings of animals and the moon and stars, and it was clear that these peaceful, gentle people were close to nature and their own ways, though most of them had been converted to Roman Catholicism by the French in the mid 1600s. As a child, Martha ran around the meadows barefoot with their children and learned alongside them how to use nature, so that she became as skilled as any Indian in using herbal medicine. Very early, too, she demonstrated that she had the Gift.

It first happened after Padraig had married Katie MacLeod, whose family had moved on from Cape Breton some years before and settled in Campbellford in Ontario. Katie and her brothers and sisters still came back to Cape Breton every summer to visit relatives, and naturally they had gone along to ceilidhs, and that's where she and Padraig had met. Padraig and Katie's house was still under construction about half a mile away, so they were staying with Ruairidh Beag and Jess in the family home. Padraig, being the man he was, had very definite ideas on every detail of the home he was building for his wife and family, going great distances to find exactly the right wood he wanted. Katie had given birth to their first son, Ranald, only a year before and now was pregnant with their second child and she wanted her own home, though everyone was joking that at the rate the perfectionist Padraig was building their house the children would grow up where their father had and never leave either. Padraig had left again to track down his ideal piece of wood, and the night before his departure Ruairidh Beag had woken in the early hours without knowing why. He found himself suddenly and completely wide awake with no thought of anything in his mind, although sometimes there would be a noise from the nearby forest that could pierce the deepest sleep. Even so, the memory of waking in the night stayed with Ruairidh Beag like a dark cloud hanging over him, and working at the desk where Donald had worked before him, he had felt cold all morning, though the weather was warm. Martha was playing with some Micmac children before lunch when she saw her Uncle Padraig approaching the house. Looking up she saw her father at the window watching as she grabbed Padraig's hand and chatted happily to him as they walked along.

'I'll have to stop, Martha,' he smiled. 'It's hot and I've hurt my back a bit cutting down a tree. Tell you what, sing me a song while I sit here.' So she sang to him as he rested, then she grew impatient and tried to pull him towards the house.

'Tell you what,' he said quietly. 'You run ahead and tell

Ruairidh Beag I'm on my way and tell him I need a warm bath for this back of mine.'

'It's Padraig,' she shouted breathlessly, running into the house where Ruairidh Beag had sat down once more at his desk, the farm paperwork spread around. 'He's just coming. He's hurt his back and wants a warm bath.' Ruairidh Beag put his hand out, caught his daughter and made her sit on his knee and, being a lively child, Martha squirmed and tried to break free.

'Listen, my little one,' Ruairidh Beag said quietly, smoothing his daughter's hair back from her damp forehead. 'There is no need to run so quickly in this heat, Padraig isn't there.'

'But he is,' she insisted, giggling, thinking this was a fine joke. 'We were talking and he was asking me if I was keeping up with my singing and I sang a little to him.'

'And what did he say?' Ruairidh Beag smiled down at her, feeling her bird's heart fluttering in her chest.

'He said it was very good, and we would sing together later, and I was to run ahead to tell you.'

Ruairidh Beag held her close and exchanged a look with his wife and Grandpa Donald who had come to investigate the commotion.

'Has she fallen again?' Jess demanded angrily. 'Martha, how many times have I to tell you not to climb trees? You're not a Micmac, you know, even if you think you are.'

'I'm as good a climber as any of them,' Martha replied defiantly, 'and I'm better than a lot of them.'

'So where are you hurt this time?' Jess demanded, advancing on her daughter as she sat in Ruairidh Beag's protective embrace. 'Or is it another torn dress? I swear, if I weren't such a good needlewoman you'd be naked by now. The number of things you rip apart would try the patience of a saint.' She pulled at Martha's skirts, examining the folds, until Ruairidh Beag put out a hand to still hers.

'There's nothing wrong with her,' he smiled. 'Martha here just ran ahead to tell me that Padraig was on his way home.'

There was something about his voice that made Martha stay

on her knees and look up into her husband's pained eyes. 'Oh, Ruairidh Beag!' she whispered and then there was a long, still, silent moment that no one dared break.

'Are you sure?' Donald asked at last.

Ruairidh Beag nodded. 'I couldn't understand why I wakened in the night,' he said sadly, 'and all morning I've been so restless and so cold, and there's a cloud, a dark shadow over me now that I can see. I looked out of the window just now and saw Padraig with Martha, and in the distance I saw Alasdair and Mairead waiting for him. He looked up and smiled, then he sent Martha ahead and just disappeared.' He shrugged his shoulders helplessly.

'But you're sure he's not there?' Jess asked, trying to control the panic in her voice. 'Maybe you just imagined it or it was a trick of the light or he's just out of sight. Did you look properly?' She ran quickly to look out of the window, then opened the door and searched desperately with her eyes. 'But Katie, poor Katie!' Jess said, giving in. 'Ruairidh Beag, are you really sure?'

'He's gone,' Ruairidh Beag replied.

'No he's not,' Martha said, looking at the faces of the adults, confused by the tone of the conversation and trying to understand. She pointed towards the outdoors. 'Look, he's coming.'

'Little one,' her father sighed, gently stroking her cheek, 'I have something to tell you. Padraig cannot be coming to see us ever again.'

Martha laughed out loud, even though she thought this fine joke had turned a little odd and scary. 'No,' she protested again. 'He's outside!' and once again she struggled to escape Ruairidh Beag's hold, this time succeeding. She ran to the door, stopped, looked around, then ran down the hill to where she had left Padraig, spinning around on her bare toes to look in every direction. When she couldn't find him she shouted his name, but there was no answer, then slowly she sat in the grass where he had been and tried to work out what was happening.

Back in the house the three adults looked upwards at the same moment; Katie, with weeks of her pregnancy to go, was resting during the hottest part of the day in an upstairs bedroom, as Ranald took a nap in his cot by her side.

'What do we do?' Jess asked desperately. 'Do we tell her? What do we tell her?'

Ruairidh Beag shook his head. 'Someone will come, that will be time enough for her to know. Let us do her the kindness of keeping her life as it was for as long as possible.'

An hour later a messenger arrived with the news that Padraig had been hit by a tree that had fallen awkwardly, it had broken his back and killed him instantly. When his young wife was told that she was a widow she immediately went into premature labour and as that drama was being played out in the house, Ruairidh Beag walked down the hill to where his daughter was still sitting. He knew she was confused, that she knew something bad had happened and didn't want to enter the house and have it confirmed. He took her by the hand and walked with her, looking out over the rolling hills to the brook, and talking to her gently.

'Padraig's gone now,' he said calmly. 'He came to you because he loved you so much, Martha. Didn't he always love to sing with you? Well, maybe he wanted to hear you sing one more time, eh? Aren't you lucky to have someone love you so much?'

'But I saw him,' she said bleakly. 'He was real. It was Padraig. He spoke to me, I touched his hand and it was warm.'

'I know, I know,' Ruairidh Beag calmed her, stroking her hair. 'No one doubts you. I saw you with him too. He really was there. You have the Gift, Martha, that's what it is, and sometimes it can make you sad.'

When they went back to the house, Jess was with Katie, where she remained for most of the day, and Ruairidh Beag settled his daughter on a sofa and covered her with a blanket. When the first cry of the child was heard Martha moved in her sleep but didn't wake.

'It's another boy,' Jess said wearily when she came downstairs.

'He's small because he wasn't due yet, but he seems healthy. How awful for the child to have his birthday on his father's death.'

Ruairidh Beag nodded. 'It isn't that awful, Jess, Padraig's life didn't stop, his son picked it up and it carries on.'

'I can't think what to say to the poor girl,' she sighed. 'What will she do now, Ruairidh Beag?'

'She'll go back to her family in Campbellford,' he replied. 'She has no close family here any longer so there's nothing to keep her.'

Jess wept quietly. 'All of them gone from here in one small day!' she cried.

'The boy will be back one day with his sons, as will Ranald and his son too,' he said, folding his arms around her.

Jess looked at her own sleeping child. 'And she really saw him?' she said quietly.

'We both did,' he murmured into her hair.

'But she's so young!' Jess said sadly.

Ruairidh Beag smiled. 'I'm told all mothers say that, all grandmothers, too, for that matter,' he told her gently. 'I was younger, Jess. It's not so bad, she'll cope, she wouldn't have it if she couldn't cope with it. Anyway, there's no way of avoiding it.'

6

They buried Padraig in the local cemetery. His father's body had never been found and his mother lay in Margeree Forks, but he had never known her and the weather was hot, so there was no time for prolonged discussions or for travelling. It was decided to lay him to rest with the only family he had ever known, with Sandy and Sarah and with Morag, the mother who had fed him at her breast along with Ruairidh Beag.

In the short time since his brother's death, Ruairidh Beag's composure had ebbed away to the point that he was going through the motions, blotting it from his mind in a kind of panic he had never felt before, trying to put it on hold until he could cope with it. He felt detached, viewing his responses and behaviour as though they came from someone else and, as a man who had always taken such matters in his stride, who had been the wise, calming influence on other people in similar situations, his self-confidence was shaken. He stood by the graveside, occupying his mind by repeating the songs his grandmother from Raasay had sung to him in his cot, and by debating points with himself to block out the minister's words. 'So here we are, in a land that gives us plenty,' he thought angrily, 'leading lives our ancestors could never have dreamed of. We build our grand houses and we fill them with things to show how far we've come, thinking life is easier and more predictable, thinking that we've tamed nature and have Fate controlled, but underneath it's still a dangerous world we have. Even an artist, a gentle man like Padraig, can die a brutal death without any warning. How can that be?'

Had the right been his, his brother's burial would have had no religious content, but like his marriage to Jess it was out of

46

his control; Padraig's wife now had that right and she needed whatever solace it brought her. He didn't grudge her this, he had never grudged anyone their beliefs, but losing Padraig had thrown his mind into such turmoil that dark feelings of a depth he had never suspected he had were stirring up emotions he didn't know existed in anyone. Mostly he was angry, but in an unfocused way. He was angry at Padraig and his perfectionist soul – why did he have to have that particular tree? A tree was a tree, wood was wood – why couldn't he have been like any other man and settled for wood that did the job? Why did he have to take everything to extremes, why, in short, had his stupid brother chosen to die for a bit of nice timber that he wouldn't now see? Mostly, though, he was angry with himself and his mind was searching desperately for any opportunity to vent his emotions. The voice of the minister was still droning on, saying nothing about Padraig that made any sense and irritating Ruairidh Beag like a hornet that won't go away no matter how often you try to swat it. He *would* swat it, he decided, and at the end of the service he dug deep within himself and produced the still quality that Grandpa Sandy had always commented on. Then he dug even deeper to heighten the stillness with as much concentration as he could, and bestowed on the minister a long, cold, dark look. Meeting Ruairidh Beag's stare the little man was so shocked by the awful expression in his eyes that he stumbled and almost fell. Ruairidh Beag had to turn away so that no one could see his laughter.

'Ruairidh Beag!' his wife whispered fiercely from beside him. 'What good did that do?'

'Well, it did me a great deal of good,' he replied calmly, 'and the only one it maybe harmed was the minister, and that did me even more good. On the day when I'm burying my brother I think I should be indulged a little, don't you?'

'I was five or six years old,' Martha would tell Nancy, every time she told the story over the years, 'and as God is my witness I saw Padraig that day, touched him, talked to him, sang to him. Your grandfather saw us together. There was nothing ghostly about him, he was flesh and blood. Padraig was the only one I ever saw, but, as my father said, I got used to the Gift of knowing the future after that. Maybe he was sent first so that I wouldn't be afraid, I could never be afraid of Padraig, but there were times after that when I wished I didn't see the things I saw and didn't know the things I knew. That kind of knowledge can hurt to carry.' And Nancy would nod because she knew her mother would never lie to her any more than Grandpa Ruairidh Beag would. But as she got older she wished her mother wouldn't keep telling the old story, because in the cold light of a logical twentieth-century day, and to anyone outside Cape Breton, how could it possibly be true?

7

After burying her husband, Kate MacDonald took Ranald and her new son, Hamish, back to Pine Edge, her family's farm in Campbellford, as Ruairidh Beag had predicted. The house Padraig had been building remained as it was, no one had the heart to complete it or demolish it – it was boarded up and covered with a tarpaulin and left as it was. For a long time afterwards there continued in Ruairidh Beag, though, an anger that he couldn't extinguish, even if it puzzled him. People had their time, he had grown up convinced of that, and he held this belief against the arguments of others.

'So we shouldn't try to save someone?' Jess had once asked, and Ruairidh Beag had shrugged patiently.

'Of course we should,' he'd said. 'What I'm saying is that we'll only succeed in saving someone if it isn't their time, if it is, then nothing will work. It is my belief, Jess, it doesn't have to be yours, just as yours doesn't have to be mine.'

Thinking back on how formed his opinions had been and how his brother's death had challenged everything he thought he believed, he felt perplexed, and that made him even angrier. He hadn't connected the warning signs before Padraig died, but he felt he should have. They had been together since weeks after birth and yet he had waved him off that morning, too wrapped up in confusion about what he was feeling to realise he was being warned about what would happen to Padraig within hours. He was not yet thirty years old; could it *really* have been Padraig's time, or was it possible that he could've saved him if he'd taken some action? He should have worked it out, he thought, and if he had, maybe his brother wouldn't have died. Well, he should've tried at any rate, that was sure, he had cheated Padraig of any slight chance there might have been not to die, crushed under that tree. But what if it *were* his time, young as he was, but yet again and worse still, what if it weren't?

The thoughts tortured him when he was awake and when he was asleep. He was haunted by the memory of looking out of the window and seeing Martha talking to his brother, of seeing Padraig's parents waiting for him and suddenly understanding; that final picture was seared into his mind, blocking out the other memories of the years they had spent together as boys. Questions twisted in his heart – was that a look of disappointment, of reproach that passed between them? Was Padraig telling him that he'd been let down? Was that why he'd come back, to look at him and ask with his eyes, 'Brother, you know things before the rest of us, why didn't you know this?' Deep in his mind he knew Padraig wouldn't have thought that way, he was too kind, gentle and loving a brother to blame him, he knew he had come back to say goodbye, but even deeper inside Ruairidh Beag's heart he still blamed himself. To the raw anger was added guilt, confusion, grief and loss, a jumble of emotions looking for release anywhere it could be found, and anyone who gave him the slightest cause risked feeling the cutting edge of his pain. It was, he thought, a gift from some higher force that John MacVicar, now a Justice of the Peace, was fated to be the one to stray unwisely into the firing line.

The little Uist man arrived unannounced and uninvited at the house in Mull River one evening only weeks after Padraig's death, and as soon as she saw him on the doorstep, Jess, knowing of her husband's dislike of him, resolved to keep them apart. The pompous little man was not to be put off, however, it was the master of the house he had come to see and, like a fly being enticed into a web by a spider, he was welcomed into the parlour with a deceptive smile from Ruairidh Beag. Jess had that minute been on the verge of pushing her brother-in-law out of the house and locking the front door behind him, but Ruairidh Beag had conveyed him out of her reach.

★   ★.   ★

'I hope I'm not disturbing you, Ruairidh Beag,' John MacVicar remarked, in a tone indicating he couldn't care less whether he was or not. These days he had a finger in every pie and was offhand with the MacKenzies when their paths crossed, a sign, Ruairidh Beag knew, of his resentment at never being accepted by them.

'Well, we certainly weren't expecting you,' Ruairidh Beag countered pointedly, closing the door on Jess with a wicked grin, 'but I wouldn't send any man away without showing him some hospitality.'

'It's about your daughter,' the little man said without any preamble.

'Really, Iain?' Ruairidh Beag replied; as a point of principle he had never called him anything other than 'Iain', because calling him 'John' implied that he believed in and respected MacVicar's recreation of himself.

Outside the closed door Jess was desperately trying to listen in.

'Your daughter and these Micmacs,' John MacVicar continued, sitting down. Ruairidh Beag looked him up and down but made no reply. He hadn't seen him lately or, if he had, he hadn't taken much notice of him, and he was suddenly struck by the illusion that his fine clothes were overcoming the MacVicar. He looked like a normal-sized man who had been squeezed smaller, there was a lot of him, but it was all short and chubby, and he seemed to be disappearing inside what he wore. Any day now, Ruairidh Beag thought, with a smile, only the dome of his head, shining with sweat and sporting two or three carefully placed strands of hair, might be all that was visible. He also now seemed to possess a great many gold rings on his stubby fingers, and there was an especially grand gold pocket watch hanging from his waistcoat on a heavy gold chain. Almost as though he had heard Ruairidh Beag's thoughts, MacVicar took the watch from his pocket and glanced at it, a gesture implying that a busy man like himself could be and should be engaged on something more important at that very moment, but he was gracious enough to make time for this matter anyway, as long as this was noted. Looking at the watch he frowned and slipped it back into his waistcoat pocket.

'There is a fear,' he said, getting up and walking about the room addressing Ruairidh Beag as he would an audience of voters, 'raised by various members of the community, and one that I have to say I share, that young Martha spends far too much time running barefoot with the Micmacs through the fields and woods, and inside their wickawams, too, I'm told.' He cleared his throat as his host stared at him benignly, but silently. 'Well?'

'Well what?' Ruairidh Beag smiled pleasantly.

'I think the fear is that her behaviour now could lead to intermarriage in the future,' said the little man, then looking away he murmured 'or worse.'

'Worse?'

'Well, their morals are not ours and we don't know what influence they could have on an innocent young girl from our side.'

'Fornication, bastard half-breeds, that sort of thing?' Ruairidh Beag asked calmly.

Jess's brother-in-law winced. 'Exactly,' he replied.

'And what business is it of yours?' Ruairidh Beag asked in a voice of extreme kindness. 'I mean, Iain, you're far too busy a man to be bothered with things like this, surely?'

'Well, I have some standing in this community, and I am a member of the family,' MacVicar stated, 'and, naturally, I thought you would prefer to discuss this with a relative.' He stopped, shocked to hear Ruairidh Beag laugh quietly to himself. 'There have already been intermarriages, as I'm sure you know,' he continued, 'and we don't want any more of that sort of thing. Each to his own, as the Good Lord would say.'

'Each to his own?' Ruairidh Beag repeated. 'I'm surprised that didn't stick in your craw, Iain. And you know that for a fact, do you?'

MacVicar looked puzzled.

'Your Good Lord has told you this, has he? Made a special trip from the heavens to share his thoughts with a wee *bodach* from Uist? Or did he convey his message through the minister you're always following around? I've always wondered about that, Iain. Does tying yourself to the minister make you more holy, or just make it easier to make money from the truly holy?'

The self-made man opened his mouth and was silenced by a look from Ruairidh Beag as he crossed to the door, locked it, put the key in his pocket and returned to his chair. Outside the parlour Jess heard the key turn and, knowing this couldn't be a good omen, regretted she hadn't followed her earlier impulse to leave MacVicar locked out of the house.

'I don't want there to be any misunderstanding, Iain,' Ruairidh Beag said quietly, sitting back comfortably in his chair, crossing his legs and clasping his hands casually in front of him, 'so I'll speak very plainly. First of all, I have allowed you into my home, though your arrival here without notice was a discourtesy, because I am a civilised man and because you are related by marriage to my wife, but don't think that you're welcome here or have my permission to repeat the intrusion. However, my own good Highland manners seem, I'm afraid, to have given you the notion that you can tell me how my family should conduct their lives. We are not related and it is no business of yours or any of your –' he paused to emphasise the word with disdain, '"friends", how much time my daughter spends with any of *our* friends, and the Micmacs are better friends to this family than any of your kind have ever been. Do I make myself clear?'

Outside the door Jess heard his calm voice, the calm before the storm if she had ever heard it.

'It is my duty –' blustered the little man.

'Your duty?' Ruairidh Beag pounced, raising his voice without losing his temper, which was somehow more threatening. 'Is this the same duty that made you and your kind give obedience to the ministers and anyone in authority at home? The same duty that kept you silent as Cumberland's men, and the traitor Scots who joined them, raped and pillaged the poor people of the Highlands, my own home on Raasay, too, for years after the '45? What were your kind doing while they were killing people's beasts, burning their houses and crops and leaving them starving, but making money from their persecution? Wasn't it your duty to speak out when they were cleared from the land and sent off on boats so crammed with people that many died, instead of singing psalms while the ministers blessed them as they were thrown in tears from their homes? I'm told that there were some who thought first of their people, but I have never met one.'

'It's your father has put these notions into your head,' MacVicar protested, 'him and his fairytales. Being transported was the making of many, they may not have wanted to go, but they thrived in their new homes, it is a proven fact.'

'Aye, isn't that just like you?' Ruairidh Beag said quietly. 'Happy to call a decent man a liar as long as he's not there to be looked in the eye.'

At that Jess tried to enter the room. She knew this would cause a rift within her family and wanted to plead with her brother-in-law to bear in mind how much Ruairidh Beag was still hurting from Padraig's death, but her husband had the key in his pocket, stopping her from coming in and John MacVicar from leaving. At last Ruairidh Beag got up from his chair, crossed to the door, unlocked it and held it open.

'Now if you'd kindly leave, Iain, and don't trouble yourself to visit with us again. I'm sure there are others who value your opinions and I wouldn't want to keep you an instant from them,' he said with great grace.

'There were others who would not have put my message as kindly,' John MacVicar blustered.

'Huh!' replied Ruairidh Beag dismissively.

'You will suffer for this, Ruairidh Beag,' the little man said, white-faced. 'They say you have the Second Sight, well if you have you will already have seen how you will suffer for this indignity to a man who came to you in a spirit of good will and kinship.'

'Never kinship!' Ruairidh Beag said in a snarling whisper.

'Never again claim that, Iain MacVicar, not in my hearing or out of it!' Then he sighed. 'Better go, Iain,' he said wearily. 'I feel a vision coming on of you leaving here with my foot firmly planted on your important backside. Now *that* would be an indignity that you'd want to avoid, surely?' As MacVicar left, Ruairidh Beag said quietly, 'Besides, I wouldn't mind my daughter intermarrying with the Micmacs. It could be worse. After all, she could intermarry with Uist folk. Now that really would distress me,' and with that he closed the door. Turning back he saw his father on the stairs, a smile on his face.

'My boy,' he said, 'you know I'm proud of you and I agree with every word, but you can be sure that in no time at all he will have spread it to everyone he can reach, and you will be snubbed by many in this community.'

Ruairidh Beag shrugged. 'The ones who side with him and snub me, well, what need have I of them?' he said quietly. 'If I have made enemies over speaking the truth then they're the sort I'm proud to have as enemies.'

As it happened he lost few friends. The respect John MacVicar commanded came courtesy of what he had achieved by using anyone and everyone to do it, the MacKenzies had earned theirs honestly and without harming another. Their standing in the area was not only a result of their wealth but because they would do any man a kindness without asking. Ruairidh Beag did lose his father-in-law, however – James MacFarlane let it be known that he would never again receive the entire family. From now on he would cut all ties with Jess, his own daughter, his granddaughter, Martha, and her younger brothers, Donald and Jamie, each named for their two grandfathers. Jess was devastated and pleaded with Ruairidh Beag to apologise to her sister's husband, and for probably the only time in their marriage she saw him truly angry with her.

'Iain MacVicar came here to tell us how to care for our daughter, Jess, to interfere in matters that don't concern him, and you're asking *me* to apologise to *him*? To change my beliefs or, worse still, to deny them, to placate that wee man and your father?' he asked her quietly.

'He's my father, Ruairidh Beag,' she wept, 'and it's not just my father. My sister will never talk to me again. Have I ever asked anything of you before?'

'I'm your husband, Jess, and you should remember that,' he replied, but his anger was mainly directed at James MacFarlane and he stormed out of the house to face him.

He found his father-in-law working in his woodmill a mile or so away.

'You're not welcome here, Ruairidh Beag,' he told him.

'It doesn't bother me whether I am or not, James,' he said in a slow, quiet voice. 'I have things to say to you and I will not leave here till you hear them. But be assured, I'm not here looking for peace and I'll be quite content if they're the last words I ever speak to you. If you cut me that's fine, the views I expressed were my own and I don't take back a word, but you have fallen in my estimation by not allowing a man to express his own opinions and beliefs in his own house. I don't agree with yours, but I would never break with you because of them, or refuse to let you have the company of my wife and children. I've respected you all my life, but I will say this. It has saddened me to see you look up to Iain MacVicar as though he deserved respect, when all he has ever done is enrich himself at other people's expense, and I find it strange that you, a Mull man, should prefer someone from Uist over your own, when you know for a fact how they look down on us.'

'He's an important man,' James MacFarlane said, 'a clever man. He'll be remembered in this town long after you are forgotten.'

'We'll have to wait to find out about that, James, we only have his word and your gullibility for it at the moment, but I'll tell you this, cause a rift between us if you must, but if you cast out your daughter and your grandchildren it's your loss, not theirs. Think on that, James.' And with that he walked away from his father-in-law for the last time.

*   *   *

Jess lived in hope that the rift would soon be breached, but it never was and it caused her a great deal of pain. Her father reconsidered and consented to see her and her children, and her sister followed suit, but neither would ever see her husband again. Furthermore, they refused to go anywhere they might meet him, which meant they never again set foot in Jess's home. It caused Ruairidh Beag no pain, though, the matter was of their doing, not of his and he was his own man and was prepared to stand by his convictions. John MacVicar, his mind still on furthering his own position, made no attempt to deepen the divide, he let others do it for him so that he could emerge unscathed, behaving entirely as Ruairidh Beag not only expected, but predicted. Over the years the gulf became unbreachable and when the time came, James MacFarlane did not attend his granddaughter's wedding. Ruairidh Beag, though, being the man of honour that he was, attended his father-in-law's funeral not many years afterwards.

8

'The minute I saw your father at the ceilidh dance,' Martha would smile, 'I knew, and so did your grandfather.'

'Yes, Mother,' Nancy would smile back, trying to disguise the sigh in her voice because it seemed to her that she had heard this and every story more often than she had drawn breath.

'Not a word passed between us, mind, not then and not for a long time afterwards, but I knew he was the one from that first moment,' and Martha would nod, smiling to herself at the memory.

Nancy would nod too at what she considered the romantic notions of an old woman, though Martha was hardly that.

Despite John MacVicar's fears about Martha and the Micmacs, she married a music teacher, a MacLeod whose family had emigrated from Skye and settled in Inverness, on the coast between Mabou and Margeree Forks. She had heard about him, of course, he was the talk of the place for a while. Even before she had set eyes on him she knew about the young man who had come to the local school to teach maths and had sent the children home singing their times tables instead of reciting them and, when they were in class, singing them in harmony no less. It was clear to all that he was in the wrong job; music dictated his life, it flowed through him, and it was prized in the community, too, so a new maths teacher was found and Tormod MacLeod was appointed music teacher instead.

Like Padraig, Tormod could pick up any instrument and play it, and that was undoubtedly the attraction for Martha when she saw him for the first time at the ceilidh when she was eighteen. When she walked in that evening she was stunned to hear the distinctive sound of one of her uncle's fiddles being played, and not just played, but played as Padraig would have played it. She could hear all his phrases, all his nuances coming from the instrument he had made, and if Padraig had still been alive she would have expected to turn around and see him there. When she finally moved her eyes from the hands playing the instrument she caught her breath; the boy even looked like him, about the same height and build, fair-haired and blue-eyed. Martha had had a special relationship with her uncle, their love of music had created a bond that had been severed on his death and the void had never been filled for her. She had missed him so much that she used to try to see him again, but it had never happened. Padraig had gone for ever, and on hearing his fiddle that evening, for an instant she was transported back in time and felt him all around her in the room. Her disappointment when she saw the fiddle in Tormod MacLeod's hands instead of Padraig's was so acute that at first she felt like snatching it away from him and hitting him for his cheek, but who could strike a man who played like that, she wondered, standing transfixed in the middle of the floor, a man with such a talent? At that moment she knew, as she told her daughter over the years, that he was the one for her, but there was such a powerful knotting in her stomach that she could barely look him in the eye. As the evening wore on the usual call came for a song from Martha MacKenzie and she stood on the little stage and tried to raise her voice but found she couldn't, because Tormod MacLeod was close by, looking at her. She tried again and heard the soft tones of Padraig's fiddle gently paving the way, and this time she couldn't sing for the tears in her throat. Then she shook her head and sang out and, as she did so, the fiddle grew in confidence along with her. Ruairidh Beag watched the two young people and there was no doubt in his mind that they belonged together, though he didn't need the Second Sight to know that, just a pair of ordinary eyes.

Even though she felt such an attraction to Tormod, Martha left the ceilidh without speaking to him that night, and for months afterwards she went out of her way to avoid him. The strength of her feelings frightened her, and his resemblance to Padraig confused her, though somehow she was still convinced that they would end up together. Then she was asked to sing with him at a friend's wedding and couldn't resist seeing and feeling the connection she had felt that first evening. Within months they, too, decided to marry and Ruairidh Beag suggested that Padraig's house, a short distance away, would make a perfect home for them. In the twelve years since his death it had lain unfinished and it stood on such a perfect setting, with views out over the valley, that many times people had approached his brother for permission to either finish it or knock it down and build another where it stood, but Ruairidh Beag had always refused. The right to make that decision lay with Padraig's widow, Katie, in Campbellford, but on her visits back to Mull River every summer with his sons she had made it clear that Ruairidh Beag should decide for her. She had remarried and had another child, but the sight of the half-built house saddened her, Padraig had meant it to be lived in and she would far rather have seen it finished and housing a family. As long as it lay there the wound remained open for her, as though life had stood still since the day he had set out after breakfast to look for a special tree. In other aspects she had moved on, but every time she returned and saw the unfinished house the pain returned as harsh and fresh as on the day Padraig had died. The future of the house was in Ruairidh Beag's hands, though, she said, whatever Padraig's brother said was law, and so he had made sure it was kept as watertight as he could manage and he had waited, though even he didn't know what he was waiting for till Martha met Tormod.

'Will Katie agree?' Martha asked when her father suggested it.

'I would think so,' her father replied.

Jess was less sure though. 'I can't help feeling it would be bad luck,' she suggested. 'It has such a sad history. I look at it every now and again and I wish it had been knocked down, that's the truth. I can see him there, so full of hope, building his house and making sure it was perfect, and that was what killed him, after all.'

Martha and Ruairidh Beag looked at each other and laughed out loud.

'Have I said something funny, then?' Jess demanded, stung by their laughter.

Her husband patted her arm reassuringly. 'We're not laughing at you,' he said, though they were. 'Maybe it would be bad luck for someone else, as you say, but if he couldn't live in it himself, there's no one in the world Padraig would've wanted to have there than Martha, don't you see?' he asked gently.

'And you wouldn't feel, well, strange?' Jess asked Martha.

'Of course not,' she replied, bemused. 'To be near Padraig, to see his work, his thoughts all around me? Of course not.'

And so, after Katie's final consent had been received, work started again on Padraig's house. It was almost as though the construction was being guided by him as ideas were rethought overnight, designs changed and different woods selected. When it was finished and ready for the newlyweds to move in it was called what it had always been called and always would, Padraig's House and, just as she had predicted, Martha could feel him all around. In time she made her children believe they, too, could feel the affectionate presence of the great-uncle they never knew, and every summer his sons, and in time, their sons, came to stay in their father's house with their father's family, so the children remained close, if not quite as close as they once would have been. As she grew older, Nancy secretly tired of her mother's fancies, as she thought of them, but the idea of Uncle Padraig being with them somehow pleased her and the presence of his sons and grandsons in her life seemed perfectly natural.

Martha's firstborn was a son she called James Donald, even though her mother's father had refused to attend her wedding because Ruairidh Beag would be there. She named her second Neil Padraig, for Tormod's father and her uncle. When Ann arrived in 1900 she was named for Annie MacKenzie, her great-great grandmother who had been buried in Clachan on the Isle of

Raasay in 1844. She had been Ann MacLeod MacKenzie, called Annie all her life, while the child who carried her name was Ann MacKenzie MacLeod, known as Nancy within the family.

Nancy and her brothers grew up with music all around them, and Tormod became one of the most important names in Nova Scotia. Padraig's House was always filled with musicians who had come to learn from him or simply to play along with him: it was, as Martha said with great satisfaction, exactly how the house would have been had Padraig lived in it himself. It was partly because Martha was a fine singer herself that she recognised her husband was in a different, higher league; she learned music faster and more deeply than other people, but he felt it coursing through his veins – music was who he was. She loved that he was a respected teacher, and she knew he deserved his renown.

With the passing years, Martha turned more and more to her interest in Indian culture and became as respected in treating people's ailments as Tormod was at treating their souls. When ordinary medicine failed, as it did many times, they would bring their symptoms to Martha MacLeod and she would invariably know just the thing to help them. Once a young Micmac man came to her during the night to say his wife was having trouble in labour. Martha set off with him to his wickawam, returning with the young woman and putting her in her own bed. Using the knowledge she had gained as a child she was able to help the woman better than her own people could, treating her with herbs and potions that eased her pain and relaxed her muscles, until her child was born alive and healthy. Word of this spread throughout Mabou and some said it was a terrible scandal, bringing a Micmac not only into her own home, but into her own bed too. 'Uist people,' her father remarked dismissively, 'and we all know how much notice to take of them.' Even in the New World, with a new life, the old clan animosities still held true.

When she was younger, Nancy MacLeod accepted her mother's healing abilities just as she did her Second Sight, or Tormod's music – all children, after all, accept whatever life they are given.

As she got older, though, she began to wonder what outsiders would make, not just of the dispensing of Indian medicine, but the Second Sight thing, and if they might wonder if it ran straight through the family to the present generation. One day, she knew, she would have friends who were different from anyone in Cape Breton, clever, intelligent people who knew things and did things, important people who would help her to change the world, and just how was she to explain her mother to them when the time came? She would sit before the dressing table in her bedroom, pulling a brush roughly through her thick, dark, curly hair – 'MacKenzie hair', Grandpa Ruairidh called it – trying to put together words that would explain Martha's little eccentricities. And just how did you explain, she wondered, screwing her eyes up as the brush fought its way through her tangles, that your mother was slightly odd and, if, for instance, you mentioned having a slight headache she would boil up a handful of berries she'd picked in the woods, throw in a few herbs and make you drink the result? Oh, and by the way, she also sees dead people about the place, but she is harmless, honestly. What bothered Nancy even more was that sometimes her mother's predictions came true, just as her berries and herbs worked, and she was determined there had to be rational explanations for both. In her mind she would remind herself that coincidences did happen, some of the potions were bound to work – look at the Indians, they were still alive – but in truth everything about her mother bothered her, even though she was the only one who was ever fazed by her strangeness. Why couldn't she be like other mothers, even if that did mean boring and ordinary? What was wrong with cooking, cleaning and looking after her family? And even though she never put her doubts into words, her facial expressions gave her away, as her father once remarked to Martha, thinking Nancy was out of earshot, 'The lass is of another age and can't be blamed for her confusion. We give them education,' he smiled, 'and what can they do but question the old ways? It's not their fault, it's ours, but what can we do but educate them?' That, Nancy thought, was precisely the point, it was all so, well, *un*educated.

Nancy was going through what most girls did with mothers, especially mothers who have a certain standing or notoriety and daughters who have a mind of their own, and Nancy certainly had that. She was stubborn, self-opinionated, her remarks could be stinging. And being a bright, intelligent, feisty female, in order to find her feet, her own identity and position in life, Nancy had to enter into a kind of rebellious rivalry with her mother. It was really an inverted admiration, not that Nancy would ever have admitted this, as she disputed anything said about her mother, and everything said by her. 'I just have to say "white",' Martha would smile indulgently, 'and Nancy will shout "black".' The strange thing, even to Nancy herself, was that she accepted her father's fame and took great pride in how much other people respected him, but somehow she couldn't quite feel as generous towards her mother. She wanted to become a doctor, she would say, before hurriedly adding that it was nothing to do with her mother's healing, if anything she had been influenced *against* her mother's ways of curing illness – she intended learning about *real* medicine, modern medicine. Boiling up a few leaves and a twig or two, she would opine loftily, was all very well before human beings knew any better, but that kind of thing was from the dark ages, before there was education and knowledge in the world, from a time when people believed in mermaids and unicorns. She knew everyone smiled when she said such things, but Nancy contrived not to notice, besides, one day she'd show them, and it bothered her not at all that there were very few female doctors anywhere; she was clever and nothing ever deterred her, so a doctor she would be. At least that was the plan, until her brothers and all the other lads she had grown up with were leaving for the war in France.

9

The 85th Nova Scotia Highland Battalion had been raised in the autumn of 1915, and from that came Cape Breton's own battalion, the 185th, Scots to a man, even if they were second- or third-generation Canadians. They adopted the motto of the 85th, '*Siol Na Fear Fearail*' — Seed of Manly Men, and they marched to the stirring tune of 'A Hundred Pipers': little wonder that all the young men in the area, including Nancy's brothers, Jamie and Neil, were keen to join up. Nancy was full of an envy she could almost taste: they were leaving Mabou, leaving Cape Breton, to have adventures, which was pretty much what the boys themselves believed, and then they would all be home for Christmas. Jamie was nineteen years old, the quiet one of the family, partly because he had some slight difficulty with his breathing at certain times of the year. In spring and summer, when the pollen from the trees and flowers was in the air, Jamie was always out of breath, his eyes reddened and his nose ran. No one knew exactly what it was, but the condition had cropped up in the family over the years and wasn't unknown to the Micmacs either, so Martha's potions had been employed many times and helped him a little. As he had grown up, though, the dark-haired Jamie had become used to retiring early from the more boisterous childhood activities during the times he found difficult, but he hated and resented having to do so and this, his mother had decided long ago, was why he was constantly looking for ways to prove himself. In winter he was the one who gave in to the cold only after the others had long abandoned snowball fights, the one who built bigger and better snowmen and created slippier and longer slides. 'Jamie always has to show what he can do and that it's better than anyone else,' she would say, shaking her head and fearing how far that attitude might take him.

When recruiting started for the war in Europe it was no surprise that Jamie was first in line, closely followed by his brother, and by Donald and Colin, sons of Hamish and grandsons of Padraig, and all their male cousins. With them in that wave of volunteers were many, many relatives from various branches of the family and different parts of the country and the US – like Gil. Donald Gillies MacDonald was the son of Padraig and Kate's firstborn, Ranald, the child who had slept in his cot beside Kate as Padraig had set out that morning looking for his special tree. Ranald had no liking for farm work, so when he was a teenager he had left Pine Edge in Campbellford to his younger brother, Hamish, and gone to work in the Boston end of the family logging business. It didn't occur to him at the time that he was handing over not only his own birthright, but that of any sons he might have in the future; but he was young, such considerations were many years away. In due course he had married, and Gil, his only child, was brought up in Boston; it was just one of those tricks of fate that Ranald's son was a country boy at heart and loved farming. Gil, like his cousins, Donald and Colin, considered himself a Cape Breton Scot, and returned 'home' to Mabou every summer, where he attached himself to Ruairidh Beag, both of them being men of the soil above all else. There were many Donald MacDonalds, so he had called himself Gil, being well aware if you didn't choose a nickname, one would be applied, and not often in a complimentary way. He was one of the family, so it was natural that Gil should join the Cape Breton regiment with the others. He had always been there in the background, a quiet, clever boy, taller and thinner than the others and with a 'big city' sophistication they all envied, even if they probably imagined it. So all of their lives there were the five lads, Jamie, Neil, Donald, Colin and Gil, who was slightly apart but friendly with everyone, moving easily between them without falling out with anyone, not even Nancy, which was a feat in itself. Like Ruairidh Beag and Padraig, though, Jamie and Donald were closer than brothers, and the coincidence that they had been born within weeks of each other was only one reason for the bond between them that was almost as strong as the one between their grandfathers. The three young MacDonalds spent at least every summer in Padraig's House in Mabou River, and by the time Donald was in his teens he was as much at home there as at Pine Edge. While Neil preferred the farm, Donald loved the places where both their grandfathers had grown up. He loved Cape Breton's easy access to the sea, the lush greenery and the hills that were so different from the flatter landscape of Ontario. As soon as he arrived each year the first thing he and Jamie did was to take a boat out, though it was Donald's obsession rather than Jamie's; for Jamie it was a means of escaping the noise and bustle Neil habitually caused, and the competition he imposed between himself and his younger brother. Sometimes Gil would tag along with the two older boys and sometimes with the younger ones, but he was equally happy on his own or talking to Ruairidh Beag, who had handed over the MacKenzie house to his eldest son and his family and retired with Jess to live in Padraig's House with Martha, Tormod and their youngsters. The old man would smile as he watched the young people who were always about the house, and the affection between his grandchildren and his brother's grandsons gave him a lot of pleasure. It was right, he thought, the thing had a kind of order about it, as though Padraig himself had come home. Donald was slight and fair and though he didn't have his grandfather's musical skills, he had a natural ability for working with wood that endeared him to the family. The boy was also quiet, even as a child he had never felt the need to rise to the usual challenges between boys, or run wildly about the place, so he was a natural companion for Jamie when, becalmed by shortness of breath, he had to sit by and watch his younger brother running around. That was what Neil did, he ran around recklessly, and mainly barefooted, a boy born to live without caution, a loud boy with a loud voice who caused fights wherever he went by simply wearing people down with his noise and energy. No illness ever brought him down, he was immune to sickness, never in one spot long enough, his grandfather said, for anything to take hold, and if he was, the old man would smile 'he'd only shout it into submission'. He was a cheerful boy, too, with no insight as to why this should upset others, and so had no means of moderating anything about how he behaved, though he was always bemused by the reaction he caused. Not that it bothered him much, he would just shrug off consequences like cuts, bruises and bumps, threats and insults, he was by then on his way to his next adventure, leaving frayed nerves in his wake. Naturally, the robust health of this boisterous younger brother added to Jamie's frustration, but it was in those times of watching from the sidelines that his friendship with Donald was forged and it lasted all his life.

'Made of granite,' Martha would say of Neil, then she would remember her own mother's worries and add with a smile, 'a bit like myself, in fact.'

'Aye,' said Tormod, 'but sometimes I think it's as well Gil's around, he acts like a buffer between Jamie and Neil, a big skinny buffer,' he laughed, 'but an effective one all the same.'

Martha nodded; she had been trying to find ways of defusing the tension between them all their lives and felt sorry for both her sons. Neil was just a big, healthy, loud lad, he didn't set out to put his older brother in the shade and didn't realise when he did, all the aggravation between them came from Jamie's frustration at not being able to keep up.

'It would've been easier if he'd been a lassie, Jamie wouldn't feel the need to compete with a sister the way brothers do.'

At that her husband would laugh. 'And you with a daughter who'll argue and fight over every word, Martha. You don't call that competing?'

'Jamie can cope with that, and the odd tussle with Nancy,' Martha smiled, 'but Neil's such a big, physical boy. Besides,' she laughed, 'Nancy only really fights with me, Tormod. With everyone else she's like a lamb.'

Tormod laughed out loud. 'You're fooling yourself there,' he said. 'Haven't you seen the lengths the lads, and the men, too, come to that, will go to to get her to look at them? They know she has a sharp tongue and won't see them in her way, but they can't help trying. I may be her father, but I can't help but feel for them when she cuts them down with a look or a sharp word. Like moths to a flame, I think, every time I see them thrown by the wayside.'

Martha laughed with him. 'But they get off easy,' she protested. 'One sharp word and she's done with them, I get sharp words all the time from our lamb!'

'Aye, but she's a clever lamb,' Tormod grinned, 'a sharp-witted, sharp-tongued lamb, who doesn't need to take anyone on physically, because she's more than able mentally for the best. You wonder what will become of her.'

'She could do great things,' Martha mused. 'She has such spirit, such single-mindedness, and she's always looking to learn.'

Tormod laughed. 'Aye, one thing's for sure, you won't see our lamb wearing a pinny and making bread, she'll do things in the world.'

Martha smiled but didn't reply.

She was restless, too, their lamb of a daughter, and never more so than when the boys were marching off to war together, leaving her behind, a fifteen-year-old girl who could never follow them and who bitterly resented it. And then it happened, though she was never sure of how or why, because there was no warning and no flash of lightning either. When she thought about it afterwards she felt it had been like waking up from a long sleep and finding the entire world changed. Only seconds had passed in real time and the same people and places were there, but in a different age perhaps. It was as the boys − the men − were leaving and she was waving and cheering with all the others in the crowd, the lump in her throat caused as much by envy as sorrow at the parting, and then, for no reason her eyes had settled on Donald MacDonald and everything stood still. Well, it wasn't quite like that, though she could never describe it exactly; *she* stood still and the world didn't, that was what it felt like, she was becalmed in the middle of the noise and the movement, and all the time the only sound she could hear was her own breathing, no shouts, cheers, goodbye greetings, only that rhythmic sound, a steady in and out, but when the moment had lifted she knew, that was all. She knew. She had known Donald all her life, had grown up with him, arguing with him and his brother as she did with her own brothers and all the cousins, till they snapped and chased her, yelling at her with boyish anger and she knew she had won again. There was nothing different about him in the days before they left for Aldershot, nothing different until that strange, silent, still moment, and they hadn't even exchanged glances, in fact he wasn't looking at her, yet suddenly she was standing alone in this quiet place no one else saw or felt, and she knew, knew it without the slightest doubt, that he was for her. It wasn't a feeling of heady romance, there was no emotion attached to it at all, it was as though a voice had spoken inside her, only no voice had; he would return from the war and this boy, this man, whose attention was elsewhere, would be with her for the rest of his life. It was, though she fought against thinking it, like a pre-knowledge. Yes, that was it; a silent, calm pre-knowledge she had only just realised she had. Nancy looked around at the others in the crowd, the anxiety in the faces of the other women, mothers, wives and sisters waving their men off. Fear was deeply etched into every expression and worry reflected in their eyes, their cheerful shouts trying to cover their true feelings; no sense leaving the lads with a last memory of crying women, even if they did know that they might be waving goodbye to them for ever. Nancy watched the tableau before her, saw the distress behind the masks and realised in a bemused, detached way that she had no such anxieties about Donald MacDonald; she knew he would be back. Then the moment passed and she quickly glanced at her mother and her grandfather, embarrassed that they might have noticed her confusion during that lost moment. She saw a look pass between them, but neither turned their attention in her direction, so Nancy convinced herself that they had more important things on their minds than her and was relieved; it would be a long, long time before she understood that look. She took a deep breath to steady herself but, just as she relaxed, there was a sensation of being invaded, of being taken over – it was the only way she would ever be able to describe the feeling – and in her mind a picture began to form of a tree with healthy branches reaching and growing under glorious, warm sunshine. Then, from nowhere a dark cloud formed over the tree, as first one branch dimmed and died, then another, and she was almost transfixed with terror and confusion.

It was May when the boys left for Aldershot, and on October 13th they boarded the *Olympic* in Halifax for the crossing to England, where a train took them to Witley Camp in Surrey. The adventure had begun in earnest. There was no national Canadian army at that stage, but many different regiments and battalions and, once in the camp, the men from Cape Breton lost their identity and became part of other divisions; some went to the 12th Canadian Infantry Training Brigade, others to the 42nd and 73rd (Montreal) Battalions, while the rest were amalgamated with the 219th, the 193rd and the 85th, though they were given official permission to call themselves 'the 185th Canadian Infantry Battalion (Cape Breton Highlanders)'. Then, in the spring of 1917, what was left of the 185th was placed within the 5th Canadian Division. Yet they weren't completely absorbed, and they wrote home describing their pride at being allowed to wear the dark green tartan of the Argyll and Sutherland Highlanders, though they would lose the kilt again when it was found that trench warfare and Highland dress didn't mix. By the time the kilt had been replaced by standard khaki uniform trousers there was a subtle change in the tone of their letters home, as the early euphoria and bravado were overtaken by the experience of the trenches. What those who fought in the First World War went through wouldn't be known by the world at large for many years, and some of the families of those men would never know. Reading between the lines of their letters, the feelings of despair and fear might be glimpsed, but the sheer brutality of their daily lives would rarely be hinted at. Partly it was to protect their families, but partly, too, because putting it down on paper, admitting that their lives were permeated by fear, brutality, blood and death might well have robbed them of any sanity they managed to preserve.

As the months turned to years, the boys fought on and, in Mabou, Nancy fought too, against what was happening to her mind. It was as though a door that had been closed all her life had opened, only she couldn't shut it again however much she tried. In an attempt to rationalise it, she thought back to the years when she was growing up and the stories she had heard of visions and trees with branches, trying to convince herself that she was imagining it all. And it wouldn't have been surprising if she was, she had heard those old stories for as long as she could remember: little wonder, when the world was falling apart, that she should construct a comforting wall of familiar tales around her. Only they didn't comfort Nancy, they scared her simply by being there. She felt as though her mind was no longer her own and she had no control over her own thoughts. There was no respite in sleep, the dreams were even worse, with voices loaded with fear, feelings of terror she didn't understand and smells that made her gag. It was the feeling that she was unable to control what was happening that frightened her most, though she was Nancy MacLeod, the strong, sensible one of the family, the calm one who had never suffered fools or their fantasies gladly, and now she was afraid to sleep. She refused to acknowledge what was happening, though, and decided it would not overcome her. It would be all right when the boys came home, she told herself, when this war was over and life was once again as it used to be and should be; she was just worried about the boys. It would be all right when the boys came home . . .

10

In Padraig's House Martha had awoken in the early hours of an autumn morning to find her son, Jamie, by her bedside, though in the two years since he had left home he had never been back.

'He stood there looking at me and saying he was sorry to cause me unhappiness,' Martha told Tormod, Nancy and Ruairidh Beag. 'He said it was his fault, that he didn't have to do it. My poor boy, there was nothing he could've done about it. I knew when they were leaving that he wouldn't come back,' she glanced at Ruairidh Beag, who nodded slightly as he met her eyes. 'We both did.'

Nancy didn't say anything. She didn't say, for instance, that what her mother had seen, she had dreamt, and that the dream had been so vivid that she had lain awake, her mind in turmoil, wondering what to do; didn't say that she had had other dreams, of Jamie coughing and fighting for breath, each time waking and looking around, the sound so clear that she expected to find him there, inches away. Even as her mother recounted the visit from Jamie, the picture in Nancy's mind of the tree with the dimming branch reappeared, but now the branch had gone. Inside her mind she was screaming, but outwardly she kept her peace, trying not to make eye contact with anyone. Then she felt Ruairidh Beag looking at her and, despite her resolve, she met his eyes. Her grandfather smiled gently at her; even if she didn't want to acknowledge it, he knew. She had never believed in the Second Sight, this Gift they prized so much, and now that it had come to her she wanted nothing more than for it to leave, for the pictures in her head and in her dreams to leave now, leave and never come back. As the thoughts raced through her mind she concentrated on other things in an attempt to distract herself, to control what she was seeing and thinking. She tried not to hear the voices of her family, but to listen to the sound of the wind in the trees outside, as it brought the first wispy snowflakes, harbingers of the winter to come. The heavy snow was a month or so away and she closed her eyes and conjured up winters past, mapping exactly where the drifts would lie, how deep they would be and how long they would stay, but recalling past winters brought memories of Jamie and how he was always the last one to give in to the cold. The tree appeared unbidden again; the branch *was* gone. Her eyes snapped open and she shook her head slightly, staring determinedly out of the window, trying to count the leaves that fell past, then she remembered that fall was one of Jamie's good times, when he could breathe more easily, only now she couldn't hear him breathing any longer. With a sudden shock she realised that throughout the last two years she had always been aware of Jamie's breathing, sometimes painful and harsh, sometimes calmer and easier, but now there was only a silence where it had been, and it was only by the silence that she knew she had heard it all this time. She turned her thoughts to the noise of the logs crackling on the fire, searching for any distraction rather than give in to this force that was taking her over, hoping desperately that if she didn't acknowledge it, if she shut it out, it might go away. Ruairidh Beag moved close to his granddaughter, put his arms around her and hugged her as he had once done with his daughter at a much younger age.

'There's nothing you can do about it, Nancy,' he whispered. 'If it's there, then it's there. But don't be afraid, you'll get used to it.'

Nancy stayed in his embrace, gritting her teeth and shutting her eyes so tightly that it hurt, but she didn't reply. It wasn't that she was afraid, or not in the conventional sense at any rate, the only fear she had was that if she admitted whatever it was existed, whatever it was might be there to stay. When the boys came home again, some of them at any rate, these feelings, these thoughts and sounds and pictures in her head would go, she decided. Only if she showed the slightest sign of believing any of it would it swoop and take root for ever, take over her life, so she couldn't give in to it now. She didn't want it, she resented it, this thing that her grandfather and her mother accepted so easily. It came from the Dark Ages and was no more than a Gaelic myth, something the old ones talked of with reverence as they told stories of the homeland they saw in their minds; it belonged in the past and should stay there. The trouble was that despite her determination to stop it, once it had made itself known in that strange, becalmed moment two years before as the boys were leaving home, it had rapidly expanded and increased, till she felt everyone could see that something had changed her. This was the twentieth century, she lived in a modern world ripped apart by a brutal war that looked as though it would never stop eating up the young men of her generation, there was no room for fancies and fables, and she felt as though she was on the edge of madness. How could anyone tell, she wondered? There were people who went insane, ran off screaming at the demons they saw and heard; who decided that one was mad and another had the Gift of Second Sight? Sometimes she only had to look at people, even think of them, for a dark cloud to appear and a feeling of restlessness, and she knew what would happen next, and it always did. In a desperate attempt to make it disappear she would retreat to her bedroom and read for hours on end to blot out the thoughts that occupied her mind, but there was no escape, they were still there.

Three days after the official notification of Jamie's death arrived, word came that his cousin, Colin MacDonald, wouldn't be coming home either. In due course the War ended at the eleventh hour of the eleventh day of the eleventh month in 1918, and in 1919 three of the five boys who left together came home again. Only they weren't boys any longer, they were men and the years spent fighting hadn't so much aged or matured them as wearied them, and that weariness had changed them forever. Neil, who had always been so loud and full of energy that everyone agreed Cape Breton wouldn't hold him for long, that the boy would leave this small, close-knit place and do all sorts of exciting things in far-off lands, was now content to stay at home and never leave. He was quiet to the point of silence now, this once annoyingly noisy boy, who used to cause arguments simply by irritating others with the volume of his voice and the exuberance of his movements. Now, instead of swashbuckling and bestriding the world, he wanted nothing more than to work quietly alongside his family in Mabou. There were those who said he would come back to normal once he had time to relax and get his strength back, but Martha would shake her head when they said this, she knew there was now a new 'normal'.

It was early summer when Donald MacDonald and his cousins, Neil and Gil, went home to Cape Breton, where all the family had assembled in Padraig's House for their return, to hear their account of the war. Those who had left to live elsewhere still returned to Cape Breton every summer: home, despite their romantic yearnings for Scotland, was still home, but in May 1919 they had made the journey slightly earlier, because the lads were due home and there was much to hear, if not much to tell, because it would be a sanitised version, edited out of kindness. There was a tacit pact among all those who had fought in the war to keep much of it among themselves, even once they had returned home: they did not want their womenfolk, and the womenfolk of those who did not come home in particular, to know the whole truth. The family that day were not told, for instance, that in 1916, when their boys had gone to Flanders to engage the Germans in what were referred to as 'local skirmishes' – intended to keep the enemy busy while plans were made for 'The Big Push' – that conditions were hell and many men died in these 'local skirmishes' – but war was war, after all. The families would hear that in August they had been sent to the Somme where the battle had been raging since 1 July, to take over a section of the front line in front of the French village of Courcelette, but not that they had been told that conditions were 'quiet' or 'normal', when in fact the fighting was fierce, with 2,600 dying before the main fighting began.

By then the Canadians had been formed into four divisions that fought together, refusing to give in to British demands that they should be disbanded and absorbed into British forces – the lads had no problem recounting that, it was part of their new pride in themselves. By the middle of September, they said, with the help of the new wonder weapon, the tank, they had taken Courcelette and defended it against constant German offensives, before attacking 'that ditch of evil', Regina Trench. Then their 4th Division arrived and the Canadians, knee-deep in mud, had to overcome fierce enemy resistance to finally take Regina Trench, and were amazed to find that it was no more than a depression in the chalk. There was always one more trench, one more hill, and next, the Canadian divisions took Desire Trench, the German support line, before the autumn rains arrived, turning the battlefield into a bog and halting the offensive. They had advanced the line a mere six miles, and for that 600,000 Allied troops, including 24,000 Canadians in only six weeks, and 236,000 Germans had died. Little wonder that the Germans called the Somme 'Das Blutbad' – the bloodbath. But even when there were no battles raging along the Western Front, when things were truly 'quiet and normal', hundreds of men died; it was called 'normal wastage'.

All of this was passed over in a few words by Gil in his quiet voice with the broad Boston vowels. He didn't tell them of the rampant diseases in the trenches caused by fleas and lice, resulting in a collection of illnesses called Trench Fever, or about Trench Foot, from standing in cold water and mud day after day, often leading to amputation. Even the Flanders soil attacked them with bacteria from generations of fertilizer, infecting the smallest graze and causing often fatal gas gangrene without a shot being fired. Their resistance to disease was already weakened by the unchanging diet of corned beef, hard biscuit, weak jam and sweetened tea, giving them boils and other skin conditions to contend with. Coils of wire as high as a house stood around them, with barbs as big as a man's thumb, catching men and holding them, sitting ducks for the enemy machine guns. They had to hack into the trench walls for a place to sleep, living in the rain and knee-deep in the mud, always the mud, with the corpses of the dead built into the parapets, rotting before the eyes of their former comrades. The mud covered everything, it sucked at their weary legs so they were always conscious of drowning in it, and it caked their clothes and kit, adding fifty kilograms to the weight of their greatcoats – some cut off the skirts, and were charged with destroying government property. They lived lives of misery, disease and fear, sent into killing fields in the face of enemy machine guns, shells and flame-throwers, and the big terror, gas. The returning men told only the barest essentials of this; bad enough that those years in hell would burn into the souls of those who had endured it, without condemning their families to suffer, too.

'Jamie got a whiff of mustard gas early on,' Donald broke into Gil's account. 'Nothing much, the wind had changed direction and it had drifted over our trench. There were some Moroccans, a whole bunch of them fighting on our side, gassed before they saw it coming. You could see it, a kind of eerie, luminous mist, and someone had shouted out a warning so we got our masks on before it really hit. But Jamie,' he shook his head and looked down. 'You know the trouble he had with his breathing sometimes, well it was worse when he had to use a gas mask, and I think the gas probably affected him worse than the rest of us as well. After that first whiff I don't think his lungs really recovered, and the weather was so bad, wet and cold, just getting through the mud dragged all the energy out of you. We said we were fighting the German generals and General Winter as well.' He laughed quietly, then paused for a long time, and Nancy, standing by the window, her eyes fixed on some spot outside, felt her heart would burst out of her chest with pity for him.

'Donald,' Martha said gently, 'you don't have to go over this all at once, you don't have to go over it at all.'

There was a silence, then Gil continued. 'After the Somme they sent us to Vimy Ridge,' he said.

Vimy Ridge would enter the souls of all Canadians and remain there for generations, yet it rose barely 150 metres above sea level between the French and British sectors. Its importance was that it gave the Germans an overview of the Allies – and would, if taken, give the Allies the same over the Germans – and it blocked the way to the mines and factories of the Douai Plain which helped them continue the war. Because of its importance, the Germans had made Vimy Ridge into a fortress of pillboxes, dugouts and interlocking tunnels linking natural caves, and despite repeated Allied attacks it had remained impregnable. Field Marshal Douglas Haig told the Canadians to take it.

'We had this British general,' Gil smiled gently, 'but he was more like us. The British were always complaining that we were undisciplined, that we never saluted, but Byng kept his hands in his pockets, and his version of a salute was moving his hand to the top of his pocket without actually taking it out. We called ourselves "Byng's Boys". He knew what he was doing when it came to battle, though, he planned everything. We even had a layout of the battlefield with every German position on it, and he made us rehearse every movement. One British officer said, "You Canadians take all the fun out of war." There were too many of his kind.'

The official records of the Vimy Ridge offensive would record that a gunner called Andy McNaughton, a McGill University professor, used the latest technology in the plan, sending in flash spotters, microscopes and oscilloscopes to locate German guns and plot them on the map. The records would also tell of how the sappers, or engineers, built 40 kilometres of roads, 30 kilometres of light railway, 70 kilometres of water pipes, 150 metres of signal wire, and 7 kilometres of tunnels from the rear to the front line, keeping the troops safe till the last minute; one of them could hold 1,000 men. It was meticulous, well-planned and rehearsed, even if it was no fun, then on 2 April 1917 the bombardment opened up what the Germans called 'the week of suffering', as 50,000 tonnes of explosives pounded them, collapsing their trenches and destroying their supply lines. At 4 a.m. on 9 April – Easter Monday – the Canadian infantry were given a hot meal and a tot of rum, then they moved forward and swarmed up the ridge, the wind and driving snow and sleet at their backs, straight into the faces of the Germans. Just as they had been trained and prepared to do, they clambered over shell craters, through pools of mud and torn barbed wire, throwing grenades into the German dugouts as they went, sergeants taking over as officers fell, then corporals, then privates. Four Canadians won the Victoria Cross that day, all but one posthumously, and by 12 April the Germans had abandoned the ridge, holding only a small bump, named The Pimple. Brigadier-General Edward Hilliam, a former Alberta rancher, led his 10th Brigade against the Prussian Grenadier Guards and threw them out within an hour. Later, writing up his report, Hilliam signed himself 'Lord Pimple'.

The repeated failures of previous Allied attempts to take Vimy Ridge made the victory of the Canadian forces shine like a rare and glorious triumph in a bloody war that would kill millions of men needlessly, but more than that, it gave Canadians a sense of themselves they had never had before. They went into the war willingly because their allegiance to the Crown was still strong, but they went from their own very separate provinces, a collection of small regiments and battalions. However, their stubborn refusal to separate the four divisions for dispersal among the ranks of the British had brought them together in a way that no one could have anticipated. They may have gone from home to the war in Europe as provincials, but they returned as Canadians, and there was an understanding for the first time that Canada was a nation. Later historians would say that the seeds of Canadian nationhood had been planted at Vimy Ridge, watered with the blood of 10,000 dead and injured, but in those early days the survivors didn't speak of blood, suffering and death to their families, as they struggled to put into words their feelings of unity and pride.

'Everyone you met was from Canada,' Gil explained. 'They were all there, the Seaforths, the Tenth Battalion Canadian Infantry – the Fighting Tenths, they were called – the Sixteenth Canadian Scottish, the Thirteenth Royal Highlanders, the Royal Canadians, the Princess Patricia's Canadians, the 46th South Saskatchewans, and others, like us, who had been collected along the way and put in with other regiments. You'd turn to some guy you'd never met before and get talking and you'd find he came from Quebec, or Ontario, and you'd discover that his people had come from near your own people in Scotland. We had things in common, we were together, and we were all one army. It didn't matter which part of Canada we came from, we came from one country. I don't think any of us had ever felt that before.'

'After that,' said Donald, 'we were sent to Ypres, to Passchendaele.' Donald shook his head. 'It was so cold and wet, Jamie was never well, no one was in the best of health, but he was worse.' He touched his chest. 'He got pneumonia and it wasn't getting better, so he was sent to the hospital by one of our officers – ours were the best, they took their lead from Byng, they didn't care if we saluted them on the battlefield,' he said bitterly. 'After Vimy we'd earned the right.' He looked up at the listening relatives. 'You remember how Jamie hated not being able to do things?' They all nodded. 'Well it was like that. He didn't want to be seen as weak, he didn't want to feel he was leaving us to it, as though any man who'd won Vimy Ridge could let anyone down. I said to him at last, "Look, Jamie, if we have to listen to you coughing and spluttering all the time it'll put us off our aim and our sleep. All the lads want you to go so badly that they'll carry you to the hospital and dump you on the doorstep!" and all the lads in the trench laughed and shouted insults at him, so finally he agreed to go. He was laughing as he went, but you could see he still felt he'd failed. He was always like that, even when we were kids. If he couldn't do something, even if it didn't matter to anyone else, it mattered to Jamie.'

'And he got better?' Martha prompted.

'Better than better, he fell in love!'

Everyone laughed quietly, happy for Jamie.

'He met a nurse there,' Donald continued, 'Catriona, a Skye lass. She was good to him, good for him, and they were so suited you'd have thought they'd been married for fifty years. When he came back to the trenches we used to tease him, "You won't have to be carried back there, MacLeod", that sort of thing, "Don't bother coughing, MacLeod, we know what you're up to". It changed him, he was so different, if ever any man could be said to be content up to his knees in mud, it was Jamie after he met Catriona.'

'What was she like?' Ruairidh Beag asked.

'Dark, blue-eyed,' Donald replied, glancing over at Gil, who smiled and looked down. 'Very calm, very gentle. She was working in all that carnage and yet she had this quiet air about her, always smiling. A beautiful smile, a beautiful girl. We kept asking aloud what she could possibly see in him, and he'd laugh, but he'd gone from us in a kind of a way, in his mind he was always with her and that made him more positive. He talked of becoming a doctor when he came home, like Nancy,' he stopped, smiling gently in her direction. 'It was because of what he'd seen in the hospital, though being Jamie he felt a fraud for being there when he wasn't actually injured, when so many men were lying there, maimed and dying. He began helping about the place, I think it made him feel better, feel that he could be of some use, and with that and Catriona, he could see something beyond where he was, so I suppose he was luckier than the rest of us. We all talked about using our leave to go back to where we had come from, Raasay, Skye or wherever, to visit family; not that we did, it was too far away and we only had a couple of days here or there, though we felt we'd been given a month off. Most hit the town or slept, but not Jamie, he spent his with Catriona and the wounded and dying, and was happy.' Donald shook his head, smiling at the memory. 'There he was in Hell and he thought he was in Heaven. The power of love.'

At the window, Nancy's hand went to her throat.

'He was at the hospital at one point, nothing wrong with him, though you could always hear his breathing. The stretcher carriers were having a hard time of it. You've no idea what those guys went through, running from the front to the field stations with the injured, risking their lives for guys they knew couldn't make it, and the mud was so bad they worked in teams of eight to carry one stretcher. Well about three teams hadn't come back and the officers told a few men they were now stretcher carriers, but they didn't need to with Jamie, he volunteered. When I heard that I remembered him in the snow, staying out longer than the rest of us – remember?' All around heads nodded. 'I was so mad at him when I heard, I thought "This has to stop. When I see him again I'm going to tell him how stupid this is, he's not a kid any more." Only I didn't see him again. No one knows what happened, well, not the details, he and the others on that team just didn't make it back. I tried to find out later, but no one knew anything; he just went out and never came back, they said. That happened to thousands of men, they didn't have to carry stretchers to disappear.'

'And the girl?' Martha asked. 'Catriona?'

Donald was silent for a long time. 'She never found out he was dead,' he said. 'She was killed by a bomb the same night.'

There was a long, painful silence, then 'My brother was killed as he got off a train at Ypres,' Donald said, and fell silent again for a moment. 'Forgive me,' he whispered, 'I can't . . .'

'Don't torture yourself, boy,' his father, Hamish, said gently from the corner of the room. 'What more is there to say?'

'There is,' Donald replied, his head down, 'but . . . not now.'

'Listen to your father, Donald,' Gil said quietly. 'You have said what happened, now let it go.'

Donald looked up at his cousin and smiled at him with an

affectionate sadness, then he suddenly got up and ran from the room, out into the chill air. Nancy instinctively went after him. She caught up with him down by the brook where Martha had seen his grandfather all those years ago, and found him standing by a tree, sobbing and talking about his brother and about Jamie.

'Jamie was in bits,' he said, his voice as taut as he could make it, but still betraying some of the horror despite himself, 'they all were. The whole stretcher team lying there, nothing more than a collection of bits and pieces of bodies. Jamie was there too, but I couldn't recognise him, all those arms and legs –' He shook with sobs again. 'I knew he was there, but I didn't know –'

'Don't,' she said.

'And Colin, that was my fault. How do I tell my mother and father that I caused Colin to die?'

'Don't,' Nancy said again, wanting to help him but feeling useless. She reached out to him and he turned, collapsing into her arms and all his weight settling onto her shoulders, so that his sobs wracked her body as well as his. From Padraig's House, Martha, Tormod and Ruairidh Beag watched the two figures melded into one, untouched by the cold.

'He'll be all right,' Martha smiled.

'*They'll* be all right,' Tormod replied, but as the three of them returned to the fireside he didn't see Martha and Ruairidh Beag exchange a look.

'Did neither of you know before they left?' Tormod asked thoughtfully, his eyes on the flames dancing in the fire. 'About Jamie, I mean?'

'It's not like that, Tormod,' Ruairidh Beag said quietly. 'It's not like knowing everything all the time, it comes in snatches, then nothing for months, even years sometimes. There are times when it's someone close and you think you should've known and can't work out why you didn't, times when you see a dark cloud over someone you barely know, and you can't work that out either. When the boys were leaving here for Aldershot, Martha and I both saw the cloud over Jamie, but I didn't see it over Colin. Did you, Martha?'

Martha shook her head. 'Just Jamie,' she said sadly. 'And later I felt his breathing getting bad. Nancy felt it, too, though she didn't say a word, I knew just by looking at her.'

'I think she might be scared,' Ruairidh Beag suggested. 'With me it was there all my life, and with you, Martha, since you were very small, when Padraig died. It must be easier to accept when you can't remember any different, but I think it only hit her that day. I remember feeling something draw my eyes to her and she looked as though she'd been poleaxed, the feeling was so strong that I even moved closer to her in case she collapsed where she stood. She still hasn't said anything to me about it, though.' He looked quizzically at Martha, who shook her head.

'I wish she'd been spared it,' she said, 'all those years I thought she had been. Nancy's a close one, she'll work it out and come to terms with it on her own, but if I say anything to her she'll bite the nose off my face. You know what she's like.'

Tormod laughed gently. 'Our vicious wee lamb,' he smiled. 'But had you no feelings about Jamie in all that time?'

'Just his breathing, as I said,' Martha said, 'I could feel that he was in trouble. Then I felt his mood lifting, though I couldn't figure out why.'

'Catriona,' Ruairidh Beag said.

'Seems likely,' Martha smiled. 'Then I woke to find him standing there, and I knew. The thought of not knowing where he's lying, though . . .' She buried her face in her hands and wept.

Tormod put his arms around her.

'That doesn't matter,' said a voice from the corner, and they looked up to where Neil had been sitting silently throughout. 'All the lads accepted that they would stay where they fell, if they got buried it would be a bonus, but it didn't matter in the end. Donald went looking for him, I think that's what he was thinking. He says it was to find out what had happened, but there was no chance of that, I think he wanted to give Jamie a decent burial if he could. But they're all there together no matter what happened to them, if they sank in the mud, if there was enough to bury, if there wasn't. None of it matters, they're together. You'd have to have been there to understand.'

'Neil's right,' Gil agreed. 'It's not easy to explain, but that's how we all feel.' There was a long, heavy silence. 'But we didn't tell you about the mutiny!' Gil said brightly, looking in vain in Neil's direction in the hope that he'd join in.

Everyone in the room looked up and smiled, lifted by the tone of Gil's voice.

'When was this?' Martha asked.

'Just a couple of months ago, March,' Gil replied; it was like him to try to make light of what had happened to them since they had last met in Cape Breton. Two of the lads had died, they had all suffered a great deal, but for Gil life had to go on, and with a smile, if possible, however wry.

'So what caused this mutiny?' Tormod asked.

'Well, it was one of those things that got out of hand, anyone half-sensible could've handled it better than the British military,' Gil grinned quietly. 'When the war ended we thought we'd be going straight home, but they sent us to a camp in Wales, Kinmel it was called. They said we had to wait there for boats to bring us home, but they didn't appear, or not for us, at any rate. The Americans had come into the war last and they were leaving first, we just waited and longed to be going home, thousands of us and more arriving all the time. And they ran this place strictly, like a proper army camp, all square-bashing and stupid routines. We'd fought a war, we'd had enough, so we weren't happy. They said we couldn't go home because Canada's railways weren't up to handling so many men at one time, next it was because of a shortage of boats, but we couldn't see why every one they had was going to America and why the Canadians never got a turn. Then the Spanish flu hit the camp and some of the lads who'd survived the war died of it. It was a bad winter and there were strikes going on, so we didn't have enough coal for heating. Things were getting worse by the day and the lads were turning angry. One night some of them went looking for a drink in town, but the bar owners refused to open up and sell the lads a beer or two. That was it, they'd had enough, and they just snapped and took what they wanted. After they'd had a couple they caused a bit of damage in a few places and there was a fight, so they say. It would've died down if the camp commandant hadn't smashed all the beer barrels in the camp. A bunch of lads were locked up, so that caused a real riot. One youngster on the army's side was killed, shot in the back by "friendly fire", and that's when things got really rough. By the end five men were dead and twenty-eight injured. How many did they court martial, Neil?' he asked, trying to bring his cousin into the tale.

'I think it was about fifty,' Neil replied quietly, 'but most of them were acquitted. I think they realised by that time it would get really ugly if they didn't get rid of us. The next thing we knew boats appeared to take us home. If we'd known that was all we had to do we'd have rioted sooner.'

'And that,' smiled Gil, 'is why we're here now instead of in that camp. The undisciplined Canadians, that's what they'll think, but it got us home. The military mind is a strange thing,' he said ruefully. 'We'd fought all those battles and won, and we still had to cause them trouble to get us home. You have to wonder if they knew what they were doing during the war at all.'

'I don't think I ever wondered about that,' Neil said darkly from the corner.

Neil never spoke of the war again. Some men couldn't stop talking about it, it was as if the only way they could survive the after-effects was to pour out their experiences and thoughts in a never-ending, repetitive torrent, and it didn't matter if no one listened. Others, like Donald, would suffer nightmares for the rest of their lives and only occasionally talk about what they had seen and done, as though every word were being dragged painfully from them, but for Neil MacLeod it was over. The war in Europe had destroyed his loud, boisterous spirit and created a distant, brooding man that none of his family recognised. At least, they mused, he had his life. He didn't though. With the passing of the years afterwards, Neil isolated himself from everyone. Looking at him there was a blankness about his eyes, as if the only way he could function was to erect a screen in his mind and hide behind it. The bottle, it soon became clear, was the only thing he cared about. Martha watched her now only son lose himself in booze, and was distraught.

'It'll only be temporary,' his father suggested. 'He's been through a lot, he's taking a little time out, that's all.'

He was a father who'd lost a son, it was what he had to believe, but though Martha and Ruairidh Beag nodded as Tormod spoke, once again neither replied; they had other considerations, they were already watching Nancy and Donald.

In the weeks that followed, the families who had come home to Cape Breton left again. Gil left with his father, Ranald, for Boston, and the other MacLeods, MacKenzies and MacDonalds for wherever they now lived, but Donald, still deeply withdrawn, remained at Padraig's House, where Nancy had appointed herself his saviour. To make sure he ate, she prepared food for both of them and sat with him at mealtimes. She took walks with him, looked for pieces of wood to try to tempt him to work again, and she read him sea stories, all the time sure that all he needed was constant care to return to normal; she was young enough to still believe that was possible. Martha watched her and despaired, knowing how her daughter would react if offered advice, especially from her mother.

'She thinks it's her calling,' Martha told Ruairidh Beag sadly. 'She thinks she's been put on earth to care for him. He has a mother of his own to do that, she's taking him over when he's too weak to protest and she's ruining her own life.'

'And that's a powerful feeling for any woman, Martha,' he replied. 'You know there's nothing will change her mind. It's there, you can see that, and it won't be resolved for a long time.'

'But she's my daughter,' Martha wept. 'She's my own child. How can I watch this without trying to stop her?'

'Because that's the way to make her more determined,' Ruairidh Beag said quietly. 'There's nothing to be done, Martha, she must find her own way.'

★   ★   ★

In due course, Nancy became the only one who could cope with Donald without realising she had created the situation herself, that anyone strong enough could have looked after him. That moment on the station platform those few short years before was all the proof she needed, though she had never spoken of it to anyone; she had been convinced that he would survive and come home, and he had – their relationship was special, meant to be. She would save him, she would heal him; there wasn't the slightest doubt in her mind that all he needed was normal family life, and she'd provide that. Against that kind of conviction no one stood a chance of changing her mind, Donald least of all.

II

Nancy MacLeod didn't become a doctor, she became a MacDonald and a nurse instead, though not a professional one. In the summer of 1919 she and Donald were married and went to Campbellford, where Donald took up the reins of the family farm his younger brother, Colin, had been destined to have. Pine Edge was 130 kilometres to the south of Campellford in Ontario, on the Morganston Road leading to Castleton.

It was a mixed farm, with hand-milked cows providing milk for the dozen or so cheese factories in the area as well as the dairies and the creamery that produced butter. On the farm, the milk was kept cool by immersing forty-gallon cans in ice-cold water, using ice cut from the river the previous winter and stored with sawdust as insulation, before being delivered to the cheese factory and the creamery by horse-drawn wagon. Pine Edge had beef cattle too, and was part of a local farm ring, each one in turn supplying an animal for butchering and eating fresh, while the rest was canned and kept for later. Vegetables and fruits that weren't used as they were picked were also kept in glass storage jars, with the refuse fed to the pigs, and there were fields of wheat, oats, barley, rye, corn, with hay, mostly timothy, red clover, alsike and alfalfa, grown to feed the animals and harvested with the horses. The two-storey farmhouse was set off the road, across an orchard and vegetable garden where Nancy immediately spotted apple, cherry, pear and plum trees as she arrived on that first day. The house was built of undressed stone with three front steps leading to a covered porch at the entrance. It followed the design of the era – a central hall with rooms leading off. On one side of the hall there was a parlour for entertaining guests and a small bedroom that in times to come would be used more often than Nancy could ever have imagined. On the other side was a family living room and, at the end, a large dining kitchen, with a summer kitchen behind, that was used for preparing hot-weather meals, 'canning' food in glass jars, and for washing clothes. In winter the back kitchen became a freezer and was cold enough to keep food frozen for months at a time. Two smaller rooms were connected to the main kitchen, serving as a pantry and a storage room, giving access to the basement, where there were screened cupboards for perishables, bins of dried fruit and vegetables and shelves of preserves. At the far side of the basement there was a furnace and a store of dry wood to keep it going, with a chute for unloading the wood from the shed outside directly to where it would be used.

In Mabou, the MacKenzies had concentrated on producing pedigree dairy cattle and sheep; the acreage they had was both big and fertile enough to divide and provide well for all of them, and they had logging interests, too. In Campbellford, over the years Donald's family had bought up smaller farms, using the farmhouses for relatives, making Pine Edge a much bigger steading than the one where Nancy had grown up. From that first day, a few months before her nineteenth birthday, she would be the sole mistress of it, her in-laws having moved out to a house a few miles away that they had undoubtedly reserved many years before for when Colin would bring home his bride. Upstairs there were four bedrooms, and from one of the front windows Nancy looked out on a much flatter landscape than she had been used to. Looking around the bedroom she was in, she touched her stomach; she had already earmarked this bedroom facing to the front for herself and Donald, and now she decided that the other would be for the child she was carrying, so that he or she would see the same view every morning that she saw herself.

All the bedrooms had angled roofs that made Nancy smile, remembering her mother's familiarity with Mabou's 'Micmac wickawams' that had led to John MacVicar's attempt to censure Ruairidh Beag all those years before; Martha would feel at home in any of these bedrooms. Outside stood the standard toilet, the woodshed and the usual outbuildings; barns with dutch roofs for keeping animal feed and hay, a dairy and housing for the animals in winter. As she looked out, she saw Hamish and Mhairi MacDonald's horse and buggy turn into the driveway and Donald walk forward to greet his parents, so she ran downstairs and hugged her in-laws in turn, feeling strange at welcoming them to the home they had lived in for many years.

'This will be different from what you're used to, Nancy,' Mhairi smiled gently.

'Well, a bit,' Nancy admitted. 'It's flatter and not so green, but we'll be happy here.' She smiled at Mhairi, who suddenly burst into tears. 'This must be hard for you,' Nancy said gently, feeling more flustered than she appeared. 'It's been your home all these years, you've brought your family up here, and now I'm taking over.'

'Aye,' Mhairi smiled, wiping her tears, 'just me being senti-mental. It'll happen to you one day, and when your boy brings home his wife you'll look back and remember this silly old woman shedding tears. It's the way of the world, Nancy, none of us can avoid change. I'll leave you to look around on your own, it's your house now, and if there's anything I can help you with, you know where I am.' Then Mhairi turned to watch Donald through a window and shed more tears. She hoped the poor lassie would have a good life here, but looking at Donald, at her boy who had returned as a stranger, she couldn't help a shiver of doubt and fear passing through her, that was what had caused her to cry, the feeling that life had changed for ever, and not for the better. As the buggy left again, Mhairi turned around to where the young couple had been standing together on the lawn, but now only Nancy was there to wave goodbye, Donald had already walked off on his own, and Mhairi felt another shiver of foreboding.

So, young Nancy MacLeod MacDonald had become mistress of a large, wealthy farm, she was already expecting an heir and, furthermore, the terrible war was over. There should have been nothing but sunshine and happiness ahead, but it became, she decided later, like one of those confusing dreams where you almost recognise a place you know well and love, only it isn't quite the same, and there is a dark, frightening side to it. In this kind of dream, too, there is always someone you know inside out, who looks the same, sounds the same, but turns out to be different in so many disturbing ways that they seem to be impersonating the real person. The kind of dream you wake from in a panic and feel relief that it wasn't real after all, though so much of it seemed real. She had known Donald all her life, had taken him as much for granted as she had her brothers; he was family in every way that mattered apart from blood, after all. Yet the Donald she had married wasn't the boy she had known, or the man she ever expected him to become. The laid-back, calm, gentle boy with a love of the sea had come back from the war a troubled man, his eyes haunted, his moods often ranging from black to blacker within minutes, and his sleep disturbed by terrifying nightmares. So she nursed Donald, that became her aim in life, to return Donald to health, and then, when he was well, when he had recovered, their life together could start afresh, that's what she thought in those early years. And the Second Sight could go hang itself, she had more pressing demands on her time and energy without giving in to that. It had just been something in the air because of the impending war and the boys leaving home, she decided, an excitement that bordered on hysteria, and she had been caught up in it. Her eyes had settled on Donald, that was true, but if one of the others had been there instead, there was just as much chance of her strange moment happening around him. Or maybe there had been an attraction there between them all along, but it was only at the moment he was leaving she had recognised it, the moment when he was leaving and maybe not coming back. She had always thought of herself as sensible and logical, but maybe, under the surface, when emotions were high and feelings deep, she was like all other fifteen-year-old girls after all, mixed up and a bit silly. She had instincts, that was all, she had feelings about things, but only if you had Scots blood would you call it Second Sight, then it would become something deeply romantic and mysterious. She laughed to herself. She had nearly fallen for it, too, thank heavens she hadn't ever mentioned it to anyone, her mother especially. What Martha would have given to have another mystic in the family!

Thinking back later, she realised that if she hadn't already been there, Donald, like her brother, Neil, would never have married and had children. His experiences had robbed him of the ability to connect to others in a normal way and he had needed someone who already had a commitment to him, someone he didn't have to get to know and who didn't have to get to know him, because after the war that process was beyond him. From that strange moment in 1916 she had been waiting for him, though she knew he had been unaware of it. Now she sensed that theirs would never be a marriage of eloquent romance, but she hoped that whatever feelings they had started with would deepen over the years. What she reckoned without, being young and full of life, was the depth of Donald's struggle with the aftermath of what he had gone through, what he had seen others go through, in those short years when idealism and adventure had been submerged by a lifetime of fear and horror. It was happening all over the world in those years after the Great War, though it was natural that those who were living through it felt only their own situations. A whole generation of men were either wiped out or survived physically, but would never recover mentally, and would go on to inflict more damage on their families, whose only wish had been to have them home again.

When their first son, Calum Ruairidh, arrived, Nancy was already a mother to her husband. She looked down at the baby for the first time, and saw a crease between his eyes, a vertical line that made him look worried or annoyed, though the midwife said it was wind. Not that he wouldn't have reason to be worried or annoyed, even if he was a healthy, happy baby. There were many times when he would take second place to the needs of his father, times when Calli slept through the night and Donald was the one who had to be held and comforted. Nancy kept hoping that normal family life would work some miracle cure for her husband, but in the darker corners of her mind she wondered if that would ever be possible; the truth was that she felt a dark cloud over Donald that never lifted. The arrival of Fearghus Donald two years later made no more difference than Calli's arrival had made, though Nancy admitted it to no one, and hints that all was not well would draw from her a blank stare or a sharp word in reply; this was their business, hers and Donald's, and no one, not even sympathetic family, would be allowed into it. But there were times when she wept in her wickawam bedroom for failing to be of any help to him, times when he would be overcome by such anger that he would rise from their bed and walk off over the fields alone to regain control over himself, afraid of what he might say. He felt out of control, afraid of his next word, and worse was his fear of what he might do to his blameless family, while he was gripped by this black fury and despair. It was an impossible concept that the anger, sorrow and memories of those men could have disappeared at 11 a.m. on the eleventh day of the eleventh month of 1918, and Donald was no different from those millions of others all over the world. He suffered not just from his wartime experiences, but from every form of guilt and remorse; the mind trying to control his thoughts, words and actions had no balance, and he suffered not only for what he had said and done, but for what he might have said and done. He knew he was inflicting his agonies on Nancy and the two, tiny, perfect little boys he could hardly bear to touch, because he was afraid of hurting them. Nancy felt adrift and unsure, there were no rules governing the kind of situations she was faced with, like the dreams about Jamie and Colin that tortured Donald more than any others. When he didn't race off into the night she would sit in their bed, the silence broken by the weeping of her husband in her arms, and all she could think to do was to let him talk, hoping that by lancing the wound the poison would be released, little realising that the words would be just as painful to say and hear twenty years later.

★   ★   ★

'We were going to Ypres by train, but we got separated, everything was always chaos. When Colin caught up he tried to get into the carriage Jamie, Neil and I were in, but I told him it was already too full, there was no point in squeezing in. "Take the next train," I said. "We'll meet up soon enough." It took us through Vlamertinghe, then we got off the train and we could see five German observation balloons watching us, so we knew we'd come under fire pretty soon. We had to unload the train as the shells landed, trying to dodge about, trying to shelter, it was total madness, then we had to march through Ypres to the Menin Gate under constant shellfire, and out on the Gravenstafel Road.' He stopped and laughed a hard, bitter laugh. 'We called it the Grab-and-Stumble Road. We were bivouacked in a graveyard, the coffins and bodies of the long dead strewn about among the newly dead; we knew most of us would be joining them soon. We kept watching out for Colin, but we didn't know then that by the time the next train arrived the Germans had got their eye in. Sixteen men in that company were killed, including Colin, who shouldn't really have been there, and forty wounded. When we hadn't heard anything for weeks we kept hoping he'd just been sent somewhere else, it happened all the time, and that we'd find him again or he'd find us. It was about a month later when someone who'd been on the train with him told me and Gil what had happened and that he was dead. Jamie was dead by then, too, so neither of them ever found out what had happened to the other. Losing Jamie was bad enough, but Colin . . .' he covered his face with his hands. 'And all because I wouldn't let him squeeze into our carriage.'

'There, there,' she murmured distractedly, stroking his head. 'There, there.' There was nothing else to say.

She was thankful in a way that these rushes of information did not come often, but she felt bad about that, because she knew Donald was in deeper turmoil than he ever told her. There were too many regrets and guilts occupying his mind to let go of times past, and there was about him an air of preoccupation, as though he were living on two separate levels and places at once and couldn't break with the one that still harmed him. There was a deep sorrow about him, that he'd let Jamie go off alone to the hospital and his Scottish nurse when they were allowed leave, while he went off to sleep for three days; that he had survived and Jamie hadn't; that Colin, too, had died and he had lived – it was, after all, an older brother's duty to look after a younger brother and instead he had pushed him onto the train that would carry him to his death. There was nothing he could've done to save Colin, but he felt he should have and if he couldn't, well at least he should have died with him. And now he was on the farm his brother had loved and had planned to take over, angry on the one hand at being trapped in work he felt he had no aptitude for and, on the other, guilty that he should feel that way when he was, at least, alive. And interwoven with so many of these self-destructive feelings and thoughts was his fear that he was short-changing Nancy and the boys because he felt too empty of good emotions to give them, and too full of bad ones that he knew he was inflicting on his innocent family. Nothing seemed to help, not even visits to Cape Breton, where he had been happy a lifetime ago, because inevitably it brought him into contact with men he had served with during the war. He would look into the eyes of others and see his own tortured feelings mirrored there without a word being spoken, and see the gaps there where friends should be; there was no escape for Donald.

Nancy threw herself into being a farmer's wife, discovering home-making skills and mothering abilities she never suspected she had. Calli and Feargie became her life, though once she would have laughed at any suggestion that she could love anyone as much as she loved her boys. Before she had them, she would never have believed she could feel so intensely as she did for her sons, two bright children who had no dark clouds over their heads – how could that be possible when they had Donald for a father? Somehow, though, they seemed to have escaped his horrors, though she worried constantly that the atmosphere must affect them in some way and she suffered agonies of guilt that they might grow up and speak of the sadness of their childhoods.

One May, leaving Donald behind in Campbellford, she had visited Mabou with the boys. It was her favourite season, when the blossoms from all the trees filled the air with colour and scent, and there was the music that filled Padraig's House, how she had missed the music in the quiet life she led at Pine Edge. She was happy and free at home. They were having a picnic by the brook that ran past Padraig's House then meandered on below the one that had been rebuilt for Ruairidh Beag and his new wife all those years ago. All the MacKenzies were there, aunts, uncles and, as usual, many, many cousins with different names, but who were still regarded and still regarded themselves, as MacKenzies. Martha was worried about her daughter, though she knew better than to voice her concerns. Nancy had always been able to close down discussions on anything she did not want to discuss and, Martha knew, it mattered little whether that meant cutting a stranger dead, or her own mother. She had been the same all her life, she often mused, Nancy was always ready for argument, but kept her own counsel over what mattered to her; 'thus far and no farther' might have been her motto. Not that this stopped her mother's natural worries, of course, her sadness at how Nancy's life had turned out. It was as if her life had stopped still, as if instead of marriage being the start of a new life, for Nancy it had been the closing down of her future. It was a tragedy, a life as wasted, she thought, every bit as much as Jamie's had been, and it broke her heart to watch helplessly as her bright, ambitious daughter's horizons contracted before her. On that trip home she noticed the subtle lifting of Nancy's mood, as always happened when she was without Donald, and decided there might be no better chance to offer a lifeline, whether it was welcome or not. They were setting out the picnic together, Nancy going through the usual routine of separating things her boys would eat from the things they would not, like children everywhere.

'They're fine lads, my grandsons,' she smiled quietly, 'and so clever too, Nancy, they pick things up so fast.'

'I know, Mother,' Nancy smiled back wryly. 'But while we're on the subject, don't think I haven't seen you sneakily filling them with the old romantic nonsense about the golden isle of their forefathers.'

'I don't know what you mean,' Martha replied a little too innocently.

Nancy smiled. 'Fairytales are one thing, but I don't want you telling them any more of those silly tales about Raasay and how it's still what you call home, and about Old Ruairidh standing on the shore all alone but still noble and brave.'

'Oh, sure everyone will be telling them about that,' Martha replied.

'Yes, but not quite with your wee bits of magic, Mother,' Nancy said tartly. 'And you know perfectly well what I mean, all that stuff about the Second Sight –'

Martha flashed her daughter a sharp, but amused smile. 'So you still think it's nonsense, do you?'

'I've never thought anything else,' Nancy lied easily, 'as well you know. I've never met anyone in my life who could put on such an act as you, when we were children you almost had us believing it, and I don't want my boys picking it up, especially not Calli, you know what an imagination he has. Everything that comes along takes his fancy, a couple of your myths and legends and he'll be wanting to be a wizard when he grows up.' She turned towards her mother and laughed. 'You're hopeless, Mother. You do know that, don't you?'

Martha laughed with her. 'But don't you see a lot of Jamie in him, Nancy?' she asked.

Nancy rolled her eyes. 'You see? There you go again! No, I don't see Jamie in him, not especially. Now stop it!'

'But his hair, his eyes –'

'– are the same as mine, Mother,' Nancy replied, holding Martha by the shoulders and staring into her eyes and laughing, 'though Calli's luckier than I was, he's a boy, he can cut this damned curly hair short, I have to contend with it falling all over the place. In a hundred years' time the same things will come out in some child or other, won't they? And they won't be Jamie, they'll be *family* things.'

Martha shrugged. She didn't agree, but she didn't want to argue and Nancy knew it.

Nancy laughed aloud as she threw her arms upwards. 'Impossible!' she said. 'That's what you are, impossible!'

'He loves animals at any rate,' Martha said firmly. 'Now not even you can say I'm imagining that.'

'He doesn't so much love them as see them as people, in a way,' Nancy smiled. 'He says "*Ciamar a tha thu?*" to dogs, cats, any creature he comes across, always has. It made me laugh at first and he'd look at me with those great big, solemn eyes. He knows every bird, and every tenth of May the first thing he does is put out some sugar water for the hummingbirds coming back; no one ever reminds him, but he never misses.' She exchanged a fond smile with her mother. 'He's not sentimental about it, though, he doesn't cry when the farm beasts are killed, he knows they're for food, but up until they are, Calli treats them like friends.'

'Now that's Padraig,' Martha said firmly, and Nancy glared a look of sarcasm at her.

'First Jamie, now Padraig?' she said, shaking her head.

'I'm telling you,' Martha insisted. 'You never knew Padraig, but anyone will tell you that animals never ran or flew away from him. He used to sit under the big tree there when he was a child, my father has told me of it often, talking to a bird or some other creature as he carved its image in a piece of wood. He was known for it, ask Ruairidh Beag if you won't believe your own mother.'

Nancy put an arm around her, hand up to avoid smearing Martha's shoulder with the food she had been handling, and hugged her, laughing. 'Mother, I love the thought of having a son with even one of the gifts that Padraig had, even if I never met him as you say. But as far as I can recall, you never once mentioned in all the fairytales you tried to fill my head with as

I was growing up, that Padraig had a groundhog, did you? Well Calli has. We've had one in the Pine Edge garden ever since I can remember, probably a succession of groundhogs, but Calli won't accept that – he's called it – them – Hamish, in honour of his Grandfather MacDonald, because he says it looks like him! Every day he waits for Hamish to climb up out of his burrow and he shouts "Groundhog up!", then, when he disappears underground again he shouts "Groundhog down!". He's so funny, but if we laugh he gives us one of those serious stares of his.'

'Padraig to the life!' Martha said firmly.

'Oh Mother! Calli's thing about animals has nothing to do with wanting to carve statues of them, he sees them as equal to himself almost. That's different from just wanting them to sit still, isn't it?'

'If there had been a groundhog around, Padraig would've been the very same,' Martha said defiantly. 'It's as plain as the nose on your face that the boy has the knowledge of the ancients, he's one of us, that's all I'm saying!'

'I wish it was all,' Nancy replied, leaning down to look into Martha's eyes, 'but I don't hold out much hope!'

The two women worked side by side in silence for a few moments.

'You know,' Martha said quietly, her eyes on her hands as she set out the food, 'that there is more than enough room for you and the boys here.' Another silence, but a different kind this time. 'If you wanted to move back home with them.'

Nancy looked sharply at her mother. 'And Donald,' she said brightly. 'You left him out, Mother. What a very strange thing to do! And I don't think Donald would ever leave Pine Edge to move to Mabou. Do you?' and with that she stopped what she was doing and joined the children where they were playing.

Ruairidh Beag, who had been listening from nearby, shook his head at his daughter. 'Now that wasn't clever,' he smiled. 'In fact it was clumsy, Martha. Whatever possessed you?'

'I know, I know,' she replied sadly. 'We were getting along so well, too, joking with each other and chatting, now the shutters have been brought down again.' She sighed. 'But she's not happy, Father.' She watched Nancy in the distance with the children. 'I always saw her out in the world, busy, happy. I never saw . . . this.' She shook her head, her eyes filling with tears. 'It's all turned out so badly, surely you can feel that too?'

'I can,' he sighed, 'I can. But there's nothing can be done about it, you know that as well as I do. Donald is a good man, he has done no wrong, he can't help what has happened to him.'

'But he shouldn't have married her,' Martha replied calmly. 'He has taken her life and crushed it. All the promise, the brightness, everything, has gone.'

'He was confused when he came home, Martha, he needed her.'

'But she didn't need him,' Martha said.

'Martha!'

'Oh, I didn't really mean it like that. I've always been fond of the boy, he's Padraig's grandson, how could I not be? And I wish he hadn't been so affected by the war, I wish none of them had gone away. My Jamie would still be here with us and —' she looked towards where Neil was sitting alone, half asleep, a bottle by his side as usual, '— my other boy wouldn't be dying before my eyes as well.' She paused for a moment. 'Was it too much to ask that one of my children would have a good life? Nancy had such fire in her, she had so many dreams and ambitions.'

'All youngsters have them!' her father teased.

'But she could've made them happen,' Martha persisted, 'and it's not as if she gave them up to be happy, because she isn't happy, is she?'

'She has her boys,' Ruairidh Beag smiled. 'Look at her with her boys and tell me they haven't brought her true joy.'

'But she has to go back to Campbellford, and I know her, she'll never give in, she'll stick with Donald for the rest of her life and she'll never admit to the slightest unhappiness. And what good has sacrificing her life done him? None at all, that's the answer, but in trying to help him she's locked herself in a dark place. It's there, I can feel it, and I can't help her.'

Ruairidh Beag put his hand over his daughter's without replying. There was no answer to Martha's fears, he thought sadly, they were well founded.

12

Almost without consciously noticing, Nancy came to understand that Donald would never get better, that whatever and whoever he used to be, he had changed into someone else and the change would be permanent. During those early nights, as he lay beside her, twisting and turning in his dreams, crying out in fear and grief, or when he had gone for a walk instead of attempting sleep, she would lie awake, making bargains with fate. If he got better, that was her first offer, then if some time in the near future he had a few good, contented years, then if the boys could at least be spared the worst of his miseries, she would do anything, anything. She didn't know who or what she was trying to make these bargains with, but over the years she came to accept that who or what hadn't been listening after all, but she had married Donald, had his children and that was that. She knew her family in Mabou saw ways out for her – she had been eighteen years old when they had married, far too young to understand what she was taking on, that was what they said, and it was true. Donald was so sunk in horrors that would plague the rest of his life that he would be the same whether she was there or not, and had she been more mature she might have understood that she owed it to any future children not to inflict this father on them. It was this that tortured her most, of course; for her husband she would've given anything, but for her children she would've given everything, and the thought that she was allowing them to be damaged was like a knife in a wound. There was no real closeness between husband and wife any longer, Donald had long ago deserted any notions of physical, never mind emotional love; soon the small bedroom leading from the downstairs parlour became his home. It made sense, he said, to sleep downstairs so as not to wake her and the boys when he'd been working late on the farm paperwork. Martha nodded her agreement, though she did most of the paperwork. And there were difficult calvings, and those walks he liked to take at night so that he could think. She nodded again, colluding with his decisions to evade her and their life as a family, because she didn't know what else to do. He simply existed and she simply cared for him as she did her children, only with less hope and even less affection, because Donald either didn't want it or couldn't cope with it. She felt that he didn't mean it, knew that if he had been in his right mind he couldn't do this to her, but wherever he was there was no place for human contact, either given or received. Maybe if he had cut off all relations suddenly it would have been easier to pack her bags and take her children northwards to Mabou. No one would've blamed her, but it was a gradual process of withdrawal over years of waiting for life to improve, until the day arrived when she knew all was lost and there was no way out for any of them.

Even his mother, who had moved out of Pine Edge all those years ago to give her new daughter-in-law the role of mistress of the house, acknowledged that Nancy was trapped. Old Mhairi had lost one son in the war, and she had been grateful to her God for not taking Donald as well. Until she saw him, that was, and knew better than anyone that she had indeed lost two. Watching him with the young lass he had brought from Cape Breton on that first day she had burst into tears. The lass had been kind, she had thought her mother-in-law was sad to be leaving her home and probably at seeing the ghost of Colin, the boy who should've been there instead, but she had cried that day with pity for Nancy herself, though it was years before they talked of it.

It was the evening of her husband's funeral. They had buried Hamish earlier that day, and the mourners had departed, apart from Gil, who had been a great favourite of Hamish's and who would be staying overnight before returning to Boston. He had made the journey often to spend some time with the old man, and Nancy's boys were used to seeing him at the home of their grandparents without knowing him well. Mhairi was exhausted. She had nursed Hamish through his long illness and, after laying him to rest, it was as if all the stress and weariness had fallen on her shoulders in one heavy load, so she had accepted her daughter-in-law's suggestion that she spend at least that night at Pine Edge. It was 1929, and the boys, then aged nine and seven, were already in bed upstairs, with Gil, their distant cousin, telling them a story. Nancy had known Gil for as long as she could recall and remembered him leaving with the others when they went to war, but standing at the bedroom door and seeing him with her sons, seeing, too, how they responded to having a man about the place who took notice of them, she had walked away, afraid of breaking down. It had been an emotional day, she thought, pausing to take a deep breath before going back downstairs, and many tears had been shed by Mhairi especially, and now that she was composed she didn't want the old woman to go to bed crying. Another breath and she went down to join her mother-in-law in the parlour, placing a tray of tea and cakes on the small table between them. Donald was elsewhere, probably, Nancy suggested diplomatically, seeing to things on the farm that he hadn't had time to do earlier. Mhairi nodded, then she trusted that her daughter-in-law's good upbringing would make her hesitate over biting off a new widow's nose.

'You know, Nancy,' she said quietly, 'Hamish had a lot of affection for you.'

Nancy smiled. 'I was fond of him, too.' She looked down into her tea as she stirred it.

'And he was grateful to you, as I am, that you never left our Donald,' the older woman said plainly. Nancy looked up, her eyes wide, and opened her mouth to reply, but Mhairi put up a hand to stop her. 'Nancy, my dear, we knew how things were, how they are now. Donald is my son, I'm not saying a word against him, I won't hear anyone else speak a word against him either, I don't need to tell you that. But you deserved better than you have.'

'I have no complaints,' Nancy said awkwardly.

'That's what I mean, you've put up with much more than we had a right to expect anyone to. We've always admired how you've stuck by him, though we wouldn't have blamed you a bit if you hadn't.'

'It's not his fault,' Nancy murmured, staring into her cup.

'Nor yours, Nancy,' Mhairi said gently.

'And maybe he'll get better.'

'Aye,' Mhairi replied softly. 'Maybe.'

The following morning, as Gil waited to drive Mhairi from Pine Edge to her own home, Nancy hugged her and whispered, 'Please, what we spoke of last night, we won't speak of it again?'

'Not a word, Nancy,' the older woman whispered back. 'As long as you know that you *are* appreciated.' She looked into Nancy's eyes, then hugged her again. 'And look at these fine boys you gave me and Hamish.'

'And Donald,' Nancy said quietly. 'Me and Donald.'

Mhairi nodded. 'And Donald,' she smiled, feeling that her heart would break for the lassie. 'And Donald, to be sure.'

When Gil returned from taking their grandmother home, the two boys pleaded with him to stay a day or two longer. He was an engineer in Boston, but Nancy knew that the downturn, what would become known as the Great Depression, was biting everywhere and Gil had already lost his job.

'Why don't you stay, Gil?' she suggested on a whim. 'I'm sure Donald would love to have someone here who understands engines, he's not mechanically minded, as I'm sure you know. You've done more with those old Fordson tractors in a couple of days than Donald's been able to do in months.'

Gil rubbed his chin with his hand and grimaced. He was slightly older than her, so he must be in his early thirties, though he hadn't changed much from the boy she remembered, taller, of course, but still thin and dark. As he thought, the two boys danced around him, tugging at his sleeves and saying 'Please, Gil? Stay, Gil?'

'What does Donald think?' he asked.

'Oh, Donald will say the same, Gil,' she laughed. 'He'd do anything to get away from the farm machinery, it drives him mad.' She thought for a moment. 'Unless, of course, you have someone in Boston you'd rather stay there for?' she smiled diplomatically. Gil looked at her blankly. 'A sweetheart, Gil!' she teased him.

'Hell, no, nothing like that!' he laughed back, but she could see he was blushing and that made her smile. A man of his age, who'd been through the war and worked in the big city, and he could still blush!

Gil rubbed at his chin again to cover his embarrassment. 'I'll maybe think about it,' he said. 'I'll have a word with Donald and I'll go back to Boston and think about it,' but there wasn't a lot to think about, Gil had always loved farming and he had a special affection for Pine Edge.

The next day he travelled to Boston, leaving the two MacDonald boys in a deep depression, but a week later he suddenly returned. For the rest of her life Nancy could close her eyes and see it, Gil's official entry, unannounced, into their lives early one hot afternoon. She and the boys were sitting in the shade of a tree at the front of the house, drinking lemonade and eating pecan pie, when they saw a biplane in the sky. Hands to their foreheads to shield their eyes from the glare of the sun, they watched as it circled over them a couple of times as they wondered aloud who the pilot could be. Then the plane came closer and closer. Each time it circled the boys became more and more excited, then suddenly it swooped down to land in the field beside them. It was only when the pilot climbed out and walked towards them, pulling off his leather helmet and gloves, that they realised the tall, thin figure was Gil, and they were so shocked by this turn of events that they were struck dumb for a few seconds. In her mind's eye she could always see the impression his arrival made on her sons, on Calli especially. Feargie whooped and shrieked with surprise and delight, but Calli had stood transfixed from the moment he saw the glorious machine descend from the sky. 'It's like a bird,' he whispered, 'just like a bird!' Then, as Gil climbed out of the cockpit and walked towards the little group under the tree, his face had flushed with affection and his dark eyes had shone with pride as he realised who it was. 'It's Gil,' he said. 'Gil can fly like a bird!' Feargie, on the other hand, immediately ran towards Gil, happy and excited, jumping up and down as he grabbed at his hand, his arm, his shoulder, till she thought Gil would land on the ground with a much harder bump than his plane had. Calli stood breathlessly watching from a distance at first, before slowly walking forward and staring at Gil, then the plane, then Gil, then the plane, his affection torn between the two. Watching the boys, Nancy knew it was a picture that would stay in their minds for ever as well as her own. To Feargie, Gil was the man who had flown this great machine into their backyard, to Calli it was the fact that he had flown, but both of them were overcome with pride that he was *their* relative, *their* Gil. It was the thing she would remember most strongly about that afternoon, apart from Gil swooping down out of the sky, the different reactions of her two very different sons, and the noise, eventually, as they cleared an outhouse to house the plane. From the younger Feargie, the questions were logical and technical. Was it his? Where did he get it? Was he keeping it? When did he learn to fly? Was it hard? What speed did it do? How far could it fly? But above that was Calli's breathless voice saying 'You were flying like a bird, Gil,' over and over again and, inevitably, when could he fly too?

'I first saw planes in the war,' he explained after dinner that first night, his speech betraying more than a slight hint of Boston's flat vowels. 'I'd be sitting in trenches full of mud, being shot at and bombed and when I looked up to the sky I could see these flying machines high above through the smoke, and I'd think "That's where I should be, up there, not down here". I vowed that if I survived I'd learn to fly, and as soon as I got back to Boston I set about finding a plane. Then this guy I knew said he knew where he could get hold of a Sopwith Camel that was almost destroyed. Someone had brought it back to the US to give flying displays, but the Camel's an unforgiving kind of plane, if you make a mistake it can go into a fatal spin before you can correct it, and that's what had happened, it had been wrecked in a crash. I looked at her that day and thought of all the war service she had done, and I thought "Right, she's a survivor just like me, I'll rebuild her". The boys were so wrapped up in the story that they had forgotten to shout, as they had been doing all day, and were just sitting at Gil's feet, their elbows on their knees, their hands under their chins, nodding as they waited impatiently for the next piece of the story. 'Been working on it for years, saving for bits I needed, had them sent over from England or collected for me by anyone I knew was going over. In a family like ours there are plenty of seafarers, that was handy,' he said, smiling conspiratorially at the boys.

'And now she's better?' Feargie asked. 'I mean, she's rebuilt?'

'And she's all yours,' Calli whispered, 'to go up into the sky any time you want?'

'Any time,' Gil smiled back.

Later that night, long after he should have been asleep and long after his brother was, Calli came into his parents' bedroom, where Nancy was alone as usual.

'What is it, Calli?' she asked, making room for him. 'Too excited to sleep?'

He shook his head calmly. 'I was just wondering,' he said. 'What relation of mine is Gil?'

She put her book down, wrapped an arm around his shoulders and hugged him gently. 'I don't really know,' she admitted. 'You know what it's like with families, if someone is a tenth cousin then they're a cousin, no one counts how far or how near they are. Let me think. He's the son of Grandpa Hamish's brother, that makes him and your father cousins, so he's a first cousin once removed to you and Feargie. I think.' She looked at him and shrugged her shoulders. 'But it's a bit of a mouthful, isn't it?' Calli nodded, his dark eyes deep and serious. 'But what made you think of that?' she asked.

'I was just making sure he *was* ours, so that I can say that to anyone who says he's not.'

'Why would they say that?' she laughed.

'People say things,' he said seriously, 'when they're jealous, and they'll be jealous of me and Feargie because of the plane.'

'Ah, I see.'

'So he is ours then?' he asked again.

'Absolutely.'

'And we're keeping him?'

Nancy laughed. 'You make him sound like one of the calves!'

'But we *are*?' he asked again.

'As long as he wants to stay.'

Calli nodded, smiling. 'I'll tell him he's not to go then,' he said solemnly, then he climbed out of her arms and wandered back to his own room. 'I'm going to be a pilot like Gil,' he said over his shoulder. 'I'm going to fly in a plane like a bird.'

13

Both MacDonald boys were bright, but as in everything else, in very different ways. Calli was the one with a thirst to know everything, 'scattergun clever' his grandmother in Cape Breton called him, describing the way he followed any piece of knowledge that crossed his path to its source. He was a cheerful, handsome boy with, as his grandmother had already noted, the dark, curly hair and brown eyes of the MacKenzies that cropped up throughout the wider family, and he was universally popular without being aware of it. Feargie took his fair looks and his nature from his father's side of the family, a cautious boy who, even when they were very small, always urged his older brother to 'wait and see, Calli', before coming to a decision or taking action, though he laughed as he said it, knowing that Calli was incapable of waiting for anything. Feargie had a settled personality, he knew where he wanted to go from an early age and never wavered; he wanted to become a doctor, whereas Calli's ambitions had changed not just by the day, but by the second, since he could talk. He was a boy of many obsessions, he wanted to do everything, learn everything, say and hear everything. In the mid-twenties, the family got their first motor vehicle, a Ford T, black, of course, converted into a truck by cutting away the passenger compartment behind the driving seat. It broke Calli's heart to see the car being defaced, and he immediately decided he'd build cars, or he'd become an engineer and build engines, or maybe he'd race cars; Feargie just decided that when he grew up he'd use one to get from A to B. The one thing the brothers agreed on, however, was that they would not become farmers. Nancy was never sure if this was a reaction to the farmer they knew best, if they knew Donald at all, or to farm life, but regardless of why, she approved and she never tried to change their minds. If her boys had the ability to go out into the world and do other things, she would make sure they got every opportunity. Their father's ambitions and plans had been thwarted, but she wanted her sons to have a clear run at life, if ever, she thought with a smile, Calli made up his mind and stuck to one thing. Until, that was, the day Gil swooped down from the sky in his plane. There was nothing else for it as far as Calli was concerned, he would grow up and fly planes. Nothing else would do, from that moment he had to fly and that ambition would never alter. Nancy smiled, wondering if those uncomfortable meetings with his teachers might be over for good. She had always known what was coming when her younger boy's talents were discussed first – the bad news was coming last, the ploy of each teacher who taught them.

'Fearghus is a model student, he knows what he has to do and he gets on with it, always producing work of the highest quality. Calum is somewhat different,' said Miss Taylor, the latest teacher at the small school, probably unaware that their mother had heard similar reports from other diplomatic young women over the years. Nancy subdued a smile as she watched the furrow in the young woman's brow, not unlike the one Calli had between his eyes when he was deep in concentration.

'Does he cause you trouble?' she asked.

'Not trouble, exactly,' Miss Taylor replied, 'but he's always asking questions.'

'Isn't that a good thing?'

'Well, a lively mind is a blessing, to be sure, Mrs MacDonald, but I do mean *everything*. He wants to know how I know every detail, where I discovered it, how do I know it's true? That sort of thing. You know?' The question was rhetorical, but Nancy did know, the problem was keeping a straight face in case this nice but earnest young woman thought she was laughing at her. 'I can't get through an entire lesson for Calum's questions,' she looked up at his mother and mistook her stern expression for disapproval. 'I'm not saying he's disruptive, it's just his nature, I honestly don't think he means it or that he can help it.'

'No, I don't think he can,' Nancy smiled back. 'He has a kind nature, Miss Taylor, would you not agree?'

'Oh, he has, he has!' the young woman replied, afraid that she had offended one of the school trustees when her job depended on not causing offence. 'I just feel that if he were to be more focused he would achieve more. He's a very clever boy, you know, he has such a wide general knowledge. There are times when he almost takes over the lesson by embellishing what I'm teaching.'

Nancy laughed out loud. 'Don't worry, Miss Taylor,' she said, 'no one's blaming you. Every teacher has said the same thing about Calum, I've said it myself. It is, as you say, how he is.'

The young woman looked visibly relieved. 'He says he's going to fly planes,' she said with an amused smile. 'It's all he can talk about these days, he seems completely taken with the idea.'

'Maybe he will,' Nancy said, 'who knows, Miss Taylor? But at least we might get him to concentrate, Gil is always telling him that he'll need to become really good at maths and geometry and geography if he's to be a pilot, and he does listen to Gil.'

'Yes, he has a real case of hero worship,' the young teacher laughed. 'I've never seen a boy so in awe of his father, Mr MacDonald must be a very special man.'

The young woman was new, she wasn't to know that Donald was Calli and Feargie's father, after all, neither boy ever mentioned him and he was never about the community, but someone had to tell her.

'Gil is a cousin, Miss Taylor,' Nancy smiled.

'Oh, I am sorry!' the young teacher replied, her hand flying to her mouth.

'No, no, please, don't feel like that,' Nancy laughed. 'My husband is a typical farmer, Miss Taylor, interested in nothing but farming.' She was lying, but who was to know? 'If you're not talking about crops and prices, especially in these times, he has little to say to you.'

'But, if I've caused any offence, Mrs MacDonald –'

'You haven't, I assure you, and how were you to know? Don't give it another thought, please, but about Calli, I know he can be a handful with his constant curiosity, but I don't want his spirit crushed, Miss Taylor,' Nancy continued, 'that's all I'm saying. I want him to grow up feeling as confident as he is now. Who knows what he'll have to face in the future?'

Her words covered a world of hopes and dreams, as well as a sea of unspoken personal unhappiness and disappointment. She didn't want him to be like his father, his real father, not the one he had chosen; that's what her words didn't say. She wanted her son to weather whatever the future held for him, as Gil had, so that he wouldn't be destroyed by what fate served up, no matter what that might be. Then, in time, perhaps Calli could be a real husband and father himself.

14

In the years just after the war Jess went into a slow decline. There was nothing specific, she simply grew older quicker than the MacKenzies. In her last years she and Ruairidh Beag had moved into Padraig's House, to be cared for by Martha, and there she died peacefully in 1924, at the age of 76; Ruairidh Beag outlived his wife by six years. It wasn't exactly unexpected, he was eighty-five years old and the family had been watching him gradually fade away over the years since Jess had gone. He died in his sleep, and Nancy hadn't the slightest inkling until she got the phone call a few hours later. She was heartbroken, of course, but deep inside there was also a streak of relief; it proved that she was right, she didn't have the Gift, just as she'd always known. If she had she would've been aware of her grandfather's death, she had been close to him and had loved him more than almost anyone else in her entire life: if there had been some extra sense it would have swung into action over his passing, and it hadn't, so it didn't exist.

The family travelled to Cape Breton immediately, with the boys pleading with Gil to fly them there.

'That's all Grandma Martha would need,' Nancy chided them, 'the noise of the plane coming down over the house.'

'But it would be fun!' Calli protested.

'It might be, if it happened,' Nancy said sternly, 'but it won't. That's the end of the discussion.'

The boys groaned and whined in disappointment, and Nancy flashed a 'would you believe it?' look at Donald for support, but there was no expression on his face. Gil, on the other hand, had to turn away to hide his laughter. Nancy felt flustered.

'Have you ever heard the likes of it?' she said.

'They're boys, Nancy,' Gil replied quietly.

'But shouldn't they be more upset about Ruairidh Beag than about not flying to his funeral?'

Gil shook his head and laughed. 'No,' he replied. 'I told you, they're boys.' He looked at Donald. 'Isn't that right, Donald? Boys are savages, they don't have feelings?'

Once again Donald didn't reply and his expression remained the same.

Nancy tried to look away quickly so that she and Gil didn't make eye contact. She didn't want to enter into any discussion between herself and Gil about Donald, she didn't want him to pick up any sign that it would be welcome. She didn't want pity, his or anyone else's, but she wasn't fast enough, and for a second she caught his look, and she was struck by the expression in his eyes; it wasn't pity, she realised, it was understanding, and in that instant she knew Gil was too decent a man to ever broach the subject, so she was safe.

They buried Ruairidh Beag beside Jess and among his Cape Breton family, his Great Uncle Sandy and Aunt Sarah; Donald and Morag, his father and mother, and all his brothers, including Padraig. The entire community turned out, those related to him in some far-out way as well as those who felt related because they held him in such affection, including the Micmacs; he had touched many lives in his eighty-five years. His immediate family were sad to lose him, but he was an old man who had had a good life, far better than if he had been born and raised on Raasay, and after all the losses of the Great War, there was something comforting in the fact that the natural order had prevailed this time – he had died because his time had come.

As his coffin was borne towards the grave by his eldest grandsons, Nancy followed behind, Martha's arm firmly tucked into her own.

'Look,' Martha whispered.

Nancy looked around. 'What am I looking at?' she whispered back.

'Over yonder,' Martha whispered, 'the stone with the cross on it.'

Nancy followed her eyes and nodded. 'Well?'

'It's John MacVicar,' Martha smiled, looking at her daughter to see if she remembered the story of the Micmac Indians.

'Ah, yes,' Nancy breathed. 'Just as well he's being buried at the other side of the cemetery then!'

'You know what your grandpa used to do when he had to come here?' Nancy shook her head and Martha giggled. 'He used to dance a couple of steps on John MacVicar's grave, said it was just for spite, to celebrate the fact that he'd outlived him!'

The two women laughed, tightening their grip on each other for support in their mirth as well as their grief, then the pipes struck up with 'MacCrimmon's Lament', and the sound defeated their mirth.

'The pipes always get you,' Martha said, wiping tears from her face. 'I don't know why that is when they can have your feet leaping in a reel, but that sound can be the saddest on earth.'

As the mourners left the graveside, Martha tugged on Nancy's arm to stay back, for a last, private farewell, she thought, but when the stream of black-clad people had ebbed away, Martha directed her daughter to John MacVicar's grave, where she proceeded to perform a little dance. Nancy gave a shocked giggle.

'Well, don't just stand there,' Martha said, 'we have a family tradition to keep up!' Then she stopped, out of breath and still laughing. 'Besides,' she wheezed, 'he was a nasty wee man who only thought of making money and looked down on his fellow men, and wee lassies, and Micmacs.'

'And he came from Uist,' Nancy added theatrically, 'and no good ever came from Uist.'

'Exactly!' Martha said, her face flushed with exertion and laughter.

Nancy would conjure up this memory of her mother many times – watching her perform that joyous, irreverent jig on top of John MacVicar's grave – and on her inevitably frequent visits to the cemetery in years to come it still made her smile. Another memory she would never shake off was the sight of her one remaining brother, Neil. She knew he had started to drink when he came back home from the war, but as she left soon afterwards for Campbellford, she had no idea how bad things were with him. She hadn't seen him every day, so the change in him was that much stronger and more shocking each summer when she took the boys back to Mabou. As with Donald, she had expected him to put the bad memories behind him one day and return to normal, but like Donald, Neil inhabited a different world after he came home.

'I had to put him out into the barn,' Martha had replied that night when Nancy had asked where he was.

'What?' Nancy replied; it wasn't a question, she had understood her mother perfectly.

'He's bad now, Nancy,' her father, Tormod, explained. 'I don't think you should let the boys near him, in fact it might be better if you didn't see him yourself.'

'What?' she asked again. Martha and Tormod exchanged looks.

'It's the drink,' Martha said quietly. 'He does nothing but drink. Doesn't eat often these days, so he's almost like a skeleton, and he causes trouble.'

'Trouble?' Nancy asked. 'What kind of trouble? Neil always caused trouble.'

'This is different, Nancy,' Martha said, her eyes full of hurt. 'He gets into fights, people don't want to fight with him, but he makes them, and he trashes places. Never remembers any of it afterwards. Folk have been good about it for the sake of your grandfather, but the police have often had to drag him away and lock him up for a few days, then they let him out again and he shakes so much he can barely hold a cup.'

'Or a glass more like,' Tormod said solemnly. 'Though to be honest, he doesn't bother with anything like that, he drinks it straight down from the bottle now.'

'I had to put him in the barn,' Martha explained almost apologetically, 'because he was messing himself, Nancy, and walking about in it for days. It was like looking after a baby again, only this was a big, strong baby who didn't know or care who he hurt. He's lashed out at me and your father when we've been trying to help him.' She saw the shocked expression on Nancy's face. 'Oh, he doesn't mean it, he doesn't even know he's done it, but we were afraid for your grandfather, if he could hit us without meaning it he could do the same to him, and he had become so frail, and anyway, we didn't want him upset by all the comings and goings. We take meals down to Neil and leave them inside the barn door, but he rarely touches a bite. Most of the time, when he isn't drinking, he's sleeping.'

'Isn't there something you – we – can do?' Nancy asked.

Martha and Tormod shook their heads.

'We've tried talking to him, we've tried keeping the drink from him, and asked the shopkeepers not to sell it to him, but he steals it instead and if they try to stop him he beats them up and takes it anyhow.' She sighed. 'The Micmacs are very good. When he goes missing for a while they find him and clean him up, and they always keep an eye on him and let us know where he is and how he is.'

Nancy smiled. The Micmacs had been indebted to her mother since Martha had brought one of their women home to her own bed and safely delivered her child. They were good friends to everyone, but especially to Martha's family, they would never see that debt as paid off.

Later, against the advice of her parents, she had gone down to the barn beside the stream and called Neil's name. When there was no answer she went inside and found him lying on the floor, partly covered with a thin blanket and snoring loudly. Nearby was a pile of clean clothes that looked as though it had been there, untouched, for some time. She took a step nearer and immediately the smell hit her like a blow. She stood for a moment, her hand across her nose and mouth, then she slowly took it away, so that she got used to the rancid smell gradually, then, kneeling down beside him, she touched his head. Neil didn't stir. She realised that if she hadn't known this was her brother, she might not have recognised him. His face was bloated and patchy red, while the rest of him that she could see was so thin that the bones showed clearly, and all over his skin was flaked and pinpricked with tiny, dark brown scabs. She stayed only a few minutes, remembering the big, strong, boisterous boy he had been, hearing in her mind his booming voice as he had rampaged through this very barn when they were children, then she got up and went outside and leaned against the wooden wall of the barn and cried. She didn't know who or what the tears were for, because she had never been a crying kind of woman: for her parents who had to watch their only remaining son like this and cope with him; for herself because in a way Neil's physical condition might have been a metaphor for her own life under the carefully applied veneer; for all the men all over the world like Neil and Donald, who had survived only to die slowly before the appalled gaze of the loved ones who had wanted them home at any price.

When she finally made her way back up to the house Nancy simply nodded at her mother; what was there to say? She suddenly felt touched by the people of the community she had grown up amongst and had taken for granted, scorned more than a little, too, it had to be said, for their olde-worlde Scottish values. Neil hadn't been to his grandfather's funeral, and those who had attended, knowing the situation and being decent people, had made no reference to his absence out of respect for the family. Why had she never noticed before what good people they were?

Back at Padraig's House there was a ceilidh after the burial, a celebration of music, storytelling and dancing in honour of Ruairidh Beag. As the singers sang, Martha went over Ruairidh Beag's final days.

'Go on,' Nancy said, 'I've been waiting for it.'

'For what?' Martha asked innocently.

'The Gift, the Second Sight. I know I'm about to hear tales

of omens, portents and dead people appearing in every corner of the house.'

'Nothing happened,' Martha said.

'So you're asking me to believe that you didn't know he'd gone?' Nancy asked incredulously.

'No, I didn't,' Martha replied. 'I knew he didn't have long, he was asleep more often than awake towards the end. I sat with him, reading him stories and talking to him, but he gave no hint that he could hear me. I'd gone to lie down for a couple of hours while your father took over, then he woke me to say he'd gone.'

'And that was it?' Nancy raised an eyebrow. Martha nodded. 'You must be losing your magic, Mother!' Nancy teased her.

'Except . . .' Martha said.

Nancy laughed out loud. 'I knew it!' she said.

'There were times as I sat by his bed when he talked to someone and when I asked who it was he said it was Padraig. He said, "Do you not see him, Martha?" and I said I didn't, and he just smiled and said, "Well, he's here".' She paused. 'Of course, it could be said that an old man dying could easily have the odd delusion, I suppose.'

'But you know better, don't you, Mother?' Nancy laughed.

There was a small silence.

'There was a time, Nancy, when he and I both thought perhaps you believed in the Gift,' she said quietly.

Nancy looked away. 'Well,' she said brightly, 'you certainly tried your best to make me, Mother, so don't blame yourself that you failed to brainwash me. But no, not me,' she said firmly. 'Never had any visions, never had a conversation with someone who was dead.' She waited a moment. 'I guess that makes me really strange in this family, huh?' and she laughed again.

As they were leaving for the journey back to Campbellford a few days later, Martha hugged her grandsons and then held her daughter for a few moments.

'Mother,' Nancy said, 'I won't say goodbye to Neil, I think I've already done that. But you will let me know, won't you?'

Martha nodded, changing the subject by looking away to where the car was being packed. 'That poor man,' she said, watching Donald and Gil finish loading the car. 'Look at Donald, his boys look on Gil as their father, they don't seem to notice Donald, and the worst thing is that Donald doesn't seem to know or care.'

'Shh, Mother,' Nancy whispered. 'He'd be like that whether Gil was there or not. I'm just grateful that Gil is there so that the boys have someone. He's wonderful with them, and he never leaves Donald out.'

'Poor Gil,' Martha said as though she hadn't heard Nancy. 'Poor Gil.'

It wasn't till they were drawing away that Nancy realised what her mother had said. She had thought Martha was feeling sorry for Donald, but when she went over the brief conversation she saw that her mother hadn't been talking about him. 'Poor Gil,' that's what she had said, and that's what she had meant. Nancy turned around in the car and looked back, making eye contact with her mother, trying to pass a question with the look, to ask what she had meant, but they were too far apart for that. She kept looking at Martha, watching the small figure grow smaller as the car drove away, then she blew a kiss to Martha and watched her return it.

15

Hot on the heels of the Great Depression came the Great Drought that lasted till 1937, turning farmland to dust and ruining thriving farms and the families that had worked them for generations. The west of Canada was the most affected, Saskatchewan hardest of all and Manitoba and Alberta to a slightly lesser degree. Families left their farms hoping to find work elsewhere, only to walk directly into the effects of the Great Depression, when commodity prices fell and the market for farm products collapsed. The MacDonalds, in the east of Canada, survived because the family had built up a chain of farms and had enough slack to turn to self-sufficiency, but even so, their wealth shrank and their standard of living fell for a time. Coming out of the worst of it they were just grateful that they had come out at all, as many they knew had not. In the intervening years, life at Pine Edge had fallen into a pattern, with Gil continuing to look after the farm machinery and the family, while giving Donald his place as head of the house. It was something that Nancy admired greatly, that and the fact that he never once referred to the difficulties of coping with Donald, or gave the slightest hint he had noticed that Nancy and her husband not only didn't share a bed, but slept on different floors of the same house. Over the years they became comfortable together, and the boys grew up happy despite her worst fears, because Gil was, to all intents, their father. She would watch them together and think back to her childhood with a kind of wonder, that the tall, skinny, dark, distant cousin she had barely bothered to notice was now caring for her sons like a father. And there were times when she felt guilty, wondering if that was why Gil, now in his early forties, had never married, because he was performing a family duty that left him no time for a separate life of his own. Not that it was unusual for the extended family to take on the duties of dead relatives, the only strange thing was that Donald wasn't dead.

Campbellford was surrounded by waterways and rivers, and it was Gil who had built a boat with the boys and gone sailing and fishing with them. He took them shooting for wild geese, ducks and partridge, too, reporting back that when Calli had shot his first and last duck he had thrown the gun down, walked away and thrown up. Gil felt guilty; he should've known that Calli had only come along on the trip because he looked up to Gil so much and hadn't wanted to disappoint him. Gil shook his head ruefully, they shared many interests, but killing any living creature was beyond Calli's comprehension, a bird especially. Gil *should have* known. He never again asked Calli to hunt with him and Calli never again handled a gun. Feargie, on the other hand, had flown in the old Sopwith Camel once and never did so again; that was his time to throw up, and his brother felt no sympathy, his only thought was anger in case Feargie had made a mess of the Camel. So Gil went hunting with Feargie, who wanted to be a healer, and he flew with Calli, who learned everything there was to know about all flying machines and hungered for the day he had his own plane.

Nancy listened to Gil's regrets about the hunting trip and nodded her head. 'You might as well have suggested he shoot Hamish the groundhog,' she sighed. 'Hamish the *many* groundhogs.'

'I feel bad about it,' Gil replied. 'Thinking about it now I can see how stupid it was, but before . . .'

'It's just a lesson learned for everyone, Gil, he'll recover,' she said gently, looking at Gil's downcast expression and laughing. 'But will *you*?'

'I'd never hurt him, Nancy, never let anyone else hurt him,' he protested. 'He's like my own son.' He paused. 'I'm sorry, I didn't mean any disrespect to Donald, I have no right to . . .'

'Gil, you know how glad we all are that you're here,' Nancy said quietly. 'If you weren't, the boys wouldn't have a father, you and I both know that.' Then, sensing that the conversation was close to matters she didn't want to discuss, not even with Gil, especially not with Gil, she changed the subject. 'He was always like that with animals. When machines took over farm work the horses were kept in luxury, because Calli hadn't imagined anything else and would've blown up if they'd been sold on. Remember how he used to muck them out, feed them and groom them himself?'

Gil smiled. 'You'd hear him talking to them as you passed by, and he didn't feel self-conscious about it, it was just his way to treat living creatures with dignity, which is why I should've known –'

'Gil, not again!' Nancy teased him.

'There's a spot, high above Campbellford, looking out over the village on one side and down to the Fairey Lake on the other, we spotted it once when we went out in the Camel. He goes up there sometimes and sits watching the hawks grabbing fish from the lake, and the raccoons and foxes going about their business. I keep telling him that there are likely bears up there, too, but I don't think he would be scared even if one did happen upon him. He'd just look up, smile and say "*Ciamar a tha thu?*" to it.'

They both chuckled at the thought. 'He says he'll build a house up there one day.'

'He's always been easily caught up in notions,' Nancy said. 'My mother used to call him Scattergun Calli, but since he laid eyes on the old Sopwith he's become so focused. And he's worked so hard, his maths and physics grades are higher than Feargie's. The teachers he had when he was younger wouldn't believe you if you told them how well he's doing.'

'He's always had a keen intelligence,' Gil replied, 'and a big imagination. If my own schooldays are anything to go by, teachers are the very ones who can't cope with that combination.'

'So you were a problem too?' Nancy asked.

'I think I had the problem,' Gil laughed back. 'I just didn't fit in, needed to learn in my own way, and they resented that. It gave me a bit of trouble, because I couldn't change and neither could they. You are what you are, like Calli. He was just looking around for something to tune in to and now that he has I don't think he'll change his mind. I hate to say it,' he smiled to Nancy, 'because I know it isn't what you want to hear, but the boy is a natural flyer.'

'Why wouldn't I want you to say that?' she asked.

'Well, most mothers don't want their sons doing anything dangerous,' he replied.

'I don't want them risking their lives stupidly, but they'll do what they do, whether I want them to or not. Do you think I could stop Calli flying?'

'It's a good way to see it,' he said, 'but you must worry sometimes.'

'Ah,' said Nancy, 'that's something else entirely, and it's my problem, not Calli's.'

By 1939, when he was nineteen years old, Calli was flying a Tiger Moth, though the old Sopwith remained his joy and was accorded its own home in an outhouse where he could work on it and maintain it as war took over Europe yet again.

'The War to end all Wars,' Gil remarked wryly. 'That's what they told us about the last one.' He and Calli were listening to the radio as they worked on the Tiger's rudder. 'That's what they told us, and a generation later we're in another.'

'Do you think we'll be drawn in again?' Calli asked.

'Well, the government says farmers' sons won't be conscripted because they're needed to produce food, but I wouldn't take any notice of that. I'd bet anything that the Liberals and the Conservatives will back down on that, I'm sure we'll be in there soon,' Gil replied. 'The Yanks don't want to get involved, but they will, unless they want Hitler to annex New York next.'

'Great!' Calli said.

Gil stopped what he was doing and looked at Calli. He had grown into a handsome boy, dark-eyed with a head of strong, curly brown hair and a compact, muscular build. He stood only five feet eight tall, while his younger, fairer brother topped six feet. Calli had an assurance about him, an attractive, calm confidence that everyone who knew him commented on, and even if he did speak his mind rather too freely than might be good for him at times, it was his own mind and not someone else's. But there was an expression about the boy's eyes that day as they talked of war that made Gil's heart jump. It was all there in Calli, he realised, the excitement he and the others had felt about the Great War, the delight at getting away from home, of seeing foreign lands, of being heroes. What was it, he wondered, about the young, that they were willing to lay down their lives so easily and readily, not for an ideal or a belief, but for simple excitement? He shook his head and grinned wryly. He had been the same, all the boys of the 185th had been. He remembered the train leaving and seeing the expressions on the faces of the women, the mothers, wives and sisters, their smiles desperately trying to mask their fear; the boys knew it, too, but it hadn't dampened their enthusiasm. The young think they'll never die, of course, he thought, but they did, and he wondered at every generation's ability to believe otherwise, especially Calli's generation, when they had witnessed the destruction of the one before. Neil MacLeod had died the year before, he had been found dead one morning in the barn his mother had exiled him to. His heart, they said, but if it was then it was heartbreak. What was he? Forty? Forty-three? A big, strong, vital boy who had survived the carnage while his friends, including his own brother and his cousin, had died around him, who had fought on, helped secure Vimy Ridge, with one thought in mind: going home. And once he was home he had drunk himself into oblivion till his heart stopped. Then there was Donald. He remembered standing with the little group at the door of the train as they waved and shouted their goodbyes, Donald, Colin, Neil and Jamie at the front, himself at the back, as usual, then suddenly seeing Nancy's face in the crowd. She was standing still, staring, he thought, directly at him, her face transfixed by something, then he had realised she was looking directly in front of him at Donald, only Donald hadn't seen her. It seemed like yesterday and yet like many hundreds of years ago.

Calli looked up. 'What?' he asked. 'What is it, Gil?'

Gil shook his head. 'I was just remembering how we all thought the last war was "great" too,' he smiled. 'It's not like that, Calli, don't be so ready to lay your life on the line. Look at your father,' he said gently, bending over the plane once more so as not to meet the boy's eyes.

Calli looked at him quizzically and shrugged his shoulders.

'The way he is, Calli, the war did that to him.'

'He wasn't always like that?' Calli asked.

'No, of course he wasn't!' Gil exploded, straightening up and staring at him despite himself. He paused a moment and tried to soften his tone. 'Your father was a gentle soul all his life, to be sure, but he was young too. He loved the sea, he loved music, he was full of life.'

Calli stared at him.

'You must've known this, boy?' Gil said, exasperated.

'I didn't know, Gil,' Calli said defensively. 'He's been the way he is all my life. I don't know him any other way.'

Gil put an arm around him. 'I'm sorry, Calli, that wasn't fair, of course you didn't know.' He sighed. 'Your uncle Neil wasn't the way you knew him either, the war changed them, it changed a lot of men. We rarely talked about it when we came back, not even to each other, but it was bad, Calli, as bad as anything you can imagine. Every day we watched men being gassed and dying in front of us, we saw them drown in mud and being blown to bits, and all we could think was that we were glad it wasn't us. If I learned one thing in that time it was that there are worse things than dying, for a lot of the survivors, like your uncle Neil and your father, I truly believe dying would've been easier than living with those memories.'

'But you've managed, Gil,' Cal said quietly.

Gil sat on the edge of the workbench. 'I know I did, and I don't really know how or why. You had to be hard, be able to detach yourself. Maybe I wasn't as sensitive as the others, maybe I just couldn't believe in anything so grotesque, so I ignored it because it couldn't be true, couldn't really be happening. But don't think of your father as weak,' he said, and saw Calli flush. He was a boy, what else would he think? 'Your father was one of the best men I ever knew, Calli, he did what he had to do and got through and all these years he's tried really hard. The way he is isn't his fault.' He shook the boy's shoulders gently. 'Remember that.'

Calli nodded. 'I still want to go,' he said, almost apologetically.

'I know you do, but any man who fought in the last war would tell you – don't go into the trenches, get as far from the trenches as you can.'

'I'm going to fly,' Calli said. 'I'll be OK, Gil. I remember what you said, about lying in the trenches looking up at the planes overhead and thinking "I should be up there, not down here". I've already put my name down for the RCAF.'

'You've what? Does your mother know?'

Calli shook his head. 'I wasn't going to tell anyone till I heard. No point upsetting my mother or anyone else before it happens. They're keeping a list for aircrew, they'll be in touch, that's what the guy said.'

A year later Calli received his Army Induction Papers telling him to report to his local Army Recruiting Depot, and he was angry enough to burst.

'I want to fly,' he protested, 'I've been flying since I was a kid. Why would anyone try to make a soldier out of me?'

Gil looked across the kitchen table to Donald. 'Your boy's an innocent,' he said, trying to include him in the conversation. 'He doesn't understand the military mind, does he, Donald?'

Donald smiled and shook his head. 'There's no sense in anything they ever do,' he said and then fell silent again.

'But I'm a pilot!' Calli said again.

'I'd say go down and report,' Gil suggested, 'and tell them you're already on the RCAF waiting list. Do you think that's the right thing to do, Donald?'

Donald nodded, then after a moment he said firmly, 'Just don't let them put you in the trenches, get as far away from the trenches as you can.' The mantra of every trench-bound veteran of the First World War.

The first time around, the men of Canada had gone to war willingly because they still had an allegiance to the Crown, but those men were now fathers and they didn't want their sons to go: a generation on, their allegiance was weaker. But it wasn't just the fathers who were less willing, the mothers, daughters, wives and sisters were less accepting of what the Crown demanded. From the other side of the table Nancy continued serving dinner, desperately blinking away tears as she did so. She wasn't sure why she was crying. Pity for Donald was part of it; being moved by Gil's kindness in deferring to him as head of the family as he always did; a natural fear for her son or, more probably, a mixture of all three, she reasoned. And the thought of the last time she waved her male relatives off to war, not knowing if she would ever see them again. Why was she having to do this again? What crime had her generation of women committed? Another reason for her tears was pity for herself then, she realised, and all those other women who waited for men to come home from wars through the ages. Then, just as they had tried to do, she closed her eyes, took a deep breath and put a benign, untroubled expression on her face, as Gil watched her from under his eyelids.

16

When Calli reported to the Army Recruiting Depot as instructed, the first thing he said was that he had already applied to train as aircrew with the Royal Canadian Air Force. The warrant officer behind the desk was unimpressed and uninterested.

'Sign anything for them?' he asked without looking up at Calli.

'No,' Calli replied. 'They put me on the list and said –'

'If you didn't sign anything for them you're in the Army now, buster,' the warrant officer replied.

'But –' Calli protested.

'Look, if you're needed as the flying ace who's destined to win the war for us they'll come for you,' he replied sarcastically. 'Until they do, welcome to the world of lesser mortals, Private MacDonald.' Calli turned to go. 'Oh, and another thing,' Calli looked back at him in despair, 'I know we're not quite as flash as your RCAF pals, but in this neighbourhood you call me "sir", and,' he suddenly barked with a ferocity that made Calli jump, 'you bloody well stand up straight when you do it! Now, hand these papers to the clerk on the way out and when you sign your papers he'll give you a bus warrant for Training Camp at Vernon. That meet with your approval, Wing Commander MacDonald?' Calli stared at him, rooted to the spot, wondering what would happen if he refused and demanded a phone call be made to the RCAF. 'Well even if it doesn't,' said the warrant officer wearily, 'do it anyway. There's a good little private.' Then he looked behind Calli. 'Next!' he yelled, and a tall, lanky young man stepped forward and took Calli's place.

Calli moved to the doorway and stood wondering what he

should do next. If he just walked away would anyone do anything? He wished he could call Gil for some advice, but that meant leaving the depot, and until he knew what action the sour-faced warrant officer might take if he did, he had better not. Just then, the tall, lanky recruit who had taken his place emerged.

'Man, oh man,' he moaned. 'Vernon!' He looked at Calli. 'Vernon!' he repeated, with even more misery in his voice. 'Jeez, I picked hops there one summer, I swore I'd never go back to the place.' He shook his head helplessly.

'As good as that?' Calli asked.

'You've no idea, man,' he said desperately.

'Where is it?'

'British Columbia,' the lanky one muttered. 'A hick town at the top of Lake Okanagan, north of Kelowna.' Calli looked at him blankly. 'Vernon, man!' the recruit repeated. 'A hot, dusty, dirty little hell of a place.' He shook his head again, then stuck out a hand. 'Rob Stewart,' he said miserably.

'Calli MacDonald.'

By the time they arrived at Camp Vernon, the latest intake of army recruits realised Rob Stewart had made no mistake, there would be no excitement to be had in this neighbourhood. The camp itself held out no better hopes. It was clinically clean, made up of single storey barracks for privates, NCOs and officers, with two administration buildings forming two sides of a spotless, square parade ground.

'Jeez,' said Rob, 'they must have guys sweeping this place every ten minutes to keep it this clean. This is gonna be just great.'

A couple of hours later the new boys sat in stunned silence, hair shorn to stubble, holding uniforms constructed of a material so rough it could only have started life as sandpaper, and boots that neither bent nor fitted.

'Jeez,' Rob protested, holding his boots at arm's length, 'these couldn't have been made to fit human feet. Look at them.'

'You're right, lad,' said the clerk happily, 'they weren't made for human feet, that's why we give 'em to you lot. Move along now.'

By the time they had finished collecting their kit, Rob had said 'Jeez' so often that it had already become his nickname. He sat on his bunk staring at the uniform.

'Jeez, why didn't they issue us with pumice stone to take the edge off?' he demanded of no one in particular.

Still in a daze, they filed out of their barracks and stood in a lazy line outside, where the ugliest man Calli had ever seen waited for them.

'What the hell species is that, Jeez?' he whispered.

'He has three stripes,' Jeez whispered back, 'so I guess it's a member of the sergeant species, my friend.'

'Did somebody say something?' the sergeant asked sweetly.

'No, sir,' Calli replied, and the others sucked in their breath.

As the sergeant made straight along the line towards him, Calli understood he had made some sort of mistake, even if he didn't know what it was.

'And who might you be?'

'Calli MacDonald,' Calli replied, 'sir.'

'Calli? *Calli?*' the sergeant rolled the word around his mouth as though savouring every letter so much that he couldn't bear to let it go. 'Isn't that a girl's name, laddie?'

'No, sir. It's short for Callum, sir, it's Scottish.'

'Oh, I know it's Scotch, MacDonald. I'm English, and proud of it, I know a bit of Scotch when I come across it and I don't like coming across it. They wear tartan skirts, don't they? And that's just the men. What we have here is a wee Scotch laddie,' he said spitefully. 'A wee *queer* Scotch laddie with a girl's name,' he said, mimicking a variety hall version of a Scottish accent. 'Isn't that right, Private MacDonald?'

'No, sir,' Calli replied calmly.

'Well, I think it's a girl's name, MacDonald,' the sergeant yelled, inches from his face. 'If I think it's a girl's name then it's a girl's name. What is it?' Calli didn't reply. 'All together, men. What is it?' the sergeant bellowed, staring into Calli's eyes.

From the new recruits came the words 'A girl's name, sir!'

He smirked, then walked back down the line. 'I'm Sergeant Grimshaw,' he yelled, 'and don't feel bad about hating me because I intend giving you miserable, useless bunch plenty of reason. And don't call me "sir", I'm not an officer, I'm a sergeant, an NCO, the backbone of any fighting force. What am I?'

'The backbone of any fighting force,' the recruits replied obediently, with a mixture of 'sirs' and 'Sergeants' at the end.

'Got that, Private Calli?' he demanded. 'What am I?'

From further down the line someone tried to cover a snigger and, as Sergeant Grimshaw departed in search of the miscreant, Calli felt that whoever the hapless creature might be, he'd be indebted to him for the rest of his life.

Breakfast was at 6 a.m. each day, parade half an hour later, then they seemed to spend all of their time marching at double-quick-time and drilling.

'It's all we do,' Calli complained on the phone to Gil. 'They say they need men to fight and all we do is march. Where's the sense?'

Gil was glad the boy couldn't see him laughing. 'Well, that's the Army, Calli, as your father said, there's no sense in much they do.'

'And no one will listen to me when I say that I should be in the RCAF, I should be flying.'

'What can I say, Calli? That's the Army. What's the food like?' he asked, trying to change the subject.

'I'm too tired from all this marching to think about it,' Calli replied miserably.

'But you're fit enough, surely?'

'Yeah, I am, but they don't seem to like that, they keep making my packs heavier. Some of the others are almost dying in the heat, they fall like flies, there's an ambulance standing by at all times. I mean, what's the sense in it? Why drill us and march us about till we pass out? How will that help the war effort? The rest of the time we have to polish our boots and constantly redo our kit. Are we supposed to kill the Germans with the shine of our boots, or will they drop dead of shock at how perfectly our kit is arranged?' At the other end of the line Gil stifled another snigger. 'And all that running at dummies and stabbing them with bayonets. I couldn't do that, Gil, not in real life, not even if it was a mad German trying to kill me.'

Gil thought back to the boy's first and last hunting expedition and didn't doubt him. 'So they did give you a rifle then?' he asked diplomatically.

'Yeah, some ancient Lee-Enfield,' Calli replied. 'We had a go with a Sten at the range as well, and we've got gas masks now. You know what they did then?' he demanded angrily.

'Tell me,' Gil replied.

'They put us in this hut full of mustard gas then told us to take our masks off and kept us in there. Nearly killed every one of us. I ask you, what's the sense in that?'

'Well,' Gil said quietly, 'it'll make damn sure you never take them off when there's gas around. It's a lesson worth learning, Calli, believe me. Just don't let the pettiness get to you, because that's what they want.'

'Why do they want it?' Calli asked.

'They don't need to have a reason, they've picked you out and that's that.'

'Well it does get to me, but I'll never let them see that.'

'That's my boy,' Gil laughed. 'Just keep reminding yourself that it's only eight weeks out of a lifetime, it won't last for ever.'

'"*Only eight weeks*", the man says,' Calli groaned. 'Eight weeks *is* a lifetime, Gil! Where's the sense?'

It went on day after day, though, as Calli was singled out and picked on by those above him in rank. He only had to look at Sergeant Grimshaw to be ordered to paint the stones around the Admin blocks with whitewash while the sun was at its hottest. He only had not to look at him to be detailed to clean out the latrines; to turn his arm in a direction an officer deemed wrong to have his weekend leave cancelled – not that there was much to do in the nearest town, Kelowna – and every unearned punishment was accompanied by anti–Scots innuendo in a concerted effort to make him hit back. Not once did Calli betray his irritation either by word or expression, until seven weeks into the eight-week course, he finally reached the end of his tether, and it was yet another kit inspection that did it. As usual, Sergeant Grimshaw accompanied the Regimental Sergeant Major around the barracks as the recruits stood by their bunks at attention, hardly daring to breathe, knowing that the tiniest infringement, real or imaginary, was being eagerly sought out; a millimetre out in the placement of one plate would be enough to consign every man to a weekend in the barracks. The Sergeant Major stopped at Calli's bunk and pointed to his perfectly laid out kit, and Calli glanced at Sergeant Grimshaw's weasel-like grin and knew it was a put-up job; all was lost.

'What's this?' the RSM asked politely, pointing to the perfectly arranged kit on Calli's bed.

'It's my kit, sir,' Calli replied.

'No it's not,' the RSM replied. 'It's a cabbage. What is it?'

'It's my kit, sir,' Calli repeated.

'I can assure you that it is not, Private MacDonald,' the RSM smiled fiercely, while Grimshaw stood at his elbow, taking down every word in a notebook. 'It is a cabbage, and I'll have no cabbages in these barracks. Cabbages belong outdoors.' And with that he bundled Calli's kit together with his bedding and threw it out of the window, leaving him standing to attention beside the bare springs of his bed. 'So what do you think of that?' the RSM asked.

Calli didn't reply. For the first time in weeks he felt no fear or anxiety, he found he no longer cared.

The RSM and the sergeant walked to the barracks door, then the RSM turned and shouted to Calli, 'Well, aren't you going to get it back in, man?'

'No, sir,' Calli replied.

'Why not?'

'Because I don't give a flying fuck if it lies there for all eternity, sir.'

The entire barrack room was frozen in silence.

'If you don't get it back inside you will have to sleep on your bedsprings,' the RSM said, and the fact that he had made no comment about Calli's language gave him a hint that he had found a chink.

'I don't give a flying fuck about that either, sir,' Calli replied calmly. 'I no longer care what you do or what you say. Isn't that what you wanted, sir?'

To his amazement the RSM and Grimshaw left the barrack room without another word, then the others crowded around Calli as he lay sprawled on the bare bedsprings, his hands clasped behind his head, every one of them afraid of the consequences for the entire room, even if they did support him.

'What'll you do?' Jeez asked. 'They're sure to put you in the guardroom, you know.'

'Couldn't care less,' Calli smiled. 'Might as well be there as anywhere else, and I won't have to march all bloody day long, or paint any more stones in the heat, or pick up rubbish.' He got up and left the room, all the tensions of the last weeks suddenly lifted from his shoulders, and went for a leisurely walk around the camp. When he came back his kit and bedding were once more on his bed and he looked around at the others, puzzled.

'Grimshaw came back in and ordered someone to bring it in,' Jeez explained, 'but they're sure to send for you. If I were you I'd be prepared for anything, including firing squad. Put your shorts on over your trousers, stick lit matches up your nose and a flower behind your ear and plead insanity, that's my advice.'

An hour later, Grimshaw appeared and ordered Calli to see the Adjutant in the Admin block immediately. Without acknowledging the order he wandered over, his hands in his trouser pockets, his battledress jacket and tie undone, and as he listened to Grimshaw's feet trying to hurry him along he grinned, realising that it was true, that he genuinely did not care. The Adjutant was shuffling papers on his desk as Calli ambled in and stood easy without being given permission.

'Both the RSM and Sergeant Grimshaw here have recommended you for Officer Training College. What have you to say to that, Private MacDonald?' he asked, solemn-faced.

Suddenly, Calli understood the game. Over the previous weeks, since that very first day in fact, he had been assessed as a troublemaker, so all that time they had been trying to break him. The 'cabbage' incident had been their last shot at making him fall to the floor and dissolve in tears, or run outside the barrack room, screaming and tearing his clothes off. He had refused to buckle, far less break, though, and as this was wartime they didn't have time to try any longer. So in the time-honoured military way of dealing with someone with a mind of his own, they would make him an officer; poacher turned gamekeeper, the best enforcer of all.

'An Army officer?' Calli said conversationally. 'Over my dead body.' There was a silence. 'Will that be all, sir?' he asked pleasantly.

'Not quite, MacDonald,' the Adjutant replied slowly and emotionlessly. He shoved some papers over the desk at Calli. 'Your transfer papers have arrived, you've to report to the RCAF Recruiting Depot in Vancouver on Monday. You can have the weekend at home. See the corporal on the way out for a clearance form and a travel voucher.'

Calli stared down at the papers, hardly able to take in the change in his fortunes and wondering how long these papers had been lying on the Adjutant's desk – pre- or post-'cabbage'? But what did it matter? The RCAF had come for him, he was out of the Army. He took the papers from the desk, made his way to the clerk's desk, signed what he had to sign and was handed yet more bits of paper in exchange.

'So that's it?' he asked the clerk. 'I'm out of the Army?' The clerk nodded. 'It's official?'

'You are now *Mister* MacDonald, son,' the clerk grinned.

'If I floor the Adjutant before I go, no one can put me on a charge?'

'If you floor the Adjutant's *wife* no one can put you on a charge,' the clerk smiled back. 'Though between you and me, if the gossip is anywhere near true, no one's laid her on her back in years, certainly not him at any rate, so she might welcome it. Take a chance, son, until you sign on the line for the RCAF you are a civilian.'

Calli turned and walked quickly back to the Adjutant's office, hoping with all his soul that he and Grimshaw would still be there. He knocked on the door, almost cried with delight when the Adjutant shouted 'Enter!', and almost danced when he saw Grimshaw standing beside him as the two men studied yet more papers.

'I just have a coupla things I want to say,' he said calmly. 'That offer to train as an officer, if it was meant as a compliment I don't take it as one. I lost two uncles in the last war, another as a result of it, and my father has never recovered from it, they were all in the 185th. Someone said that the men in the trenches were lions led by donkeys, and from what I've seen here I don't think much has changed. Right now I look at you people and all I feel is anger on their behalf. I never felt that before, so I guess I should be grateful that you donkeys have given me new respect and pity for the lions.'

The Adjutant looked at him steadily, a fixed smile on his face. 'For what it's worth, MacDonald –'

'*Mister* MacDonald,' Calli interrupted. 'I'm not in your bloody army now.'

'– I think you'd have made an excellent officer too. You have leadership qualities.'

Calli returned his gaze for a few moments. 'You haven't heard a word, have you?' he asked. He took his battledress jacket off and threw it violently onto the Adjutant's desk, scattering the all-important paperwork across the room like Cape Breton snowflakes, then he walked out of the office, Sergeant Grimshaw at his heels.

'I know you won't accept it, MacDonald,' the little man said smugly, 'but we've done you a favour, you've learned things here that will stand you in good stead in the future.'

'*Pòg mo thòin*,' Calli muttered. 'That's "Scotch", by the way, Gaelic to be precise. It means "Kiss my ass". Now *you've* learned something, Englishman.' And with that he left Camp Vernon and the Army for ever.

If Gil had witnessed that last performance he'd have shaken his head and said 'That's Calli, does whatever he thinks is right, but doesn't think it out very far.' But if his mother or his grandmother had been there, they'd both have seen something, someone else. They'd have looked at each other, smiled, and said 'Ruairidh Beag lives on.'

When he arrived back in Campbellford to spend the weekend with his family before reporting to the RCAF, there was a difference in Calli that everyone noticed. He was harder and less innocent in some ways, yet more sensitive in others. He was, as Nancy and Gil both saw, more attentive to his father and he kept trying to make some sort of contact with him. Unusually he sought Donald out in the downstairs bedroom and attempted to talk to him. He wandered about the room, telling his father of his experiences from the last weeks, turning them into amusing stories against himself, trying to reach him, he supposed, because he felt guilty about not trying before. Being young he now blamed himself for the gulf between them and left with tears in his eyes because there had been little response from Donald.

'It's as if he doesn't know me,' he told Gil later, as they tinkered with the old Sopwith Camel. 'I've spent almost every day of my life feet from him, and all that time I haven't looked at him properly.'

'It's not just you, Calli,' Gil said sadly, 'it's everyone. Everything's locked up inside him and as the years have gone by that's got worse. Think how your mother must feel. She married him when she was a teenager, thinking she could help him, no one explained to her that no one could, not that she would've listened, she was always stubborn.' He smiled at the memory. 'But it's changed her too, if you had known her when she was young, Calli, you wouldn't believe she was the same person.'

'What was she like?' Calli asked.

'Bright, sparky,' Gil laughed, 'didn't suffer fools gladly, as they say, didn't suffer them at all! She was going to go out into the world to do great things, she wanted to be a doctor, as I recall. As tart as you like with your grandmother, always arguing.' He sat down and looked into space. 'All the stuff about the Second Sight, the Gift?' he said, and Calli nodded, smiling. 'Well, your mother wouldn't have any of it, never missed a chance to tell your grandmother what a load of nonsense it was, told everyone. I can see her now, refusing to have anything to do with what she called "the myths and stories" about Scotland.'

'Granny used to tell me and Feargie those stories and tell us not to tell Mother she had,' Calli laughed. 'Then Mother would ask us when we left if she had and we'd say "No", and snigger between ourselves. Do you think there's any such thing as the Second Sight, Gil?'

'Well, how would I know?' Gil replied. 'All I can tell you is that when Ruairidh Beag saw things it seemed perfectly natural and real, he never made a great big production out of it, it was just a part of his life.'

'And he really saw the future? And dead people?'

'He said he did and he was a good, decent man. Why would I doubt him? When he and your grandmother saw Padraig, every member of the family was there and saw them seeing him, if you see what I mean. He only saw people a few times, though, he said he had fewer visions as he got older, but when he was a boy he had no idea of what a burden it would be and didn't question it. He reckoned that he managed to block a lot of it when he grew up because he had other things to think about and that made him less open to it. He was a fascinating man, Ruairidh Beag, he didn't think there was anything magical or mysterious about it, he reckoned it was a kind of heightened intuition. Anyway, they say it runs in the family, boy, so you'd better be careful!'

Calli nodded seriously, but said nothing more.

* * *

When the time came for Calli to leave Pine Edge he walked into the kitchen and found his mother examining her blue suit. She had little use for 'best' clothes, she lived and worked on a farm, so she rarely needed them, and when she did, it was the blue suit.

'Going somewhere?' Calli asked.

'Well, yes,' she laughed. 'I'm coming to the station to see you off.'

'No you're not!' Calli replied, shocked to the core. 'Dear God! The blue suit!' he slapped a hand over his eyes. 'Is this a blue suit do? I didn't realise I'd become a blue suit project!'

Nancy looked uncertainly from Calli to Gil, her face colouring slightly. This was a new Calli, a grown-up Calli. Before the Army got hold of him he would never have spoken to her like that, and she was confused, unsure how to respond.

'Put it away, Mother,' he said, 'and you can forget about fond goodbyes at the station.' He gave a theatrical shiver of distaste, grimacing. 'Gil,' he pleaded, turning to leave the room, 'talk to her.' Feargie, up from Toronto to see his brother off, had been sitting in the corner of the kitchen, a text book in his hands, waiting for Calli to come downstairs. He stood up.

'And where are *you* going?' Calli demanded.

'To see you off,' Feargie replied.

'No, you're not!' Calli almost shouted. 'What's with this family? All of a sudden every time someone goes out the door it's some kind of occasion?'

'I promise I won't wear the blue suit,' Feargie mocked him, 'If that's what's bothering you.'

'Yeah, very funny,' Calli muttered. 'Pick up a bag and carry it out to the car, but that's as far as you go, little brother.'

'OK, big brother,' Feargie said, saluting Calli as he followed him outside to the yard.

When he'd gone, Gil laughed out loud. 'You should see your face!' he said to Nancy.

'I don't know what's come over him,' Nancy said, still not sure whether she should laugh or go after her big son and tell him off.

'He's grown up, Nancy,' Gil said gently. 'Or he's growing up; he's not quite there yet. He's not his mother's laddie any longer though.'

'He'll always be that,' she smiled quietly. 'Doesn't matter how old he is, he'll always be my laddie.'

'But you still have to let him go, Nancy,' Gil said. 'And you know how he's always hated fuss, he's never had any time for social niceties, now has he?'

Nancy laughed and sat down with a sigh. 'No, I suppose that's true,' she said. 'I just thought I should make an effort, do something, you know? I've never had a son go off to war before.'

'You can do something,' Gil explained, 'you can let him do this his way. Maybe the memory he wants to take with him is of you in the kitchen, baking as usual.' Nancy nodded thoughtfully. 'So put the blue suit away,' he teased her.

'Yes, well,' she said bemusedly. 'I don't think I'll ever be able to wear it again after *that*. I didn't know there was such a thing as "a blue suit do".'

'Of course there is! We all cringe when we see the "best blue suit", we know the situation is serious when it comes out.'

Nancy lunged at him, laughing, trying to slap his arm, but Gil dodged out of her way and ran around the kitchen table as she chased after him. Just then Calli came back in with the last of his bags.

'This is how I'll remember you,' he said, smiling wryly, 'running around the kitchen like kids while I'm out there fighting a war. Aren't you two supposed to be adults?'

Calli's refusal to allow his mother to wave him off at the station wasn't what it seemed, Gil knew, he was downplaying the event for Nancy's sake. The boy was being sensitive to her feelings in a way that Gil understood and admired.

Calli spoke briefly to his father and emerged shaking his head, with a pained look on his face.

'Don't take it so personally,' Gil said. 'He doesn't mean it that way, he can't help it. It's not his fault and it's not your fault either. Remember that.'

'I know,' Calli replied, 'but all these years I've never tried.' He shook his head again. Before he climbed into the car he turned to Feargie and hugged him, making Feargie laugh as he looked down at his big brother.

'Stick in at university,' he ordered. 'No nonsense about joining up.'

'Oh, the war just needs you, does it?' Feargie asked.

'It certainly doesn't need *you*,' Calli replied seriously. 'If I ever find out . . .'

'I won't let you find out then,' Feargie teased.

'I'm serious, Feargie,' Calli said. 'You've got to finish medical school.'

The two boys looked at each other for a moment then hugged again.

'And look after Mother, and Father and Gil, and Hamish.'

'What about the Camel?' Feargie laughed.

'Oh, you'd be no good at that, I wouldn't let you near her,' Calli laughed opening the door of the station wagon and climbing in. 'You just look after Gil and Gil will look after the Camel. OK?'

'OK!' Feargie shouted, then slowly went into the kitchen again.

'What's wrong?' Nancy asked.

Feargie shrugged. 'Damned if I know,' he replied. 'It's just the strangest thing seeing him go off like that and not knowing when I'll see him again. Makes me feel a bit guilty, I suppose.'

'What do you mean?'

'Well, I'll be safely back here reading my books, and he'll be off fighting a war.'

'So,' Nancy said quietly, 'you'd rather have me worry about two sons, one isn't enough for any mother?'

Feargie looked at her sharply. 'You know, Mother, I think that's exactly what's in his mind. He didn't say it, but I really believe that's what he was thinking.'

Gil pulled up outside the station, where he and Calli talked for a few minutes before the train left.

'Will you look after my father?' he asked.

'Of course I will, haven't I always?' Gil laughed back. 'You're getting serious here, boy, are you planning on not coming back?'

'Who knows?' Calli laughed back uncertainly. 'And my mother, make sure she's OK.'

'She always will be as long as I'm around, Calli.'

Calli nodded again. 'Feargie will take care of himself, but make sure he stays at medical school and keeps out of the war.'

'Check!' said Gil, holding up an imaginary list. 'Anything else? No favourite bull or cow you'd like me to keep safe till you come home again, a special apple tree you'd like ring-fenced?'

'No, nothing like that!' Calli smiled. 'But make sure Hamish is OK, that no one disturbs him and don't let the Camel collapse.'

'Sometimes I think you believe that plane is *yours*!' Gil snorted, shoving Calli's shoulder. 'That I only delivered it to you that day!'

'But my mother, Gil, make sure she's happy,' Calli said seriously. 'You can do that.' Gil met the boy's steady gaze. 'You know you can do that, Gil, don't you?' he asked again solemnly. 'Don't let her duck out of what life she has in front of her.'

'You talk as if she's an old woman,' Gil said, trying to lift the conversation, 'she'd have your hide if she heard you. She's what? Barely forty years old?' Calli nodded solemnly again, and it seemed to Gil that he was ticking his own imaginary checklist as they talked. 'You know, you'll find that there's always something that will keep you going in war, don't let the bad stuff get into your head.'

'Like my father?' Calli said. 'And Uncle Neil?'

Gill nodded. 'I remember once at Passchendaele I came across this tiny shrub with green leaves, I almost cried when I saw it there. All that blood and bits of bodies and mud, and there it was, still alive, and the sight of it kept me going. I used to fall asleep and dream about that little bit of greenery being destroyed and wake up in a panic, but there it was each time, clinging on to life.'

'What happened to it?'

'Oh, it was destroyed one day, but just knowing it had stayed alive so long gave me some satisfaction, some hope, I suppose.' They sat in silence for a moment. 'Here,' Gil said, taking off the gold ring with the MacDonald clan crest that he wore on the pinky of his left hand, and holding it out, 'take this.'

Calli looked at it. 'But it's yours,' he said uncertainly.

'Well strictly speaking it's *ours*,' he laughed. 'It belonged to Alasdair, Padraig's father, and has been handed down to eldest sons. I got it from my father, Ranald, who got it from Padraig, right back to the man himself, God knows what its history is before that. The motto is "*Per mare, per terras*", it means "By sea and land", they obviously didn't think of people flying in those days,' he laughed. 'I don't have a son to hand it down to, but I think of you as my own boy, Calli, so you'd get it in due course anyway. I'd like you to have it now. Go on, take it, it would make me happy to know you're wearing it.'

'Padraig wore this?' Calli asked.

Gil nodded and smiled. 'Alasdair left it at Mull River for him. Neither of them had much luck in life,' he said, 'but I don't think we can blame the ring for that. It hasn't done anyone else much harm and it brought me safely through the First War. I used to lie in the trenches during the mayhem, hoping that the next bullet or shell wasn't mine, then I'd twist the ring on my finger and remember who I was and where I came from and, more importantly, where I would be going back to. This is our green shrub, Calli, may it bring you safe back to us, boy,' he said, gently patting Calli's shoulder.

Calli took the ring and placed it on the same finger of his left hand. 'Thanks, Gil,' he said, overcome by the gift and the affection he knew lay behind it. 'I won't take it off till I come home again.'

As the train left Gil stood on the platform and felt as though he had been transported back in time. 'So this is what it was like for the relatives?' he thought, watching Calli being taken away, as he and the lads had been more than twenty years before. 'They must have felt like I'm feeling now.' He looked down and blinked. 'I never realised till now how hard it must've been for them to wave and smile as we left to go to war.'

'Gil! Gil!' the boy shouted from the open window, and Gil put his hand to his ear to hear better. 'What Ruairidh Beag said about the Gift – he was right, it's a kinda feeling.'

'What?'

'Like a kinda cloud you sometimes see over some people, that's what it is.' Then he laughed, waved, and was carried beyond reply.

Not that Gil had a reply. He stood transfixed, watching the train long after he could no longer see Calli. On the drive back to Pine Edge he relived that final remark over and over again. That was what he had said, wasn't it?, he wondered. He hadn't misheard him, had he? But he knew he hadn't; that *was* what Calli had said. What had he meant? Was he harking back to their conversation of the other day, about Granny Martha telling him and his brother the old stories and swearing them to secrecy lest Nancy should find out? Or did he mean something else entirely? He had always been a serious kind of lad, yet he was laughing – was that an affectionate chuckle at the secret he kept for his Granny, or because he had kept something else from his family, had put one over on Gil and everyone else all these years?

He arrived back at Pine Edge and wandered into the kitchen, still deep in thought. Nancy was sitting at the big table, a magazine in one hand, a coffee mug in the other.

'Well,' she said, 'you're back, and you look as though you've seen a ghost.'

'Oh, just thinking, you know, the way you do,' he replied, with a quiet little smile. There was a silence, then, 'Is it away?' he asked lightly.

'What?'

'The dreaded "best blue suit". Back in mothballs, is it?'

'Oh, yes,' Nancy smiled a hard little smile at him, glaring at him from narrowed eyes, 'very funny. Did it take you all the way back from the station to think that one up?' They both laughed. 'The coffee's fresh,' she said, 'and the cookies are just cooled.'

Gil nodded, sitting in a chair by the door. 'I can smell them both.'

'Did you get the talk, then?' she asked brightly, looking down at the magazine.

'The talk?' he asked, bending to pull his socks up.

'Did he tell you to look after everyone?' she laughed gently.

'Oh, that! He did indeed.' He looked up. 'You too?'

'We *all* got the talk,' Nancy smiled. 'Feargie's to look after everyone I've to look after, and you've to look after as well.' She was smiling, but her eyes were filled with tears.

'He even talked to his father,' Gil said, trying to fit in with the mood she had chosen.

'Really?'

Gil nodded. 'Didn't get far, poor lad, and felt bad about it.' There was a silence. 'I told him it wasn't his fault, but I don't know if he believed me. Had that wee line between his eyes, you know the one,' he put a finger between his own eyes and traced a vertical line, laughing.

'He had that line when he was born,' Nancy murmured. 'I looked at his face that first time and thought he must've had a premonition about the world he'd been born into.'

Gil deliberately bypassed the premonition line of thinking. 'As you say,' he said, pouring himself a mug of coffee, 'our Calli was always a serious lad who took everything seriously.'

'He called my mother,' Nancy said, 'made her cry but couldn't understand why.'

'What did he say to her?'

'That he'd try and get to Raasay.'

Gil took in a long, whistling breath.

She looked up at him. 'That's what Jamie said to her when he went away.'

'I remember,' Gil replied quietly.

'Do you?' she asked, surprised.

'I was there, too, Nancy,' he said curtly.

She looked thoughtful. 'Of course you were,' she said after a moment. 'Behind the other four on the train.'

'Only you were looking at Donald,' he teased. 'I actually thought you were looking at me for a minute.'

Nancy looked up at him sharply; all these years she thought no one had noticed that strange moment when the world had kept spinning and she had stood still, her eyes on Donald.

Gil felt the silence and added, 'I remember wondering what I'd done to offend the tetchy Miss MacLeod and preparing to duck! You were quite a firebrand as a youngster, if you remember, not someone to offend unless you were sure you could defend yourself.'

They both laughed quietly without looking at each other, but somehow a sudden tension had entered the room making every normal conversation seem difficult. The silence stretched.

'I didn't tell him that,' Nancy said eventually, in a determinedly casual tone, 'about Jamie I mean. I just said she was crying because she was an old woman and he was her eldest grandson, so she'd miss him.'

'That was probably for the best,' he nodded.

There was another silence. Gil sat at the kitchen table and placed his cup down.

'Your ring,' she said, looking at his hand.

'Oh,' he murmured absently. 'Must've left it somewhere.'

She looked down at her magazine again. 'Did he say anything else before he left?' she asked.

'He told me to look after Hamish and the Camel!' he laughed, and Nancy chuckled. He didn't tell her what Calli had said about the Second Sight.

Later, in his bedroom, lying awake in the early hours thinking about Calli, he wondered why he hadn't, and though he couldn't decide why that had been, somehow he felt he had done the right thing. In her bedroom across the landing Nancy slept fitfully, each spell of sleep full of disturbing images. Dreams of the lads of the 185th leaving for France, only now her son was standing there among them, and Donald on the train, only his face was intermixed with Gil's till she couldn't tell them apart. And caught up in all of the dark images were even darker clouds and trees, and the trees had branches, some strong, some weak.

17

As he left on the train for the long journey to Vancouver and the Air Force Recruiting Depot, Calli felt his life was back on course. During his time as a private in the Army he decided that he could cope with anything, even that hell, if at the end of the day he was allowed to fly, and now it was about to happen; he had been rescued by the RCAF. On his arrival in Vancouver he had a medical, but that was no problem, he was fit and healthy, then an aptitude test that didn't exactly tax his abilities, and after that, he was sure, he would be able to fly.

'Your tests show that you're very strong in maths and physics,' said the officer behind the desk. 'Just what you need to train as a navigator.'

Calli looked at him aghast. He didn't want to be a navigator, he wanted to fly. He reined in his natural lack of caution and said, as calmly as he could, 'I want to fly, sir.' What he'd wanted to say was 'Get a grip, man, I'm a pilot, surely you can see that?'

The middle-aged officer squirmed in his chair without looking across the desk at him. How many times had he had this conversation with some innocent boy, he wondered? They all wanted to fly, they all wanted to be sitting in the cockpit becoming flying aces.

'Well, the thing is, old boy,' said the officer kindly, 'that we're very short of navigators and we have all the pilots we can handle for the present.' Then he looked up at the young, enthusiastic face before him and saw the disappointment in his eyes; how often had he seen that? 'Did you know,' he continued, going through the usual motions, 'that the Dutch Air Force actually make their navigators captains, not their pilots, most of us believe we should do so, too, in fact.' Calli didn't reply. 'You see, most people think there's something special about being a pilot, but in reality it's just like driving a bus. The navigator calls the shots, he tells the pilot what to do, he's the man in charge at all times. Mark my words, the key man in any plane is the navigator, not the pilot, and if you want to serve your country in your best capacity, and I know that you do, young MacDonald, you'll train as a navigator.' When he looked up the boy's expression hadn't changed, so the officer sat in silence, save for an occasional little cough to remind Calli that some reply was expected, twiddling his thumbs and leaning forward to glance at the papers on his desk as though they were of the utmost importance and needed his immediate attention.

'I'd still like to fly, sir,' Calli said eventually.

'Yes, well, for the moment, perhaps you could start off as a navigator, and if the opportunity should come up for you to cross over, well, then . . .'

'OK, sir, I'll be a navigator,' Calli said quietly, and the officer relaxed. 'For now,' Calli added.

'Jolly good, MacDonald,' the officer said brightly. 'It'll be Initial Training School in Winnipeg then on to Navigation School after that.' Then he breathed a sigh of relief that there wasn't going to be any unpleasant scene, and shut the file on his desk. Once the boy got into navigator training it would fill his every moment, he wouldn't have time to think of being a pilot, but as he left the office, Calli had already read that thought and added one of his own: 'We'll see about that!'

Outside Winnipeg Station a blue bus with RCAF – ITS on a sign waited for the next bunch of twenty recruits from all over Canada, and when they arrived at the old armoury building that served as their training HQ they were separated into potential pilots, navigators, wireless operators and gunners. As a sergeant took names, he directed them to stores, to be equipped with sheets, blankets and a pillow. 'Take any bed,' he said, 'we'll sort you all out tomorrow,' but he *said* it, he didn't bellow inanely, and Calli realised that this regime was far more relaxed than the Army.

The following morning they were given shoes, caps and uniforms with no badges – there were none for lowly AC-2s – Aircraftsmen, second class.

'Aircraftsman MacDonald?'

'Here!' Calli called out, delighted to be rid of Private MacDonald.

'Report to the office.'

'This is it,' he thought as he hurried along, 'they're going to let me be a pilot.'

The warrant officer he reported to said casually, 'Stand at ease,' without looking up from the paperwork on his desk. It had begun to seem to Calli that the most important aspect of the forces and of warfare was the paperwork. 'I hear you've been to boot camp?'

'Yes, sir,' Calli replied.

'Thank God,' the warrant officer replied. 'We don't have anyone here who knows how to march. You're now an acting, unpaid Corporal Drill Instructor, draw a couple of stripes from the stores and the sergeant will lead you to your squad.'

'But . . .' Calli protested.

'That's all, Acting Corporal MacDonald.'

'But, sir . . .' he tried again.

'Run along now, there's a good chap, I'm busy,' said the warrant officer wearily, his head already down among his paperwork as he spoke.

Calli was so disappointed he had a hard time not hitting something or screaming out loud. He'd just escaped the Army and joined the RCAF, then he'd discovered that instead of flying he'd be a navigator, and now he was being used as a Drill Instructor. Who ran the forces, he wondered, if anyone? He decided not to tell Gil any of this, because he knew Gil would laugh and make some kind of comment about the forces being like that. They *shouldn't* be like that though, that was the point, why did no one else but him see this? He collected his two unwanted stripes and went in search of the sergeant who took him to his squad, all of them as young and bewildered as himself. He took a deep breath and started to push them into some semblance of order, then the sergeant turned to go.

'Sergeant?' Calli asked before he left.

'Yes, son?' the sergeant said kindly.

'How long will I be doing this?'

'Oh, a couple of weeks, that's all. A proper Drill Instructor will turn up one of these days,' and with a grin he departed.

Having become rapidly used to the Army, however, Calli could see his dream of training as aircrew, *any* aircrew, disappearing before his eyes, and decided that he would be a Drill Instructor only in the very loosest terms of the job description; if he was too good, even adequate, he knew he could kiss goodbye to flying in a plane. Without any difficulty he found that his squad of fellow navigators was as reluctant to march about as he was himself, so they came to an arrangement that they would drill expertly only within the environs of the armoury building, where eyes would be upon them. When they went out on route marches they ended up outside the local ice-cream parlour, where they would stand for considerably longer than the allotted ten-minute break, eating ice cream and watching the girls go by. In this fashion the two weeks passed and, much to Calli's surprise, a real instructor arrived, as promised, and he was free. Joyfully he returned to being an AC-2, and rather quickly thought better of it, as he joined the others being inoculated against every disease known to the medical world, plus a few he was sure they'd made up. As raising so much as an arm was out of the question for days, the RCAF took the opportunity to educate their young recruits in the horrors of every form of venereal disease. This was followed, with indecent haste, Calli and his fellow recruits thought, by a film on female genitalia that was intended – and succeeded for a considerable time – in making them wince to a man if they saw a female of any age in the far distance. To complete the lesson they were told about possible infestations of crabs in their pubic hair, which ensured that for days afterwards every one of them examined himself minutely without any reason, which led them to the delights of a 'short arm inspection'. In other circumstances, young, healthy men might have reason to dread, even to refuse having their private parts prodded and examined by other males, whether they were medicos or not, but the recruits were so shocked by what had been laid before their eyes and imaginations in the days before, that they subjected themselves to it if only to be told they were OK.

Next they were sent to No 7 Observers' School, in Portage la Prairie (navigators at that time being called observers), one of the bases formed by the Commonwealth Air Training Plan, where some 28,000 aircrew would be trained every year of the war. An instructor explained that the first three weeks of the four-month course would be taken up with basic maths, geometry and navigation, then there would be the small matters of maps, charts, airmanship, meteorology, wireless, compasses and instruments to master. After that, he informed them gloomily, there would be mid-term exams, beyond which some of those present would no longer be there. Still, even though he fully expected few of them to need them in the long run, they should now report to stores for issues of log books, notebooks, pens, pencils, compasses, dividers, protractors, rulers, slide rules and all manner of other equipment they might need during their short stay.

That evening the AC-2s sat dejectedly in the canteen, drinking watered-down beer and feeling sorry for themselves. Out of the window Calli saw a Tiger Moth parked on the runway and felt a stab of homesickness. He had been flying since he was in his early teens, he had just jumped in the old Camel and flown, then progressed to the Tiger, what possible need could there be for all this stuff on paper? Weather he knew about, every pilot knew about the vagaries of the weather, flying would be easy if there were none. There was wind, rain, hail, sleet, snow, turbulence, lightning and, above all else, ice to contend with, but did it really have to take algebraic equations to take a plane through any or all of that? There were times during the next few months when he felt like climbing aboard the Tiger outside and heading for Campbellford, but he couldn't do that, they'd only drag him back, and to punish him he'd end up in the Army again. Besides, there was the promise of the top five recruits being commissioned as pilot officers. The rest would become sergeants, putting up only three stripes and a half wing with an 'O', which other aircrew delighted in calling a 'Flying Arsehole'. At that time the importance of being an officer was one of pride, Calli wouldn't understand for some time yet that there were other considerations. Passing the course would also lead one day to flying in a twin-engined Avro Anson aircraft, that was the carrot as far as Calli was concerned, he hadn't been this long out of the air since he'd first climbed aboard the old Camel. The idea was that they would gain 100 hours flying experience while they honed their navigational skills, flying with mainly American civilian pilots who were there for the money long before the US entered the war. So it was that snowy November, that Flying Officer MacDonald finally made it inside a plane, and even if it was a slow, draughty, creaky Anson, at least he was in the air again and flying at night, his favourite time, with the stars above and around him. Once they were only stars, but now they had names and functions – Polaris for latitude, the bright Aldebaran, Capella, Arcturus, Antares, Vega and Sirius, and he felt really proud of himself when he could look up to Orion and find Betelgeuse and Rigel in its belt. Now the stars meant more than being in a world of his own, they were the tools of his trade.

Next came No 3 Bombing and Gunnery School in Manitoba, where they flew in ancient Fairey Battle aircraft with civilian pilots once again, firing .30 calibre machine guns at ground targets and at a drogue pulled by another Fairey Battle. Learning about high- and low-level bombing meant dropping 25lb practice bombs in freezing February temperatures of -35F – the pilots refused to fly if the temperature reached -40F – where they also learned that the accepted practice of wearing many layers of clothing to stave off the cold also meant you couldn't move.

Finally that course, too, was over, and Calli was posted to Halifax, where he would have two weeks leave, and then depart by ship for England. It was too good an opportunity to miss, so near to Cape Breton and Mabou, where he might not set foot again for years to come. He would, he decided, call Pine Edge and his mother could arrange a family get-together at Mabou, one of those huge family affairs with all his cousins, the kind of outing that he remembered from when he was a child. It was still April, so it wouldn't be as warm as the usual Mull River gatherings, but he would see as many of his relatives as he could before he went overseas, and there were bound to be others there in the same position. Before he could make the call, though, the plans were changed and he was told to report immediately to the RCAF station in Dorval, near Montreal; he wouldn't be sailing to England, he would be flying the Atlantic instead. His mood swung between elation at that thought, sorrow that he wouldn't see his family before he left and relief that he hadn't already called home to arrange it, then had to call again to cancel. But he could still phone.

Nancy answered. She had been baking and stood with the phone cradled in her neck as she wiped her hands with a towel.

'England? That's great, Calli!' she enthused. 'Flying right across the Atlantic? Wait, I'll get Gil.' She had to get Gil because her mind and her emotions were all over the place and she didn't want Calli to hear it. He heard a bustling noise and imagined her running to the back door, then a distant voice calling Gil's name and a muffled conversation coming ever nearer before Gil's voice came on the line.

'Hi there,' he said breathlessly. 'So tell me.'

'Not much to tell, I'm travelling to Dorval and flying to England.'

'And you say that's not much?' Gil laughed. 'It'll be a bit different from trips in the Camel and landing in the field!'

'How is she?' Calli asked. 'The Camel, I mean.'

'I didn't think for a minute you meant anything else,' Gil teased. 'She's fine, doesn't get much flying, but I'm tinkering with her, making sure you won't have any complaints when you come home. The Tiger's fine, too, and the groundhog is happy and healthy, before you ask as well.'

Calli laughed. 'So all's well with the world,' he smiled.

'Should I try to find your father?' Gil asked tentatively, a token gesture that he hoped Calli would understand.

'No, no,' the boy replied, 'don't bother him. Just tell him I called and said . . . um, I'm fine and I'll see him when this is over. And tell my baby brother to keep at his studies, I want to meet Doctor MacDonald when I come back.'

'OK, I'll pass the messages on. Well, take care and come back safe, boy,' Gil said brightly. 'Your mother wants another word.'

Hearing the familiar voices, picturing them at Pine Edge, almost smelling the place, Calli suddenly felt near to breaking down and wanted to tell Gil not to put Nancy on, but before he could chicken out he heard her again.

'Write home as often as you can,' she said, 'and write to your grandmother, and look after yourself, and –'

'Make sure I eat well, sleep enough and wear clean underwear?' he laughed.

'Well, I suppose that's what I'm saying!' she laughed back.

There was an awkward moment of silence. 'Well, I have to go, Mother,' Calli said. 'I don't know yet when I'll be off, it could be any time really. I'll call again if I can, so that should give you time to come up with a few more instructions. 'Bye.'

''Bye, Calli . . .' Nancy said, ''bye, and be careful. OK?' adding a silent '*Mo ghaol*, come back safely, my love.' As she put the phone down she turned and left the kitchen and headed for her bedroom.

'You OK?' Gil asked quietly, watching her haste.

'No,' Nancy threw over her shoulder. 'You?'

'The same,' he said.

'Well, then!' her voice said angrily.

In the distance he heard the noise of her retreating footsteps on the stairs, then the closing of her bedroom door, then the creaking of the rocking chair where she did her thinking. He sat in a chair by the stove, cupping a mug of coffee in his hands and gazing into space. Gil had never married, had never come anywhere near close and doubted he would now, so maybe he didn't understand about things between couples. But one thing he did know for sure was that if any relationship existed between Nancy and Donald he would be in there with her right now, comforting her. But he wasn't.

18

The train journey to Montreal was Calli's third trip across Canada, and by now he had become a seasoned hand at long-distance travel. Without the smallest twinge of conscience he faked a bad leg to get a lower bunk, knowing that no one would dare question a man in uniform in those times. He observed all the rules; he carried his wallet in his inside pocket, put his valuables under his pillow at night, went to the first meal sittings instead of the second before the food ran out and, no matter how bored he was, he didn't play poker, thereby avoiding falling into the clutches of the con men who regularly worked the trains.

It didn't surprise him that when he reported to the RCAF Administration Office on his arrival in Dorval, he was informed that the Hudson that would carry him to England would not arrive for a couple of weeks. Nothing, it seemed, ran to time or as planned in the forces, just as Gil had said, and he felt a pang of anger, knowing that if someone, somewhere, had passed on news of the delay he could've been on leave after all. He was caught between congratulating himself on always expecting the unexpected these days and annoyance at not seeing his family one more time before he left Canada.

Until the Hudson arrived, he would make up a crew of four, pilot, co-pilot, wireless operator and himself, in a C-87, the military version of the Liberator aircraft, transporting supplies and equipment from one base to another, where, he told himself, there would undoubtedly be some other disenchanted airman waiting to take it back from whence it had come. The C-87 would fly between Presque Isle in Maine, 300 nautical miles from Dorval, to Goose Bay in Labrador, 600 miles north of

Presque Isle, and it would be Calli's job to measure the tracks and distances and make a rough flight plan. He looked at the maps provided and saw that the whole of Labrador carried the legend 'Unexplored'; suddenly what had seemed so easy in the classroom became daunting. When the cloud cover over Dorval broke he saw why it was labelled 'Unexplored', it was a landscape so tedious that probably no one could carry out a survey of it without going mad with boredom. Below the aircraft a picture of true desolation unfolded, mile after mile of small lakes, scrub and rock with no vegetation and no habitation, with the steady drone of the plane's four engines as background noise. Soon it became a milk run, as routine and uninteresting as the cargo they carried – wooden and metal beams, doors, windows, concrete and sand, and the endless paperwork without which it could go nowhere; it wasn't Calli's idea of war. Then, one day in June 1941, he was told he would be flying to England the following morning.

'That our Hudson?' he asked as nonchalantly as he could, as he walked across the tarmac with the civilian pilot, Bill, and the radio operator, Paul, both of whom were in their thirties.

'No,' Bill replied, 'it's the military version, a Ventura, got different engines. Took it up for a spin yesterday, it's OK.'

'Oh,' Calli said, wondering if anything would ever again prove to be what it was supposed to be. 'Where's our co-pilot?'

Beside him Paul and Bill exchanged looks and laughed. 'Haven't got one,' Bill told him. 'Didn't you know there's a shortage of pilots?'

'You're kidding,' Calli muttered sourly. 'I wanted to be a pilot, but I was told they had too many, they needed navigators.'

The two older men laughed out loud again. 'That's the Air Force for you,' Bill said, 'nothing they do surprises me. Glad I'm not in it!'

'The worst of it is,' said Calli with feeling, 'I *am* a pilot.'

'You are?' Bill asked.

'Yeah, been flying solo since I was about fourteen.'

'How in hell did you manage that?'

'My father –' it slipped out before he could stop it '– had an old Sopwith, I learned in that. We have a Tiger now.'

'Never flown a Camel,' Bill smiled. 'Wonderful aircraft though, I envy you. Did you tell them you could fly?'

Calli stopped in his tracks. Had he? 'When I first put my name down for aircrew I did,' he said. 'I was called up for the Army a year later and the RCAF came for me at the end of boot camp. I just thought it would be passed along.'

Once again the older men laughed out loud; it seemed to be his lot in life to make people laugh, he thought wryly.

'Did no one warn you, boy?' Paul asked. 'No one in the forces passes anything on. Chances are no one knows but us. If I were you I'd mention that to someone on the other side of the pond when you get there.'

The Hudson that was really a Ventura landed first at Gander then the crew filed a flight plan for the Great Circle route, which would take them over Ireland and then to Prestwick, on the west coast of Scotland. They were told not to believe signals from radio beacons from the British Isles, because the Germans could bend the beams, so that the planes ended up elsewhere. 'A couple ended up in occupied France recently, so I'm told,' Bill smiled cheerfully.

Then the Met Man informed them that once they reached 10,000 feet there would be no cloud. 'Don't believe that,' Bill whispered. 'I was once told by a Met Man that there was little chance of rain. It was running down the windows as he said it. Take it as it comes, that's my advice.'

It wasn't entirely surprising, therefore, that they were still in cloud at 12,000 feet and had to climb higher so that Calli could get to work with his astro to plot a course by the stars. 'Better put on oxygen, guys,' the pilot suggested. At 16,000 feet the cloud remained unbroken, and Calli looked anxiously at Bill as the speed fell.

'I know,' he smiled calmly. 'We're starting to pick up ice on the wings. The de-icers will deal with it soon.'

Just then there was an almighty cracking noise that made Calli go weak at the knees, as he imagined a wing being ripped off the fuselage.

'There it goes,' Bill said. Then he switched on the landing lights so that Calli could see the snow and sleet in the beams. 'There you go,' he said encouragingly, 'it's not that bad, is it?'

Calli didn't reply, he contented himself with a hard swallow. At 19,000 feet the aircraft was feeling jumpy and unstable.

'We can't go much higher than this,' Bill said, then suddenly they broke through to clear sky with thousands of stars so bright that Calli felt like singing. Bill grinned. 'You can get busy with your sextant now.'

When Calli reached the glass astrodome halfway down the fuselage, he discovered that there was no oxygen outlet, and without oxygen he would pass out at that level, so he held his throat mike and informed the pilot.

'Oh, that's a bugger,' Bill said, as though he'd been informed there was no sugar for his coffee. 'I'll try to keep her steady and you can have a stab anyway.'

At the end of two minutes Calli made his way back to the cockpit and flopped into his chair, breathless and exhausted.

'Knew you could do it,' Bill remarked happily, and nodded to the controls. 'You wanna go?'

'Really?' Calli gasped, still trying to recover his breath. 'You sure it's OK?'

'Well, I'm the pilot and I say it's OK. You sure you can handle it?'

Calli nodded and, as Bill eased himself out of the pilot's seat and into the one for the missing co-pilot, Calli took his place.

'That's it,' Bill smiled, 'just keep her steady till you get the feel of her.' He watched as Calli got to grips with the controls. 'And you didn't tell them you were a pilot, boy?' he asked, shaking his head. 'I'll mention it to someone when I get back, you should be flying.'

Over the next six hours the oxygenless procedure of gathering their position by the stars had to be gone through repeatedly until they broke back through the cloud and eased down to 7,000 feet, to see a bright, sunny day ahead of them as they approached the Irish coast.

'We've come in between two large bays,' Bill remarked. 'The one to starboard is narrower and extends further inland.'

'That's Shannon Bay,' Calli replied. 'The one to port is Galway Bay, we're only fifteen miles out.'

'Well done, young MacDonald,' Bill said.

'Wait a minute, if you've flown this route before you must've known that,' Calli said suspiciously.

'I suppose that's perfectly true,' Bill laughed, looking at Paul, 'but we haven't.'

'What?' Calli exclaimed, looking from one to the other. 'Neither of you?'

The two men shook their heads and grinned.

'If I wasn't so drained I'd punch you both at the same time!' Calli moaned.

For the next hour they flew over the Emerald Isle and watched the different shades of green unfolding below them in the morning sun; the name made perfect sense. Just before they landed at Prestwick in Ayrshire, it crossed Calli's mind that they weren't far from Skye and Raasay. He could see islands spread out in the clear distance, but he didn't know what any of them were and it struck him that one of them could be the very island where Old Ruairidh had stood watching his family leave for Nova Scotia a hundred years before. They were so close that just a little detour further north would take them there, but that would have to wait for another time; they had been in the air for nearly eleven hours, and Calli had a raging headache from lack of oxygen and sleep.

'Wanna add insult to injury?' Bill asked as they parted.

Calli nodded sleepily, shaking hands.

'How much will you get paid for this flight?' the pilot smiled.

'Oh, I dunno,' said Calli, 'about $4.25 I think. Why?'

'Because I've earned $1,500, and Paul here $750. Now doesn't that make you feel better, young MacDonald?'

Calli shook his head in disbelief as they went their separate ways, Bill and Paul to make their return flight to Canada, and Calli to find an aspirin and a bed.

There wasn't much time for sightseeing in Scotland, and the following day he and a bunch of others who had arrived from Canada were on their way once again, to Bournemouth this time, where one of the seaside town's hotels had been taken over as a reception depot. Looking out of his bedroom window on arrival, he saw the beach crisscrossed with barbed wire and skull and crossbones mine warning signs, but the rest of the town looked reasonable, with a theatre, pubs and movie houses. Not that Calli was interested in having a good time, at least not in the conventional manner of young men away from home for the first time. All he had on his mind was getting into the war, yet here he was, doing yet more training, and as a navigator, not as a pilot. Still, he could choose between Coastal Command or Bomber Command after this stint was over. If they wouldn't let him fly his own kite, the least they could do was allow him into the thick of things at Bomber Command, and with that in mind he intended applying himself fully to the course. It didn't work out of course, nothing in this war ever did. The course proved to be pretty much a repeat of what he had already done in Vancouver, but at last it came to an end and a few days before graduation he was called in to the Chief Instructor's Office, where Squadron Leader Mackie, a tall, thin Dundonian, asked him what his preference was.

'Bomber Command, sir,' Calli replied without a moment's hesitation.

'Now that's a pity, laddie,' said Mackie calmly, 'because we rather want you to go to Coastal Command.'

'Sir?' Calli said, trying to control his disappointment.

The squadron leader lounged in his chair and looked at him, sighing deeply. 'That's the trouble with sending boys to war,' he said thoughtfully, as Calli wondered who he was actually addressing, 'they all want to be heroes.' He sighed deeply. 'The thing is, young MacDonald, that no matter what you've heard, Coastal Command is no soft option. Reconnaissance, anti-submarine patrols, convoy protection and anti-shipping strikes add up to serious and essential work, we need top people for this every bit as much as Bomber Command does.'

Calli didn't reply, his heart was in his boots.

'Anyway,' said the squadron leader, 'you're to report to RAF Turnberry in Scotland for operational training on Beaufort torpedo bombers. You'll crew up there. Anything to say?'

Calli considered the question, bit his tongue for once in his life and decided a degree of discretion might be in order. 'No, sir,' he said miserably.

'That's all,' said the squadron leader, and with that he turned back to his paperwork.

Turnberry, fifteen miles south of Robert Burns' town of Ayr, was one of the leading links golf courses in the country, celebrated by the world's golfers for its majestic scenery and its beauty, but you wouldn't have known it in 1941. The RAF had taken over for the duration and the station ran straight through the middle of the course, with taxi strips, aprons and two hangars completing the desecration. On slightly higher ground nearby stood the once luxurious Turnberry Hotel, which served as accommodation for the staff and forty students of No 5 Operational Training Unit, with officers and NCOs from all over the Commonwealth sharing the same facilities. The idea was that they would form crews as they wished, and even once they had done so, they would change around several times, just to be sure, because it was intended that they would spend a lot of time together. In the mess Calli got talking to an Aussie civilian pilot from Victoria whose name was also MacDonald, Gus MacDonald, and they discovered that their families had both come from Skye.

'I think,' said Gus cheerfully, 'that mine were probably a bit more firmly encouraged to leave than yours, I suspect they embarked with iron bracelets around their wrists and ankles,' and he laughed a loud, raucous laugh that made heads turn all over the mess.

'How much flying time have you got?' Calli asked, already lining him up as his pilot.

'I dunno,' Gus replied thoughtfully. 'Probably a thousand or more. You?'

'I dunno either,' Calli smiled. 'We've had a succession of planes on the farm at home, been flying since I was a kid.'

'So what the hell you doing navigating?' Gus demanded, and another wave of noisy laughter ran round the mess, like uncontrolled machine-gun fire.

'I'm still trying to work that out myself,' Calli replied. 'No one listens,' and with that he shrugged his shoulders.

'Well, as far as I'm concerned, if I have to be ordered about by a navigator, I'd rather be ordered about by one who knows what it is to fly, and a kinsman at that. Deal?'

Calli considered what it could be like in the confined space of a plane with that great noisy laugh coming at him, then he stuck out his hand and said, 'Deal. If you can't trust a Skye MacDonald, who can you trust?'

'Well, you obviously haven't studied our history, Calli. The Skye MacDonalds were famous for backing both sides in the '45, while sitting firmly on the fence,' and throwing his head back he joyfully strafed the area once more.

After that they found a gunner from Liverpool, Dave Smith, who had been an engineer and had expected to continue being one in the RAF, only he'd been made a gunner; it was, Calli mused wryly, a familiar story. Finally a wireless operator was found, a London Irishman called Pat Muldoon who had worked for BBC Radio – well, sometimes their masters got things right – but who seemed to spend his every waking moment bedding each female he saw, and thinking about bedding the ones he had yet to see.

'The trouble is,' said Gus, 'the blighter's so bloody good-looking and he knows every workable line, the rest of us won't get a look-in.' He stood up in the mess and yelled, 'Any ugly bastard wireless operators here?' then sat down and attacked his embryo crew with his terrible laugh.

'Jesus Christ,' Dave protested, shaking hands with each of them in turn, 'it's worse than that. What did I do to deserve this lot? A Canuck navigator, an Oz criminal for a pilot and some crumpet-machine by the name of Muldoon! Is anything called Muldoon? I thought that was one of those joke names.'

Muldoon, a handsome, dark-haired six-footer, gazed at him benignly. 'How do you think we feel?' he asked. 'We'll need a translator on board to understand every word you say.' He looked at the MacDonalds and said, 'You sure this is a good idea? Isn't there a non-English-speaking Pole somewhere instead?'

'A sense of humour,' Dave said gloomily, 'that's all we bloody well need. I didn't want to be here, you know, it's all a mistake. I wanted to spend the war making rotten pies in the mess.'

'Why rotten pies?' Gus asked.

'Because that's what they make, must be, it's all we get.'

'So were you a baker in Civvy Street?' Muldoon asked.

'Was I hell! I conducted the Liverpool Philharmonic,' Dave lied.

The others exchanged amused looks.

'So why did they make you gunner?'

'Buggered if I know, I told you, it's a mistake. Don't get too used to me, because someone will realise and they'll come and get me to make rotten pies.'

'So what's the connection between conducting an orchestra and making rotten pies then?' Muldoon persisted.

'Weren't you listening, cloth-ears?' Dave asked. 'There is no connection, it's all a mistake!'

19

The training at Turnberry consisted of getting used to the Bristol Beaufort Mk 1, an aircraft, the instructors assured the students, that could take a lot of punishment and stay in the air.

'Oh hurrah,' muttered Dave darkly. 'Let's hope we get to prove that.'

It did, however, 'fly like a brick', if one of its two engines stopped working 'for any reason'. A knowing look passed between the crews. The Beaufort had one set of pilot controls with a jump seat beside the pilot's seat, where Calli would sit for takeoff before he disappeared down the entry to the Perspex nose on the right. Behind the pilot and separated by armour plating, was where Muldoon operated his wireless and dreamed of his previous female conquests and those to come. Further back, on top of the fuselage, was the rear gunner's power-operated turret, again protected by armour plating, where Dave, Tail-End Charlie, would try to stay alive and think of pies. It was a broad aircraft, though, with plenty of room to move around, and it even had an Elsan chemical toilet, but despite this luxury it was a machine built for battle, carrying machine guns and bombs. As well as navigating, Calli was bemused to discover he would have to man a machine gun and master a large, hand-held camera to capture the accuracy of their strikes. 'And if you've got any time left over,' quipped Dave, 'you could serve a hot meal and drinks and mop my brow.'

On their first flight they tried to be very professional, walking around the plane as Gus checked for external problems, and then they all kicked the tyres.

'What the bloody hell are we doing this for?' Dave demanded. 'What does a bad tyre sound like?' and they all laughed nervously.

As they climbed inside the aircraft, Dave glanced at the airman on the tarmac holding a fire extinguisher, waiting for the port engine then the starboard engine to be started up.

'Do you know something we don't, mate?' he shouted gloomily.

In the cockpit, Calli read out a list of items for Gus to check, then they taxied to the end of the runway.

'Everyone ready?' Gus asked, looking around, and three voices responded. 'Here we go,' he said calmly.

First he pushed the throttles forward and the plane responded, then the control panel to bring up the tail wheel. Calli brought up the two big wheels, the gear, tapping the lever to stop them rotating as the doors closed over them. At 500 feet a minute they soon reached 6,000 feet and Calli climbed into the nose to give Gus his first heading, a triangular route to the north of Glasgow.

'Blimey,' came Dave's voice over the mike as he surveyed the bleak landscape, 'welcome to bloody Scotland. No wonder your lot left it.'

'Careful, pieman,' Calli replied. 'Have you checked your parachute?'

'In fact, are you sure you *have* a parachute, smartarse?' Gus added.

In the background, Muldoon, who could've dismantled his radio and put it back together again before the plane had taken off, sang along to a programme on the BBC as he awarded stars in his little black book.

The rest of the course consisted of navigation, bombing and gunnery exercises by night and day, then they were told to take ten days leave and report to Abbotsinch for torpedo training. Dave and Muldoon went home, but Gus and Calli, both too far from their immediate families for a Christmas visit, took up the offer of a home from home, with a great-uncle of Gus's in Glasgow. Dr Alasdair MacDonald lived in the West End, in a large, redstone villa in the leafy cul-de-sac of Redlands Road, just off Great Western Road. A veteran of the First World War, he had become a doctor afterwards, a thought that occurred to many after the carnage of the trenches. He was of average size, fair hair now fading in colour as well as quantity, with bright blue eyes and a pink face. He was the picture of health in a colder country, Calli thought, looking at him: had he lived in a warmer climate, somewhere the sun shone on a regular basis, he would be tanned instead of pink, and he always had a pipe in his mouth, though it was hard to decide if he was actually smoking. He welcomed both young men with a torrent of excited Gaelic and large glasses of whisky.

'I thought you couldn't get this stuff,' Gus said.

'There are ways,' the good doctor winked, and as they drank, family trees were dissected.

'Skye and Raasay, Calli?' Dr MacDonald mused. 'Well, you could scarcely have a better pedigree, my boy. And who do you have?'

'MacKenzies, MacLeods and MacDonalds,' Calli replied.

'And the MacKenzies would be from Raasay?'

'Yes,' Calli smiled.

'There was a great man there called MacKenzie,' Dr MacDonald said, screwing his eyes up and removing his pipe from his mouth, 'a legendary seer. Ruairidh MacKenzie, you wouldn't know if you're related to him, now would you?'

'Yes!' said Calli delightedly. 'He was my great-great-great grandfather, my great-grandfather was called after him and my middle name is Ruairidh.'

'Well now, fancy that!' said Dr MacDonald. 'I'm honoured to meet you, my boy! I've been hearing tales of his Second Sight all my days. And has it been passed down?'

'Well, to hear my mother, it's all nonsense, something from the Dark Ages, but my grandmother still claims to have it. Where we come from in Cape Breton the culture is still strong, I think it's easier to believe in it while you're there, though my mother has rejected it all her life, long before she married my father and moved to Ontario.'

'Tut, tut,' said Dr MacDonald, troubled by this heresy. 'But tell me, have you ever had any signs of the Gift yourself, Calli?'

Calli shuffled uncertainly. 'Och, a feeling now and again, that's about all I can claim,' he grinned. 'If I'd ever had a vision, I'd never have admitted it anyway, my mother would have disowned me!'

'But you still have the Gaelic, she didn't outlaw God's own language?'

'Everyone up there has, and my mother and father were both native speakers, so it was the first language I heard.'

Dr MacDonald looked at Gus. 'My, my, now, isn't that something?'

Gus nodded. 'We still have it, too, but it's not as strong as in Cape Breton by the sound of it. I have to admit that I think in English now, though I'd never tell my mother that.'

'Ah, well,' Dr MacDonald smiled sadly, 'mothers are magical creatures, we have to keep on their right side till the end of our days. I'm a man of more years than I care to tell you, but I become a laddie again when my mother comes into the room. They're born with this ability to see into your soul, you can never fool them,' and they all laughed, as they thought of their mothers. 'And this war, how is it going?' Dr MacDonald asked seriously.

'Well, if we ever finish training we might find out,' Gus complained.

'I saw some things in the first show,' Dr MacDonald shook his head. 'I was a pilot, but I was hit a couple of times and had to go to the makeshift hospitals. Brutal places, they were, not that they wanted to be, mind, they couldn't help it. I swore that if I survived I'd become a doctor after the war, that was what kept me going, and now my own lad is talking of following in my footsteps. Those nurses were angels, I tell you, how they managed to keep their sweetness with what they had to do and how they had to live, I'll never know.'

'I lost two uncles in the first war,' Calli told him. 'My Uncle Jamie wanted to train as a doctor, too, if he got home, but he was killed at Passchendaele. He'd fallen for a nurse from Skye, instead of going on leave he stayed around the hospital to be with her, and when they asked for volunteers as stretcher bearers –'

'Heroes,' Dr MacDonald whispered, 'heroes to a man. Some of them were conscientious objectors, cowards the Army bigwigs called them, but they were heroes.'

'Well, my Uncle Jamie volunteered because he was there and he was blown to bits.'

'Shocking, shocking,' Dr MacDonald said sadly. 'And the nurse?'

'She was killed too, hit by a stray shell.'

Dr MacDonald shook his head. 'They said there would never be another war, you know, and now look at this mess we're in. I still see men today who never got over the first one and now their sons are in the second.'

'My father's never recovered, so I'm told,' Calli said quietly. 'I've never known him any other way, but he was close to my uncle and then he lost his own brother. It's been like . . . well, like living with a ghost, I suppose,' Calli murmured, realising it was the first time he had ever really put those thoughts into words. 'His cousin, Gil, runs the farm back home, though he gives my father his place,' he smiled, seeing Gil's lanky frame in his mind's eye. 'He managed to get a Sopwith Camel when he came home from the war, and one day he just came down from the sky, landed this beautiful machine in the field while we were playing.'

'And you wanted to fly ever since?'

'Right! Learned to fly in the Camel, went on to other planes after that, but the Canadian Air Force made me a navigator.'

'Why in hell's name would they do anything so foolish?'

'No idea,' Calli sighed. 'I can't seem to get it through to the right people that I'm a pilot, yet they're always saying how short of pilots they are, I can't even seem to find the right people, come to that.'

Dr MacDonald sucked thoughtfully on his pipe. 'I'll see if I can do something about that,' he said.

★　　★　　★

After Christmas and New Year the two lads still had a week's leave left.

'What do you want to do?' their host asked.

'Well, I don't know if it's possible,' Calli suggested, 'but I promised my grandmother I'd try to get back to Raasay to take a few pictures.'

Dr MacDonald slapped him on the back. 'Where there's a will, my boy,' he laughed, 'there's a way. Leave the details to me.'

And so they found themselves transported to the Isle of Skye, first by car and then by boat from Mallaig, thanks to Dr MacDonald's excellent contacts, all relatives. They took many pictures without being questioned because they were in his company. After the bleakness of a war-hit city, they travelled through mountains and glens of such beauty that they would have brought tears to the eyes of an Englishman, and Calli began to understand why emigrant Scots still felt such love for their native land. What was it one of them had said? 'It wasn't the land itself that treated us badly, it was those who owned it.'

From Skye it was a short hop by rowing boat to Raasay, in the company of one of Dr MacDonald's many cousins many times removed. Everyone they encountered was told by Dr MacDonald of Calli's relationship to Old Ruairidh and there would be sharp intakes of breath, looks of reverence and awed remarks that 'He has the MacKenzie hair and eyes!', followed by handshakes so enthusiastic that his hand ached all day.

The island was tiny, that was Calli's first impression, and pretty bleak, too, mainly scrubland, and he wondered how anyone had ever made a living on this harsh ground. Down the middle ran a mountain called Dun Caan, but there were no real roads, just tracks, and they didn't even try to reach Arnish. Dr MacDonald took many pictures with his box camera, including one of Calli on the shore where Old Ruairidh must have stood to wave goodbye to his son and family as they left for Canada a hundred years before. It felt strange to Calli. This was the fabled land of his forebears, the place that had been the backdrop to the stories he had grown up hearing from Martha, despite his mother's embargo, and he knew the landscape so well that he felt he could identify every stone, was sure that if he turned his head quickly he might see the ghost of Old Ruairidh smiling at him.

At the cemetery he found that no headstone had been erected to him or to Annie, they had been the last of their family on Raasay after Donald had gone with his family and there was no one close enough to do them that duty, no money either, he suspected. Old Ruairidh's name was still known all those generations later, though, and the local people pointed out to him the piece of earth where he lay, indistinguishable from any other piece of ground. For some reason this brought him close to tears, and as there wasn't time to consult parish records on that short trip, he made a mental note to come back here one day, find where they lay and mark it with a headstone.

'If you give me your family's address in Canada, dear boy, I'll make sure they get their pictures of home,' said Dr MacDonald, on the way back. 'I have my ways.'

They then had a couple of days to look around Glasgow and found it pretty dreary.

'Is it always like this?' Gus asked.

'Oh, no,' Dr MacDonald replied. 'It's a good place full of decent people, believe me, this is it under war conditions. It's been hit by the Luftwaffe a couple of times and its menfolk are fighting elsewhere, hardly surprising that it's a little depressed. Nothing as bad as Clydebank a few miles away, mind you, where the big ships are built. It was hit in March and May this year, totally decimated. The Luftwaffe went for the houses, the factories were mainly left untouched, almost every house destroyed. Those who survived were evacuated, but do you know, they kept the factories running? A lot of them had been turned over to munitions and the people just travelled in from where they'd been evacuated, often many miles and hours travel away, and kept right on going. Many didn't even know if their families were alive or dead in the rubble, you have to admire them.' He shook his head. 'I work in the Western Infirmary, we got a lot of the casualties, terrible, terrible injuries. Poor people, they had no defences either, sandbags and stirrup pumps, totally useless.'

'I guess that's what we forget,' Calli said quietly, suddenly feeling a little ashamed. 'Our families and homes aren't being hit, we don't have any reason to complain about the war the way these people have.'

'True, my boy, true,' said Dr MacDonald. 'I imagine you don't have much that you can tell your family, what with the censors?' Both young men shook their heads. 'Well, I was thinking,' said Dr MacDonald, 'and as I said, I might have a way out of that. I have a friend in the Canadian Consulate in Edinburgh, we've known each other since the last war. There's no way you could use the telephone, they'd listen in, and even if you spoke Gaelic those ignorant folk over the border would jump to the conclusion that it was Irish and we'd be had up for consorting with the enemy. You could write a letter though, and I'm sure my friend would get it to your people.'

So the evening before he reported to Abbotsinch, Calli sat down in the big house in Redlands Road and wrote three letters: one to his grandmother, telling her that he had actually stood on Raasay and how respected Old Ruairidh's name still was. He told her that there was no headstone marking Annie and Old Ruairidh's resting place, and that one day he would make sure that was corrected, then he wrote another letter to Nancy, Gil and Feargie at Pine Edge, the last one would go to his father. In the one to his mother and the others he wrote of the strange people he had met, the Aussie MacDonald with the amazing laugh, the scouser who should've been making rotten pies, and the BBC radio man who spent all his free time chasing women, and with great success. He told them where he was, what he was doing, but most of all he told them of how much home meant to him now that he was far away from it and faced with the sight of other people's homes that had been damaged, destroyed in many cases. 'I know now what you meant about the little green shrub, Gil,' he wrote. In his note to his father he tried to convey feelings he knew he should have but didn't, not through his own fault, though he felt now that it was, but because of what his father had gone through all those years before. His own experiences had given him a feeling of affinity with Donald, though he couldn't express it properly. At one point, sitting at Dr MacDonald's big dining-room table, he stopped writing and reread the letter. It was about what he had been doing, padded in places with detail that his father wouldn't be interested in and probably wouldn't understand, and he pictured him sitting there in the downstairs bedroom off the parlour that had become his world, his place of safety over the years, and he felt ashamed that he couldn't think of anything more, anything better to write. He reflected on how short it was compared to the others and agonised over how to make it a decent length, and when he couldn't – they had no relationship that made words, written or spoken, come easily – he almost crumpled it up and threw it away. Then he thought again, folded it carefully and put it with the other two in an envelope and handed it to Dr MacDonald before he left Redlands Road.

The small station that was RAF Abbotsinch was a few miles out of Glasgow and could be reached by tramcar, and there they would learn all there was to know about torpedos short of dropping them. Sitting in class one day, having the delights of torpedo innards explained yet again, Calli mused that it was his eighth course since joining up and wondered if he'd see some action, then his ears pricked up as he heard that to deploy a torpedo successfully they would have to fly straight and level at only a thousand feet. He nudged Gus beside him and they exchanged glances.

'Pardon me,' Gus said politely, 'I may be wrong about this, but there again, maybe I'm not.'

'Is there a problem?' asked the instructor.

'This thousand feet. Am I right in thinking that we won't find a nice sitting duck all by herself? I mean, a nice big ship out for a stroll on the ocean all alone?'

'The whole convoy will be in attendance, I should think,' the instructor replied, every tooth on show in a wide smile, 'guns blasting away. Plus, of course, whatever air defences the convoy might have. That's usually how those naughty Germans like to do it.'

'And we'll be under fire from all of them as we're flying straight and steady *at one thousand feet*?'

''Fraid so, old man,' the instructor smiled back. 'Congratulations on exposing so precisely the dilemma of being on Coastal Command.'

'Not at all,' said Gus sanguinely. 'Don't say another word.'

'We will be giving you some practice at dropping dummy torpedos at dummy targets while you're here with us, of course.'

'But there won't be naughty Germans firing back?'

'Oh,' grinned the instructor, 'that would hardly be cricket, now would it?'

'I shouldn't be here,' Dave whined, from beside Calli. 'It's all a mistake, I should be –'

'Aw, shut up!' Gus muttered, leaning across Calli and jabbing Dave in the arm with a pencil.

At the end of the course in July 1942 they were sent to Malta, the home of the Royal Navy and of strategic importance. A thousand miles from both Suez and Gibraltar, it was a stop-off point in the trade route between Britain and the Far East, with natural attributes, like a narrow, easily guarded harbour, and its coast of coves and inlets that provided ready-made wharfs and dry docks. Mussolini had decided he would be in Grand Harbour in a few weeks, Malta had to be wiped off the map. The Italian Air Force had first hit the island in 1940 and the barrage had been kept up ever since, with the Luftwaffe joining in and forcing the people to live in tunnels and caves for protection. By the time Calli and the crew arrived there, Malta was low on all supplies, thanks to attacks on Allied convoys trying to bring provisions to the beleaguered and starving Maltese people. Even for the military, life wasn't easy, they were short of fuel for planes, and repairs were done using whatever could be salvaged and recycled from crashed aircraft, even tin cans served as fuselage patches. More importantly, perhaps, was the Spitfire problem, or the problem with their 20mm Hispano cannon, namely the dust and sand that got into the cannon while the Spitfire was taxiing. The best idea was to paste paper over the outlets, keeping them clear till the planes were airborne and the first bullet fired, but there was no paper. Then the solution was suggested: toilet paper, but the stuff issued to the rank and file was too rough. More thinking was done, and it came to the attention of the Armaments Officer that HQ and civil servants only, were given soft toilet paper. He knew if he asked for it he wouldn't get it, even for a cause like this, so he got himself a bike and travelled around, stealing what he needed and bringing it back to base. A solution to the lack of food was harder to dream up, though, and Calli found himself surviving on a piece of bread, one sausage and tea for breakfast, cabbage soup and a hardtack biscuit for lunch and bully beef and perhaps one vegetable for dinner, with the shortfall in fruit and vitamin C made up for by ascorbic acid tablets. So it was in the interests of the men of Coastal Command to do the job they had been sent out to do, which was protect Allied convoys en route to the island with much-needed supplies, and to attack the German convoys trying to deliver fuel to the Western Desert, where the Allies were losing the war.

The first job handed to the new crew in 39 Squadron was to take off with another plane and plant mines in Tunis Harbour, about two hours' flying time away. There was more kicking of tyres but a great many more butterflies in their stomachs. This time it was for real, this time they could die, only they wouldn't; they knew this because they were young and knew that the young couldn't die. And Fate confirmed this by giving them a bomber's moon and no opposition, apart from a bit of flak way off in the distance that didn't bother them. They arrived back feeling euphoric with relief, they had proved themselves, they could hit more than dummy targets and were now combatants in the real war. A few days later word came in that a German convoy had been spotted leaving Messina for Benghazi, a tanker, a small merchant ship, two destroyers and two flak ships, and once again Calli and the others took to the air in a force of twelve Beauforts and ten Beaufighters, the aircraft the Germans called 'Whispering Death', keeping radio silence and using light signals to set a course. There was elation at sighting the convoy, followed by shock at the high level of flak coming towards the planes. From his position in the Perspex nose section Calli suddenly realised how exposed he was, watching the bright flashes that could kill coming straight towards him. He saw one of the destroyers hit, and then it was their turn to attack the tanker, first coming in at thirty feet, then climbing to seventy-five to drop their torpedos, swooping so closely between a flak ship and the tanker that Calli could see the gunners firing at him. Survival instinct took over and he fired his machine guns back at them, and whooped with joy to see them duck for cover, it seemed almost irrelevant that the tail of the Beaufort had been hit. Then his joy turned to terror as he saw a Beaufort ahead of him slam into the water, then another was shot down, followed by a Beaufighter. From the tail came Dave's voice, 'We didn't get it,' he said miserably, 'the bastard's still afloat.'

The following day it was decided to try again. This time another plane hit the tanker, but it was Calli's crew who launched the torpedo that passed through both sides, then he struggled to take pictures showing oil spilling from the crippled ship, with Dave yelling delightedly, 'We got her, we got the bastard!'

It wasn't till they had landed and the adrenaline was seeping out of their systems that they realised more of their planes had been lost; in all, three Beauforts and two Beaufighters and their crews had been lost to cripple the tanker and damage one destroyer. Morale was hardly high.

'Well,' said Gus in the mess that evening. 'How do we all feel about the second run?'

'The first one was a disaster,' Dave said. 'There's no getting away from that. What the hell happened?'

'The intelligence was wrong,' Calli replied. 'The tanker was higher in the water than we'd been told, so our torpedo settings were wrong, our torps ran harmlessly underneath her.'

'The Intelligence Officer should be fucking shot!' Dave shouted. 'We lost five planes and crews because he got it wrong, it could've been any of us, all of us.'

'Well,' said Muldoon, 'we did get her the second time.'

Dave grinned. 'Wasn't that a sight?' he asked.

'Were you scared?' Muldoon asked, looking around.

'Out of my wits,' Calli replied. 'I kinda wished I'd stayed on the farm.'

'Yes,' Muldoon mused calmly, 'I found myself counting the number of women I'd had and thinking "Is that *all* I'm ever going to have?"'

'Meanwhile,' said Gus, 'I was wondering if I had a clean pair of shorts back at base,' and he hit them with one of his laughter attacks.

20

And so it became the norm: they got up, attended briefings, attacked convoys or attacked Germans who were attacking Allied convoys and took as much pride as they could when their efforts paid off. Calli, who had vomited as a child on his first and only hunting expedition, and knew he couldn't put a bayonet into another human being, found it considerably easier if he couldn't see or hear who he was shooting. It was the coward's way out, he supposed, but that's how it was and so he got on with it.

Back in Campbellford his letters had arrived while he was still at Abbotsinch, thanks to Dr MacDonald's endless contacts, and there had been a great air of excitement at Pine Edge. When Nancy phoned her mother and told her there was a letter for her, Martha insisted that it be read to her, then wept at the contents. Her grandson on Raasay, his physical resemblance to her great-grandfather and him so well remembered, made it impossible to talk.

'Will you pull yourself together!' Nancy teased her, desperately trying to control her own tears. 'I'm glad it wasn't *bad* news if this is the way you react to good news!'

'And what did he say in your letter?' Martha asked, and that, too, was read down the line.

'He sounds more grown-up,' Martha remarked. 'Wasn't that a good thought to put a headstone on the graves of Annie and Old Ruairidh? Imagine him thinking of that in the middle of all he's doing. He was always a kind lad, Nancy, even when he was a child there was never any of that silly male nonsense of trying to appear tough. My father was like that you know, even as a lad and a young man he was always his own man, you got what you saw. That's where Calli got it, he's always been just Calli, and he has never minded who knew it.'

'We were all just saying that,' Nancy replied, smiling at her mother's affection for her son without reminding her mother, as once she gleefully would, that the old woman saw Calli as resembling every male member of the family for generations. 'He sent a separate note to his father,' she said quietly.

'What did he say?'

'I don't know,' Nancy replied. 'I took it to Donald in his room and there hasn't been a word about it since. Gil thinks Calli's trying really hard to reach him.'

'As I say, he is a kind lad, our Calli, a thoughtful lad,' Martha said softly. 'But how did he get the letters past those censor fellows? I heard they are being very strict.'

'The same MacDonald who took him to Skye and Raasay, a doctor, a relative of his pilot he says. He got them to us through a diplomat friend.'

'Isn't that wonderful? He goes all those miles away and meets up with Highland people. I wish Ruairidh Beag had lived to see this day.' Then she started crying again.

'Not again!' Nancy howled down the phone. 'I'll send your letter in the post today.'

'Can't you send your letter too?' Martha asked.

'How can I do that?' Nancy demanded. 'Then you'll have two and I won't even have one.'

'Oh, yes, I see that,' Martha said sadly.

Then Gil took the phone. 'Granny Martha,' he said, 'don't worry. We'll come up instead and bring them both.'

'Oh, that's a clever thought, Gil,' Martha said happily. 'I was just saying to Nancy that Calli is just like my father, kind and thoughtful, but you've always been like that, too. It obviously runs through the family.'

As he hung up, Gil shook his head and laughed.

'What is it?' Nancy asked.

'I think all she can see today are kind and thoughtful males in the family,' he replied. 'But she's right, it was good of him to send a separate letter to his grandmother and to tell her about his trip to Raasay, though he probably doesn't understand how much it means to her.'

Later, sitting at the kitchen table having dinner, as Nancy and Gil went over the letters again, dissecting each syllable, Nancy seemed to become quieter.

'What is it?' Gil asked. 'You were happy enough earlier on.'

'I know,' she smiled, 'but then you think of how long ago he wrote the letters and you wonder what's happened in between, where he went after Glasgow, where he is now, how he is now.'

'I think that's how it is for all the people at home, everywhere,' Gil replied.

'Doesn't make it any easier,' Nancy replied.

'I know, I know.'

She picked at her dinner. 'What did he mean about the shrub?' she asked.

'Och, just a thing I told him once.'

'What?'

'Man's talk,' he grinned at her.

'Are you telling me I should mind my own business?' she demanded, in a mock angry tone.

'I suppose I am!' Gil laughed.

There was silence for a few minutes.

'I suppose I'm feeling that it's all so familiar, you know?' she said. 'Waving the first lot away, waiting all those years. Now we're waiting again, it doesn't seem fair to be doing it again.'

'It isn't fair,' Gil said. 'If there's one thing it isn't, it's fair.'

After that there were more letters in reply to his and from him, but they couldn't be as informative or as long as the ones that had arrived courtesy of the diplomatic bag. In all his other letters the censor had blue-pencilled any mention of where he was, how long he had been there, how long he would stay or what he was doing, all in the interests of national security, and all they could deduce from what was left was that Calli was still alive, or was when the mutilated letter had been written. Donald never mentioned that first note he had got from his son and had listened impassively as Nancy read the other one to him before going to Mabou. Calli always sent separate letters to them, an unconscious statement of Donald's distance from his family, though that never occurred to Calli, he just wanted his father to feel special. The farm work went on, the seasons turned as they waited for the war to end. Feargie went to Toronto to become a doctor and life ticked by. Though life seemed to continue as before, there was an air of distraction and expectation, as there always is in any family when one is away, especially in a dangerous place. Nothing would have made Nancy admit it to anyone, but she felt a connection with Calli, as though there was a line between them that gave each of them a basic communication; she felt she would know if anything happened to him. Had she mentioned it to her mother it would have been taken as Nancy's acceptance of the Second Sight, but she wondered if what she was feeling was what all mothers felt about their sons. He was there, in her mind, waking or sleeping, quietly, but constantly there, that's the only way she could have described it – if wild horses could've dragged it out of her, which they couldn't.

In Malta, life also continued, but as if in a parallel universe. The sorties became almost routine, though the older, more experienced men advised against this thinking because it was precisely the state of mind you had to be in for some dark 'something' to find you. They were all slightly superstitious, most had tokens they relied on to get them through and they wouldn't fly without them. It was less to do with magic and more to do with something to hold onto, something from home that made them feel they existed outside the war and would return one day to that existence. One man wore one of his wife's silk stockings around his neck and never took it off, not even when showering, another had a tiny doll belonging to his small daughter, and as long as he had it in the plane with him he felt no harm could come to him. And Calli, who thought they were slightly insane, was amused to find himself twisting his ring with the MacDonald crest on it around and around on his finger during sorties, just as Gil had done a generation before. That was his talisman, he supposed, everyone needed something. He had often thought Muldoon's constant tales of sexual conquest, or supposed sexual conquest, were pretty much the same thing, something to ground him, to remind him of that other life.

He remembered later that he had been twisting the ring on his finger the day they went out in search of a reported 5,000-ton tanker off the toe of Italy. It was considered crucial to Rommel in the Western Desert because the Afrika Korps was running short of fuel, and though it had the protection of seven fighter planes and a destroyer, it also took the precaution of hugging the shoreline. Nine Beauforts attacked from landward and from close range in the shallow water, while the Beaufighters battled with the tanker's fighter escort. At only five hundred yards a Beaufort ahead of Calli's got an unexpected direct hit on the tanker, and their plane, flying directly behind, was suddenly caught up in the resulting fireball. Flames and black smoke billowed up and around as the plane was thrown about by the blast and peppered with debris. Then everything went into a kind of slow motion, as though the rest of the world continued in real time, but Calli was becalmed in the middle of it with all the time in the world. Almost a bystander, he watched what was happening. A Beaufighter went down, crashing into the sea. He heard the delighted shouts of the others as the tanker burned beneath them. He was aware of Gus trying to take the damaged plane higher and out of danger, watched as he found a welcome cloud, but as he came out the other side, a Macchi fighter seemed to be waiting for them. He heard the noise of the plane being strafed, saw the bullets crack and slice through the fuselage, heard Dave scream as one ripped into his stomach upwards and through his chest, and Muldoon's cry that Gus had been hit. It seemed to last an hour, but it could only have been an instant, and all through it there was a calm and utter certainty in Calli's mind that he would survive, never for an instant did he think of death. The plane was in a dive and he had to climb upwards out of the nose, where he knew without looking that Gus was dead, so he dragged him out of the pilot's seat and heaved him sideways, then sat down and struggled with the controls. Still the plane was diving, but again Calli had no doubts, he simply kept doing what he was doing and, as the plane neared the water, it came out of its dive and started to climb again.

'What the hell are you doing?' Muldoon asked, his voice cold with terror.

'Well,' said Calli calmly, 'we're not going back until we drop this torpedo.'

'Are you mad?' Muldoon screamed at him, then a little oddly, 'Let me off!'

Calli laughed. 'You know how to let a torp go, don't you?'

He could sense Muldoon nodding dumbly as he took the plane within striking distance of the destroyer.

'Let her go *NOW!*' he shouted, then pulled the plane away as rapidly as he could and headed home, smiling as he heard the explosion of the destroyer being hit as he did so. Leaving the rest of the wing to carry on with the attack, Calli nursed the plane back to base.

'See how Dave is,' he told a shattered Muldoon. 'Muldoon, wake up! There are too many women out there waiting for you, come on, wake up! See how Dave is in the back.'

'What about Gus?' Muldoon asked quietly.

'Gus is dead, see to Dave, he's in a bad way.'

Back at base the story of how the Canadian kid – a navigator at that – had not only stopped the plane from crashing, but had climbed again, dropped his torp and hit a target then flown the plane home was all everyone could talk about. Calli was deeply embarrassed by the attention and more concerned about the loss of Gus, his fellow MacDonald, and the serious injuries to Dave. He watched Gus's locker being cleared and knew that among his effects there would be the standard letter he had written to his family in Australia just in case, and decided to write to Dr MacDonald himself. A few days later he went to see Dave in the hospital and knew he wouldn't return to flying, in fact Dave's war was over. As he was leaving, Dave said, 'Didn't I tell them it was all a mistake? They should've let me make rotten pies.'

'I'll pass that on,' Calli grinned. 'I've been told to report to the Adjutant, I'm sure that's exactly what he wants to discuss!'

'How's Muldoon?' Dave asked.

Calli shrugged, wondering what to say. He had watched the tall, good-looking womaniser collapse to five-feet-nothing, watched him deflate and be carted off to a psychiatric unit with a breakdown. 'Who knows?' he said. 'He's pretty shocked.'

The Adjutant sat behind his desk, his hands clasped across his stomach, as Calli walked in.

'You wanted to see me, sir?' he asked.

'Yes, well, MacDonald, I suppose someone has to congratulate you officially on that piece of bloody schoolboy bravado the other day.'

'No one has to, sir . . .'

'You realise you could've lost the plane and what was left of the crew? What in hell possessed you to carry on with the mission, boy?' the Adjutant asked in a gentle, warm voice, and Calli relaxed.

'It seemed the natural thing to do, sir. Gus was dead and I could fly the plane, so I did. Then I thought if we crashed on the way back we'd still have the torpedo on board, so I'd better get rid of it or we'd lose the plane and what was left of the crew, as you say, and if I was going to get rid of it, why not drop it on a decent target instead of wasting it?' He looked at the Adjutant and shrugged.

'Since when could you fly the plane?'

'Always, sir. I've been telling everyone since I contacted the RCAF a year before my call-up that I've been flying since I was a kid, no one would listen.'

'Well, I don't know how to tell you this, and I have no idea how it happened, but this signal has been lying around somewhere for months.' He looked at a piece of paper on his desk. 'It's actually followed you from Glasgow, but you are now, and have been for several months, a pilot officer.'

Calli smiled broadly. 'They'll let me be a pilot?' he asked.

'Strictly speaking you were a pilot when you brought the Beaufort home, but neither you nor we knew it. I have no idea where the order came from, we didn't put you in for it, obviously, as it came through while you were in Glasgow and then got lost. These things happen in war, I'm afraid, but you'll get the back pay sometime.'

As far as Calli was concerned they could keep the back pay. He wondered how this had happened. The pilot who had brought him across the Atlantic? Dr MacDonald? Or had the word just filtered through official channels that he could already fly, or was it a combination of all three? He decided to accept that he'd probably never know, but who cared?

'We've been thinking,' said the Adjutant, 'how would you feel about moving onto Beaufighters?'

Calli took a deep breath and chanced his arm. It was one of those moments when his brother would've said 'Hold on, Calli', but that was in another life. 'If it's all the same to you, sir,' he said, 'I'd like to volunteer for Bomber Command. It's what I've wanted to do right from the start.'

'We'd rather like to keep you here. You do know that there's some talk about putting you forward for a gong over the other day's escapade? A gong would be some recognition for Coastal Command, too. God knows, we deserve it.'

Calli's face creased with horror. 'I don't see any reason for a gong, sir,' he said, shocked. 'The pilot was dead so another pilot who happened to be there took over, that's all that happened. I don't want a gong, if I'm put up for one I'll refuse it,' he said, the initial shock giving way to annoyance. 'I'd rather forget all that rubbish and go to Bomber Command, sir. I hear they've got the new Lancaster operational.'

The Adjutant watched him for a few moments. 'Well, I've

never heard anyone be so upset at the prospect of a medal,' he laughed quietly.

'I didn't do anything to merit it,' Calli said desperately. 'The whole thing was quite routine and logical, there was no bravery involved, sir. Lots of guys do braver things every day and no one notices, I'd feel a fraud.'

'OK, MacDonald,' said the Adjutant in a bemused tone, 'have it your own way. I'll see what I can do about Bomber Command. You've been messed about a bit and after the other day we owe you one. I'll see what strings can be pulled.'

That day Calli sent a telegram to his family at Pine Edge. 'Now a pilot,' it said. They wouldn't hear of his exploits in the Beaufort till after the war was over.

21

When Bomber Harris – a sanitised version of Field Marshal Arthur Harris's real nickname, Butcher – took over as Commander-in-Chief of Bomber Command in February 1942, the aircraft that would become his main weapon was about to become operational. The Avro Lancaster Heavy Bomber was an updated version of the troublesome Avro Manchester. The Lanc was constructed of five separate sections and put together almost like a kit by a workforce of as many women – some conscripted – as men, all putting in sixty-six-hour weeks and turning out 150 Lancs a month. The Manchester's wings had been made longer to accommodate four Merlin engines, the kind used in the Spitfire and Hurricane fighters, instead of two manufactured by Rolls-Royce, a rare failure from the mighty company. Extra fuel tanks had also been incorporated, but the Lanc that emerged was still fast, strong and manoeuvrable. Along her belly was a thirty-three-foot bay that could carry a variety of bombs, it could fly over a range of 250 miles, which meant it could attack all of occupied Europe. The aircraft would be, said Harris, his 'shining sword', and a month after his arrival he knew how he would use it, a decision he never regretted, though he carried the stigma of it till the day he died and beyond. The gloves would be removed, as far as Harris's RAF was concerned; they would adopt the policy the Germans had routinely employed in Britain and every country Hitler turned his attentions to, and saturation bombing of German towns and cities would commence immediately. There would, Harris decreed, be a thousand bomb raids in future, and not necessarily aimed at industrial targets, but against the German people in their homes, starting with

Cologne in May. There would be new bombing techniques, greater concentrations of aircraft over targets, greater use of incendiaries, and a 'Pathfinder' force of specially chosen men to mark the targets for the heavy bombers coming behind, to make raids more effective. They would bring about 'the progressive destruction and dislocation of the German military, industrial and economic system, undermining the morale of the German people to a point where their capacity for armed resistance is fatally weakened'. By achieving this between 1943 and 1944 he would shorten the war and save the lives of millions of fighting men, and though his volunteer crews would remain loyal to him, he would for ever be vilified for bombing civilians, for doing what the Germans were already doing.

Into this, in late 1942, came twenty-two-year-old Calli, desperate to fly a Lancaster, the plane every pilot talked of, whether they were supposed to or not. After initial training he was posted to 207 Squadron at Langar in Nottingham, a happy choice, as there were already a large number of Canadians at the squadron. His feelings when he saw ED498, the Lancaster Mk 1 he would fly in combat, were of absolute adoration, and when he climbed into the pilot's seat his chest ached so that he could hardly breathe. It was like the sensations he felt as he had watched the Sopwith Camel soar out of the sky and land beside him all those years before, and he didn't feel disloyal to his first love, the Camel, because he knew that even the Camel herself would've fallen in love with his Lanc. And he was in love; totally, completely and to the exclusion of all other emotions, convinced that he had been created to fly a Lanc one day. Not that he was alone, every Lanc pilot adored his machine, every member of every aircrew loved every Lanc, and every Lanc was a 'she', never an 'it'. A collection of metal bits and pieces weighing in at 16,330 kg empty and capable of carrying, if need be, a bombload of 32,660 kg the Lanc might be, but she was very definitely 'she', a lady to every man who ever flew in one. She was a thing of such beauty that Calli immediately decided to name her 'Groundhog', because she looked like Hamish, short, squat and, well, beautiful.

*   *   *

When he arrived at the squadron he was immediately claimed by the large number of resident Canadians and his history, both family and service, extracted. One was friendlier than the others, a tall, thin, blue-eyed man with fair hair and, Calli soon discovered, forever wrapped in cigarette smoke. His name was Graeme Shaw, a pugnacious twenty-five-year-old flight engineer from Toronto, a veteran compared to most aircrew.

'You'll be glad you were an officer before you came here,' he told Calli in the mess that night. 'There are some weird bastards among the RAF.'

Calli looked at him, raising an eyebrow.

'Not so much here,' Shaw said, 'though you'll always get it I guess, but in some other squadrons it's pretty much "them and us", they think flying is a nice, clean sport and the RAF is a gentlemen's club that shouldn't be letting in riffraff like us. Happened during the Battle of Britain. I had a cousin came down from Aberdeen, a young lad, nineteen he was. He had a couple of hours' tuition on flying Spitfires as soon as he arrived, then they sent him straight up. When he came down again he found the officer pilots living in luxury hotels and mansions, while the sergeants lived in tents and huts beside the runway. When the Luftwaffe came calling, they got it.'

'I heard something about that,' Calli recalled, 'but to be honest I didn't believe it.'

'It's true,' Shaw replied. 'If they were forced to share accommodation, some of the officers hung a blanket over a rope down the middle of the sleeping quarters so that they didn't have to see or hear the sergeants, the guys they flew with. It was the officers who wouldn't let them become officers, threatened to resign if they did, so if a sergeant pilot was killed, his wife got a sergeant's pension. Group Captain Peter Townsend, you know the great ace? He threatened to resign his commission if they even let enlisted men into the RAF, said flying should remain "for gentlemen". Stupid bastard.'

'Have you found it much here?'

'Not much, the odd idiot who thinks he's better than the rest of us because he went to some fancy school, there's an Adjutant you should watch out for, but on the whole it's OK. Took me a bit of getting used to when I came to England at first though, I got quite a reputation for fighting.'

Calli thought for a moment, the whole thing seemed alien to him. 'What happened to your cousin?' he asked.

'Killed the second time he went up,' Shaw replied. 'Dead within twelve hours of arriving. One of the officers said, "What can you expect of a sergeant?" One of his mates told me about it and I made sure he was the first guy I slapped about when I got to England. Went looking for him when I arrived, found him in his fancy country house and taught him some manners.'

Calli smiled and decided he'd like this guy on his crew if it was possible. 'How many times you used your fists?' he asked.

Shaw blew out a long stream of cigarette smoke and looked thoughful. 'Not many,' he said. 'I've lost count. The others think they're smart calling me Bruiser, but, to be honest, not that many.'

Lancasters carried seven crew: the bomb aimer, Jake, an Australian, lay flat in the Perspex nose watching out for the target and ready to let the bombs go; Calli, the pilot and skipper, sat on the port side with the flight engineer, Bruiser, who was really the co-pilot, beside him; the navigator, Frank, who hailed from Dorset, sat behind the skipper with a curtain around him to black out the screens of his trade; with the wireless op, Bill, a Norfolk man, behind him. The mid upper gunner, a Welshman named Arthur but, inevitably, called Taffy, perched in a Perspex bubble halfway along the top of the fuselage and the tail gunner, Tail–End Charlie, who really was called Charlie Trotter and came from London, sat in another at the rear. As it worked out, and maybe because they met first and were both Canucks, Bruiser Shaw remained the closest friend Calli had, the longest, too, given the high rate of mortality in the Lancs, that forced crews to change about and reform frequently. The general rule was that they got one week in every six off, but as members of other planes were killed, other crew members moved up to fill the gaps and, volunteers to a man. They learned to take it in their stride when an Adjutant emptied a locker of possessions, including the all-important last letter home, and they trained themselves not to dwell on the sight of those empty bunks that night. After the war, when the losses were added up, it was discovered that almost half of the 7,000 Lancs produced and their crews had been lost in action, and if the number killed in training was added on, the deaths rose to sixty per cent. The official number of missions required was put at thirty, but few survived that long, and if you got over seven it was considered you were living on someone else's time. Even so, they were absolutely certain that they would survive, and never thought 'it' would happen to them. 'It' only happened to other guys, even in the midst of their worst fears they had to believe that, and to keep 'it' at bay they carried the usual selection of mascots and charms. Bruiser had a green scarf given to him by his sister, though the others insisted green was unlucky, and one or two had religious medals or rosaries, or small, knitted dolls.

At the beginning of each briefing they would gather together, trying to work out whether this was a long mission or a short one. A short one was indicated by how much fuel had been ordered for their Lanc – 1,150 gallons meant short, 2,154 gallons meant long, and short could mean they were acting as decoys for the real raid and would only be going part of the way, but they would still be under fire, that was their job, after all, to draw the night fighters' bullets away from the planes doing the real business. So it might not do them much good to know which was on the cards, but somehow they felt they had control of the situation if they knew, not that they did, of course. They would file in to the briefing and sit before a curtained wall map, waiting for the CO to arrive and remove the curtain, then they could see the target area outlined in ribbon, and every eye immediately looked for the end of the ribbon. The CO would give them details of their mission, the Meteorologist would give his opinion, usually being regarded by many jaundiced eyes as he did so, because weather forecasting was slightly less accurate than thinking of a number. Then there was the long wait before takeoff.

Once aboard, Calli checked his meters and gauges then started the engines one at a time, first starboard ones, then the port, and got them synchronised, listening to the rhythmic, comforting purr of the Merlins. As they took off from Langar the planes were guided by an aircraft marshaller signalling with a handheld Aldis lamp to preserve radio silence and stop the Germans from tracing them. The heavy Lancs took off thirty seconds apart, each one carefully picking its way along the narrow tarmac, knowing that if a wheel touched the grass on either side the others would be held up and the mission compromised, possibly even aborted. Then full power, pushing the manual control panel hard forward and having to use so much effort to keep it there that Bruiser automatically added his hand as well. Halfway along the 1,300 yards the heavy bomber needed for takeoff there would be a gentle bounce, then another, then a bump as she became weightless and climbed into the sky, with the next one right behind. Planes from other squadrons would join them and form up precisely on time, then they would reach the French coast, where the enemy night fighters were prowling the skies and the terror would begin to gnaw at the stomach of every man. 'Anyone says he's not scared,' Calli remembered from his training, 'he's either a liar or a nutter,' and it was true. Ahead of them, if the Pathfinders had been accurate, the target would be ringed by coloured incendiaries and it was down to the bomb aimer to decide when they were in the right position. Calli had to hold the plane level and still, knowing that a night fighter could appear from anywhere, and the fifteen or thirty seconds it took for the bomb aimer to feel happy would drag like so many hours in the tense silence. The bomb aimer checked the wind speed and direction and waited some more, till he was completely happy he would hit the target. 'Let them go, you sick bastard,' Bruiser would mutter every time. 'What the fuck's keeping you?' another voice would demand, 'he does this on purpose, you know.' Then the release button would be pressed: 'Drop it.' A shout of 'Bombs away!' and every face would instantly light up as the Lanc shot up in the air with the sudden loss of weight, and Calli would throw the plane hard to port, sending it corkscrewing in the air as it took evasive action. On the way back to base they were still in danger from the night fighters that had hunted them all the way over. They would watch out for them, see others being hit, usually from below – the Lanc's weak spot and the Germans knew it – wincing at the flames and desperately looking for parachutes, and if they appeared, counting them. With every mile nearer home there was the fear that a giant hand would appear behind the plane and drag it back, then contact would be made with the plotters in the Ops Room who had them on the end of that magic piece of string and were pulling them home. Once they'd landed, they'd climb out and pat the Lanc and thank her, she had brought them back safely again, and they hoped she'd do it again tomorrow.

It was at the end of one of those terror trips that a name was demanded for the beloved Lanc by her crew. They got down from the Lanc and handed her over to the ground crew, and as usual when they came back safely from a successful mission, they were high on adrenaline, shouting, laughing and pushing each other around.

'She has already got a name,' Calli said quietly.

'Well don't keep it to yourself, you Canuck bastard!' Bruiser yelled, trying to slap him and light a cigarette at the same time.

'It's Groundhog,' Calli grinned, waving away the smoke.

'It's bloody *what*?' Tail-End Charlie demanded.

'Groundhog,' Calli repeated. He laughed self-consciously. 'I didn't tell you before because I knew you had no imagination. She's always been called Groundhog.'

'You're serious, aren't you?' Frank, the navigator asked. 'How in hell can you call our Lanc *Ground*hog? She's a high-flying lady, for God's sake! "Airhog" if anything.'

They had grabbed him, pushed him down and were all rolling around on the grass aiming blows at him as Calli tried to fend them off.

'I want to call her after that gorgeous and well-upholstered WAAF, the big blonde one with legs and curves and everything,' Bruiser said softly. 'I don't know her name and she won't give me the time of day, but that's who I want on my Lanc.'

'I know the one,' said Taffy dreamily in the dark. 'She's a Geordie, so they say.'

'What the hell is a Geordie?' Jake asked.

'Means she comes from Newcastle,' Taffy explained.

'Where's Newcastle?' Bill wondered.

'Up north, but not as far as Scotland, you ignorant lot,' Taffy commented.

'Do they have people up there?' Bill asked again. 'I have trouble believing they have people in London and Wales!' he laughed, shielding himself from Taffy's blows.

'Do you know what she once said to me?' Bruiser asked softly, lying on his back and staring up into the sky.

'What did she once say to you?' Calli asked, and Bruiser aimed a punch at him.

'This is not for your ears,' he said sternly. 'You don't appreciate real beauty so you've no right to listen, cover your ears immediately!'

Calli lay still and covered his ears.

'Tell us, Bruiser,' said Frank.

'Well,' said Bruiser in a warm, gentle tone, 'she caught me looking down her blouse in the mess, you know the way you do, if you get the chance?' The others nodded. 'And she said to me, "Don't bother thinking about it, sonny, you couldn't cope with what's down there". Wasn't that beautiful?'

'Beautiful indeed,' said Taffy with feeling. 'She did tell me to fuck off when I kind of squeezed past her once —'

'As you do,' said Bruiser dreamily.

'As you do, indeed,' Taffy continued, 'and I've carried those words with me ever since, but what she said to you was far more poetic, Bruiser, you lucky bastard.'

'Yes, yes, God was generous to her from what I glimpsed down her blouse, I can tell you, but as I say, she won't give me the time of day.'

'I don't think I've ever noticed her,' Calli said innocently and they started throwing blows at him again. 'Wait a minute!' he shouted. 'Wait a minute! You just don't know what groundhogs are like. They're strong and compact, real survivors, they never let you down. I've got one in my garden at home, he's called Hamish, and he survives the hardest winters and the hottest summers, he's indestructible. He's better than any big blonde.'

The crew lay on their backs in the dark, giggling and breathless, waiting for the adrenaline to subside.

'You're a twisted individual, you do know that, don't you?' yelled Bruiser. 'Nothing's better than that big blonde! I hereby excommunicate you from Canada, no Canadian could prefer a furry rat to the big blonde!'

'A groundhog isn't a rat,' Calli protested.

'What is it then?'

'A groundhog!'

'Well it had better be Lady Groundhog, you mad bastard!' muttered Tail-End Charlie.

The next day the Lanc's name was painted on the fuselage in red, with a maple leaf beside it.

'Look at it,' Frank said gloomily. 'Everyone else has a decently naked woman in an indecent pose. We have something called a groundhog, and I'm not even sure there is such a thing, he's probably making a fool of us. I think I'll drag him out of his bed and kill him!'

From March to July Lady Groundhog was involved in the Battle of the Ruhr, where later the records would show that 23,000 sorties were flown, 57,000 tons of bombs dropped and 1,000 aircraft lost. All the crew knew was that they were scared and tired and grateful to make it home in one piece. They hit Hamburg in July, too, almost destroying the city and killing thousands.

Harris was unrepentant. 'They have sown the wind,' he said of the Germans, 'now they are going to reap the whirlwind.'

Calli never thought of what or who the bombs were dropping on, or what damage was being done, he just got the Lanc to the target, and headed home once the bomb aimer shouted 'Bombs away!' It was the flying he loved, it was always the flying, and that indescribable moment his Lanc left the earth behind, he had never known such a feeling of joy. Then he met Eileen.

The crew were on their week's leave, and though technically it didn't start till the next morning, they had jumped the gun, and strictly speaking he didn't meet Eileen – he discovered her laughing at him in a pub where RAF personnel gathered outside the base. She was one of the wireless operators working in the airfield tower; he'd spoken to her many times as he was bringing the Lanc home, without knowing it was her, a Scottish voice, he knew, but the accent was harsher than the ones he was used to. The Adjutant Bruiser had promised to point out to him was in full flood again, about how if there wasn't a war on the kind of people who were in the pub at that moment wearing officers' insignia wouldn't even get a guided tour of the squadron. They were all trash, they were worth nothing, they had no class, he was saying loudly, mainly because he was drunk; when he was sober he said the same things, only less loudly. Bruiser wanted to hit him, but Calli said he wasn't worth hitting. Instead he told the Adjutant to fuck off, and that he was the result of a coupling between an ignorant sassenach bastard and a deformed she-goat, only he said it in Gaelic. He had said similar things before, usually to the Adjutant, though he had to admit that the insults were becoming more extreme and obscure the longer he was with the squadron. Then he had noticed the lovely girl with the glorious light red hair and sparkling blue eyes sitting at a table nearby and laughing. He had registered her laughter, but it didn't occur to him for a second that she had been laughing at him. This time, though, she was looking directly at him and laughing out loud.

'One of these days you'll meet someone who understands exactly what you're saying,' she said and laughed again, and when he heard her voice he recognised her as the Scottish voice in the tower, one of the girls holding the piece of string that brought them home at the end of each sortie. To Calli, she suddenly became the only one.

'How do you know what I said?' he demanded. 'You're not a Highlander, judging by your accent.'

'Well, neither are you by yours,' she replied.

'I am!' Calli replied indignantly.

'You are not!' she laughed. 'You're a Canadian! You're that Canadian with the Lanc that's got the daft name, that's who you are.'

Encouraged mainly by his good friend, Bruiser, Calli had recently taken to drinking the odd pint of cider, in the mistaken belief that it was a soft drink. After a half pint, to his crew's considerable amusement, he became quite gregarious and happy; Calli just thought the world had turned into a nicer place, except for the Adjutant, of course. He decided, anyway, that his mind was too fuzzy at the moment to reply to the insult to Lady Groundhog's name, he'd deal with that another time. 'As I said,' he said very carefully and precisely, 'how can you possibly know what I'm saying to the nice Adjutant there? Do you have the Gaelic?'

'I don't have Scottish Gaelic, I have Irish Gaelic, a bit at least. There's not that much difference, I get the gist of it, and one day you'll be caught out.'

'How come you have the Irish Gaelic when you're not even Irish?' Calli persisted.

'How come you've got the Scottish Gaelic and you're not even Scottish?' she countered, and even though his mind was slightly fuzzy – lack of sleep he thought – Calli once more took offence.

'I bloody well am!'

'You bloody well are not!' she shouted back, and he noticed the other WAAFs were gathering around her and egging her on, including the one Bruiser had wanted on the side of the plane, and suddenly he could clearly see why.

'I think you're a very argumentative kind of female,' he said, returning to the problem of the red-haired girl with the sparkling blue eyes.

'And I think you're a very stupid *Canadian*!' Eileen retorted.

'And I think —' Calli said, desperately trying to find a way through the mist in his head for the witticism he knew must be forming there. He straightened up and stared at Elleen for a moment. '— I think I might marry you,' he said, and fell flat on his face, feeling so exhausted that he decided to sleep where he lay. The last sound he heard, apart from the noise of the WAAFs cheering, laughing and jeering, was Eileen replying 'Stupid idiot!' but she said it in Gaelic and he smiled as he fell asleep.

Lady Groundhog's crew felt slightly let down by their defeated skipper, but they knew the only way to retain a little dignity was to lift him off the floor and carry him homewards. Bruiser knelt beside him, initially in an attempt to rouse Calli by yelling obscenities directly into his ear and, entirely by accident, he found himself staring up the skirt of the beautiful blonde of his dreams. She stood on the edge of the throng of jubilant WAAFs, her arms crossed under her magnificent chest, watching the performance, the rout of the Fly Boys.

'Eyes down, sunshine,' she growled at Bruiser, 'that's if you want to see out of them tomorrow. As far as you're concerned, that's the forbidden zone.'

The following day the others got their revenge by teasing Calli. They told him he was as good as married, that the 'bride' had been around three times before he woke up, ready to go shopping for a ring, that he had better pray he ended up in a POW camp, because that was his only chance of safety. But Calli was in a place of his own, with a headache, but still happy. He had fallen deeply in love with every aircraft he had ever laid eyes on since he was nine years old, but this was the first time he had fallen in love with a woman, and as with all things Calli did, he did so seriously and single-mindedly. He was coming up for twenty-three years old yet he was still an innocent boy, untouched by any woman save his mother and his grandmother, though he'd picked up enough savvy not to advertise this fact to the men he now lived among. Morals may well have relaxed, even disappeared, around him, but

Calli MacDonald had devoted himself to one thing since Gil had landed the Sopwith Camel at Pine Edge all those years ago. Before that, his grandmother had called him 'Scattergun', and she'd been right, but afterwards he proved to have rigid concentration for what interested him, and so far that had been flying, the love of his life. There was nothing else, it was his one and only obsession, and if he had to apply all his thoughts, time and ability to realising his dream of living in the air and had to exclude everything else from his life to do so, then so be it. In matters of the heart, and of the groin, he was a total novice, there hadn't been time, so it was inevitable, therefore, that when he finally succumbed he would fall like a lump of lead.

As soon as he had showered and dressed, he set off in search of the beautiful Eileen, much to the shock and horror of his crew. She'd laugh at him, the word would spread around the squadron like wildfire, the WAAFs would make sure of that, they said, he was in danger of making himself – and, more importantly, them – a laughing stock, he must still be under the influence of too many soft drinks, would he just sit down and think this thing through? For God's sake, Skip, we're on the first day of a week's leave, why are we still here? But it all fell on deaf ears. The first WAAF he encountered was driving a tractor-train of bombs towards one of the Lancs that would go out that night. He waved the tractor down and all the armourers sitting on the bombs looked around and followed the conversation with keen interest. He wanted to see Eileen, he said, where could he find her?

'Eileen who?' the WAAF asked coolly, trying not to laugh, and Calli knew his crew's worst fears had already been realised; everyone knew about the night before.

'You *know* which Eileen,' he replied.

'Would that be the Eileen you proposed to last night?'

'Yes,' Calli said.

'Jesus Christ, Skip,' one of the men shouted out, 'you didn't, did you? I refused to believe it when I heard. So it was true, then?' and all the others laughed.

'And you don't even know her surname?' the WAAF asked, smiling.

'What difference does that make?' Calli demanded earnestly.

'You must still be drunk, why don't you have a lie down?'

He grabbed the keys from the tractor and made ready to throw them into the grass. 'If these keys get lost, who gets the blame?' he asked.

'Tell him for God's sake,' yelled another of the men as he chalked another message to Adolf on a huge cookie bomb. 'Hey, Alf,' he said to the man beside him, 'how do you spell fornicate?'

'F–U–C–K,' replied Alf, returning to the conversation.

'So last night, when you'd had a few, you proposed to this Eileen who doesn't have a surname, and this morning you want to find her,' teased the WAAF. 'Have I got that right?'

'Just tell the soft bugger,' Alf shouted.

'Yeah, he's his own worst enemy,' yelled another airman. 'Big Daisy will cut off his balls before he gets near Eileen anyway, tell the daft sod!'

The WAAF laughed. 'I can tell you where Big Daisy is; in the mess. She might tell you where Eileen is,' she said, leaning across to reclaim the keys.

'Hey! What is it?' Calli called after the departing train.

'What's what?' the WAAF shouted back.

'Her surname?'

'Oh, that. Reilly,' she called over her shoulder.

'Thanks!' he shouted, and blew her a kiss.

'And Skip,' the WAAF yelled back, patting her hair and smiling coquettishly, 'if she's not interested, give me a call!' and as the tractor pulled the line of bombs towards the waiting planes, all the men hooted and whistled.

When he went into the mess, Calli was directed to the big blonde so adored by Bruiser and the others, sitting at a table by herself. She looked up, shook her head in disbelief, and turned away from him.

'Where's Eileen?' he asked.

'Go away, sunshine,' she advised wearily.

'I will when you tell me where she is.'

'Would you like your balls removed with a fork?' she snarled.

'Maybe later,' he smiled, 'but first I have to find Eileen.'

'She didn't take your proposal seriously, if that's what you're worried about,' Daisy replied without looking at him, and he sensed she was trying to hide a smile.

'She didn't?' he said mournfully. 'Why not?'

Daisy sighed, put out a long leg and, in a wonderfully unladylike manner, pushed a chair from the table and motioned for him to sit down.

'Look,' she said firmly, 'don't fuck about or I will use that fork. Even if you are serious you must be mad, she's been well warned about getting involved with Fly Boys. You don't have a chance anyway, there is a childhood sweetheart in the Navy somewhere, damn the bastard, and she's the most innocent girl you'll ever meet, so if you think –'

'Why "damn the bastard"?' Calli asked.

'That's all you heard?' Daisy demanded incredulously, pushing herself back from the table on outstretched arms, so that her uniform shirt and tie strained tightly across her chest.

'My God,' said Calli, 'they really are magnificent. I'd never noticed them before. Sorry, did I say that out loud? I really didn't mean to. So why "damn the bastard" then?'

Daisy looked at him in silence, then started to laugh. 'I have a theory about childhood sweethearts.'

'Let's hear it then.'

'They're parasites, leeches. Like all men, they want to be looked after when they get older, they know this even when they're boys, so they identify a likely lass early on and decide she meets requirements. Then they hang around for years, making sure nobody else gets near her, all the time having a go at every other girl in sight, and then they marry the lass, so that she never gets a chance to think for herself or to sample other merchandise. I hate the bastards.'

'Have you met him?'

'No, I don't have to meet him to know he's a bastard, I've met enough of other lasses' childhood sweethearts to know what he's like.'

'Anyway,' Calli said nonchalantly, 'he doesn't matter now.'

'You reckon?' Daisy asked, laughing at him, eyes wide.

'Yup. What would you say about a Canadian Scot with no childhood sweetheart at home?'

'Yeah,' said Daisy knowingly, 'and I'll believe that! Those big soft brown eyes, the dark hair falling over your brow, and you don't have some poor sap waiting at home for you? Yeah, I'm sure to fall for that one!' She brought her face close to his. 'What would I say? I'd say fuck off!'

'But it's true,' Calli said quietly, meeting her stare. 'It's true.'

Daisy drained the last of her cold tea from her cup and grimaced. 'OK, stay here, I'll get her, I suppose she has to get to grips with other men some time, but if you fuck her about –'

'I know, I know,' Calli grinned, lifting a fork from the table and handing it to her.

Daisy laughed and walked out of the watching mess, returning ten minutes later with an embarrassed-looking Eileen, dressed, Calli noticed, in civvies, and his heart sank. Just his luck if she was going home on leave to the childhood sweetheart.

He stood up and held his hand out. 'Miss Reilly,' he smiled, 'how nice to see you again.'

Daisy groaned and looked skywards. 'You're supposed to be impressed by the fact that he knows your name,' she told Eileen.

'Be quiet, you horrible old crone,' Calli said in Gaelic, smiling sweetly at Daisy, and Eileen laughed.

'What did he say?' Daisy demanded suspiciously.

'Um, he said you're like a mother hen,' Eileen replied, flashing a look at Calli.

'Mm,' Daisy muttered, 'I just bet the fucker did!'

It struck Calli that he had never met a woman who swore, not ever in his entire life, yet he wasn't shocked by Daisy, it was just how she was. 'Can we go somewhere?' he asked in Gaelic, 'I mean without the, er, mother hen?' Eileen laughed again.

'Is he taking the mick?' Daisy asked. 'Tell him to speak proper.'

'Kiss my arse,' Calli beamed at her in Gaelic, then he said in English, 'sorry about that, Daisy, I forgot you weren't blessed with the language of the Garden of Eden. I was just saying how nice you are.'

'Yeah, I'm fucking sure you were,' she replied.

'I've got a couple of days off, I'll meet you outside in half an hour, OK?' Eileen asked.

'Eileen!' Daisy said, shocked. 'Are you mad?' but even as she said it she knew Eileen wasn't listening.

Calli dashed back to the hut to change out of his uniform, ignoring the questions of his crew and evading their grabbing hands. Then he made his way to another hut, looking for a fellow Canadian he knew who wasn't on leave, and asked to borrow his car. He departed with the keys and angry, envious oaths about his head, jumped into the low-slung sports car so beloved of all Second World War pilots and drove to the main gate, where Eileen was waiting for him. They looked at each other and laughed, both thinking how different they looked out of uniform, then they drove out into the countryside.

'Do you know where you're going?' Eileen asked.

'Haven't a clue,' Calli said happily. 'It's a road, it must lead somewhere.'

They ended up at an inn with a small lake beside it, a custom-made setting for talking, and it seemed to both of them that they had known each other all of their lives, though neither voiced that thought. Eileen asked where he came from and he told her the long story about the family migration from the Scottish Islands to Cape Breton, and then his parents' further migration to the Campbellford farm.

'What's it like?' she asked, and he told her about the wildlife and the space and the hot summers and deep, deep snows in winter.

'Every year on the tenth of May, the hummingbirds arrive,' he told her.

'Hummingbirds?' she giggled. 'I don't believe you! They come from tropical countries, don't they?'

'I promise you, it's true,' he laughed. 'Tiny things, you'd think they were butterflies, maybe, or extra big bees, if you didn't know better, brilliant green with scarlet throats.'

'And on the tenth of May, every year?' she asked. 'Precisely?'

'Yes, why won't you believe me? We have squirrels, too, only not the red or grey fellows you have here, ours are black. There are other birds as well, blue jays with incredible patterns and shades of blue, and blackbirds like the ones here, except ours have red flashes on their wings. Sometimes we get golden orioles passing through, and there's a hill above Campbellford that looks down on a lake, and you can sit there and watch the hawks swooping down and grabbing fish, then flying off with them in their claws. I'm going to build a house up there one day. And then there's my groundhog,' he flashed a smile at her.

'Ah, the Lady Groundhog, you've no idea the conversations we've had about *that*! Daisy reckons it's a filthy name for a woman of low morals.'

'Daisy would,' he said. 'The Lady part was to placate the crew, but the Lanc's called after the groundhog that lives in my garden.'

'Are groundhogs pigs?' she asked.

He screwed up his face. 'I dunno, really,' he said. 'They're more like a cross between a small bear and a beaver, about the size of a small dog, but more muscular.'

'And they live for a long time?'

He looked at her suspiciously. 'Have you been talking to my mother?' he demanded. 'She says it's a succession of groundhogs, but how would she know that? It's one groundhog: Hamish. What about you? When is it my turn to laugh?'

'Oh, nothing as exotic as your life,' she sighed. 'My grandfather left Wexford in Ireland with his family when he was about twelve years old. In fact some of his relatives went to Nova Scotia, but his family only went as far as Scotland. His father found work with a furniture maker in the South Side of Glasgow, in Darnley Street, though that won't mean anything to you. Irish emigrants couldn't get apprenticeships in Glasgow because they were Catholics, it was just lucky that his father had already served his time in Ireland, so the only work my grandfather could get at first was sweeping up, though he was taken on and properly trained later, when people saw what he could do. He was far more artistic than his father, so they say, and in his spare time he carved things, made little men and birds and things. He couldn't resist the urge to include them in his furniture either, we still have pieces all over the house. There are little people sliding down banisters and sitting on the backs of the chairs, we even have a couple of mice running up the legs of the dining-room table. He was commissioned to make a grandfather clock once and got so carried away that he couldn't bear to part with it. On one side there's a tiny figure of a boy climbing a ladder, and on the other side there's a girl, and as they climb they get steadily older. Your eyes follow them to the top and there they are, an old couple sitting in rocking chairs, holding hands, so it's more of a grandparents' clock really. I've told my father that if the German bombers arrive he's to save that clock for me no matter what!'

'I knew someone who did exactly the same thing!' Calli said in an amazed voice. 'Well, I didn't know him, I knew of him, Padraig, my great-grandfather. He was killed by a falling tree when he was looking for some perfect piece of wood for a house he was building.'

They smiled at each other, delighted to have discovered a connection.

'So what happened to your grandfather?' Calli asked.

'Well, eventually he became one of the most skilled workers in the factory. He specialised in making fancy bits, ball and claw feet, carved wooden spiral legs for tables and chairs, thistles and flowers, you know the kind of thing. The man who owned the factory was getting on and had no one to leave it to, so my grandfather gave him every penny he'd saved over the years and the owner let him have a half share, and he sold the other half to his foreman, Samuel MacLean. My father and Samuel's son eventually became partners, they still are, and that's the story really.'

'But what about you?'

'It's pretty boring,' she smiled, 'nothing like your land of hummingbirds and aged groundhogs.'

'I'll try to stay awake,' he replied seriously, pretending to stifle a yawn, and she slapped his arm.

'I suppose I grew up in privileged surroundings, thanks to my grandfather's hard work, he saw me as a princess of Ireland's exiled Royal Family, so all things Irish were drilled into me, the language, the songs, all that, and I was dragged along to Irish dancing lessons almost as soon as I could walk. I was a little doll in my embroidered dress and cape, I can tell you.' She rolled her eyes.

'I'd like to see that one day,' Calli said, pretending to be serious.

'Well don't hold your breath, you won't!' she retorted. 'He always said he'd go back one day, that we'd regain the throne of Ireland, but he never did. He and my grandmother lived in a tenement in Govanhill Street, but it was a higher-class tenement than most, it even had an inside toilet. My parents moved to a big white house in a very posh area called Whitecraigs before I was born, it's the only home I've ever known, sits in its own grounds with a swing and a very small garden pond – nothing like your lake, no hawks! The house has a big, sweeping staircase with a grand piano below it that my mother used to play, but I don't remember much about her, she died when I was five years old. I went to a fee-paying school that turns out future wives for doctors, lawyers and businessmen, and as far as my father was concerned I'd marry his partner's son and we'd each be given our fathers' halves of the business when they died.'

'Ah, so he's the sailor childhood sweetheart?'

'Daisy's been talking! I don't know if that's what you'd call Alex —'

'Would he?'

'Oh, he would, he does, just as my father and both families do, always have. I suppose it seemed such a nice, easy pattern to follow, a boy and a girl from each side of the partnership, what could be handier than that? More of a business merger than anything. I kind of went along with it — why not? He's a really nice guy and I didn't know any better. Then the war broke out and two years ago, when I was nineteen, I was walking down the street one day when I saw the RAF recruiting office, so I went in and asked if I could become a WAAF.'

'Why?'

'I don't know! It was a spur of the moment thing, I suppose I began to feel stifled, as though my life had been mapped out for me since the day I was born, and now here was this chance of freedom. I wanted to get away from home and the war came along and gave me the opportunity. You know?'

Calli nodded. 'What was the reaction to that?'

Eileen rolled her eyes. 'Need you ask? Panic, a lot of screaming and hysterics, how could I do this to Alex, to his family, to my family, to the business? I promised to come back after the war, told them I'd have been called up anyway, this way I got to choose what and where.'

'And Alex?'

'Cut to the quick, supposedly. Couldn't understand why I'd choose to go sooner than I needed to, it was all awful. Then he came over all understanding, and I felt even more insulted somehow, as though he was willing to indulge me as long as it was on his terms, as long as I didn't go too far.' She looked down. 'Do we have to talk about this?' she laughed.

'What do you miss about home?' he asked.

'Shopping!' she giggled. 'Walking down Sauchiehall Street from Daly's to Pettigrew's, carrying lots of packages, that was my only real occupation before the war. What do you miss? — no, don't tell me, Hamish?'

'You guessed,' he laughed.

'I can't see me going back,' she sighed. 'How do you settle down to shopping in Glasgow after this?'

'You don't have to,' Calli said softly. 'Come back to Pine Edge with me.'

So they went for a walk and found they couldn't stop talking and finding coincidences that took on the aura of magical portents. His mother's name was Ann but she was called Nancy, while Eileen's mother had been named Ann but was called Annie, and furthermore they both had grandmothers named Martha. It didn't occur to either of them that these were popular names at the time, to the young couple it was proof that they were meant – fated – to be together. He told her about Mabou and the freezing cold and the blizzards in winter.

'I'll take you to see Cape Breton for the first time in May or June,' he said, his eyes soft, 'when the blossoms from the fruit trees fall as heavily as the snow in winter and as gently, too, and the breeze smells sweeter than any perfume. The flies come in June, mind you,' he laughed quietly, 'but they're gone by August.'

'You sound like a poet,' she laughed.

'Cape Breton's like that,' he grinned, slightly embarrassed. 'It makes poets of even dumb people like me.'

'But I thought you lived in Ontario?' she asked.

'Well, that's about it,' he smiled, 'I was born in Ontario, I live in Ontario, but home will always be Cape Breton.'

He told her of his family in Mull River, of his grandmother and Ruairidh Beag and the Second Sight, and his parents in Campbellford and his brother who was going to be a doctor any day now, and he described Gil descending from the sky over Pine Edge in the Camel. As an afterthought he asked her when she wanted to get married. She blushed and said he was being stupid and she wouldn't listen to any more of his nonsense, and he said he was serious, both of them believing they were unique, as all young lovers do, as indeed they should. The war had provided an extra element, of course, in allowing romances to move quickly, and they were both aware of that, they had watched it happen to many others. Somehow the uncertainty of war made people feel they had to grab happiness when they could, because tomorrow the chance could be gone, and you might live forever wondering if you had missed the love of your life because of the fear that in a second either one might be killed. If there was one thing the generation following the First World War had learned, it was that the mayhem might last for years more, no one knew what would happen. There were hundreds of thousands of young people in situations and locations they couldn't all have been ready to cope with, they just happened to be the required chronological age. So it was inevitable they would behave in ways they wouldn't have had they been at home, with the restraining morals of their parents and backgrounds. In that era youngsters didn't set up in flats together or even separately, they remained in the family home until they married, so for the vast majority, the war provided the chance to get away for the first time in their lives. Everyone knew that the normal rules of courtship had been suspended for the duration, but even so, Calli suspected he would've felt what he was feeling for this girl wherever and whenever he met her. Again, like all innocent, newly-besotted young men, he was touchingly startled by what he thought of as the glaring similarities between their lives, though had he been older and wiser he would've known that you find such similarities when you want to. Eileen's mother had died when she was young, and to him it seemed that he had lost his father, even if he was still there to a degree; her artistic grandfather had been a skilled woodcarver, like Padraig, and her family considered themselves to be exiled Irish Royalty, just as his felt they were displaced Scottish Royalty, they had even left their original homelands around the same time. Not for one moment did he think there might be millions of others from countries and cultures all over the world with similar coincidences – he and Eileen were special, somehow intended to be together.

They spent the remaining three days of Eileen's leave together at the inn, in separate rooms, of course, because they were young and inexperienced enough still to believe that their love was different, it was pure and unspoilt, not some grubby couple of days with no intention on either part of ever meeting again. When they arrived back at the squadron, Calli had another four days left of his leave, but he stunned his crew, who had waited patiently for him to return from his dalliance, by refusing to leave Langar. The crew couldn't believe it, they were as close as family, they always spent their leaves together, but Calli wanted to stay where he could be with Eileen as often as possible.

'Listen, Skip,' Bruiser said, sitting beside Calli on his bunk and putting his right arm around him, while smoking with his left. 'I've asked around about this girl and she's already been out with two pilots who were shot down. Did you know that?'

'So?' Calli asked, waving the smoke away with his hand, as he always did and as always Bruiser ignored.

'Well,' Bruiser said, looking at the anxious faces of the others for support, 'we reckon she's a jinx and that you should dump her.'

Calli looked around the nodding heads and laughed out loud. 'Who else would she go out with?' he asked. 'We're all here together, working these odd hours. We can't take the risk of mixing with outsiders, who else would she go out with but Air Force people? If we ruled out dating girls who had dated crews who were shot down, that would rule out a fair number of them, don't you think?'

The crew looked at him, perplexed.

'Look, Taffy, how many times have you played darts with someone who then got shot down? But we don't think you're a jinx, do we? A bloody nuisance, granted, but we still fly with you, don't we?'

Taffy didn't reply.

'And you, Bruiser, how many times have you cheated some poor sod at cards and they didn't come back from the next mission?'

Bruiser looked bewildered, then, 'Ah, but, there's more!' he suddenly remembered. 'We've been told she's frigid, she wouldn't do the deed with any of them. Now that shows a hard nature!'

he said triumphantly. 'I mean, those poor brave boys going off to be killed and in need of comfort, and word has it she gave them nothing. Now you don't want to be stuck with a dame like that, do you?'

Calli fell back in his bunk and laughed till he choked. 'Your blonde, Big Daisy,' he said eventually, wiping his eyes, 'is she frigid or does she give it away to anyone who asks, or almost anyone, seeing as she won't give any of you a sniff?'

'That's different, Skip,' Taffy protested, slightly offended. 'We see her as a challenge, you see this jinx female as a wife. That's the difference.'

'Oh, get out of here,' he told them, 'go and get drunk and find yourselves a few women, I'm staying put.'

They could still hear him laughing as they left the hut.

On her way back to the WAAF hut Eileen knew she would be put through a similar attack from Daisy, and she had no answers for her, except that it felt right with this boy. When she first came down from Glasgow it was Daisy who had adopted her and protected her; she really was a mother hen, though she didn't realise it. Daisy's version was that she was against men taking advantage of women, and men always did. Eileen remembered the first time she saw her, and was aware Daisy was the kind of person she would never have met in her life in Glasgow, or if she had, she'd have been warned to keep away from her. The woman oozed sex, there was no other description. She very probably had similar measurements to other women, but the inches seemed to have been distributed differently; her body flowed sensually and provocatively inside her skin; even the awful uniform that reduced them all to sexless drones seemed to enhance her curves. Sensible black leather tie-up shoes with thick soles, worn with heavy black lisle stockings, made frumps of everyone else, but they showed off Daisy's shapely legs in a way that was hard to understand. Shirts and ties made to fit men's physiques were ugly on women, but on Daisy there was a suggestion of womanly wiles about to be unleashed, of a hot sexuality simmering and straining just under the surface, and it was the same with the rest of the uniform. Cotton vests and brassieres that fitted uncomfortably where they touched, were transformed by Daisy's body into feminine garments. She never wore the regulation long knickers with elasticated legs, grey ones dubbed 'twilights' and black ones called 'blackouts'. She wore them in bed under the striped pyjamas that were part of the issue, because it was always cold in the hut which housed twenty-four beds, two pot-bellied stoves and a supply of coal that was never enough. No, under the heavy grey-blue skirt, and against regulations, Daisy wore lace-trimmed silk cami-knickers, and admitted that men were good for the odd thing, especially the Yanks who seemed able to get anything, but only on *her* terms. Wherever she went men's eyes followed her and women sighed, because those male eyes had been distracted from them, and yet they couldn't dislike her, she was her own person.

More than that, she had the ability to remain absolutely calm in a crisis, which was why she, like Eileen, was a wireless operator, though nothing in Eileen's background had suggested she had this talent. When they were on duty they sat waiting for calls from homeward-bound planes, often in the most desperate trouble, and they kept up contact as they tried to bring them home, reeling them in with that long piece of string. Sometimes it worked, but often it didn't, and they would go off duty with the last words of some terrified boy who knew he was about to die ringing in their ears; sometimes they screamed all the way down, all the way to their deaths. It took a special kind of mental toughness to deal with that and to go back on duty the next night, and the next, when it could, and probably would, happen again. Daisy could handle that, despite her hatred of men on the ground, probably, Eileen thought, because they couldn't see her and she couldn't see them seeing her. Daisy taught Eileen how to handle it, too, taught her how to handle everything about the tower and about service life. In the tower Daisy was an efficient, able, calm voice trying to get them safely back home when they had been hit in the air, but God help the aircrew who thought she would be any better disposed to them once the emergency was over. The tales of Daisy's retribution were passed around as eagerly as her fierce putdowns of prospective suitors. Often it would be some unsuspecting rookie who hadn't yet encountered Daisy who approached her, a Fly Boy she had helped through the latter stages of the last mission who wanted to thank her, encouraged by his sadistic colleagues, a patsy set up for their amusement. They never approached Daisy again, though, they just waited for the next rookie and set him up. There always was another rookie, too, it was as if they couldn't help it, when they set eyes on Daisy, somehow they couldn't appreciate that there was a human being inside that fabulous body. The thing was that Daisy was a shy soul who hated the attention, and it was partly because she knew it risked her friendships with the other girls that she went out of her way to be aggressive with the men – but only partly. The others quickly realised that Daisy was doing nothing to attract the attention she got, realised, too, that whether they just saw her in passing or had some reason – or permission – to talk to her, the eyes of all the men never strayed as high as her eyes. You only had to see that to understand why Daisy was as she was, it was her way of taking control of a situation she didn't ask to be put in, one that was unfair but couldn't be righted, and that was bound to make anyone slightly prickly on the outside. She came on like Mae West, but inside she was Mary Mouse, and Mary Mouse was protected by Mae West and, unusually in female relationships where one is singled out by men, she didn't have an enemy among the other girls. Daisy looked after them, but in their own way they looked after her, without ever making her aware of it. Daisy had a mother's heart and reached out to any young girl, Eileen knew that at first hand.

When Eileen first arrived from Glasgow and saw what she was supposed to call home, she felt she had made the biggest mistake of her life. She had tried to work out why she had joined up, and the only thing she could come up with was that she was different from the other girls she knew at home. In the 1930s and 1940s women didn't question their role in life, not women from Glasgow at any rate, where the society of the whole West of Scotland was ruled by a patriarchal regime. Girls grew up with one thought in mind, marrying and having a family, because in that era there were few other avenues open to the majority of women, but Eileen had never thought in those terms. Most girls planned their wedding day when they were still in primary school, putting net curtains on their heads and practising the long walk down the aisle, even choosing names for their future children when they were still children themselves, but Eileen didn't join in. It just wasn't the big thing on her mind. There was no big thing on her mind, though she'd often wondered if that was because she had never known her mother. There was no female role model in her family, only a series of shadowy memories she was never sure were real or if she'd dreamt them or been told about them. She thought she remembered sitting on the piano stool under the big sweeping staircase as her mother played for her, but even though she could hear the music in her head still, she couldn't be sure the memory was hers or if it had been placed there by her father. When she came home from school it was to a maid or a cook who went off duty soon afterwards and went home to have dinner with their own daughters, while Eileen sat down to eat with her father – that was the Reilly domestic life. Quiet and loving, that was how she remembered her childhood, mainly just the two of them, everything orderly but nothing like she knew the family lives of the other girls at her school to be. They had fathers *and* mothers, and those fathers and mothers related to each other, she knew that from the conversations of the others, and their talk of their mothers – mothers were a big feature in the lives of girls especially. Eileen had never known that kind of relationship except for her grandparents, but grandparents were very different from parents, that much she knew, so there was nothing to follow, no idea of what she should aim to be. Instead there was a growing restlessness she couldn't explain, and frequent dreams of being choked and of trying to stretch. Throughout her childhood she had a recurring dream that she was trapped and couldn't get free, couldn't breathe, and she would wake up in the middle of the night naked, with her bedclothes in a heap and her pyjamas lying in a tangled mass on the floor. Sometimes in the dream her clothes were closing around her and she was trying to cut them off with a pair of scissors, it came so often that she kept scissors by her bed, just to be sure, just in case. Maybe that was what joining up was all about, being free, and joining the RAF in particular – reaching for the sky. The war for her, as for many young people, was a means of breaking away, an older version of those scissors by her bed. According to the political leaders of the day, Hitler and the relentless march of Fascism across the globe had to be stopped, and defending home, family, country and democracy was the duty of all citizens of service age, but few young people saw it that way, they just grabbed at the chance to be free of kith and kin at a time when no one left home till they married.

That first night, however, she had felt like going AWOL. Her bedding, she discovered, consisted of a mattress of three large, joined slabs, like outsized Weetabix, she remembered thinking miserably, that parted as she moved about and left her lying on the hard iron bed. On top were a few thin, grey blankets and a pillow stuffed with straw, and there was nothing as sophisticated as a wardrobe or a chest of drawers, there were hooks on the wall if you were lucky; it wasn't what they had been led to expect. The recruiting office had shown Eileen leaflets with sitting rooms and easy chairs, with smiling, relaxed WAAFs who weren't shivering with cold, and by the chorus of sobbing around the hut that first night she knew she wasn't alone in feeling cheated and shocked. Twenty-four beds were arranged against the two walls, with two round, closed stoves in the middle and a cylindrical black chimney that went through the roof. The stoves were lit when they arrived, but no one told them it would be their responsibility to keep them lit, till next day, when they had gone out. That was their only source of heating, and they soon learned that when Daisy wasn't around to coax extra coal from some vulnerable male or other, they would have to mount lightning raids themselves. The stoves were their salvation, and they spent many evenings sitting around them in a circle, sewing, chatting, polishing their ugly shoes and Brasso-ing the buttons on their tunics and one-size topcoats. The gathering by the stoves produced memorable performances from Daisy, especially when there were newly-arrived recruits who were wishing they had stayed at home. She would hold a sanitary towel in her hand and give a lecture in the manner of all the lectures they had to endure, and the girls joined in with frequent rounds of applause.

'This is a gift from Lord Nuffield,' she would begin seriously, in a mock Austrian professor voice for some reason, 'the man who owns Morris cars, who seems a sad sod, because he has nothing better to do with his millions than fund the sanitary towel allocation of the WAAFs. In the near future I intend paying him a visit, my friends,' she would say, wiggling her hips, 'in the hope that I can give him other ideas. Now we come to the various uses of Nuffield's sanitary towels, and I know it just looks like a sanitary towel to you, my friends, but it has a multitude of hidden uses, don't just think of them as groundsheets in the world of the Curse,' and she would pick up a can of Brasso. 'Use one: shining the buttons of tunics and coats, you will find it attracts liquid, Brasso of course, girls, like nothing else. Now, split them open, remove the tissue paper inside, and now we have the perfect hankie, and cotton wool interiors are ideal for removing the make-up we're not supposed to wear, and the gauze is just dandy for straining coffee grounds.' She would stop about there to acknowledge the applause, bowing and throwing kisses. 'But there is one more use, my dear friends,' she would say slyly, 'and we all know what it is, don't we? That's right, and I'm now going to give a practical demonstration.'

'Oh, Daisy,' Eileen would shout in a suitably appalled voice, 'I really think you're going too far!'

'Now, Eileen, there may be girls here who have never come across these items before, we owe it to them to show how they should be used correctly,' she would reply sternly in her fake Austrian accent. Then she would put the towel across her eyes, place the loops around her ears and declare, 'They are of course intended for helping you sleep after night duty.' She would then retire from the 'stage' with many more gracious bows to her audience.

It all helped in making the adjustments to this new and harsh life that much easier when Daisy was around. On Eileen's first day she had been placed in a different hut from Daisy, and she knew what it was to feel despair. Breakfast that morning had consisted of a mug of tea and a spoonful of golden syrup poured onto a slice of bread, earned after marching in a long line through squelching mud and heavy rain in their civvies. Then it was time to be kitted out with their twenty-six-piece kit, uniforms, tin hats, gas masks, and two identity discs that had to be worn around the neck on a cord, one yellow and one red; if they died they would be buried with one, while the other would be sent to their next of kin. They soon found that individual sizes meant little, though you were free to give measurements if it made you feel better. Skirts and belts were too long or too short, and the two tunics issued with them were covered with brass buttons that had to be kept shining like gold, just like the heavy, unisex topcoats. Tent groundsheets were supposed to double as raincoats, but every girl hoped one day to meet the idiot who had thought of this great wheeze, because he – and they were sure it had to be a he – had obviously never tried it out, or he would've discovered that rain dripped from all four corners directly into their shoes. Yet the dry, wrinkled shoe leather had to be very shiny and smooth, and even the most delicate and ladylike female soon learned that vigorous buffing did not produce the regulation effect and accepted the spit and polish routine or faced the consequences.

Next came the medical, where the girls had to parade naked except for a towel around their waists in front of a room full of men, and it didn't really make it any easier for modest and well-brought-up young women of their time that the men were doctors. X-rays were taken, eye tests performed and armfuls of vaccinations given, before they were allowed to slink, red-faced and miserable, back to the safety of their cold, bare hut and their uncomfortable beds. Eileen had lain that night and wondered why she had given up the life of an exiled Irish princess for this, and was far from sure she could stand it. As it turned out, the other girls got her through, they got each other through, till they were given proficiency tests and assigned to various jobs within the RAF. To Eileen's bemusement she had been told she was a natural born wireless operator and sent to the tower, and that's when she had met Daisy and come under her protective wing. She wouldn't have managed without Daisy, she knew that.

The one thing everyone was in agreement about was that you shouldn't get involved with aircrew, partly because the girls resented the notion that they were there to satisfy the lusts of the men, and partly because that way lay heartbreak. Men died, that was a fact; of the 7,000 or so Lancs in Bomber Command, nearly half never came back, and only a lucky few of their crews ended up in POW camps. Dating was all right in moderation, the odd drink maybe, but serious fraternising was not encouraged, not by the WAAF officers, not by the more experienced girls themselves. But it happened, and there were always a few girls walking around with eyes red from crying. And some of them got pregnant and had to go to their WAAF officer with the news, only to find themselves packed and despatched homewards to shocked, ashamed families before they had finished the sentence. Others opted for secret backstreet abortions; when a girl borrowed money from the others, as Daisy always said, you knew what was going on. A girl called Celia had died in Eileen and Daisy's hut, after being found bleeding heavily in her bed one morning, the result of an abortion that had gone wrong. Her family was told she had died of a burst appendix, but all the girls knew what had happened.

'How do they actually do it?' Eileen asked Daisy.

'The usual self-help method is gin and a hot bath, but I knew of an old woman down our street who used tree bark,' Daisy replied.

'How does that work?' Eileen asked, puzzled.

'The bark gets pushed into the neck of the womb, it gradually expands till what's inside falls out,' Daisy shrugged.

Eileen's eyes widened with shock.

'Then there's knitting needles,' Daisy continued. 'I knew a girl once who'd been brought up in an orphanage where the girls were taught to knit. At the end of every day, though, all the needles were collected and locked up. She didn't understand why and no one would tell her, till she fell pregnant by one of the boys.'

'You mean . . . ?'

'Of course I mean!' Daisy said. 'I don't have to draw you a diagram, surely? Now you know why I keep saying never fall for a Fly Boy, never, never.'

They fell for her, of course, and she used their interest for her own good, or that of the other girls. Daisy might look like a sex bomb, but she wasn't. When she was young, she confided, she hadn't known how to deal with the reactions and the brazenly crude, not to mention uninvited, approaches of men. As far as they were concerned, if she had a body like that then she was automatically loose, easy and fair game; that was when she had assumed Mae's hard, cynical shell. Men were only after one thing, she told the others, and in her case it was entirely true. Eileen, like the others, admired her but also felt sorry for her. Out of desperation she had harnessed the attention she attracted, but she hated men and assumed every one was up to no good on principle, it saved time, she said, she was on permanent attack as a means of defence. Too often it was justified, too, Eileen knew that. She had witnessed how openly predatory men were where Daisy was concerned, how she winced at the assumptions they made about her and, though Daisy would never have admitted it and would have been embarrassed had she known anyone else had, how she cringed as the next guy came along, egged on by his friends, to chance his luck, as though she were some initiation device, or some game they had to try.

22

When the crew of Lady Groundhog returned from leave it was back to the old routine of bombing Germany, and three weeks into their six-week block their luck began to run out. They had dropped their bombs over Berlin and the bomb aimer had whooped with delight in the Perspex nose as he watched the explosions spread out rapidly from where they had hit, then it was 'Bombs away!' and turn for home. They were always euphoric on the journey home, even though they knew that anti-aircraft guns and German night fighters lay in wait for them once again. They were just about clear of the French coast when Charlie shouted.

'Skip, a JU-88 coming in on the tail! Prepare to dive port! Prepare to dive port! Prepare to –' and as Calli turned the Lanc over hard into a corkscrew dive to evade the German fighter, he heard the sound of tracer fire passing close below him, and simultaneously, screams erupted from Charlie in the tail then from Taffy, the mid-upper gunner on top of the fuselage. Calli found that the dive was too steep to hold, so Bruiser also grabbed the control panel in a desperate attempt to correct it, and between them they managed to level at 6,000 feet. In the confusion of still being chased by the German fighter and the cries of the injured gunners, he relaxed too much, and once again the Lanc went into a steep dive, but they managed to pull up from it at 2,000 feet. Calli saw a cloud and headed into it to lose the fighter, but leaving the French coast he was having major problems controlling the plane.

'Bill,' he called to the wireless operator, 'send out a Mayday to Langar. Frank, try to find us a new course, she's drifting to port all the time, I can't get her to starboard, I'm afraid I'll pull the rudder off.'

'Mayday, Langar, Mayday. Papa 1 calling Langar. Over,' Bill's Norfolk tones repeated, then they heard Daisy reply.

'Langar calling Papa 1, what is your position? Over.'

'On our way over the Channel heading for Langar. We've been hit, both gunners hurt and plane drifting to port. Possible hydraulic damage, gear may not come down. Over.'

'Papa 1, this is Langar. Is a landing here possible or do you want to divert? Over.'

Calli took over the conversation. 'We can make it there, Langar, but I'm not confident of the landing. Over.'

'Papa 1, emergency services will be standing by, Skipper. Over.'

Beside Calli, Bruiser smiled. 'My big blonde,' he said dreamily. 'We'll be all right now, Skip, my big blonde will save us.'

'You are in need of help,' Calli grinned wryly, still struggling with the crippled Lanc.

Two hours later they were within reach of Langar. Two long hours during which Calli knew his gunners were both badly injured and that time was crucial to whether or not they survived, though Bruiser and Frank were trying to help them.

'Give the tower an update, Bill,' Calli told him. 'Tell them part of the wing's missing as well.'

'Papa 1 calling Langar. Skipper says we are missing a lump of wing. Over.'

'Papa 1, relax boys, we're waiting for you. Over,' Daisy said almost casually.

'I'm going to land fast and hope she doesn't flip over,' Calli said as he saw the runway. 'Any of you lads want to bale out now with your 'chutes, that's OK.'

'We're staying with you and Lady Groundhog, Skip,' they all replied.

The Lanc bumped off the tarmac several times before she caught the ground, with fire tenders and ambulances racing alongside her, but luckily the gear did come down, and when they came to a stop Charlie and Taffy were quickly unloaded and taken to hospital. Up in the tower, Daisy and Eileen watched as the rest of the crew sat on the ground as the ambulances raced off. The boys were feeling sick and exhausted instead of the usual adrenaline rush, but now that the emergency was over they were trying to create the usual atmosphere.

'Were you trying to scare me?' Frank demanded of Calli.

Calli laughed. 'No, that wasn't in the plan,' he replied.

'Well you *did*, Skipper,' Frank complained, 'you *did*! Promise me you won't do that again?'

'I'll try,' Calli laughed, as relief turned on the adrenaline taps and the usual horseplay took over.

'Did I ask you to try?' Frank demanded, aiming a punch at Calli as Calli dodged out of contact. 'I said don't – *don't*!'

'He's right,' Bruiser said wearily as they climbed to their feet, already sucking on a cigarette and deliberately blowing the smoke into Calli's face. 'That was as close a call as I ever want, you Canuck bastard!' he shouted. 'Don't fuck around like that again, OK?'

Calli nodded and grinned weakly, throwing in a theatrical cough for good measure and grabbing at his throat.

Bruiser smiled back and threw an arm around his shoulder as they staggered away from the plane. 'Well done, Skip,' he said quietly. 'That was as fine a piece of flying as I've seen, but the boys are both bad. I think next time we go for a spin we'll need two new gunners.'

'I know,' Calli said. 'Poor Charlie, he looked worst. I don't know how these tail-enders do it, climbing into that space, mission after mission. I couldn't do that,' and he shook his head. Then, knowing that Eileen was on duty with Daisy in the tower and would have been following every minute of the hours it had taken them to get home from their dangerous situation, he set off to find her.

The near disaster had an effect on all of them, as that first brush with real danger always did. They were used to the silent figure of the Adjutant arriving in their huts at the end of every mission and removing the belongings of those who would not be coming back, they were almost used to the sight of those empty bunks, but nothing banished bravado more effectively than a near miss. The unplanned leave that came along afterwards, giving time for new crew members to replace those who had been lost, and for damaged planes to be repaired, was not always a good thing either. It gave them time to think, to build up a fear that couldn't be dealt with and, hopefully, banished, till they were once more in the air under battle conditions. There were some who welcomed the extra rest, but some, also, who would have preferred to go up again straight away, to salvage their confidence before it had a chance to run out completely.

As it was, Calli's attitude had already changed in the weeks since he had met Eileen. For the first time he now felt there was more than him at stake. He always carried thoughts of his family at home, but this was different, this was nearer. For the first time in his life he had looked beyond returning to his old life after the war, now he could see ahead to a future out there with a wife and children, and felt under an obligation to stay alive. He wasn't responsible only for someone else's happiness, but for the children they would have together, when all this was over. So he thought more about his own mortality during that enforced leave than he had ever done before, and wondered if he should update the 'goodbye letter' that had lain with his belongings since he had first started flying. Being true to his superstitious Highland roots he decided not to, though, in case it might tempt Fate. There was already a cloud hanging over his thoughts and he wondered if it might be to do with his father, then he put it out of his mind because there was nothing he could do about it if that were the case. Besides, there had been a dark cloud about his father for as long as he could remember. Probably it was due to the apprehension and anxiety caused by having this extra time to mull over everything, he mused, and grinned; waiting to get back into the air had been enough to be going on with.

Soon Lady Groundhog was repaired and Calli's crew would

rejoin the six-week block of missions. It would seem strange to be without Charlie and Taffy, he thought, but it had happened to other crews, and at least the boys were both alive. The replacement gunners had only just arrived. One was a Scot, but he hadn't had time to do more than shake hands with him, he'd catch up with him after the mission. The day before his leave was up, he borrowed his friend's car again and took Eileen out, he wanted to make sure she wasn't anxious about the upcoming mission, the first since the Mayday incident, and if she was, to calm her down. Eileen wasn't the hysterical type, he knew that, that's why she was picked for the job she did, but there was a tension between them in the car. They got out at the inn they had visited that first time, and the tension didn't ease as they sat in a booth by the window. He asked her what was wrong.

'You know how Daisy lectures us on not falling for the old "I may be dead tomorrow, give me my oats tonight" routine?'

Calli laughed. 'You think I'm going to try that one on you?' he asked, tightening his grip on her right hand.

'No, listen, Calli,' she said, and he saw tears in her eyes. 'I've been thinking a lot after the last time –'

'It won't happen again –'

'Will you shut up for once, MacDonald, and let me talk?' she said angrily.

He pulled an imaginary zip across his mouth and she laughed.

'I was thinking, that if anything happened I'd rather we had . . . you know . . .'

'Are you saying, Miss Reilly,' he said in a shocked voice, 'that *you* want *your* oats?'

'Yes, Calli,' she said softly and seriously, turning in towards him and placing her left hand very gently on his chest. 'That's what I'm saying. I want you to be first, whatever happens.' She put her head down and blushed and his heart ached at how innocent she looked as the colour spread across her cheeks.

'Nothing will happen,' he said brightly.

'Don't say that,' she said seriously. 'You know that's not true, Calli, don't say it.'

'Eileen, there's a lot to consider,' he said quietly. 'Think about it.'

'I know. Didn't I say I'd been thinking?'

They got a room in the inn and she took an RAF towel out of her bag and insisted on putting it on top of the sheet, and laughed when he clearly didn't understand why; he was as inexperienced as she was. He was gentle, and scared in case he hurt her, and she had to reassure him. Still she had to push harder against him than he was prepared to, and then it happened and she cried, which scared him even more until she laughed as well. She had heard so many scare stories about the first time, about the pain, about how it was always awful, you just got it over as quickly as possible. But they were all wrong. She couldn't imagine anything more sweet, more tender, more complete, they truly felt as one. They lay together in silence afterwards, then he asked 'Are you OK?'

'Yes,' she replied happily. 'You?'

'Better than OK.' When he got up to go to the bathroom his eyes went to the towel she had put on the bottom sheet and he was horrified to see the blood. 'I did hurt you,' he gasped. 'Why didn't you say?'

Eileen lay on the pillow and laughed at him. 'It's always like this the first time, you idiot, you great big boy!' she giggled.

'So you brought the towel with you because you knew this would happen?' he asked.

Eileen nodded.

'Have you no shame, woman? You came here ready to seduce me, didn't you?'

'Yes, I did, you great big boy,' she grinned again.

'A great big boy, am I?' he asked.

'A great big country hick of a boy!' she giggled.

'In that case,' he said, getting back into bed, 'I think I'd better show you what a big boy I'm not, at least not in the way you mean.'

*   *   ★

When they returned to the squadron he found it strangely more difficult to leave her, they weren't two separate people any longer, so they shouldn't be parting, they should be going home together. He was relieved she wasn't on duty till the following day, he didn't want her in the tower tonight, waiting fearfully for another Mayday call; that would be one less thing for him to worry about ahead of the mission.

At the briefing they discovered their target was Milan, they were Italy-bound for a change, and because of what had happened to them last time out, they took extra notice of every detail. The manifest was clinically detailed. The armourers' tractor-train had loaded Lady Groundhog with one 4,000 lb. High Capacity Bomb – a 'Cookie'; one batch of 150 x 4 lb. Incendiary Bombs; one batch of 16 x 30 lb. Incendiary Bombs, and one batch of 90 x 4 lb. Bombs. In other words, armed to the teeth and pretty much par for the course. The mission of the 199 Lancs on their way to Milan that night would take them over Selsey Bill, Cabourg, the north end of Lac du Bourget, to the factories and railway installations that were their target, then back by the same route. The Met Report mentioned 'small amounts of cloud over France with uncertain conditions over the Alps; possible layers of cloud between 12,000 and 18,000 feet, well broken with good clear lanes. Peaks may be obscured. Return similar, with Alpine cloud more broken still.' Calli, Bruiser and Frank exchanged looks.

'Talk about fence-sitting,' Bruiser muttered to Frank.

'I've never understood why they don't just say "We don't fucking know", and be done with it,' the navigator replied.

The attack was to take place between 2357 and 0022 hours, with zero hour fixed at 0000, by which time the marker planes should have put down a precise series of green, white and red flares, with release-point flares of red and green if there was cloud cover obscuring the target, which was the centre of the town. When the flares were sighted from up in the air they would show the area where the bombs should fall. Although Milan was new ground for

Lady Groundhog, their mission on the 14th and 16th of August 1943 was the fourth leg of a cumulative attack that month. The three earlier raids had already inflicted considerable widespread damage to railway operations and installations, especially on the area between the central station and Scalo Farini goods yards to the north of Milan, and another area to the southwest. Fires had burned for two days following the previous raid and, said the report, forty-four per cent of the fully built-up areas had been destroyed, and fourteen per cent of the less built-up areas. In excess of 239 factories had been partially destroyed or damaged, including Alfa Romeo, Isotta Fraschini, Breda and Pirelli. The majority were concerned with engineering, but some textile and electrical factories were hit, and in all nineteen industrial concerns were totally destroyed and forty-seven completely devastated. In addition, transformer and gas works, tram depots, post office and other public buildings had been hit, together with several barracks and military targets. The fourth attack was expected to complete the destruction.

It was raining as they taxied into position, waiting for the sergeant with the Aldis lamp to show them the green light. Lady Groundhog lumbered down the runway till she reached that joyous moment of weightlessness. It was 2032 when they took off from Langar and the outward journey was the same as usual, fear as they dodged the fighters and anti-aircraft guns over France, relief when they reached Italy because everyone knew Italian defences weren't worth bothering about, unless your luck ran out, of course, and there was nothing anyone could do about that in advance, so why worry?

When they reached Milan the flares had highlighted the targets fairly well, though the timing wasn't perfect, nothing ever was. They waited as ever for Jake to line up his sights and be satisfied, calling out their traditional threats to him to get on with it, which he ignored, before finally yelling the much-loved words 'Bombs away!' They felt the familar leap into the air as the weight of the departing payload released the Lanc, then Calli corkscrewed into another lightning getaway and headed for home, with the comforting rhythmic throb of the Merlin engines warming the ears of every man.

The attack came from underneath the port wing as they were nearing the town of Caen on the French coast. There was a sudden hard thump, then one of the crew, Calli didn't really register who, shouted, 'We've been hit by flak, Skip! We're on fire!' In his mind he thought it was more likely a hit from an anti-aircraft gun than a fighter that would now be chasing them, and he felt better about that. All he had to do was get her out of this dive, pull her back to level and reach the sea, where he could ditch if he had to. Bill was already sending out another Mayday call, so any station listening would pick it up, get a fix and then they would be rescued. Simple, as long as they didn't hit the ground first. He and Bruiser were struggling to pull the Lanc out of the dive, but it occurred to Calli that the fire had a better hold than he wanted and he realised the plane wasn't responding and they were spiralling downwards towards the ground. Parachutes, bale out, he thought, but they were too low for 'chutes to open properly, it was too late, the only chance they had was to gain control and reach the sea. In the background, Bill was still transmitting Maydays as Calli and Bruiser fought with the ailing Lanc.

'We've got to make it, the sea isn't far, get to the sea.' Thoughts and images jumbled about Calli's head as the desperate battle continued. So was this the reason for the dark cloud? He saw the faces of everyone who mattered and said their names in his head. 'Eileen . . . Mother . . . Gil . . . Father . . . Granny Martha . . . Feargie . . . Oh God, not like this! The flames . . . the ground's coming faster . . .'

There was an almighty impact that jarred every cell of his body and forced the air out of his lungs, and in the background a loud cacophony of different materials crashing together. Then, nothing.

Back in the underground Ops Room, the filter plotters watched the blip of a plane nose-dive and disappear, and the word was given to the plotters at the big board to remove the marker that showed the plane's position in that sector. The WAAF responsible acknowledged the instruction into the microphone attached to her earphones, leaned forward with her long stick and pulled the marker off the board. Six other Lancs from Calli's group were lost that night, and when the surviving planes returned to Langar their crews gave as much detail as they could of what they had seen. They had watched Lanc ED498 of 5 Group 207 Squadron hit the ground near Caen, already well on fire, they thought the pilot was trying to get to the sea to ditch and hadn't made it. They had watched for parachutes as usual, but there were none. On the Squadron Report the names of the crew were recorded with their ranks and numbers, and beside each one was written 'Dead'. At twenty-six, Bruiser was the old man of the crew, the others were all twenty-two or twenty-three. There was nothing more to say.

The following day, the Adjutant Calli liked to insult in Gaelic cleared out the personal belongings of those who hadn't returned, telegrams were sent to their families, and Daisy had to go back to the hut and tell Eileen that Calli was dead.

23

She had taken the news calmly, Daisy told the others, but she hadn't known the boy long – six, seven weeks? – so she'd get over it; what was the alternative? They had all seen this kind of thing before, and let it be a lesson to them all – keep away from aircrew.

At Pine Edge, Gil was working on a tractor that had stopped in the field. He had hoped to get one of the new Ferguson Fords everyone was talking about before the war, but production had stopped for the duration, so he'd had to keep patching up what he had. Nancy was shopping in the town, due back any minute. He straightened up and bent backwards, his hand on the small of his back, winced and stretched, and then he noticed someone making his way towards the house. He knew who it was: Tony MacKay. Everyone with a relative in the forces knew who he was and dreaded seeing him. Tony said they averted their eyes when they met him, even if he was in church or working in his garden, even, he meant, when he wasn't carrying a telegram that might be for them.

Gil instinctively broke into a run, his aching back forgotten as he jumped the wooden fence and reached the front door as Tony was still approaching from the other direction. He looked guiltily at Gil, knowing that he wanted to be told this was good news, or maybe not too bad news, as long as it wasn't *this* news. He held the telegram out reluctantly.

'Gil, I'm sorry . . .' he started to say, but Gil grabbed it from his hand and ripped the envelope open savagely. Tony looked away as Gil read it, he had witnessed this scene too many times to watch it again, the taut face as the panic-stricken eyes darted about, scanning desperately, not really reading, trying to take in the important words to prove it wasn't what they hoped it wasn't. After a long, silent moment, Tony slowly looked back again, and saw that Gil was standing in exactly the same position, looking at the telegram, his face expressionless but with tears running down his cheeks.

'Gil,' Tony said, and Gil held a hand out to silence him. Tony waited a little longer. 'Gil,' he said softly again, 'I saw Nancy in the town with the truck full of groceries. I didn't let her see where I was headed, but she looked like she'd be on her way home any time soon.'

Gil looked up and stared at Tony for a moment, then he silently nodded his head. He knew he had things to do and had to work out the sequence in which he had to do them, but his head wasn't functioning properly.

'Can I do anything?' Tony asked miserably. 'Can I help in any way?'

'No,' Gil replied huskily, then he cleared his throat. 'No, thanks, Tony,' he said.

Tony's eyes went to the telegram still held in Gil's hands, as though they were paralysed.

'Well, if you're sure, Gil,' he said uncertainly. 'I'll head off towards Castleton, I wouldn't want to pass Nancy on the road to Campbellford and have her panic out there on her own.'

'Yes,' Gil replied distractedly. 'Do that, Tony, that's good of you. Do that. Thanks.'

Gil stood on the grass in front of the house, trying to collect his thoughts, trying to put together a plan. People had to be told, Nancy would have to be told, Feargie in Toronto, Martha and the rest of the family in Mabou. Donald. He swung around, looking in the direction of the downstairs bedroom that Donald rarely left these days, and saw him standing by the window, watching, then saw him step back out of sight. Donald could wait, he decided. Nancy. God almighty, how was he to tell Nancy? he asked himself, and as he was wondering, he heard a single, loud sob, and realised it had come from himself. He decided he couldn't do that, and desperately tried to bite back the others welling up in his throat. She would be here soon; what was he to say? Just then he saw the truck come around the bend in the road, heading for Pine Edge. He would have to get her into the house, he decided, if he told her outside and she collapsed – no, he couldn't cope with that. He turned away, looking for some normal thing to be doing. 'Normal!' he thought. 'How can there ever be normal again?' He grabbed a rake and tried to co-ordinate the motions needed to use it and discovered that he had somehow forgotten how. As the truck came nearer he looked up briefly and away again with a slight wave, still trying to look as though he was doing something ordinary so as not to give her any clue. Keeping his back to her, playing for time, he heard her get out of the truck and slam the door, then her footsteps sounded on the wooden planking leading to the front door of the house. There was the squeak of the bug screen that he kept meaning to oil, then of the inside door shutting behind her. Gil put down the rake, slowly walked towards the house and let himself in, still trying to work out how to tell her this news, and found her standing at the big kitchen table, her back to him.

'It's Calli,' she said flatly.

Gil didn't answer; he hadn't expected this and was annoyed that despite Tony's efforts she must've seen him, or had spoken to someone who had seen him head this way.

'It's Calli, isn't it?' she asked again, and turned her head to look at him, briefly making eye contact before turning away again.

'Nancy . . .'

'It's OK, Gil,' she said softly. 'I know.' Then she turned and walked past him without looking at him, climbed the stairs in the hall, went to her room and almost silently closed the door.

In her bedroom she sat in the rocking chair by the window and looked out at the scene as she had on the day she'd arrived some twenty-four years before, expecting her first child, Calli. It was her favourite place to sit, and during her pregnancy she had put the rocking chair there, where it had sat ever since. Next door, looking down on the same view, was the room she had chosen for Calli months before he was born. Now he was gone; that was all she could think about, the enormity of what she would now have to accept. In the three years since he'd left, the room had still seemed to be Calli's, it had been waiting for his return, as they all had, his presence seemed to inhabit it even without him being there. Now, in a strange way it seemed lifeless, in the blink of an eye it had become a thing lost in the past; it was no longer waiting. She didn't know how long it was before there was a gentle tapping on the door and Gil came in.

'Nancy,' he said uncertainly, 'is there something I can get for you, something I can do?'

She shook her head.

'We have to tell people,' he said. 'Do you want me to start doing that?'

'Who?' she asked distantly.

'Well there's Donald for a start,' he said.

She had forgotten about Donald, completely forgotten that he existed. She would tell Donald.

'Would you rather I told him?' Gil suggested.

'No, thanks,' she said. 'That's all right.'

'And what do we do about Feargie?' he asked. 'I don't think he should hear over the telephone, do you? I was thinking, if I get one of the family or a neighbour to stay here with you, I could drive to Toronto and tell him myself, if you agree?'

'I don't need anyone else here, Gil,' she replied.

'I don't want to leave you on your own,' he said, then corrected himself, 'you and Donald I mean.'

'It's OK, Gil, I'd rather be on my own anyway.'

'And there's your mother and the family in Mabou,' he reminded her.

'My mother will already know,' she said quietly.

'But how . . . ?'

'She just will, Gil, don't worry about it.' She fell silent again, sitting in the rocking chair, staring out of the window. 'Gil?' she said.

'I'm still here,' he replied quietly.

'I've changed my mind. Would you tell Donald, please? I'm being a coward, I know, but I'd rather not face him. Is that OK?'

'You're not a coward, Nancy,' he said tenderly. 'You only have to say what you want, whatever it is, you know I'll do it.'

Before he told Donald, Gil went into the kitchen and called one of Nancy's cousins in Mabou and told him what had happened. Then he apologised for asking this of him, but Nancy would be obliged if he would pass the word around the family up there, but most importantly, if he would visit Martha first with the news. As soon as things were clearer he would call again, he said, but make sure Martha was taken care of and ask her to stay up there, for the moment, he and Feargie would look after Nancy. He suspected that Nancy would want to travel home to Mabou shortly to be with her mother, there being nothing to be done in Campbellford. There was no funeral to arrange, after all, Calli wouldn't be coming home. Then he visited Donald in the lower bedroom, and gave him the brief details contained in the telegram, that Calli's plane had crashed and there were no survivors, that his eldest son was dead. Donald's expression didn't alter, he looked at Gil with a steady, empty stare, as though it wasn't any great surprise, then he remembered seeing the figure at the window as Tony had arrived with the telegram and supposed that Donald had already worked it out. He asked the usual questions, if he wanted or needed anything, and got a slight shake of the head in reply, told him what he planned to do next and if he agreed, and this time Donald nodded. He was in the truck and driving towards Toronto before he realised that Donald hadn't asked about Nancy.

The Lancaster and her crew had been officially missing for two weeks when Eileen's next weekend pass came up. The wording was routine, but everyone else knew Calli and the others to be dead, other crews had watched as the plane was hit by flak, set on fire and plummeted earthwards, a few quietly mentioned watching the deathly crunch as the Lancaster hit the ground. Other than that there was little discussion and no pause in what they were all engaged in. The loss of a plane and crew was a common occurrence after all, and the shock over Lady Groundhog's downing had been superseded many times in those two weeks, and many more families of very young men had been plunged into grief. For those still engaged in warfare in 207 Squadron and countless others, there was no lost sleep to be wasted over any of them, they didn't have time. Eileen, though, couldn't bring herself to believe it, as long as there was no absolute confirmation otherwise then, to her, there was a chance that he was still alive somewhere. Some kindly French people could have rescued him and be taking care of him, it happened all the time, or he might have been taken to a prisoner of war camp, either way she'd see him again when the war ended. Without realising it, though, she began to make the little concessions that would bring her to the truth; she was willing to contemplate that perhaps he had been injured, possibly badly injured, but he wasn't dead. Couldn't be. No. Slightly burned, badly burned, even, but not dead. And as her hopes fought with logic in the deepest part of her mind, she went on with her job in the tower; listening to radio conversations, talking with pilots, watching them go out and guiding them back again, delivering them safely at the end of each mission, her calm, efficient words travelling through the air and wire connecting her earphones and mike to theirs, the fabled 'piece of string' all air-crew knew reeled them home from every raid. Every time there was a Mayday with a successful outcome she would smile and think 'There you go, all safe. Calli could be out there safe and sound, too,' while ignoring the rescue missions that failed.

Slowly, though she betrayed little emotion, reality was seeping through no matter what tactics she used to block it, and underneath the calm façade, her mind was beginning to turn into turmoil and panic. At night she dreamed of him, standing before her so vividly that she would wake and shed disappointed tears when she found he wasn't there, and dreams of hearing his voice calling to her. The other girls exchanged looks and turned away, they had seen similar things many times, and often it was best to leave the girls to work through it themselves. Daisy noticed, of course, and though she was closer to Eileen, she didn't mention it either and neither did Eileen.

Despite the warnings not to get close to aircrew it had happened to them all, this loss of some young pilot or gunner during that first flush of romance, and somehow in those days when romance progressed faster than in peacetime, they all had to get through it, that was all. Still, Daisy watched Eileen, kept an eye on her without asking questions, gave her private time. Maybe the weekend pass would help her, she thought, leaving the base would remind her that there was another world outside waiting for them to return to, one day.

'So, where are you going?' she asked brightly, as Eileen packed a bag that Saturday morning.

'Down to London,' Eileen smiled.

'You lucky dog!' Daisy howled. 'London in September, it'll be wasted on you, it's a place for bad girls like me, let me go in your place?'

'I'd be happy to,' Eileen replied, 'but I'm meeting Alex down there.'

'Oh Gawd, not the childhood sweetheart?'

''Fraid so!' Eileen said brightly. 'He's sailing in a couple of weeks, got some leave, so I said I'd meet him down there.'

'I didn't know he was back on dry land,' Daisy said. Normally at this juncture she would also come out with one of her vicious remarks, like 'I hoped the bastard would drown before now', but this time she thought better of it.

'I said I'd spend some time with him before he goes.'

'And you can't get out of it?' Daisy asked, her face screwed up with distaste.

Eileen laughed. 'What do you have against him? You don't even know him!'

'I don't have to know him,' Daisy said darkly. 'They're all the same, childhood sweethearts, you know that. They latch onto a lass early on and leech off her for the rest of her life.'

'I think I've heard that lecture somewhere before, now where was that?' Eileen said, waving her hand across her mouth and pretending to yawn. 'Besides, that's not fair and you know it!' she laughed, returning to her packing.

'I'm telling you,' Daisy protested, 'keep your distance. Don't do –'

'– I know, anything you wouldn't.'

'Oh, to hell with *that*! You know me, there's nothing I haven't done or wouldn't think of doing, if it suited me, but I'm a bad girl, bad girls get away with it. As well you know,' she said, and for both of them Celia's name hung in the air, 'it's innocents like you who get caught, so just don't do anything.'

'What? Nothing?' Eileen teased.

'Not as much as a button undone, his or yours. Promise me.'

'Look,' Eileen replied, holding up a pack of sanitary towels. 'Lord Nuffield's little present. The Curse is about to hit, I won't get much chance to do anything you would or wouldn't do.'

'Well, thank God for that,' Daisy grinned, 'and God bless Lord Nuffield.'

Eileen reached London at lunchtime on Saturday and Alex was waiting at the hotel for her; he looked strange in his Navy uniform, but he wasn't alone in that, the entire world was wall-to-wall uniforms. She was surprised how young he seemed too, he looked much younger than his twenty-one years, all gangly arms and legs attached to a thin frame and topped by a long, thin face, with brown hair and eyes. He looked entirely different from Calli, only the colour of his hair and eyes was the same – stop, Eileen. *Stop.*

'I could only get one room,' he burst out nervously, without even saying hello, 'and it's not a twin, but don't worry, I'll sleep on the floor.'

'Relax,' she smiled, suddenly feeling decades older than this large boy standing before her, then in an instant she felt that she was standing outside watching herself and Alex. There was something wrong with this scenario; she shouldn't be here, at least not with Alex, it was wrong, all wrong. It was as if the voice of reality was twisting a knife in her bowels, asking, 'Well, who *should* you be here with, then?'

All through their lives they had fitted together easily and happily, but she didn't feel at ease with him now. The weeks she had known Calli, their last night together before he'd flown to Milan, had changed everything in her life, the way she saw things, the way she felt. She wanted to close her eyes then open them again, and see Calli there in the room with her instead of Alex, it was how things should be, the natural order, she belonged with Calli, and again the voice inside her head demanded, 'So where is he? Why isn't he here?' She looked down, trying to quell an impulse to run by controlling her breathing, but it was taking all her strength not to obey her instincts.

Alex was keen to see the sights, so they went out into the streets and walked around, taking in all the usual things, Buckingham Palace, Trafalgar Square, the bomb-damaged buildings. Calli had been to all the places they saw, and something like a hundred years ago, or maybe yesterday, she remembered how unimpressed he had been. 'Never been so bored in my life. What's so good about them?' She heard his comments about each place she and Alex now saw, it was as though they were retracing his footsteps and she resented Alex for being there. Then she realised she was actually looking for Calli in every face in the crowd, in the back of every head, too, come to that, and she felt a physical pain and wanted to fall to the ground, curl up in a little ball and stay there for the rest of her life. She was losing it, she could feel that, and even more so at this moment and with this boy, but then she remembered that her period was due and it always made her more emotional, so it was all right, there was a logical reason. She decided to make an extra effort to be pleasant to Alex. They sat in a café and he told her the news from home that he'd collected when he was briefly there the week before; everyone was fine, though one of the workshop workers – Mr Devine – did she remember him? No, she didn't. Little man, middle-aged, dark receding hair, moustache, kind of shy? He had worked on those Rennie Mackintosh chairs that needed to be repaired, kept saying the only people who should design furniture were furniture makers, though they all said that, to be honest. Remember? No, she shook her head, she still didn't remember him. Well, anyway, he had fallen down the stairs of the tenement where he lived during the blackout and broken his neck, someone had found him dead after the all clear. Alex said he'd visited the workshop and everyone had made a great fuss of him, and they were missing her, too, said to pass on their love, they were worried about her and about him, and they were both to come home safely because everyone was looking forward to a good wedding. Eileen smiled but didn't reply and Alex, noticing that she wasn't quite herself, thought she was worried that they might not see each other again. He put a hand over hers and said softly, 'Don't worry, I'll come home again safe and sound.' Eileen nodded, tears in her eyes. She felt like a harp that someone had decided to destroy by slowly tightening one string at a time till it snapped under the pressure.

They went to the theatre; someone had given Alex tickets for something that was, presumably, hilariously funny, as everyone laughed loudly at every remark from the actors on stage. Afterwards they went to a pub and she realised that Alex must be nervous, or else he had never had a drink before, because he drank quite quickly and became slightly unsteady and a bit giddy. Back at the hotel bar he drank some more and found that he couldn't stand up, so the porter helped Eileen carry him to their room and dump him across the bed. She looked at him lying there and wondered what to do for the sake of propriety, then she sighed and decided propriety could take care of itself. She removed all his clothes and heaved and shoved him under the covers, where he snored heavily and unconsciously. She sat in a chair, the only one in the room, for a while, her mind a blank, save for the feeling that she shouldn't be there, that none of it mattered and please, let tomorrow come soon so that she could be out of this awkward situation. It suddenly struck her as odd and sad somehow, that any situation that included Alex could be awkward, but it was, and, feeling deeply weary, wearier than she had ever been in her life, she took off her uniform, placed it over the chair and slipped into bed beside him. What the hell? She had known him all her life, if it hadn't been for the war they'd be married by now and, anyway, there was no chance of anything happening, he was dead to the world.

When she woke in the morning she found him dressed and sitting in the chair watching her.

'It's OK,' he said sheepishly, the palms of his hands towards her. 'It's only nine o'clock. I was just sitting here watching you while you were sleeping.'

'Why?' she asked groggily, and as she moved she felt her breasts ache, as they always did before a period, only slightly worse, she thought.

'Because it's a sight I won't see again till the war's over,' he said solemnly. 'Stay where you are, I'll get you some breakfast.'

'No, don't,' she said, 'I'm not hungry.' As usual, slight nausea was part of her period pattern, too, and she wanted to complain at how unfair the world was. On the way back to the base she was bound to be crushed into a train carriage with every kind of humanity pushing and crushing her, with sweating bodies and smells she didn't want to think about. Wouldn't that be just the time for the floodgates to open, wouldn't it be just her rotten luck? She made a mental note to put on the sanitary belt in her case and pin one of Lord Nuffield's little presents to it before she left, whether she needed it then or not, just in case. She noticed that he was pacing about the room.

'Look, Eileen, about last night,' he said, and by his tone she knew he had been rehearsing this speech as he sat in the chair watching her. 'I'm sorry it was like that, it's not how I planned it.'

No, she thought, it wasn't high on my list of how to spend a precious weekend pass either.

'I'd always wanted our first time to be special, you know?' he looked at her then looked away quickly again, embarrassed, as she desperately tried to work out what he was talking about. 'The awful thing is that I can't remember a thing about it,' he tried to laugh but it sounded pained. 'All these years I've been planning romantic, um, things, and it happens when I'm too drunk to remember. I don't blame you for feeling annoyed and out of sorts this morning, I only hope I wasn't, you know, rough or anything.'

Eileen didn't reply, partly because she couldn't think of anything to say, and partly because her silence seemed to be what he wanted. She sank back against the pillows and shut her eyes, wishing she could be anywhere else, wishing whatever time they still had to share together would fly by quickly.

'If anything, you know, happens, we'll get married before I go overseas,' he continued, still pacing, looking down at the floor as he did so. 'I was thinking we could anyway, I mean there must be ways of getting married quickly in wartime.' He looked up at her again, she could feel it even though her eyes were closed. 'Look, I'll take off downstairs while you, er, get yourself ready, OK?' he said, and almost ran from the bedroom.

When he'd gone she lay in the bed and pulled the covers right up to her chin, feeling completely and utterly relaxed for the first time since she had left the base the day before. So, he thought they'd done the deed. She imagined him wakening, naked, and finding her beside him, naked too, and naturally he had come to the obvious conclusion, and she felt so embarrassed for him that she couldn't think of any way of explaining it to him. What could she say? 'Well, actually, you were too drunk to manage it'? The thought brought Calli so sharply to mind that it hurt and she rolled over into the pillow and cried. In her head she was still fighting to believe he was alive, but that dark, cruel little voice deep inside kept telling her he wasn't, and no matter how much she protested, it wouldn't make things any different. It was like being slowly encompassed by a cold liquid, feeling it first at her toes, then her calves and her knees, moving relentlessly up her body till she risked drowning in it, while remaining calm and composed on the outside. There must be a point where it would break over her head and she would have to swim for her life, but so far she had managed to keep afloat, just, though the spells of tears were gradually increasing. The Curse, she thought again, it did that to you. The only times she was homesick was when the Curse was about to strike, which said more about the methods the Curse employed to upset her than it did anything about home. If she ever got into Parliament, she mused, she'd make sure the Curse was outlawed.

With a sudden start she jumped from the bed and hastily grabbed her clothes, her fingers turning to thumbs as she tried to pin Lord Nuffield's little present to the ugly, uncomfortable sanitary belt before getting dressed. She had to get completely buttoned up as quickly as possible in case he thought better of his chivalry and decided 'in for a penny, in for a pound', instead, and came bounding through the door intent on a more memorable 'second' time. In fact, if she was really smart she would heave her things into her case and be out of the room and downstairs in the lobby before the thought had time to occur to him.

Their goodbyes were swift and they both promised to be in touch before he left the country, with the thought that 'something might, um, happen' uppermost in his mind, no doubt. He tried to kiss her at the station, but she gave him a 'people will see' look and he just hugged her instead. Then he found her a seat beside an older woman with a gentle, polished pink face and greying hair, who smiled sympathetically as the young couple parted. The train was just as cramped as she had feared, and the journey just as hellish, the train stopping every two minutes for some reason or other, but she felt happy to be free of him. Now there was a thing to think – happy to be free of kind, loving, devoted Alex –

what on earth had he done to deserve that? He hadn't been Calli, that's what he'd done, she realised with a start, and instantly tears coursed down her cheeks.

'Don't worry,' said the older woman beside her, offering her a handkerchief. It had been folded and ironed into a triangle, so that the embroidered flower edge with its lace trim was on show. 'See?' she said gently. 'They're forget-me-nots, that's an omen. So don't you worry, dear,' the woman said kindly again. 'I lost my young man in the first war, so I know what you're feeling, but you'll be seeing yours again in no time,' and Eileen collapsed on her shoulder and sobbed.

Eileen had been back on the base for a week before she realised that the Curse still hadn't arrived, and instantly she sought out Daisy, who was busy delivering the routine 'Keep Away From Aircrew' lecture to a new intake of WAAFs. Eileen caught her eye and motioned with her head to a corner of the hut.

'Did you see them?' Daisy asked, shaking her head.

'Who?'

'The new lot. God, but they're green. That little one on the right, Pearl, will be working with us in the tower, which is just as well, because she's a good-looking little thing. They'll be around her like vultures: we'll have to look out for her.'

Eileen glanced at the girl and then looked away.

'Listen, Daisy, I have a problem, and I need your attention,' Eileen said quietly.

By the slow, deliberate way Daisy turned to look at her, Eileen knew her friend had already guessed. It wouldn't, after all, be the first time Daisy had heard very similar words from some scared girl, or the last either. They all brought their problems to Daisy. Eileen held her gaze, and nodded.

'Yes,' she said solemnly. 'I think I'm caught.'

'You can't be!' Daisy wailed. 'You wouldn't be that silly, and what did I tell you before you went? Anyway, you said the Curse was about to strike, you're worrying about nothing, you only saw him last week. It's just guilt talking, you good girls are always full of guilt, it does you no –'

'It happened before him,' Eileen said quietly, 'and I *know*, Daisy, I've never been as much as a day late in my life before.'

Daisy stared at her, thinking, then a look of understanding passed over her face and she slapped a hand across her forehead. 'The lovely boy?' she whispered. 'The Canadian boy, Eileen?'

'Eileen nodded and Daisy immediately put her arms around her and hugged her.

'Please don't be too kind, Daisy,' Eileen choked, 'I'm barely in control as it is.'

They stood in silence for a while, then, 'So what are we going to do?' Daisy asked. 'An abortion?'

Eileen shook her head firmly.

'I know what you're thinking, about Celia, but it's not like that every time,' Daisy said. 'That was just bad luck.'

'No, it's not that, Daisy, I want Calli's baby.'

'But how will you manage?' Daisy asked. 'What will your family say? Eileen, you really have to think about this.'

'I have a plan,' Eileen said, freeing herself and leaning her back against the wooden wall, her arms folded over her uniform shirt and tie. 'But I need to know if you think I've turned into a really bad girl.' She tried to smile, but tears overcame her again.

'You could never be that, Eileen,' Daisy said. 'Remember what I always said? It's only the good girls who get caught out.'

'You might change your mind about me when you hear what's in mine.'

'Try me.'

'Last weekend, when I saw Alex,' Eileen started.

'The childhood sweetheart,' Daisy interrupted with distaste.

'Him,' Eileen nodded. 'Well he got so drunk he passed out and I had to put him to bed. I think he was hoping to suggest we sleep together since he was going to war and all that.'

'The old story,' Daisy snarled. 'You'd think they'd try something more original, wouldn't you?'

'But he got nervous,' Eileen continued, 'and drank to give himself courage, only he overdid it.'

Daisy chuckled bitterly. 'Good!' she said.

'Well there was only one bed, so I took his clothes off, then I got in beside him,' she looked up and saw that Daisy was laughing. 'He was out for the count, unconscious, not just sleeping,' Eileen explained, smiling despite herself. 'Anyway, next morning he thought we'd actually done it, and I didn't tell him otherwise. He said we could get married if anything happened, as he put it.'

'A bun in the oven,' Daisy supplied.

'Exactly. Well, there is a bun in the oven, but it's not his.'

'And you're asking if I'd be shocked if you let him think it was his and you married him?'

Eileen nodded and lowered her head.

'Eileen,' Daisy sighed, 'I sometimes wonder what kind of people live up there in the Highlands.'

'Glasgow isn't the Highlands,' Eileen laughed.

'Might as well be,' Daisy said dismissively. 'If it's over the border then it's the Highlands, that's official.' She thought for a moment. 'Marry him,' she said. 'Marry the bastard. Not that I think you should, but if you really want to have this baby you have no choice, marry him.'

'Really?'

'Of course, you idiot,' Daisy said. 'Look on the bright side, you might get lucky, the bastard could still drown and you'd have the baby *and* your freedom.'

'Daisy! Don't say that! He's nice, it's me that's changed. And you don't know him.'

'I know the type, though,' Daisy said darkly. 'He's a man, isn't he?'

★　　★　　★

And so a week later Eileen married a delighted Alex in London by special licence with the complete understanding and blessing of the families at home; it was wartime after all. There were times when Eileen wondered what would happen to the world when that excuse was no longer available. There was no time to consummate the marriage, she was relieved to discover, Alex and his best man had to rush back to their ship to prepare to sail. Instead they had a couple of hours in a pub for a meal with a few friends. Daisy was the bridesmaid, and was on her best behaviour till the best man grabbed at her breasts and she broke his nose with a bottle. 'Pity we're not having pictures,' she muttered to Eileen, as the groom tried to staunch the best man's blood.

Eileen feigned disappointment that she wouldn't be carried over the threshhold, and would have no wedding-night passion.

'Doesn't matter,' Alex whispered, hugging her. 'We did that earlier.'

When she repeated this to Daisy later she muttered, 'Smug bastard.'

Two months later, Eileen was released from the WAAFs in respectable fashion on account of her pregnancy, and went home to Glasgow, to be greeted by two equally delighted families.

That's when her grief for Calli began to close in, when she arrived at her in-laws' home and became an expectant mother whose every need was indulged to the point where she had nothing to do but think. The family doctor was called in when her grief reached its lowest ebb. He advised Mrs MacLean that it was understandable that she should be deeply worried about Alex so far away and in constant danger, especially with a baby on the way, but there were thousands of women in the same position, she just had to get on with it as they were doing. Besides, he chided, all of this couldn't help the baby, and unless she pulled herself together she might lose it.

The thought of losing Calli's baby snapped Eileen out of her depression, that she couldn't bear, so her feelings about his death – she now accepted that he was dead – were cut short. She went on to deliver a healthy girl, and it did no harm that she was two weeks late. The baby had a mop of brown, curly hair and she was the image of her father, everyone said so, the little girl had Alex's dark hair and brown eyes, the curls were just a bonus, though Eileen knew they came from Calli, her real father, the real father she would never know, that no one would ever know about. Except for Daisy, of course, who used up a weekend pass to travel to Glasgow with an American Army major whose grandfather had come from the city.

When she saw mother and child she wept. 'She's Calli's double,' she sighed. 'You did the right thing, Eileen. You really loved that boy, didn't you?'

Eileen nodded.

'Well, it's not much consolation, but even like this you're lucky. I wish I knew what love meant.'

'What about the Yank?' Eileen asked.

'Oh, that's a union blessed by the Bank of America, as far as I'm concerned. Get the bastards before they get you, that's my aim, or get them and don't *let* them get you, that's even better!' And she threw her head back and laughed so loudly that her dyed blonde locks shook and the baby stirred and squirmed, a little line of annoyance appearing between her eyes.

'What are you calling her?' she whispered.

'Her name's Ann Martha,' Eileen replied. 'Calli's grandmother and mine were called Martha and our mothers were called Ann. I call her Annie.'

As they waved goodbye the two friends promised to keep in touch, but Daisy knew it wouldn't be true, their lives would be too different in future for that, but at the time they both meant it. It had worked out, then, Daisy thought to herself, Eileen and her daughter were safe and no one suspected anything, but she was married to the childhood sweetheart, God help her, a union she had lobbied against since Eileen told her of his existence; who knew what it would bring? Sitting beside the Yank on the car journey south again, she wiped her eyes.

'Never mind, honey,' he told her kindly, 'one day that'll be you, nicely set up with a husband and a baby of your own.'

Daisy smiled and blew her nose. 'In your dreams, sunshine!' she said in her head.

24

At Pine Edge life was changing so quickly that Gil was having trouble keeping up.

Still reeling from the shock and grief of losing Calli, Nancy had gone into the downstairs bedroom with a meal for Donald a week later, and found him dead in bed. She came out, the tray still in her hands, and walked to the kitchen, where Gil was sitting at the table.

'Not hungry?' Gil commented, pushing his own meal away. 'I suppose it's natural, Nancy, I don't think any of us will feel like eating normally for a while.'

'He's dead,' she said, putting the tray of food on the table, and for a moment he thought she had suddenly been overcome by the enormity of Calli's death. She had been so composed that he'd been waiting for something like this, he thought, she was only human, she had to break down sometime. If there had been something to bury, the ritual of a funeral to arrange and go through, that would have released the pain, but all she had was a telegram with a few terrible sentences on it, there was no tangible proof. He got up from the table and made to put an arm around her.

'Nancy, I know it's hard –'

'No,' she said, looking up at him sharply. 'Donald's dead.'

Gil ran through the house to the bedroom and found that it was true, then he sat down on the bed and looked at Donald, at the bluish tinge on his face against the premature whiteness of his hair – when did that happen? Donald was forty-five, the same age as himself, when had his hair gone so entirely white? He walked back into the kitchen and found that Nancy had cleared the table and was washing the dishes.

'I've called the doctor,' she said over her shoulder.

Gil didn't know what to say. Donald was his cousin, he had his own feelings, but he knew Donald had died many years ago, that if Nancy hadn't sacrificed her own life and breathed it into him he would've gone much earlier. When he thought about it, as he often did, he wondered if Nancy had done him a disservice in marrying him, if it would've been better all round for everyone if she had let him go when he came back from the first war. The man had wanted to go, as had Nancy's brother, Neil, both of them too damaged to take the pressures of normal life. Was it really a kindness to try to provide for him and look after him physically and keep Donald hanging on long after he had a right to go? They had produced those two perfect sons together, that was true, but Donald had been unable to take part in their lives or relate to them in any way, and lingering on as he had must've been a kind of purgatory for him. For Nancy, too, Nancy most of all, perhaps, because she had the capacity to live and she hadn't, not normally at any rate, instead she had wasted all that vitality he remembered so well from when she was a girl. She and Donald had had no married life as anyone else would've understood it, they had slept alone for all the years Gil had lived at Pine Edge, and many more before that, he suspected, so she had brought her boys up, cared for Donald and that was it. He had never spoken to her about any of this, he knew that discussing the arrangements that had evolved was mainly off limits, and only rarely did she say anything about her life. But now, surely, he thought, waiting for the doctor to arrive, there would be some relief for Nancy, now she could resume her life, but the truth was that he didn't really know what Nancy's feelings were or ever had been for her husband.

They buried Donald beside his parents in Campbellford. It was a well-attended funeral, everyone in the area knew of Calli's death and turned up as much out of sympathy with the family for their loss, as they did out of respect for Donald. He had grown up in the area, he was a local man from a well-known family, but little had been seen of him after he had brought his bride to Pine Edge, and it had always been assumed that he was in poor health after the first war, the gas and all that. Then his boy had been killed and that blow, on top of his poor health, had undoubtedly caused Donald's death, the poor man had died of a broken heart. All eyes were on Nancy, of course, the grieving mother and now widow, who looked withdrawn, very pale and near to breaking point as she stood with her remaining son, accepting the usual sympathetic condolences and, in a barely audible voice, thanking everyone for attending.

As Gil had suspected, as soon as she could gather her thoughts, Nancy had headed for Mabou to be with her mother. He had wanted to take her there, but she said she wanted to go alone and he respected that. After he had seen her off on the train, he went back to the farm and cleared out the bedroom where Donald had lived, it was a chore he didn't want Nancy to face. There he found all the letters Calli had sent home to his father and was shocked and a little saddened that not one had ever been opened. What did that signify, he wondered? A personality that was completely incapable of emotional contact with others, or a man rendered emotionless by circumstances? Either way he decided not to tell Nancy and at the same moment he was glad Calli had never known, even if the boy had come home again and his father's death had occurred years hence, the boy would have been hurt by that discovery. Gil was so grieved by Calli's death that he found it hard even to think about him without dissolving in tears, for Nancy's sake he had held himself together, but he felt dangerously adrift and wondered what fate would throw up next. Everything, he realised, had been geared to Calli's homecoming, when life would return to normal, and now that prospect had gone, everything was in limbo. He had no idea what Nancy wanted to do with the farm, though when he had spoken with Feargie before the boy had returned to Toronto, he had confirmed that he didn't want it.

'I think my mother sees it as your farm, Gil,' he had said. 'I think it's possible she might stay in Mabou.' And that had thrown Gil even more, he had to admit. He had been trying to hold on to some scrap of normality after losing Calli, but now the boy's death seemed to have been a catalyst for the loss of all normality. Gil's life had centred around Pine Edge and the family for so long, now all that was left was Pine Edge, the family he considered his own had disappeared before his eyes and he didn't know what would become of any of them, not least himself. Maybe it was a good thing overall for Nancy to spend some time in Mabou, it would give them both time to think.

When Nancy arrived at Mabou she moved back into her old room in Padraig's House, the last place, she felt, where she had been herself, the place she had escaped to when she had so often despaired of her odd mother. The times she had retreated there following some argument or other – and there had been plenty of those when she was growing up – walking up and down on the beautiful wooden floor that Padraig had cut the wood for but hadn't got around to completing all those years ago, towering with indignation about Martha's nonsense. The Micmac medicine, the mythology about their 'real' home, and the Second Sight, all of it had infuriated and embarrassed her. There was something missing from the bedroom now, though, from the house, too, and at first she couldn't work out what it was – her father's music. No matter how angry and irate she had been about her mother's determinedly strange ways, as she had fumed in her room there had always been music in every room of the house; now everywhere she looked in her life there seemed to be loss.

In the weeks since the telegram had arrived she had felt saddened at how she had treated Martha. Casting her mind back to the years when the boys were off fighting in the first war, she could recall only that Martha had kept life on an even keel, but when Calli first left she had suddenly realised that how she was feeling must've been how Martha had felt when Jamie and Neil were at the front. Now Nancy felt ashamed of herself for not being more understanding and sympathetic at the time, your child going off to war ripped your heart out, she knew that when Calli went off. Then there was the news of Jamie's death, she had never given Martha credit for dealing with that as well as she had, now that she stood in her shoes she understood that her mother was as brave and fine and special as everyone around her had always said. After that she had to watch the disintegration of her only remaining son and bear the failure of all her efforts to help him. Now there they were together, in Padraig's House, two widows, two bereaved mothers, and it had taken all this tragedy for Nancy to respect her mother.

They rubbed along quietly together, both of them recovering, the days turning to weeks, late summer changing to fall, as they sat outside in the weakening sunshine, looking down over the brook and the orchard, discussing all that had befallen the family over the years.

'The first thing Gil worried about was how to tell you about Calli,' Nancy said, 'but I told him you'd know. Did you?'

'Of course,' Martha replied. 'I heard him calling out.'

'Me too,' Nancy said quietly. 'I just wish I could bring him home.'

'I felt the same about your brother,' Martha nodded. 'To this day it seems so, well, unended, somehow, but I feel you will hear more of Calli one day.'

'Oh, Mother!' Nancy sighed. 'Not more of your hocus-pocus, I can't be doing with it.'

'I can't explain it,' Martha protested, 'I wish I could. I just have this feeling, Nancy.'

'Then feel it, Mother,' Nancy said angrily, 'but don't tell me about it. You know as well as I do that Calli won't be coming home, he's gone.'

'Yes, I know that,' Martha replied.

They fell silent, then, 'He's a good man, Gil,' Martha said, out of the blue.

'Yes, he is,' Nancy replied. 'I don't know how my boys would've fared without him.'

'And you, too,' Martha smiled.

'Yes, well, me too, I suppose. He took over the entire running of the farm, so he was a big help. Donald just retired, just faded away. It was strange, he just did less and less, left his room less and less, but it happened so gradually that I hardly noticed. I keep thinking now that it was as if he was waiting to die.'

'He would've died a great deal sooner if you hadn't married him,' Martha said. 'I know you meant well, but I don't believe you did him any favours, Nancy.'

'Oh, Mother, not that again!' Nancy said. 'My husband's just dead and you're going on about how I shouldn't have married him. Doesn't that strike you as slightly insensitive?'

'The fact that he's gone doesn't change anything,' Martha smiled back at her, 'and I had nothing against Donald, he was always a pleasant lad, he just wasn't for you nor you for him, it wasn't meant. And don't come the grieving widow with me, my girl.'

'Mother!'

'Stuff and nonsense,' Martha replied. 'You always did have your head in the clouds.'

'I did not!' Nancy retorted. 'If anyone had their head in the clouds it was you, I was the logical one, if you remember!'

'Nancy, Nancy,' Martha said, leaning forward and patting her daughter's knee, 'that day at the station, when the boys were going away, you made a mistake, it's as simple as that.'

'I don't know what you're talking about,' Nancy said loftily.

'You do,' Martha stated flatly. 'You made a mistake, girl. You looked at Donald and settled on him – didn't it ring any bells that he wasn't looking at you? You were looking at the wrong man.'

Nancy looked away, flustered. 'I didn't think anyone had noticed that,' she said quietly.

'Well, that's not true,' Martha said. 'You know perfectly well that your grandfather noticed, he as good as said to you, and I saw it, too, but I knew how you'd react if I'd said anything – straight up in flames, am I right?'

Nancy laughed despite herself. 'I think that's fair,' she said. 'In those days if you'd said black I'd have said white, you used to say that yourself.'

'Exactly,' Martha replied. 'Gil was standing behind Donald that day, I thought you were looking at him just as he was looking at you, the feeling was so strong you could almost see it. I didn't know you'd made a mistake till Neil and Donald came back, and by then you'd settled on the one you thought it was and there was nothing I could do to stop you. You should've been looking at Gil that day.'

'*Gil?*' Nancy laughed. 'Mother, I was just beginning to think I'd been wrong about you, but now you're off on another planet again!'

'Nancy,' Martha said sternly, 'you were always far too smart for your own good and you ruined your life because of it. Now you have a chance to make the rest of your life happy, so you must listen to me. Gil was the one for you right from the start, even when you were children it was obvious. You have always been far too headstrong –'

'As well as too smart?' Nancy suggested, sarcastically.

'– they tend to go together, Nancy, now be quiet and for once in your life, listen to your mother.'

'I feel like a child!' Nancy protested.

'That's because you're behaving like one. Now listen to me. You needed someone who could handle you, and Donald was never up to that, never, not even if the war hadn't happened. Gil was, he could always talk to you when you were off on one of your strops and refused to talk to anyone, Gil was able for you. All these years in Campbellford, the two of you have worked together, bringing up the boys, managing the farm. Isn't that right?'

'You make it sound as though there was something going on, I can assure you –'

'Oh stop it, Nancy,' Martha said angrily. 'Don't try to distract me, you know perfectly well what I'm talking about, you've known for years. Remember when you were all leaving here once and I said "Poor man, poor Gil"? What I meant was that something *should* have been going on, but nothing was.'

'Mother,' Nancy said, flustered, 'I really don't need this, I can't deal with your fantasies. How can you talk to me like this after all that's happened recently? I came here to rest and —'

'Oh, Nancy,' Martha groaned wearily, 'you are still such a fool! I actually thought you'd grown up a bit, but there's still no talking to you.'

Nancy looked away. 'Mother,' she said quietly, 'if I ever admit to myself that there was nothing between me and Donald, it means my life has been meaningless, that I've wasted all those years. Don't you see that?'

'I know that's what you think, Nancy,' Martha smiled at her gently, 'but nothing in life is ever wasted, nothing. Maybe you'll have to live longer to know that, but I assure you it's true. Besides, you had those two fine lads, how can you have wasted all those years?'

When Nancy went back to Campbellford she did so to make arrangements for the future. She and Gil sat at the kitchen table as she explained what she had in mind. She would, as Feargie had said, return to Mabou, so she proposed signing the farm over to him entirely.

'It's yours by right anyway, Gil,' she said quietly. 'If your father hadn't given it up it would have come to you in due course and none of us would have been here. And there would be no farm left if you hadn't taken over when Donald couldn't cope any longer.'

'I don't want it,' Gil replied firmly. 'Not like this.'

'Gil, it's not like you've stolen it from me and my children,' she laughed nervously. 'Neither of the boys wanted it.'

'I don't want it like this,' he repeated.

'I don't understand.'

'Nancy, I stayed here because we were a family. The boys weren't really mine, but I could pretend they were, and you weren't my wife, but there was nothing I could do about that.'

Nancy stared at him.

'I stayed because you were here,' he explained. 'I just wanted to be near you, Nancy.'

Nancy coloured and he smiled. 'I never thought I'd see that,' he said. 'When you were young you only blushed when you were angry, all those boys didn't embarrass you, they just annoyed you.'

'Gil, I'm sorry if I ever gave you any reason –' she said quietly.

'Stop it, Nancy,' Gil sighed, getting up and walking about the kitchen. 'You've always known, maybe not when we were young, but in the years I've been here. We've been like husband and wife except we didn't share a bed, but you didn't share a bed with Donald either and you still called him your husband, didn't you?'

They stared at each other in silence.

'Look,' he said eventually, 'I don't want the farm, sell it, do what you want, but I'll be moving on now. I'm not staying around here, it would be too embarrassing for both of us now, and the last thing I could put up with is watching you marry someone else.'

'I'm not marrying anyone!' she laughed.

'But you will,' he replied wearily. 'You're still a young woman, Nancy, someone will come along in time and I don't want to be here when he does. I'll find you someone to work here before I leave.'

Over the next week they avoided each other as much as possible, Gil even went off elsewhere for his meals, then he told her he'd taken someone on to do the farm work and would be leaving the following day.

The next morning she was working about the kitchen, her mind in turmoil, when he came down with his bags.

'I'm off now, Nancy,' he said quietly, 'take care of yourself.'

'Gil, I feel as though I'm pushing you out of your home,' she said, trying to smile.

'You're not; I am,' he replied, and headed for the door. He

was putting his bags in the truck when he heard the door open behind him.

'Gil,' she said softly. 'Gil, please don't go.'

He sighed, about to tell her there was no alternative, but when he turned to face her he saw her arms open wide and tears on her cheeks.

25

Ann Martha MacLean was three years old when Alex came home
to Glasgow in 1946, and both of them were instantly enraptured
by each other, having only seen each other in a succession of
photographs up till then. Annie had the same colouring as Alex
and she was a tall child, too, but her mother knew she was the
image of Calli, and she knew, too, that there were tall people in
his family in Canada. Eileen had got away with it; she had Calli's
child and Calli's child had a father, even if she had paid for the
arrangement by becoming Alex's wife. She didn't want to be his
wife, but as there was no one else she wanted to be wife to either,
what did it matter? She would be the best wife any man had ever
had, she decided, she would do everything in her power to make
Alex happy and to give her daughter a family, even if half of it
wasn't Annie's own. Still, those first sexual encounters with Alex
were torture. She hadn't expected it to be so bad, it was just a ritual
to be gone through, she had decided, nothing like what she had
experienced with Calli, but that was a once in a lifetime thing and
she knew from talk with friends that there were plenty of women
out there who just went through the motions. It wasn't that he
was rough, as once he'd feared, it wasn't that he was inattentive
or didn't care, it was just that he wasn't the right man. She tried,
she never refused him nor showed anything but pleasure at his
advances, and she met him thrust for thrust, smiling lazily and
happily afterwards to his face until the muscles in her own face
froze and ached with the effort. Then, when the light was turned
out and he lay snoring beside her, she would move as far away
from him as possible, roll into a foetal position and cringe with
horror in the blessed darkness. Darkness was her friend, where

the real Eileen hid. Occasionally, but only occasionally, she would pretend to be asleep to discourage him, even the odd excuse of a headache worked, because he would never have forced her, Alex was a kind man. It was inevitable, though, that over the years the fact that she hated having sex with him added a new guilt to those she already carried and made her even more anxious to please him in any way that she could. She was guilty about so much, most of all that he was bringing up another man's child without knowing it, without consenting to it, even if he loved the child more than life itself, and he did, and the child loved him. 'Where's the harm?' her conscience would ask, then, 'It's wrong, that's all,' she would reply. 'Plain wrong,' till she felt it eating into her soul.

Slowly she felt the marriage becoming unbalanced by her guilt and her attempts to make everything right. She had a debt to pay, but in doing so she became subservient and anxious, in case somehow the secret should leak out; there would be many losers then, she realised, Calli's daughter more than anyone, if she should lose a second father.

Both Eileen and Alex's fathers had happily retired and handed their halves of the business to the young couple, but after the war the Scottish Co-operative started to buy up all the small furniture makers, and by the fifties they had closed them down, ending a once thriving export trade and the traditional Scottish style of furniture that had travelled over the Empire in its day. Alex had seen what was happening and had already started changing the business into one that accepted contracts for special pieces of high quality furniture, and financially they were thriving. They had a beautiful home with modern conveniences most would not have for a decade or more, plenty of foreign holidays and a thriving social life, she even had her own little car when few women drove; everything, in fact, was as perfect as she wanted it to be, or nearly everything at any rate. Before she knew it, she fell into a pattern of dressing the way Alex liked, of having her hair as he preferred it, never questioning, far less disagreeing with him, in her quest to become the perfect wife; anything and everything about her had to be sacrificed to keep the secret and the guilt at bay, even her personality. Everything about her days as a WAAF was destroyed, every scrap of paper burned, every memory erased, in case something might be found or she might let slip some detail that could be traced. The world, she knew, was a very small place, all it would have taken was a mention of her work in Bomber Command for someone, somewhere, to have had a relative or friend who had worked there too, and before she knew it her carefully constructed existence could unravel. So her life in the WAAFs hadn't happened; she had married Alex and stayed at home to await the arrival of her baby while he was abroad in the forces, just as millions of other women had done. Home free, that's what they called it. Home free.

Gradually, though, she noticed a strange change in Alex, she could feel it happening, but in the circumstances, she couldn't risk challenging it. It was as though there was a subliminal game being played between them, a game that neither of them ever acknowledged openly, though she would lie awake at night and try to work out what his next move might be and how she should counter it, if she should counter it. Slowly he began to find little ways of humiliating her, she realised, of making her feel more guilty than she already was, and she wondered why, which made the secret all the more important to keep secret. If she cooked his favourite meal in the state-of-the-art kitchen, he decided he didn't want it just then after all, put it in the fancy new refrigerator, he'd have it later, only he never did. It would lie there, curling at the edges and drying up to a brick, as though it was rebuking her, a testament to some crime or other she had committed, before being thrown out. Then suddenly it was the way she ironed his shirts that was wrong, so that he could say in company, 'My wife is lovely, but she can't iron a shirt!' and he'd laugh affectionately so that everyone else would laugh too, only she sensed a certain edge to his voice sending barbs instead of affection. Next her driving became the butt of his attention and there were many tales told of the supposed lack of clear thought that stopped her being a competent driver. 'Women,' he would say, to general laughter, 'women, eh? And I have the dizziest one of the lot! No logic, no sense, maybe it's the thick Irish in her,' and he'd reach over and ruffle her hair, affectionately, of course. Eileen would smile but say nothing. What defence did she have that wouldn't seem like open warfare? That a few short years ago she had worked in a tense wartime situation, doing a demanding job under great stress, and had never been considered dizzy? It was only then that she realised he had never mentioned her war service, that he had blotted it out as effectively as she had, and of course she was pleased about that on one level. But she had had a reason for doing so – what was his reason? Inside she panicked but on the outside she smiled instead. His next ploy was to accuse her of losing things, the house keys, her purse, which she never did, and with a few acceptable exaggerations he'd turn supposed incidents into amusing anecdotes for everyone they knew, recounting them in front of her and laughing at his forgetful little wife, so that gradually he had altered everyone's perception of her. Still she smiled without answering back – what could she say that wouldn't sound petty? When they were in company, as they often had to be for business reasons, he was all attentiveness and 'Darling's, making sure she had a drink, that she was warm or cool enough, that she wasn't too tired, while at home they spoke rarely and only for practical reasons. He was good at that, using silence as a weapon; there was never a raised voice, that would've betrayed some emotion. It was all intended to demean her, she knew that, and somehow she knew that he knew that she knew, and he despised her even more for knowing and not answering back. Answering back might lead to anything, she decided, and she had Annie to consider, she didn't want her life disrupted.

The final straw was his impotence, not so much the reality of it, but what she felt was behind it. In the early 1950s, no man mentioned the word, it was strictly taboo and shameful; any man who suffered from it felt less of a man, and any man who knew of another saw him as less of a man, too. Not Alex though. He shrugged, said how terrible it was, how sorry he was, yet underneath he was – what? Smug? Yes, smug, that was the word. In some subtle way he managed to convey to her that it was her fault, he never said it, but he let her know he believed it, though he didn't, and Eileen was cut to shreds, not knowing which way to turn. For a start she was relieved that those awful nights of pretending it was all fireworks and earth movements were over, but there was the ever-present threat that he could make a miraculous recovery and they would return again, the power was all his. There was a feeling he transmitted to her that this most awful situation that any man could endure had been inflicted on him by something she had done, or not done, though he was forever cheerfully forgiving about it. She wasn't sure how to handle the problem. Did she do the wifely thing and lovingly urge him to seek medical help when the last thing she wanted for herself was a return of his erections, or did she ignore it? And yet how could she? And all through her agonies she knew, knew without a doubt, that he was watching her and laughing at her, he was punishing her. *Why?* He didn't have an inkling that Annie wasn't his daughter, she knew that for certain, he even managed to hint that she should be grateful to him for giving her this wonderful child, a gift from him that she didn't really deserve. In company he would say that Annie was the joy of their lives and though they had dearly wanted more children it simply hadn't happened, 'But we're still trying, aren't we Eileen?' he would ask devilishly, and everyone would laugh, 'We try all the time, don't we, darling?' and they would laugh even louder, never suspecting that they lived a celibate life by his choice, by his imposition. Eileen would lower her head and blush out of embarrassment for what he was doing, though no one knew this, except Alex; everyone thought she was blushing because he was talking of their wild and steamy sex life.

At times she felt angry over his battery of calculated little barbs, but she felt new guilt too, because he wouldn't be behaving like this – what man glories in his own lack of manliness? she thought – unless he was deeply unhappy, and that must be her fault. Alex was by nature a kind man after all, so why had he changed towards her? She had given him a much-loved daughter, she tried hard in all wifely areas, but where there had once been warmth between them there was now politeness, even if, more and more, it was a cool politeness. So it was her fault, when you boiled it right down, she had brought him to this vicious point, what was she to do that she wasn't already doing? She didn't love him, and by all the signs, if he had ever loved her, he no longer did, so she began to hope he might find someone else. But that was his final, deepest barb; he would not find someone else, he would not be happy, he wouldn't give her that satisfaction, and he wouldn't give her the chance of happiness with someone else either. And so they continued, on the surface a loving and happy couple; they had their own business and financial security, a beautiful child and a fine house, but underneath there was a cold, contained bitterness from Alex and a calm acceptance from Eileen that was every bit as cold.

26

In 1952, Nancy and Gil received a letter from Dr MacDonald in Glasgow. Dr MacDonald was attending a conference in Toronto and asked if he could call on them, he had met Calli during the war and had some photos he thought they should have. In due course he arrived, and discovered that he had the right Mrs MacDonald, but that she was now married to another Mr MacDonald.

'Don't tell me,' said the good doctor, 'it's Gil, isn't it?'

Nancy and Gil laughed.

'Look at us,' Dr MacDonald smiled, 'a house full of MacDonalds, could there ever be anything better? And who are these beautiful children?'

'This is Ceitlin Martha,' said Gil, presenting his seven-year-old daughter, 'and this,' he said nodding at his six-year-old son, 'is Padraig Calum.'

'Ah well,' said Dr MacDonald, 'if he's anything like his older brother he'll grow up to be a fine chap. Which brings me to why I'm here, as if the company of so many good people wasn't reason enough. I managed to get a package of letters from Calli sent to you by a diplomat friend during the war.'

Nancy nodded, he had mentioned in the letters that he had met this doctor. 'We were very grateful to you for that,' Nancy said. 'It was such a kindness.'

'Not at all, not at all,' smiled the doctor, waving away her thanks. 'The diplomat fellow was a kinsman and kinsmen do these things, don't they? And Calli was with another kinsman of mine, Gus, perhaps he mentioned him?'

'He did,' Nancy smiled. 'The Aussie with the laugh.'

'That was him to a T,' he grinned, remembering that laugh,

'like being machine-gunned with good humour from close range. He was killed when they were stationed in Malta together, you know, did Calli tell you? No? Well then, that's a story you must hear, because your boy was a hero.'

He told them of how Gus and Calli had been on Coastal Command, of how Gus had been shot during an attack on a tanker, and Calli had taken over the plane, dropped the torpedo and then flown the plane back to base, though he was officially the navigator.

'I found this out after the war, Gus's family in Australia wanted to know how he had died and I made some enquiries. Calli sent me the most beautiful letter when Gus died, you know. He had the soul of a poet, your son, and he was a kind and thoughtful lad, too, I have such happy memories of him. Anyway, it seems that Calli was told he could be put up for a medal for what he had done that day, but he was so horrified at being the centre of so much fuss that he turned it down flat, seems he became quite angry about it.'

Gil and Nancy looked at each other and laughed gently, picturing Calli's annoyance, both of them remembering a similar reaction of horror over Nancy's 'best blue suit' on the last day they ever saw him.

'All he asked for was a transfer to Bomber Command, apparently,' said the doctor, digging into his case. 'I saw them both when they were training at Abbotsinch outside Glasgow, just before they were posted to Malta. The only thing Calli wanted to do was to visit Raasay and Skye, and you know what we Highlanders are like, I knew people who could arrange it. We took these photos on that trip and I promised Calli I would get them back to his family, but I held on to them because I knew they would be precious to you so I wanted to give them to you in person.'

He handed a bundle of photos to Nancy and watched her looking through them, then her hand flew across her mouth and nose and she handed them to Gil and turned away.

'There are some of him on the shore at Raasay, he said his

grandmother would be anxious to have those, so I had copies made of all of them. Mrs MacDonald, I'm sorry if I've upset you with this, I do apologise.'

Nancy shook her head and held up a hand.

Gil smiled, putting his hand over hers. 'Look there, now,' he said softly, 'the lad on Old Ruaridh's shore on Raasay. You're mother will be so pleased to see these, won't she, Nancy?'

Nancy nodded.

Dr MacDonald winked at Gil. 'Calli told me he had a working Sopwith Camel, Gil, I don't suppose you still have her, do you?'

Gil put the pictures on the table in front of Nancy and took Dr MacDonald outside to the barn.

'I thought it might be better to leave her to look at the pictures alone, Gil,' he whispered.

'You're right,' Gil replied. 'I regard him as my son, too, I was anxious to see them, but his mother should have her own time with them.'

'So tell me, how did this marriage come about?' smiled the doctor. 'Do forgive a nosey old man, but I would like to know.'

'Calli's father was my cousin, he'd been ill for a long time, and a week or so after Calli died we found him dead in bed,' Gil explained.

'He told me that his father hadn't recovered from the first war,' Dr MacDonald said. 'I was in that show, too, which is why I was so envious of the Camel when he told me.'

Then Gil pulled back the covers and revealed the Camel in all her glory.

'My word!' sighed the doctor. 'What a beauty, I can tell you now, I feel tears in my eyes, Gil.'

'I haven't taken her up since Calli died,' Gil admitted. 'I used to tease him that he thought I'd delivered the Camel to him when I landed that day, and the truth is that he was right, she's still his. He loved her so much that I'd be afraid to damage her, it's a bit of him still with us in a strange way, all we have left of him except our memories.'

'And did you ever hear the details of how he died?'

Gil shook his head. 'All we know is that he was coming home from a raid, was hit by flak somewhere over France and crashed while on fire.'

'And was the plane recovered?'

'No.'

'Now that is sad,' the doctor said, shaking his head. 'Of course, you'll remember as well as I do, Gil, there are bogs in France that could swallow ten planes.'

'It's something that still bothers Nancy, though,' Gil said. 'Her brother Jamie was killed in the first war and his body was never recovered, and now her son. I think she would like to be able to bring him home and bury him beside his family, but it won't happen.'

'No, it won't,' Dr MacDonald said sadly, 'but look at the two of you, so content here with your new little family, think how happy that would have made Calli.'

Gil nodded, smiling.

Back in the house Nancy picked up the pictures again. He looked so young in his uniform, she thought, but then he was just a boy, as so many of them were. She was glad his grandmother had lived to see the pictures of him on Raasay. For generations the family had carried the guilt of leaving Old Ruairidh alone on the Raasay shore as his family sailed away, but Calli had travelled to Raasay and stood on that same shore, perhaps even in the old man's footsteps. Calli had gone back to him.

Calli's personal effects had been sent on shortly after his death, together with his last letter, but it had told them little more than he had said before he left. There were no great revelations, probably because he didn't really believe it *was* his last ever contact with his family, Gil said, he was too young to believe he would die. The pictures said so much more, somehow, even if it upset her to see him there, smiling, handsome, so much Calli that she traced his features on the paper as she used to do when he was little. Still, there was something bothering her, something she knew would be bothering Martha, too. When she thought of Calli, as she often did, in her mind's eye she would see the tree everyone back to Old Ruairidh talked of. If you saw a dim or a dead branch then nothing could be done, but if there was still life there, that was a different kind of sign. And when she thought of Calli the branch was still alive – why was that? Was it because she was his mother and didn't want to give up on him, especially as there had been no body, no identification, and no funeral, and until then she couldn't accept it? She had heard his voice that night in 1943, she knew he had died and she wasn't stupid, she didn't expect any longer to see him again as she had at first, walking through the door and saying it was all a mistake. So why was there still life in the branch? Looking at the pictures it appeared in her mind again, and she didn't know why.

27

In the years that followed, life went on, as people all over the world adjusted to the end of the war and hoped, as they had after the first one, that it wouldn't happen again.

Nancy's second brood grew up as her first lot did, living at Pine Edge and spending as much time at Mabou as Campbellford life allowed. Eventually, Feargie became a heart surgeon of some renown and when she grew up, Ceitlin married a doctor who was on her older brother's staff and moved to Toronto.

After the war the natural order had been restored and deaths occurred as they should, according to age, though that was no comfort to the family when Martha died in 1961, at the age of ninety-six. Like all families who lose someone who has been there for ever, it seemed to them that a prop had given way in their lives, but Martha had lived to a ripe old age and, after the loss of her two sons then Calli, she had still known joy in her family.

In that other family in Glasgow, it was noticeable that Annie and her mother, and Annie and her father, were close, but that there was a distance between her parents.

There was a special friend Annie hadn't mentioned since she was old enough to understand that no one else saw what she did. All her life he had been there, the dark, curly-haired young man who sang to her in her cot and watched over her, she couldn't recall a time when he wasn't there. Not every minute of every day, of course, but most times, and even when she couldn't actually see him, she knew he was there and felt comforted by that. She couldn't remember when she had first noticed what the man in the corner was wearing, he had always been as he was and that had been enough, but somewhere along the line she knew he was dressed like a pilot, with a fur-lined leather jacket and zip-up boots, a leather helmet and gloves, and there was an oxygen mask hanging around his neck. When she did notice, she simply accepted it; why shouldn't he be a pilot? Luckily, though, when she was very young, she had referred to him as her 'friend' to her parents, and they had laughed, accepting that many children had imaginary friends, especially only children, and predicting that as she got older, her 'friend' would recede into the far distance. He wasn't like the imaginary friends of other children, though, he wasn't an elf, a clown or Mowgli from *Jungle Book*, but a man, a flesh and blood man. Neither did he scribble on walls or knock over flower vases, or break cups, he just stood in the corner and smiled at Annie. Every night before she went to sleep she would look for him and say 'Goodnight, man,' and he would smile back and nod his head, and as she did her homework he would look on encouragingly. He never spoke, that was the only thing she wondered about, he had sung to her when she was a baby, but as she got older he just appeared now and again, watched and smiled, a quiet, encouraging and, in a way she couldn't explain, a loving companion. And if he had been an imaginary friend, it would have been no wonder the child had need of him, because the tense, cold atmosphere between her parents was palpable to a child extra-sensitive to such things, and it confused her. As she grew, she noticed that they spoke freely in the presence of others, but on their own at home there was a silence that frightened her when she was small. Like all children, Annie's greatest fear was that her parents might split up, even in the 1950s in Glasgow she had heard such horror stories, and that if they did it would be her fault because she had failed to keep them together, obviously. So each time Eileen and Alex had company and spoke to each other she thought everything was better, only to find the situation returning to normal, or normal for the MacLean family, when they were alone again. She would retreat to her bedroom where the man in the corner awaited her, making her feel warm and cosseted, and wonder what she had done to bring about the latest coolness, though she never did figure it out. All her life there had been that tension and confusion, as she wondered and worried if this might be the day one of her parents, or both, walked out. The last thing she wanted was to provoke a situation that might bring this about, so Annie went to extremes to be a good child, who did well at school and was never naughty. There were no tantrums and no misbehaviour, because she just never knew what would happen, yet the man in the corner, though he didn't speak, seemed to understand and was always sympathetic to the child. But somehow Annie sensed that if she had mentioned that her 'friend' was still there, it would add more pressure to a situation already straining at the seams, so the man in the corner became and stayed her secret.

When she was ten years old her parents decided to move to the fashionable West End of Glasgow, and went house-hunting. Annie's only fear was that if they lived in another house the man might stay in the old house. By then she accepted that no one else could see him and, though she didn't analyse this, she still didn't want to lose him. The round of house viewings was boring, but it seemed to be the way of things for her parents, they had to have some diversion to be able to speak to each other, to be able to live together almost, and it made Annie feel happy for a brief spell to see them talking as though they belonged together – after all, if they were buying another house, they couldn't be splitting up, could they? – so she always tagged along. They looked at a big house in Dowanhill, a huge red sandstone building set off a quiet, leafy avenue. Annie liked this one, even if there were too many rooms to keep track of, it was different. Leading off the corridors were odd little rooms at strange angles, giving constant surprises. As her parents were led around the house by the estate agent, Annie opened a door at the top of the stairs that from the outside looked like a cupboard, and found herself in a tiny bedroom. From the wall on the right was a bed that came to the middle of the room, in front of the inward opening door, with a dressing table against the left-hand wall. She walked in and sat on the pink velvet-covered stool in front of the dressing table, and found to her joy that it was covered with the forbidden prizes of perfumes and cosmetics; she decided that this would be her room. Then she heard her mother calling her, so she got up and stepped carefully around the bottom of the bed, turning to give 'her' room a last look as she put her hand on the knob to close the door behind her. Then something happened. She could hear the sounds of her parents and the estate agent, their footsteps and voices, but muffled, as if they were in another house, and there seemed to be only Annie and the room in focus. Sitting on the bed now, staring at her, was a little old lady with a very pale, wrinkled face. Her white hair was caught up behind her head in a bun, with little wisps framing her face, and she was dressed in black, except for a high-necked, white blouse with a pie-crust collar piped with delicate lace and stitched pleats running down the front. Clasped in her hand and rolled into a ball was a handkerchief, but Annie could see that it, too, had lace edging, and the little lady was looking straight at her with sad, blue eyes that were awash with tears. They stared at each other for what seemed a very long time, the child and the old woman, then suddenly she felt her mother behind her, taking her hand from the doorknob and closing the door.

'There you are!' Eileen said. 'You mustn't go wandering about people's houses on your own like that, Annie, it's very rude.'

'It's OK, Mrs MacLean,' the estate agent said beside her. 'There's no one living here. The lady who owned it died three weeks ago, in fact that was her bedroom . . .'

Annie stood still, looking at the closed door inches in front of her, but she could still see the little lady and the little lady was still looking at her and crying.

'The family just want to sell everything,' the estate agent was saying as he left with her parents, 'so if you like any of the furniture do say.'

'She doesn't want to sell her house,' Annie thought desperately, making her way rapidly downstairs and out into the front garden. 'The lady wants to stay here, she doesn't want us in her house.'

She ran to the car and sat inside, looking up at the window of the tiny room, where the lady was looking out. 'Poor little lady,' she said sadly, 'she doesn't know what's happening.'

When her parents came out they had already decided that the house wasn't what they were looking for, and as they drove away Annie knelt on the back seat, watching the figure at the window wave a sad hand to her till she was out of sight. When she got back home Annie told the man in the corner about what had happened; he wasn't there, but she knew he was nodding sympathetically. Annie didn't understand when things like this happened to her, and they had always happened, just as she didn't understand the man in the corner. Gradually she realised that other people didn't see what she saw, but even then she didn't doubt it or feel afraid, though as she grew up she would wonder about that and still not be able to come up with an explanation, it was just part of being Annie.

Before long the quest for a new home came to an end and they moved into a house not far from the one the old lady hadn't wanted to sell. It was built of natural red and blonde sandstone and had arched windows and little turrets everywhere, and it stood on the corner of Kirklee Road, opposite Kelvinside Academy. Her mother had liked the house because it had a sweeping staircase like the one she had lived in when she was a child, though she didn't put a piano underneath it, but her Irish grandfather's grandparents' clock. All Annie could think of was losing the man in the corner, but when she bounded upstairs and burst into the room that had been earmarked for her, there he was, smiling at her as usual.

Alex was immensely proud of his daughter, a pretty, serious but intelligent child, with deep, brown eyes, though he wished something could be done about that lock of dark, curly hair that kept falling over her brow, spoiling, he thought, her perfection. Eileen would make token attempts to anchor it, but she knew where it came from and for her it was a link with Calli that she wanted to keep, there being little enough pleasure in her life. Despite the stubbornly wayward lock of hair, Alex took

Annie everywhere with him, to show her off. This included the workshop, where she grew up watching the men working and was always full of questions about what they were doing. Alex was primarily a businessman, he had no inherent skill with woodwork, but he knew how to keep together people who had, most of whom had worked for his father and Eileen's over the years, or were the next generation, and gradually he adapted the business without the profits going down. Postwar Britain was not the promised land fit for heroes, rationing still existed into the 1950s, and few people could afford custom-designed pieces, so Alex had shrewdly moved the emphasis from making furniture to conservation, restoration and repairs, so that the business became the automatic choice for large collectors and museums with priceless antique furniture that had become distressed. He did all this without consulting Eileen, though she owned half of the company in her own right, behaving pretty much as any man of his era would. It still irritated Eileen, though given the situation, she couldn't risk voicing her objections to being ignored, to not being given a voice in what was happening, however successful it was.

Annie was absorbed by the skills she saw and she learned fast, listening to the men explaining what they were doing and telling her stories from the past, about her grandparents and people who had worked in the business before. Stuart Devine, son of old Mr Devine, who had specialised in renovation many years before, would tell her how his father had despaired of Charles Rennie Mackintosh's designs. Rennie Mackintosh was becoming slightly better known in Glasgow, though it was some years before his name was known all over the world, it was the way of things that the poor man's genius had only been recognised by a minority of his fellow Glaswegians while he was alive. His beautifully designed furniture would eventually change hands for millions, and even reproductions of his exquisite high-backed chairs cost the earth, though they were better to look at than sit on. The originals did indeed have all the flaws that had so frustrated the late Mr Devine, Stuart would chuckle to Annie, the design was inspired, but not practical, and not just for sitting on, they didn't really make sense from the construction point of view either, and frequently had to be discreetly nailed together to keep the elegant lines from falling apart, something that would have appalled the minimalist designer had he known. Added to that, the original workmanship wasn't always well done, which always surprised people. Most people would have assumed that as Rennie Mackintosh had designed his furniture for the wealthy, it would be constructed by master craftsmen. It wasn't though, perhaps because he was so ahead of his time that few furniture makers appreciated or understood his artistic genius, so a lot of their work was botched, and that would show up later, keeping the MacLean family business in work.

Annie attached herself to Stuart especially because he was so open about his work and loved teaching her about beauty, he didn't guard it jealously as though no one else should have any knowledge of it. She liked the fact that he could admire a particularly fine piece of wood for hours, though no one else could see what he saw, and in Annie he had a captive audience. She would come home, dark eyes alight under the unruly hair, and announce to her mother that Stuart had a special job on at the weekend and she was going in to watch, as though it was the most natural thing in the world that she should be there to see it done. 'After your homework,' her mother would say, and Annie would nod, her eyes gleaming in a way that reminded Eileen so much of Calli that she had to blink away the tears.

There was the restoration of an eighteenth-century cabinet, that Annie remembered for the rest of her life because of how it looked at the beginning and how beautiful and proud it stood when Stuart had finished with it.

'It's sad,' Annie sighed, looking at it.

'I know, I know,' Stuart replied, rubbing his hands, eager to get started, 'but just you wait till it's done.'

The rosewood cabinet was decorated with laburnum oysters and had originally come from a country house, but had been stored in a damp garage for years before someone doing some clearing out had found it and wondered if it was 'anything'. Stuart had examined it with pained eyes, noting the veneer lifting and bubbling in places, completely loose in others, as though an old friend had arrived down on his luck, ill and wearing ragged clothes. As Annie watched, he carefully removed the loose and damaged veneer.

'You're breaking it more, Stuart!' she wailed.

'No, it's all right, it all has to be cleaned, you see, I have to take off all the dust and the old glue.'

She watched him place a cloth soaked in hot water over the old glue to soften it, before removing it gently with a chisel. Stripped of much of its decoration, the cabinet looked lifeless and Annie urged Stuart to put it all back on again. He had great patience and concentration with things he cared about, though.

'It has to dry first,' he smiled. 'If I put all the nice bits on now they'll just come off again.' When he was sure there was no moisture left on any of the surfaces, he replaced the veneer pieces using fish glue. 'Now we have to clamp it very carefully,' he breathed, delicately and carefully placing small blocks of wood under the biting edges of the clamp.

'What's that for?' she demanded.

'To make sure I don't scratch the wood under the clamp,' he told her, 'and to make sure there aren't any gaps.' Then he removed all traces of the new glue before it set, and examined the cabinet from every angle, checking and rechecking every aspect.

After twenty-four hours they went back to the workshop, both full of excitement, and with great care and gentleness Stuart removed the clamps.

'What do you think?' he smiled.

'It's still dirty,' Annie replied. 'It's not shiny.'

He caught her nose between two of his fingers. 'You're never happy, are you?' he joked, smiling at her. 'It still has to be cleaned.'

'Do you use a scrubbing brush?' she asked, knowing this would produce a shocked, hurt expression from Stuart.

'I most certainly do not!' he gasped, and she was delighted at having caught him out. 'I use a very soft cloth with tiny bits of water and do it very slowly.'

'A scrubbing brush would be faster,' she said solemnly, then laughed out loud at his mock serious expression. Then she watched the process and how gently he used the cloth, stopping every now and again and holding it up to let her see the dirt he was removing.

'See?' he asked happily. 'And now for the wax,' and once again he took great care, working in tiny circles on one small area at a time, until he had completed half of it, then stopping to let her see it. She loved that part, the comparison between how it looked with wax and without, until finally the task was done, and a thing of great beauty stood before them, its high shine mirroring Stuart's satisfied smile.

He was the cleverest man in the world, that's how she had always seen him, a man who made things beautiful, who looked deeply hurt at the sight of a fine old chair or table with woodworm and who couldn't resist sorting it out and making it better. One day she would do that, she decided, one day she would make things beautiful like Stuart did, and he became her hero, much to Eileen's amusement.

When she was about twelve years old, Annie was waiting for Eileen to drive her to the workshop to watch one of Stuart's special jobs, when she looked out of the window of her upstairs bedroom and saw him walking up the driveway towards the glazed white door of their house. Thinking the arrangements had been changed and Stuart was collecting her, as he sometimes did, she jumped down the stairs of the long staircase three at a time, reaching the front door as he was about to ring the bell. She turned her head to shout 'Stuart's here!' then, as she turned back towards him again there was another of those moments she didn't understand. Everything around her slowed down, the noise of the traffic outside seemed to fade and the house went out of focus. In the distance she heard the phone ring in a muted way, and when she looked out of the glass in the door Stuart had disappeared; one moment he was there, the next he wasn't. She heard her mother answer the phone and took in every word, but from a long, long distance.

'Oh no! Not Stuart!' Eileen's voice said. 'How is his wife?' then there was a pause. 'Yes, yes, I'll tell her, but I don't know how, she adores him. Thank you for letting me know.' Just then Eileen looked up and saw Annie at the door. 'Did I hear you shout something to me, Annie?' she asked gently.

Annie shook her head.

'I could've sworn I heard you,' Eileen said distractedly.

'I saw a pal from school,' Annie replied.

'Oh, well, that's all right then,' Eileen smiled tightly. 'Um, that phone call, Annie, it was your father. About Stuart. I'm afraid it's very bad news, Annie.' Eileen moved closer and drew her daughter to her. 'He took ill at work this afternoon. They got an ambulance, but when it arrived at the hospital I'm afraid it was too late, Stuart was already dead.'

'Oh,' said Annie.

In 1971, Alex was diagnosed with cancer; Annie had known for some time that there was something wrong, because she could see a dark cloud over him, and when she thought about him a image of a tree would spring into her mind, a tree with a withering branch. She had had these feelings and thoughts so often over her twenty-seven years that they no longer bothered her. Once they had, because they were so confusing and no one else seemed to have them, as far as she could tell, but it was only when the strangeness had happened a few times that she was able to see a pattern and then the consequences. For instance, it wasn't till Stuart had been dead for years that she understood why he had had a dark cloud over him for weeks before he died, and she only understood it because it had happened again with someone else. Yet, strangely, she never felt afraid, never doubted what she was seeing or feeling, but it made her feel sad because by then she knew what these things meant. By the time Alex's illness became terminal she was married and had a baby on the way.

It had all been very strange. She had been in the workshop alone when a young man called, a doctor from the nearby Western Infirmary. At one time she had thought of becoming a doctor herself, but that was before Stuart Devine had introduced her to the joys of working with beautiful wood, so she was always half-interested, half-envious, when she met a doctor. This one was tall and fair-haired and wondered if she might be able to help him with an old piece of furniture that had belonged to his great-grandmother. He remembered playing with it when his grandmother had the piece, but his father had never liked it and since she had died it had lain in a basement for many years. It looked like a standard bureau with a rolltop lid, but Annie's eyes lit up as she opened the various drawers and compartments. As usual there was a secret drawer, a little trick, but it didn't stop there, this bureau had many compartments, and inside each one was a surprise, a mouse, a little man, a cat; whoever had made this bureau had become completely carried away.

Annie laughed. 'I know who made this,' she told young Dr Johnstone. 'Your great-grandmother's bureau was made by my great-grandfather.'

'Well, he was a genius,' Dr Johnstone said admiringly. 'I still haven't discovered all of the secrets of his creation.'

'Would you like to see more of his work?' she asked. 'Our house is full of it.'

And that evening, watching him delight in the grandparents' clock, the chairs with owls and other birds and the table with mice running up and down the legs, Annie decided she would marry David Johnstone.

'You can't make a decision like that based on the fact that he likes my grandfather's furniture!' Eileen told her, aghast.

'Yes I can,' Annie smiled.

'But did this young chap make the same spontaneous decision?'

'Oh,' said Annie, 'he doesn't know yet.'

'Annie, this is madness!' her mother exclaimed. 'You're not a silly person, you don't give in to fancies like this!'

'I know I don't,' Annie said quietly, 'but I know I'm right

about this man, Mum, I can't explain it, I just feel that he's the one.'

Eileen nursed Alex throughout his last six months, and though he was pleasant enough to other people, to her he was ill-mannered and sometimes abusive, despite everything she did for him, or perhaps because of it. When the end finally came, he said his goodbyes to his pregnant daughter, then asked for a moment alone with his wife.

'You never loved me,' he said bitterly to Eileen. 'I gave you everything, I gave you Annie, but something happened before you joined up, you met someone else, that's why you were so desperate to get away. You never loved me.' So that was why he had never mentioned her wartime service, he had sensed that his rival, real or imaginary, lay back there, though he was wrong about the timing. She had joined the WAAFs to get away from him, that was true, though it was fair to say she was getting away from her life and he was a part of that, but the someone else she had met arrived during those years. Still, she could see Alex's point, in his mind someone had taken the love he regarded as his by right, so he had been cheated of a possession. She could see it now but, nevertheless, she was stung by his rebuke. He had thought she had met someone else before she had joined the WAAFs, yet he had still insisted that she married him, as though her feelings had to come second to what he wanted.

'And when did you ever ask me if I loved you?' she demanded just as bitterly. 'You decided if I didn't then I had to be made to. You're like all men, you decided I had to fit into your life, into whatever you wanted. In all *my* life, when did you give me a choice about anything? And that's why you've tortured me all these years, because you thought I left Glasgow with another man. Well, I'll tell you now, it wasn't true, you made our lives miserable over something that wasn't even true.' It was the only time she had ever given voice to the pent-up anger she felt at how he had tortured her mentally during what passed in the eyes of others as their marriage, the first and last time she would answer him back, because Alex didn't reply, he simply turned his head away, closed his eyes and sank into a coma; he died that night.

He was right, of course; she had tried, but she had never loved him. Maybe she would have if she hadn't known Calli, or maybe if she and Calli had known each other longer, the first madness of romance would have worn thin and she would have gone back to Alex and loved him; who could tell? She doubted it, but it was just possible; anyway, life was as it was. What she did know was that she had tried with Alex, the stumbling block to the kind of love Alex wanted was that she *had* experienced it with Calli, she had some measure to judge by, and what she felt for Alex was entirely different. It was no one's fault, it was just how it was. And not once had she grudged him Calli's child, he was the father who had brought Annie up, so he was her real father in every possible way, and the two were devoted to each other. In all the time they slept together, before she 'caused' him to become impotent, she had never again become pregnant though, and she often wondered if he had been able to have children, and if not, then she had done him a favour, and not the other way around. It was a strange thing, but now that he was dead she felt such anger and longed to tell him what she thought of him and his petty, childish mind games. They had cheated each other, that's what she would have said to him, should have said to him. He had treated her as a possession, like something he had bought that hadn't lived up to expectations, but he had lost the receipt and couldn't return it, so he had abused it instead. But he had been a good father to Annie, so she could forgive him everything he had ever done to her.

After Alex died, the big house in Kirklee Road was divided into two separate flats, the top one for Annie, David and their son Gavin, the bottom one for Eileen, with both parties knowing that in due course the young people would have it all. It was the perfect arrangement, separate but not apart, and Eileen would be able to help with her grandchild. Not that it quite worked out that way, though, because she only seemed to rest there between foreign trips. Annie noticed a huge change in Eileen once she became a widow, there was a sense of freedom, of relief about her. Alex's half of the business had been left to Annie, and Eileen had signed over her half, too. She had always had her own money inherited from her parents and grandparents and from the business profits up till Alex's death, and from now on she intended to do what she had always wanted, to travel on her own to all the places she had never seen; the bitterness in her life had gone.

28

When the phone rang in the Ministry of Defence's Laycon House in Holborn, the home of the RAF History Unit, one rainy Tuesday early in 1975, it proved to be the kind of call that the officers working there loved and hated at the same time. On the other end was some anonymous junior diplomat in the British Embassy in Paris, passing on some information from the French authorities. Excavation work had just started in an area of Normandy to lay the foundations for a new motorway after a prolonged debate and many heated exchanges; there would be many more in the years to come, and always for similar reasons, but no one knew that at the time. The objections had come mainly from those who still remembered the dead of two world wars, and considered the building of the proposed motorway on top of thousands of unmarked graves to be sacrilege. Countless war dead lay where they had fallen, either because there hadn't been time to bury them during battle, or because they had simply been swallowed up by the all-pervading mud of the infamous trenches. Young men, boys, lay there, never having been afforded the dignity of a decent burial, unlike their comrades who lay under acres of nice white crosses in well-tended cemeteries across France and Belgium. They were, nevertheless, said the protesters, human beings who had given their lives and should be shown some respect, not covered with Tarmac and forgotten. The French government had decided to go ahead anyway, stating that the needs of living drivers were more important, in their eyes, than honouring the fallen and being sensitive to the families who still grieved for them. When they had just started digging, however, they had come across the wreck of a British plane with human remains inside, so they were forced to stop work and inform the British Embassy, who in turn informed the RAF.

The female officer, Janet Ross, who took the call, had the mixed feelings everyone had on these occasions. Sometimes you traced relatives of the dead and they expected to be presented with a perfectly preserved body, when all that they found were a few bones. You often contacted someone who, against all the odds, against reason, had never really given up hope and was devastated to hear the words that would bring it to an end once and for all. Not that many such calls still arrived in the 1970s, they had steadily decreased every year since the Second World War, but there was still one or so a year, from somewhere or other. Only the year before a British plane had been found at the bottom of a lake in Archangel in Russia and when it was identified it cleared up a mystery that had probably haunted the families of the crew all those years. It shouldn't have been there, that was the point, it had been delivering supplies somewhere and had veered well off course and got lost, so that when it had disappeared no one knew what had become of it. So it was satisfying at least to tell the families that it had been found and to arrange funerals and lay the crew to rest. And that was the next problem, persuading people that no matter what they did or who they spoke to, the remains could not be brought home, but had to be buried in the country where they had been found. It was only natural, of course, to want a son or a husband to be buried at home beside the mothers, father and wives who had grieved for them, but it couldn't be done, not even if the families offered to pay all the costs. The reason was simple, after the war no country could have afforded the cost of bringing so many dead home, which had prompted many relatives to remark that they had been only too happy to pay the costs of taking them to their deaths in the first place. Since the First World War, there had been an international agreement that everyone should be treated the same; regardless of how poor or rich their families were, the remains of fallen servicemen from both wars must be buried in the country where they died, but a full military funeral would be arranged in accordance with the wishes of the families, and the RAF would pay for two family members of each aircrewman to attend. It was the best they could do, the rule couldn't be broken, though Canada had passed a one-off law for an unknown Canadian soldier to be taken home to represent all those who never would, on the strict understanding that it would never again be permitted.

The procedure was always the same. There was a record of all missing aircraft kept at Hayes, in Middlesex, and if there were enough markings still on the plane, it could be identified and matched with the date of its last mission. Then, regardless of how many years had passed, the History Unit would attempt to contact families, by writing to the last known address, placing adverts in local and national newspapers and appeals on television and radio. Usually someone turned up, a grandchild, a brother, someone who had grown up hearing the sad tale of the one who never returned and had wondered for years where their relative might be, and would be grateful that at last the waiting was over. Some of them expressed great relief, others broke down completely, as though they had been told of a death that had happened minutes ago instead of years, but it was amazing how long people could hold out hope, how many impossible scenarios they could invent in their minds.

By the sound of it, this might be one of the easier jobs, the plane had dived into a bog and was well-preserved, and the numbers were clear. It was a Lancaster Mark 1, serial number ED498 EM-0, and, according to the records at Hayes, it had crashed on the way back from a raid on Milan on 15/16 August, 1943, piloted by skipper Calum R. MacDonald of the RCAF. The French would continue to excavate the site and recover the human remains inside the wreck, while the RAF Historical Unit tried to contact relatives.

And so, some weeks later, Young Padraig MacDonald found among the farm equipment circulars and Reader's Digest mailshots, an official letter from the RAF in England, addressed to Mr & Mrs Donald MacDonald. He wondered whether or not he should open the letter. It clearly concerned his half-brother,

Calli, a revered name within the family, but Calli's father had died shortly after he himself had been killed, and the mother Young Padraig and Calli shared was a lady of some seventy-five years. She came from long-lived stock and her mind was clear and sharp, it was true, he thought, but seventy-five was seventy-five, after all. She and Gil had handed the farm on to Padraig when he and Val had married the year before and they now lived in happy retirement in the house on Calli's Hill, high above Campbellford, while in Pine Edge Val was pregnant with her first child, which brought back memories for Nancy, of course. Young Padraig wondered what to do with the letter, he had noticed that it didn't take as much to knock her off her stride these days, and whatever this letter contained, he felt sure it must have the capacity to do just that. He turned it over in his hands, as though that would make it divulge its message without opening it, then he decided to call Feargie in Toronto.

'Feargie, I don't know what to do about this,' he explained. 'Do I open it?'

'Only if you want a thick ear,' Feargie replied. 'Mom won't take kindly to being treated as too far gone to open her own letters.'

'But it's bound to be about Calli, and what more is there to say about him after all these years? What if it's just some scam, you know, give us a thousand bucks and we'll put his name on some roll of honour, that kind of thing?'

'If it is she'll see them off,' Feargie laughed, 'but I see your point. Look, hang on to it and I'll come up, if it's about Calli I want to know what's in it, too.'

The next day, the two MacDonald brothers drove up the hill together to Gil and Nancy's home, the letter from the RAF sitting on the dashboard of Young Padraig's station wagon. When Gil and Nancy had built their home here they had been on their own, but now there were houses all around, not surprising really, as it was such a prime spot, and it had been renamed High Street, though it would always be Calli's Hill to the family. They found Nancy at the back of the house, filling the bird feeders all over the garden, getting the hummingbird feeder ready to fill with sugar water for the tenth of May, which wasn't far off now, while Gil continued what had become a major obsession with him these days, hunting down and killing dandelions. When Nancy saw her two sons she froze, afraid of bad news, then she saw the letter in Feargie's hand and looked from one to the other.

'By the look of the two of you,' she smiled, 'I'd better sit down.'

'I don't think it's bad news,' Feargie grinned.

'But you've come all the way up here anyway, on the off-chance, I see,' she chuckled.

'You are a nasty old biddy, Nancy MacDonald,' her eldest son replied. 'All the stories I've heard from Gil are obviously true.'

'What stories?' she demanded, staring at her husband, who calmly smiled back at her.

'You know perfectly well what stories,' Feargie teased her. 'And everybody in Mabou has confirmed them over the years, too. I've heard them all, the tongue of a viper they say up there, would argue with her own shadow and shoot people down in flames for fun.'

'Only if they are idiots,' she said meaningfully, 'so I'd be careful if I were you, Fearghus MacDonald.'

Feargie laughed and put the letter down on the table in front of her. 'It's from the RAF in England and it's addressed to you and my father,' he said quietly, 'so it can only be something to do with Calli. If it is, I want to know, too, that's why I'm here, Mom.'

As they looked at it in silence for a few moments, Feargie could almost read what was in his mother's mind and had to look away. Whatever the letter contained it was not news that Calli had been found alive and well and still aged twenty-three, and that's what she had wanted all these years, what he had wanted, too, he suddenly realised.

Nancy put her glasses on to open the letter, then changed her mind and handed it to Gil. 'You open it,' she said.

Gil tore open the envelope and read the letter in silence.

'They've found the plane,' he said quietly, 'or at least the wreck of it, and the remains of the crew are inside.'

'They've found Calli,' Feargie said, almost in wonder. 'After all these years, they've found him.'

Gil put the letter down and put his hand over Nancy's. There was a long silence. It was as though they were becalmed in the sunshine, the only sound, the cries of the birds around them.

'What do we do now?' Nancy asked at last.

'I don't know, Mom, what does the letter say?' Feargie asked. He picked it up, read a couple of lines then, finding he couldn't go on, he handed it to Young Padraig.

'Someone should contact this Janet Ross woman,' Young Padraig said. 'There's a number here. Should I call?' He looked at his watch. 'Just after 10 a.m., so it'll be, what? 3 p.m. there?'

Feargie nodded.

'Call this woman,' Nancy said, 'and tell her we'll make arrangements to bring Calli home.'

Janet Ross's heart sank when she heard what the Lanc skipper's brother said on the phone, it was going to be one of those ones. Briefly she explained the procedure, that there were no exceptions, it was an agreed international law, every country had to abide by it, and she did understand the family's feelings, but there was nothing anyone could do, then she braced herself for the inevitable protest. Young Padraig said he'd get back to her. There had been positive results in the search for the families of the other crew members, though details of the two gunners, one a Scot who'd just joined the crew, had to be broadcast on television before there was any response. A woman with a Scottish accent had called and asked the names of the other crew, then she had burst into tears and rung off. Sometimes it was like that, they called back once they'd composed themselves and taken it all in, though she hadn't so far.

*   *   *

'They say we can't bring him home,' Young Padraig told Nancy, Gil and Feargie.

'Did you say we'd pay?' Feargie asked.

Young Padraig nodded. 'It's some international agreement, apparently, no exceptions, he has to be buried where he was found.'

Gil nodded silently.

'He's ours,' Nancy said to him, horrified. 'When he went away that day we didn't say he belonged to the military.'

'He signed the papers, Nancy,' Gil said quietly. 'That means he signed himself over to them.'

'But it's not right!' Nancy cried. 'Why did they bother telling us they'd found him? We knew he had crashed and was buried in French soil, what difference does it make if they rebury him in French soil?'

'Look, Mom, you have a lie-down,' Feargie suggested, 'and Young Padraig and I will find a way around this, if we can.'

She wanted to say, 'Who are you talking to? Some ancient old crone?' She even wanted to give him a clip around the ear, but instead she felt suddenly weary, weak even, so she must be that old crone after all. 'OK,' she said meekly.

Over the coming days Feargie fought the battle to bring Calli home as Gil kept his own counsel; he knew this had to be gone through for Nancy's sake, but, equally, he knew what the outcome would be. Feargie looked up all the contacts he had made in his days as a surgeon, he called in every favour, but he had to admit defeat and, worse, to admit defeat to his mother.

'The RAF say they'll pay for two family members to attend the funeral in France,' he told Nancy, 'and we can have any kind of ceremony we want.'

'But not here,' she said darkly. 'Not among his own people.'

'No,' Gil murmured. 'But, Nancy, he died with his crew and he'll be laid to rest with them. All the men in the first war thought that was the right thing to do, the men of the second would've thought so, too.'

'I'm sure Gil's right, Mom,' Feargie said quietly.

'But that's the point, Feargie,' she said, annoyed with herself for being near to tears. 'My brother, Jamie, and your father's brother, Colin, never came home. I don't think your grandmother or any of the family ever resigned themselves to the fact that they were lying in some far distant land. My brother's lying in France, now my son, too.'

'Well then, Nancy,' Gil said gently, 'Calli will be in good company, won't he?'

Nancy smiled sadly; Gil was right. 'Well, I'm going over there,' she said firmly, and Feargie looked at her sharply. 'Forget it, Feargie,' she warned him, seeing what was in his mind, 'I'm not one of your patients, I'm not scared of you. If I can't see him laid to rest here at home, I'll see him laid to rest over there. And don't you dare say I'm too old to travel, just don't you dare!'

Gil looked at Feargie and laughed softly. 'You won't win, Feargie,' he said, 'and I'm going too.'

'So am I,' Feargie replied. 'Ceitlin's too near to having her baby, but what about you, Padraig?'

'He was my brother, too,' said Young Padraig, 'so I'll be there. I'm sure Val will be OK.'

'Of course you'll be coming with us!' Nancy replied. 'You've carried his name all your life, of course you'll be there to see him laid to rest. I know it's Val's first baby, but her family will be here for her, and we won't be gone long. Besides,' she smiled gently, looking at her eldest son, 'someone will have to hold Feargie's hand on the flight.'

Feargie shivered. 'I just can't believe those great heavy things can possibly stay in the sky,' he said defensively. 'I mean, it's not natural, is it?'

Nancy laughed. 'And you a man of science!' she mocked gently.

'I'm a surgeon, Mom,' Feargie smiled wryly, 'and whatever else surgeons may be, they are not men of science, believe me. They're just high-class butchers, if the truth were known.'

'But you go to all those overseas conferences,' Young Padraig laughed. 'I don't understand how you can be scared of flying yet you fly all over the world.'

'I do it in a state of mindless terror, that's how!' Feargie grimaced. 'And I'm not scared of flying, the flying bit's a fine idea, it's the thought that suddenly the aircraft will say to itself "Wait a minute – this doesn't make sense", and fall out of the sky.'

The four MacDonalds were suddenly silent, all of them thinking of Calli and his plane falling out of the sky all those years ago.

'Do you remember the time Gil took me up in the Camel, Mom?' Feargie asked, his voice quiet and gentle.

Nancy smiled and nodded.

'I panicked so much I'd have climbed out of the darned thing while it was in the air if Gil hadn't held onto me. So I compromised,' he laughed out loud, 'I threw up all over her instead!'

'And Calli was so furious that you'd made a mess of her,' Gil remembered, 'that he wanted to box your ears.'

'Yes,' Feargie nodded, looking into the distance, 'he really did love that old plane, he flew her like he was born to fly.'

'And look where it got him,' Gil said sadly. 'I often wonder what would've happened if he'd stayed in the Army instead.'

'No point in going down that road,' Nancy suggested gently.

'I know what Gil means,' Feargie murmured, 'I often think that, too. After he was lost, I was angry with him for the longest time. I kept thinking "Why the hell didn't you stay in the Army? Why the hell did you always have to push your luck, Calli?" I swear, if he'd been found safe and sound and walked up the driveway to Pine Edge, I would've welcomed him with a right hook to the jaw.'

In the quiet at the top of the hill, the family then sat in silence for a while, watching the birds flying around them.

*   *   *

Much to the RAF's disappointment, the damage to the Lancaster was too great to allow them to recover her for reconstruction. After the war, the majority of planes had been scrapped with indecent haste, people wanted to forget the long years of fear and hardship and no one thought then of conserving anything, not even a beloved Lancaster with its glorious Merlin engines, for future generations, no one even thought that those future generations might be interested. There was a Lancaster in the Battle of Britain Flight, the collection of planes that performed flyovers on special occasions, anniversaries of the end of the war and that sort of thing, but it had never flown in combat and so didn't seem 'real' somehow; a genuine Lanc with a history would have been a real find, a prize to the RAF. Still, as part of their investigation they had collected more details that were typed up and sent to the families a few weeks later. The plane had crashed in the early hours of 16 August 1943 at Beuzeval in Calvados, 1 km east of Houlgate, in France, not very far from the sea. The crew had completed a successful raid on Milan and were on the way home when the Lanc was hit by flak and set on fire, with the loss of all the crew, but the force of the impact had extinguished the fire, which was why there were so many human remains recovered.

'The crew named their Lanc "Lady Groundhog", it was still visible on the fuselage,' Feargie read, and they all laughed quietly.

'I wonder whose decision that was!' Gil said.

'Hamish is still at Pine Edge, you know,' Young Padraig smiled.

'What?' Nancy asked. 'The same groundhog?'

'Absolutely!' Young Padraig said.

'So who's that one?' Gil asked, nodding out of the window to a mound of earth in a corner of the back garden, where an odd, furry little animal stood on its hind legs and peered about. 'I thought Calli's groundhog had followed us into retirement!'

'The same one after all these years?' Feargie laughed.

'Absolutely!' Nancy mimicked her youngest son.

Young Padraig smiled. 'I think that one's the brother of the one at Pine Edge,' he said. 'Anyway, they're obviously closely related, they even look alike!'

29

In Glasgow, the sleep of the mystery Scotswoman who had called Janet Ross had been disturbed for weeks. Eileen didn't understand why she had been so affected by the news that the plane had been found after all these years; he had lain where it had crashed and now he would lie somewhere else. Maybe that was it. While the plane lay undiscovered, Calli and the boys were still officially 'missing, presumed dead', the file had remained open in her mind, but now the file would finally be closed. She realised that against all sense and logic she had been keeping him alive in her mind. He hadn't been brought back as a corpse, identified and the public burial rites gone through, so for decades he had inhabited a limbo state, remaining her young, handsome lad while she had grown older, and the truth was that she didn't want to let him go, not even now, though she knew she would have to. Eventually she called Janet Ross.

'You probably won't remember,' she said, 'but I called when you were looking for relatives of the crew of a Lancaster that had been recovered in France.'

'Oh, yes, I do remember,' Janet Ross replied. 'I wondered if you would call back once . . .'

'Yes, I'm sorry about that,' Eileen smiled over the phone. 'Your job must be hard enough without some old woman blubbing over the phone.'

'It happens all the time,' Janet Ross said kindly. 'Why shouldn't it, after all?'

Eileen closed her eyes tightly, she was still so close to tears, kindness wasn't what she needed. 'I worked with Bomber Command at Langar during the war,' she said brightly, and on the other end of the phone the young officer heard the catch in her voice and bit her lip. 'I knew most of the crew of the plane, and I wondered if friends could come to the funerals?'

'Yes, yes, of course,' Janet Ross replied. 'I'm afraid we only pay expenses for two members of each family to attend –'

'That doesn't matter, it isn't an issue.'

'Well, then, of course you can attend. If you give me a contact number I'll call you with the details when we have everything arranged.'

'That's very kind, thank you,' Eileen said, putting the receiver down quickly and subsiding into another bout of tears.

In Laycon House, Janet Ross stood with her hand still on the receiver, wondering what story lay behind the woman's grief, because she was certainly affected by the finding of the plane and her crew. You'd think it would be good news that relatives and loved ones could at last be laid to rest, but it didn't always work out like that, sometimes you almost felt guilty for stirring up emotions and memories that you couldn't really understand. It was one of the things the job had taught her. Every day she passed men and women from that era in the street, people of her parents' age, without giving them a first, never mind a second glance, at least she used to. These days she looked at them and was aware of what they had at least lived through, and she wondered what stories they had to tell that they never would, because people of her generation usually weren't interested.

They buried what was left of Calli and the crew of Lady Groundhog in Houlgate Communal Cemetery more than thirty years after their deaths, with representatives of all their families, and at the request of the MacDonalds, a piper played the lament 'The Floo'ers o' the Forest'. Eileen watched from among the crowd of people who had turned up, grateful for a place to hide. The families had opted for full-sized coffins, though there could be little of their men left to bury. Still, she thought, it concentrated the mind, emphasising that there were human beings inside, not just a collection of bones. The families all mixed easily as though they were old friends, bound together by this event, but you could tell them apart by the way they lingered near the boxes containing their boys. The old lady must be Calli's mother, and the older man, she presumed, must be Gil. And was that Feargie, his younger brother? Strange to think of Calli being older than him, but then Calli had never lived to grow older, Calli was still twenty-three, so his younger brother was now older than he would ever be. She didn't know who the other man was, but he looked disconcertingly like Calli, but Calli only had one brother. A cousin, maybe, or Feargie's son? She glanced at him again, but her mind was too full to think beyond that. Seeing them felt strange, unreal in a way, and being faced with Calli's reality brought the cover-up of the last thirty years into sharp focus. They had never met, but she knew these people, yet they didn't even know of her existence, despite the fact that they had all been part of his life and had loved him, still did. And there was Annie back home in Glasgow, she didn't know them and they didn't know her, didn't even know of her, and she had no idea that was why Eileen was really here, burying her father. All those years ago she had made the decision to hoodwink Alex into thinking Annie was his, but now she realised that she had also hoodwinked Annie, and had she had the right to do that? It had been a solution to the predicament she had been in, of being pregnant by a man she loved and couldn't marry because he was by then dead. She had only thought of her pregnancy in terms of it being a child she didn't want to abort because it was Calli's child, she hadn't looked beyond that, visualised a person with thoughts and feelings, with rights. Now here she stood, watching Calli's grieving family. She thought of herself in the same position, if she had had a son and that son had died, she knew she would have given anything to know that something of him lived on, to know his child and his grandchild; that's what she had done to these people, she had deprived them of Annie and Gavin. She had lied to her own daughter too, denied her the knowledge of her own identity; what kind of mother would do such a thing? And there was no way out, that was the awful thing, there was no way of taking from her daughter the only father she had ever known, the one who had loved her beyond everything, and replacing him with the contents of the coffin she was watching being lowered into a grave in Normandy. What would Annie think of her for deceiving her for all these years over something as fundamental as this, she wondered, and a shiver of horror ran through her body as she imagined the hurt and anger in her eyes if she ever found out. Eileen couldn't bear that; Annie was everything to her, she couldn't bear her disappointment and disapproval. She looked up and made eye contact with Calli's mother for a fleeting second as the old lady glanced around at the crowd of mourners, and they exchanged a brief, tight smile. Eileen put her hand over her mouth to stifle a sob, understanding for the first time the full consequences of what she had done. Beside her a woman patted her arm. Eileen turned and looked at her, a small woman about her own age who, by the looks of her, had been darkly pretty in her youth. She didn't know her, so she was a kindly woman as well to offer comfort to a stranger. As the final tones of the Last Post sounded, a sigh rippled around the tiny cemetery. It was over. The painful, sad thing that had brought them all here had finally ended and they stood in little groups, talking and weeping. The woman who had patted Eileen's arm slipped her own through Eileen's and led her a few steps to the side.

'You don't recognise me,' she said, staring into Eileen's eyes.

Eileen shook her head. There was something familiar about her smile and the way she held her head to the side, but that was all.

'I'm not asking you,' the little woman chuckled, 'I'm telling you! I'm Pearl. I started in the tower at Langar around the time you got married. After that I suppose you were worried about your husband and then there was the baby to think about, so we never really got to know each other.'

Suddenly Eileen remembered the day she told Daisy she was pregnant. Daisy had been lecturing a bunch of new arrivals and was worried about one in particular: Pearl. 'Yes,' she said. 'I remember

Daisy warning your bunch off aircrew. She did it to every new intake, but she felt she had to protect you most of all.'

'Did she? She terrified the hell out of me, I remember that!' Pearl said.

'She terrified the hell out of everyone,' Eileen said, 'but she really did have a good heart.'

'I was due to go on a date with one of the new gunners when he came back from that last mission,' Pearl said wistfully. 'I was too scared to tell her, and he didn't come back, of course, so she never did find out. I was on duty with her the night the plane was lost. She ran off to tell you before you heard from someone else.' She looked at Eileen. 'You had gone out with one of the crew a couple of times, hadn't you?'

'Yes,' Eileen replied, 'a couple of times.'

There was a silence.

'That's why I came, too,' Pearl said softly. 'I never really knew that young gunner, he'd just arrived at the base, but I remember those days and the people more vividly than any others in my entire life.'

'I think we all feel that,' Eileen said. 'Those years were the most intense of our lives. We faced the life and death thing every day. We never really lived so fully again, did we?'

Pearl shook her head. 'I saw the appeal for relatives on TV,' she said, 'and I thought, 'Well, I *nearly* knew him, so I'll go over there and say a proper goodbye. He deserved that, I thought . . . silly really, when you think about it.'

'No, no,' Eileen protested, grasping her hand, 'it's not the least bit silly. I often think back on those boys and remember how special they were, all of them.'

Pearl nodded again in agreement.

'We were there, we *have* to remember them.'

'You're right,' Pearl said and threw her arms around Eileen. 'But isn't it strange to think of Daisy of all people remembering them, too?'

Eileen looked around. 'Daisy?' she said, puzzled. 'Daisy's here?'

'No,' Pearl laughed, 'maybe that would be expecting too much, but she sent a wreath of white roses for each of them. I suppose she saw it on TV the same as us, but who'd have thought it of Daisy, eh?'

Eileen had noticed the wreaths earlier and assumed the RAF had arranged them. 'Daisy sent them?' she asked, bemused.

'Yes, strange, isn't it?' Pearl replied. 'There can only be *one* Daisy, can't there?'

Eileen walked forward to examine the flowers. Bruiser's wreath had a Maple Leaf, one had a blue and white saltire, and the others had red and white crosses of St George. Attached to Calli's flowers was the same Canadian flag and a ribbon of MacDonald tartan. Daisy had remembered them all, even the new gunners she never knew. There was a card on Calli's flowers, inscribed 'For the lovely boy, and all the other lovely boys. Daisy.' Eileen was almost overcome with affection for her old friend.

'We were so close,' she murmured. 'We promised to stay in touch yet we never did. I've always regretted that. I wonder what became of her.'

'Well, all I know is that she got married,' Pearl sighed.

'*Daisy?*' Eileen gasped. 'Daisy *got married?*'

'Yes, I know,' Pearl laughed. 'That's what I thought. I saw it in the WAAF Association booklet. Someone had written in asking if anyone knew what had become of her after she married. Could've knocked me down with a feather, but maybe she found one who was *so* rich she couldn't turn him down!'

On a whim Eileen copied down the address of the florist on the back of the card attached to Calli's flowers and then the two women exchanged adresses and telephone numbers and vowed to stay in touch.

'This time we have to *mean* it,' Pearl said, hugging Eileen as they parted, 'and we should try to find Daisy.'

'Yes,' Eileen said firmly. 'Yes.'

At the other side of the cemetery Nancy stood with her sons, leaning on Gil's arm, looking at all the people who had come along, wondering which were representing organisations and which were relatives or friends. Despite losing her fight to bring Calli home, she was touched that he and the lads would be lying among some of the people they were fighting to liberate from German occupation. Now that she saw the reality, it did indeed seem fitting somehow. Behind where they now lay together was another row of graves from the First World War, Moroccan soldiers, they discovered, who had been gassed accidentally by their own side. Gil shook his head in surprise; remembering a similar incident that had happened near the Cape Breton lads in the early years of the first war. When they had said their goodbyes to Calli and were preparing to leave the cemetery, a woman approached.

'I'm sorry to bother you,' Eileen said uncertainly, 'but I understand you are Mrs MacDonald, Calli's mother? I worked with Bomber Command and I knew your son.'

Nancy looked up and smiled, remembering how they had caught each other's eyes earlier, then she took Eileen's hand and held it between both of hers.

'He really was a wonderful young man,' Eileen continued, 'everyone liked him. I just wanted you to know that.'

'That's very kind,' Nancy replied. 'This is my husband, Gil, and my son, Fearghus, Calli's younger brother, and his much younger brother, Padraig Calum. His sister, Ceitlin, couldn't make the trip, she's expecting her second baby any day now.'

Eileen shook hands with them all, meeting their eyes in turn.

'They call me Young Padraig,' the much younger brother grinned.

Looking into his face she suddenly realised that up close there was a strong resemblance not only to Calli, but to Annie as well.

'I'm Eileen MacLean,' she smiled nervously. 'During the war I worked in the tower, I was a wireless op.'

'Would you like to have a coffee, Mrs MacLean?' Feargie asked, partly out of courtesy, but also because this woman had seen Calli long after his family had, she was a link to those last days they never got to share with him.

Eileen looked uncertain.

'Please,' Nancy smiled encouragingly. 'We have to go back through the village anyway, and I know Gil and I would welcome something warm and a chance to sit down.'

So there she was, in the midst of Calli's family, knowing how much she could say, wondering how not to say it, and trying to avoid looking at his younger brother in case she stared. How could she have missed his likeness to her daughter, she wondered, to Calli's daughter?

They climbed into the car Feargie had hired and drove the short distance to the village, between high hedges with wonderfully Gothic homes beyond. Some of them were huge chateaux, built at a time when families were larger as well as richer but which were now in varying states of gentle decay, like elderly ladies declining in genteel poverty, but determined to wear their best gowns till they fell apart.

'I've never come across roads like these in Normandy,' Feargie muttered. 'They undulate every way, up and down and across, it's an adventure just getting from one place to another.'

They passed the town hall, a typically fairytale confection, and on through the village, stopping at a café near the outskirts, beside a shop selling tacky tourist merchandise, with plastic buckets and spades, postcards and cheap trinkets, spilling onto the pavement and hanging on the shop frontage from anywhere a hook or a piece of string could be attached.

'You always expect the French to have such good taste, don't you?' Feargie smiled. 'But this is as bad as what's grown up around Niagara Falls.'

'In England, Blackpool is the epitome of tat,' Eileen replied, 'but I honestly don't think it's any worse than the Scottish seaside resorts I know, there's just more of it there.'

There was a silence.

'The other thing that surprises me,' Eileen said brightly, 'and I don't know if you've noticed, is that you don't have to stop for people on pedestrian crossings, which seems strange. I was crossing the road the other day and by the look in the eyes of the drivers they seemed to be daring me.'

'You don't have to stop at crossings?' Young Padraig asked.

'No,' Eileen laughed quietly. 'Look, there's one behind you.'

They all turned around to watch pedestrians risking their lives on the striped road, dashing across as brakes screeched.

'Why do they bother having crossings?' Young Padraig mused.

'I've been wondering the same thing since I arrived,' Eileen replied. 'I still can't work it out.' With his profile to her she looked at him, thinking that he must be around Annie's age, then she looked away in confusion. 'But if you do knock them down it's still your fault, apparently. It's just that you have the choice whether to do it or not, it's not really about pedestrian safety.' She laughed, surprised that her voice sounded so normal.

'Have you seen Paris?' Feargie asked.

Eileen shook her head.

'I was over at a medical conference once, and I sat on the Champs-Elysées for an hour,' he laughed, 'it was the funniest thing I ever saw, like watching a Keystone Kops movie. They don't obey any rules, they just weave in and out of lanes inches from each other, and they stop to chat to each other on roundabouts, it's amazing. I saw at least six collisions, but the French don't get angry like we do, they just jump out of their cars, exchange details, then jump back in and drive on with a friendly wave of the hand, till the next one. All the cars have bumps and dents in them, no one seems to worry.'

'You made it,' Eileen thought. 'You did become a doctor.' Then she said to Feargie 'So you're a doctor? My son-in-law is a doctor, an anaesthetist, he works at the Western Infirmary in Glasgow quite near to where we live.'

'Really?' Feargie replied. 'What a small world. We had an old family friend who worked there, another Dr MacDonald, he died several years ago unfortunately. He would've wanted to be here today, he was very fond of Calli. His son is a doctor, I think he works in the same hospital.'

Eileen remembered Calli talking about old Dr MacDonald and their trip to Raasay and Skye a few years before he died, but she couldn't mention that; there was so much she couldn't mention.

When they had exhausted every other topic they came to the one that had brought them all together in this foreign land. Eileen explained about her wartime job in the tower at Langar, and how she had spoken to Calli many times on the air long before she met him, then their actual meeting, when he cursed the Adjutant in Gaelic. Because of her Irish Gaelic-speaking grandparents, she explained, she had understood enough of what he was saying to know it wasn't praise. She told them about Bruiser, who was perfectly amiable but reserved the right to thump those who annoyed him, and how he had hoodwinked Calli into drinking cider, telling him it wasn't alcoholic, and how Calli got merry and cursed the Adjutant with even more gusto. Gil and Nancy smiled at the picture of their innocent lad she was bringing to life. Then Eileen told them about the incident weeks before Lady Groundhog was lost, when the plane had been badly damaged and two of the crew were injured, and how Calli had brought her and them safely home.

'We watched them from the tower,' she laughed. 'They tumbled out of the plane onto the runway, laughing and wrestling with each other, and then they lay on the concrete, smoking and shouting cheerful insults. Then they got up and went off to their hut, their arms around each other. They were so young.' She lowered her eyes. 'So very young.'

'Did he have many friends?' Gil asked.

'His crew, mainly,' she replied. 'They were all like that, crews really were as close as family, they'd do anything for each other.'

'And there was no girl?' his mother asked.

'There wasn't much time for that,' Eileen said evasively. 'It was pretty intensive stuff, they were either flying or getting ready to fly. The only girls they really met were WAAFs, and every

WAAF knew better than to get involved with aircrew, and anyway, most of us had sweethearts back home, as I did myself. I got married before my husband went abroad on active service; luckily he came back, though he was a different man.' She held her breath as she sipped her coffee, wondering if she'd negotiated the thin ice convincingly.

Nancy exchanged a look with Gil, smiling sadly. 'It was the same in the first war,' she said, nodding. 'Calli and Feargie's father never recovered from that one.'

'I spend a lot of time travelling since I was widowed a few years ago,' Eileen explained. 'It was a bit of a relief, to be honest, though I shouldn't say so.'

'I know what you mean,' Nancy said softly. 'Young Padraig here never knew his brother,' she explained. 'I was widowed not long after Calli died and later married Gil, my husband's cousin. He was the one who taught Calli to fly as a boy.'

Eileen nodded. 'I know,' she thought, trying not to betray that she had heard all the names and was familiar with the circumstances.

'Calli never lived to see us married,' Nancy continued. 'So he never knew Young Padraig here, or his sister back home.'

Once again Eileen bit her tongue, as she thought, 'But he'd have been happy about it, really he would.' She thought about saying how affectionately Calli had always spoken of Gil, but stopped herself in time; that would have shown a closer relationship than she wanted them to know about.

'I've been hearing about him all my life,' Young Padraig grinned, 'so I feel like I know him.'

Eileen felt a great pressure welling up inside her, as though she was losing control of her carefully constructed alternative story and it was about to burst forth, so she decided to bring the meeting to an end, citing travel plans as her excuse.

'Well, thank you for giving us your time,' Nancy said, embracing her. 'It was kind of you. It's brought him closer, my dear, filled in some of the gaps after he left home.'

Eileen felt overcome with another wave of guilt and emotion.

Here was Calli's mother thanking her, yet she was deceiving her by keeping from her not only his daughter and grandson, but the everyday, minor events in the months before he died that she knew they hungered for. Only someone who had shared them would have those details; she had them, but if she disclosed them too much might unravel. She had to keep all of that to herself, but she was aware that she was keeping something precious from his mother and the rest of his family.

They exchanged addresses before they parted and Nancy invited Eileen to visit them at home. 'You should see Canada,' she smiled. 'We would all be happy to see a friend of Calli's any time, and a Scot would be doubly welcome.'

Eileen felt flustered. 'He was a fine young man,' she said in a tearful rush. 'I know everyone says that, but he was, they all were, every one of them.' What she wanted to do was apologise for what she had done, albeit with the best of intentions, but she couldn't, so after returning Nancy's embrace and shaking hands with Gil and Calli's brothers, she made her goodbyes, turned and quickly walked away, her eyes blinded by tears.

Nancy watched her go. So the loss of her boy was still affecting people he had briefly known all those years ago, she thought. All mothers think their sons are special, of course, but maybe Calli really was. She couldn't believe how badly she herself was affected; her boy had been dead for over thirty years, yet she had just buried him. Somehow it felt as raw as if he had died days before, and just as obscene, too; mothers shouldn't bury their children. Her arm was through Gil's and, sensing her emotions, he put his free hand over hers and squeezed it.

'You know what I was thinking?' he asked. 'About old Dr MacDonald in Glasgow. What a pity he didn't live to be here, he had such affection for the lad.'

Nancy nodded. 'He was a good friend,' she agreed. 'I wish Mother could've been here, too. I remember looking at her at

Neil's funeral all those years after the first war, and the expression on her face that said "Why not me? I'd have gone instead". It's only now that I truly understand how she felt.'

Gil nodded; there was nothing to say.

'You remember when I went home to Mull River after Calli was lost?'

Gil nodded again.

'Well my mother told me I'd hear of Calli again one day, she said it was a feeling she had and I got angry with her, told her I'd had enough of her Second Sight nonsense.'

'As you always did,' Gil smiled thoughtfully.

'True,' Nancy laughed. 'Now here I am, an old crone in my seventies with a son in his fifties, and I can finally say she was right all along, yet I felt so embarrassed by her while I was growing up.'

'I'm sure all children feel that about their parents,' Gil laughed. 'We don't know what we have till it's too late to appreciate it.'

'I suppose that's life, oh wise one,' Nancy mocked.

'Anyway,' Gil said, 'she knew you understood.'

'You think so?'

'Of course she did,' Gil replied reassuringly. 'Looking back I think she knew everything.'

Nancy nodded. 'There were things I never told her, though, things I should've said.'

'She knew that, too,' Gil said.

'What?'

'That you loved her.'

'I should still have told her,' Nancy smiled sadly. 'But you're right, she would have known anyway, Martha of all people. I still wish I had said it, though.'

'If wishes were fishes,' Gil sighed.

'What?' she demanded, laughing up at him.

'It's an old saying of your mother's, you would've refused to register it, being the uppity madam you were,' he said. 'If wishes were fishes we'd all cast nets in the sea.'

Nancy rolled her eyes. 'Yes,' she said, 'nice and mystical. It certainly sounds like one of my mother's!'

Before they returned to Canada, Janet Ross had some things of Calli's to give to his family. First there was one of his dog tags, the other had been buried with him, then his medals, but there was nothing to mark his exploits with Bomber Command. By as early as the end of the war a grateful nation was ashamed of what the men of Bomber Command had done and there was no word of thanks, nor a single mention in any of Churchill's eloquent speeches, far less battle honours for Bomber Harris, the young men who died and the few who had lived. Finally, there was the one thing that had identified Calli's remains beyond doubt: the gold signet ring with the MacDonald clan crest that Gil had given him the day he left for the war. A look of pain passed over Gil's face when he saw it. Seeing it took him back to their last parting at the railway station all those years ago; it seemed strange to be seeing it, touching it again. Nancy looked at her husband in surprise.

'I thought you'd lost it,' she said, remembering noticing it had disappeared from Gil's finger at the time.

'I gave it to him before he left,' he said quietly, turning the ring in his hand. 'I hoped it would bring him safely home again.'

'Well, he's given it back to you,' Nancy smiled gently. 'Put it on again. He would want that.'

On the flight home, Feargie sat rigidly in his seat across from Gil and Nancy, his face white with fear.

'Would you look at the state of him,' Nancy said to Gil, shaking her head.

'Why don't you try to sleep?' Gil asked him.

'Then I'd miss the aircraft realising it was doing something impossible,' he replied tightly.

Then Nancy dozed off. She slept nearly all the way home, dreaming of them all, her grandfather, Ruairidh Beag, her parents and her brothers, of Donald and Calli, all branches of the tree that had lived, dimmed and died. Only Calli's still hadn't. She had seen him buried, knew and accepted beyond a shadow of a doubt that it was him, yet in her mind his branch was alive.

30

On the plane home from France Eileen dozed, her mind filled with images and memories. She thought about Daisy sending flowers, of her thoughtfulness towards the aircrew all these years on when she had made it her purpose in life to keep them away from 'her' girls. Eileen had always known there was a sensitive side to Daisy, but it was so deeply hidden; what could possibly have mellowed her to this extent? She had obviously gone out of her way to make sure the flowers were perfect, and then there was the card. When she had told Daisy she was pregnant all those years ago she had asked, 'The lovely boy?', meaning Calli, and there it was again on the card. She swallowed hard, wondering how she could have lost touch with her. She knew how, of course; Daisy had been part of the life she had had to put behind her in order to protect her secret. And Daisy married – she could hardly believe it. The flowers could be traced, she thought, she could find Daisy again, but for the moment she would have to clear her mind before the plane landed or Annie would spot the redness around her eyes and the air of sadness surrounding her. She was always good at sensing that kind of thing, Annie. Even as a small child she picked up feelings and moods no matter how you tried to hide them.

At that moment Annie was rushing around the kitchen, trying to get Gavin to eat his breakfast so that they could set off for the airport to meet Eileen. The latest trip had been to France, though it was easy to lose track of where on the globe Eileen was at any given moment. Gavin was being particularly annoying, finding distractions, taking too much time to do everything, and he was irritable, too. She felt his forehead, wondering if he might be coming down with something, and he squirmed away from her, screwing up his face in annoyance. She shrugged, supposing it was reasonable behaviour for a nearly four-year-old boy; things would improve once he saw the planes at the airport, if there was one thing guaranteed to perk him up it was the sight of a plane.

'Gavin,' she said, 'what is wrong with you this morning? You know we have to be quick, that Granny Eileen is coming home.'

The little boy pulled a face.

'And you'll see the planes,' she wheedled, trying to brush his curly hair. 'You know you like planes.'

'Planes are silly,' he said sullenly.

'Since when?' she laughed. 'And Granny Eileen will have a present for you, so be a good boy and hurry up.'

'Don't want a present,' he protested, slapping his spoon down on his bowl of cereal, sending milk and soggy cornflakes splashing around.

'Well I don't want that mess everywhere, so stop it,' she chided.

Gavin put the spoon down and sat with his hands in his lap, staring at the bowl as though it was his worst enemy. Annie tried again; life was easier when he was in a good mood.

'What is it?' she asked gently. 'Tell Mummy.'

He got off his chair and climbed onto her knee, allowing her to fold her arms around him.

'He's gone,' he said simply.

'Who has?' Annie asked. 'Daddy? Is that why you're in such a bad mood? He's just gone to work, silly, he'll be back as usual tonight!'

'No!' Gavin shouted, striking out with one hand. 'You're being silly! The man, he's gone!'

'I don't know what you mean,' she said. 'Man? What man?'

'The man in the corner of my room, silly!' he shouted again, then he buried his head in her chest. 'He's not there any more,' he protested, the words muffled against her. 'I've looked everywhere, but he's not there, he's gone!'

Annie sat holding her son, her heart beating hard in her chest, her mind in turmoil. The man in the corner of his room, that's what he'd said. Her mouth felt dry. She reached one shaking hand out for a glass of orange juice, holding her son tightly on her knee with the other.

'Gavin,' she said quietly. 'What man in the corner of your room?'

'You know!' he replied, pulling himself back from her to look into her face, the little line between his eyes deepening with irritation.

So what was she supposed to do now, she wondered. Tell him he was making it up, that he had an imaginary friend that no one else could see and that that was OK, a lot of people had them, she'd had one herself? She'd be lying to him if she did that, or half-lying at least. She looked at the clock; they were pushed for time as it was.

'Gavin,' she said gently. 'Could we maybe talk about this after we pick Granny Eileen up from the airport?'

Gavin didn't reply.

'Besides, maybe he'll have come back when we come home again,' she said brightly.

'He won't!' Gavin shouted. 'I've just told you, he's gone!'

'Yes, yes, all right,' she said, trying to calm him down. 'But we'll talk about it when we come home with Granny Eileen, OK? Now, quickly, get your jacket and, Gavin, don't say anything to Granny Eileen about the man. It'll be our secret.'

What on earth was she doing swearing her son to secrecy? She had been determined she wouldn't have secrets, all her childhood she had felt she had been a prisoner of whatever secrets had divided her parents, now here she was forcing them onto her son.

All the way to the airport her mind was racing. Gavin could see the man in the corner and he knew, absolutely knew, that she saw him, too. And he had gone, she knew that, too, she hadn't seen him recently either. Not that that was significant, he had never been there every minute of every day, but she hadn't felt him there, that was the difference now; even when she hadn't seen him, she had always known he was there, but Gavin was right, he had gone. She cast her mind back to when Gavin was a baby and recalled how he would look behind her and gurgle to himself. 'You'd swear he was seeing something we can't,' her mother used to say. 'You were just the same, Annie.' At the time Annie had nodded; she knew perfectly well what she had been looking at, but even so, it simply hadn't entered her head that her son was seeing the same thing – the same person. Thoughts crowded her mind, thoughts she'd left unattached to each other probably, she realised now, because she hadn't wanted to connect them. As a toddler, Gavin would sing sometimes in what sounded like garbled words. All children did that, of course, they made sounds as they learned to speak, dadada, mamama, then abadabadaba, the noises parents liked to believe were actually words but weren't, they were just the easy first sounds all babies made. They picked things up from people around them, too, and from the television, but she had noticed little snatches of melody she remembered singing herself and wondered if he had heard them from her. Maybe she had sung them about the house without realising it, of course Gavin could have learned them that way, but she couldn't remember doing so. The man had sung them to her when she was a baby, she had never told anyone that, and the words weren't garbled, they were proper words, only not English words, they were Gaelic, she had known that for a long time, and to this day she still knew those words, though there was no reason why she should, except for the man in the corner.

She looked at Gavin in the rear-view mirror as she drove along, wondering how she was supposed to deal with this, her mind racing. Past the BBC and the Botanic Gardens in Queen Margaret Drive, trying to make up time, then down Byres Road.

'Look, Gavin,' she said excitedly, pointing to the Western Infirmary on Church Street, 'that's where Daddy is.' She waved a hand and shouted brightly 'Hello, Daddy!' as they always did, but this time Gavin only gave a token silent wave towards the grey building, instead of his usual happy yell and boisterous gestures.

Across Dumbarton Road, heading for the Clyde Expressway and the Clyde Tunnel. 'And there's the hospital where you were born,' she called, looking towards the Queen Mother's Maternity up on the hill to the left, but Gavin couldn't have cared less. Maybe he really was coming down with something, she thought, the hand on the forehead method of gauging temperature wasn't exactly spot-on accurate, or maybe she was making far too much out of this. Still, the last thing she wanted was for him to say something about the man to her mother. She needed time to think, to find an acceptable way of making sure he didn't, but how was she supposed to do that? Through the tunnel. She hadn't intended using the tunnel, he had always hated it, he got restless being closed in, but because of the earlier tantrum she hadn't any choice, so she was relieved and surprised when he didn't seem to register it this time. 'Nearly at the airport, look, there's a big plane coming down!' Gavin dipped his head to see under the roof of the car and gave the British Midland jet a cursory glance, then went back to looking out of the side window again, his little face irritated.

When they reached the car park he didn't want to get out of the car, so there was another mini-tantrum over that, and time was passing. Luckily the flight was late — weren't they always? — and Annie chided herself for expecting anything else. Maybe that was what was wrong with him, she thought, he was a little under the weather and she had hassled him when he wasn't feeling up to it. Yes, that's what it had been; she had blown the whole thing out of proportion. There was no time to think up a diversion, so now she'd have to bribe him into good behaviour, good *silent* behaviour, till she had collected and delivered her mother and they were home on their own again. Dear God — bribe him! She shook her head and frowned; another parental promise to herself gone.

Gavin perked up when he saw Eileen. How come, Annie wondered, smiling to herself, grandparents were so much more demonstrative with their grandchildren than they ever were with their children? Not that Eileen was cold, but the way she swept this little boy into her arms and smothered him with hugs and kisses, well, it was different, that was all. She watched them together, thinking how much happier her mother was these days, and freer; maybe that was the key, she was free to be herself, free from whatever anxiety had stopped her before, free from Alex. She was in her fifties, but she was still a good-looking woman, especially now that the worry and stress lines had softened, it would be nice to see her happy with some nice man, though Annie doubted that would happen; what Eileen now had she wouldn't be in any hurry to give up again, Annie reasoned. She had brought Gavin a model plane, something that always went down well, but she wasn't sure today, and there was a bottle of Calvados, the apple brandy of Normandy, for David, and Calvados liqueur chocolates for Annie.

'So they're big on apples?' Annie teased her as she drove home-wards, relieved to hear plane noises coming from Gavin in the back seat.

'You should see the open fruit flans,' Eileen replied. 'I tell you, just looking at them makes your mouth water.'

'And was it a good break? I mean, did you see much in a week?'

'Yes, it was worth going, I think,' Eileen said evenly. 'I'd always wanted to see France, and the Eiffel Tower was worth it on its own, except for this officious woman who worked there, yelling her head off at everyone in the queue to keep moving, a rude creature. I gave her one of my stares and said, rather imperiously "*Je ne pas parle français*". I hope it was right!'

'Isn't it *parle pas*?' Annie smiled, she could just imagine her mother's dismissive look.

'I have no idea,' Eileen said, 'but she must've got the general idea, it shut her up at any rate.'

'So where's next?' Annie asked.

Eileen shrugged. 'To tell the truth I'm not thinking that far ahead just now, I'm feeling a bit low in fact, in need of my own bed, I think.'

'Anything wrong, or are you just tired?'

'I think I might have picked something up, I feel a bit achy and shivery,' Eileen said.

'I think Gavin's coming down with something, too,' Annie said. 'What a palaver getting him through breakfast and out this morning. I think I should put both of you down for a sleep when we get home,' she smiled.

'That's my plan,' Eileen sighed, 'a cuppa and a bun and a couple of hours in bed.'

Annie didn't reply, but she sighed with relief inwardly; she wouldn't have to worry about Gavin repeating his earlier performance in front of her mother, not yet, anyway.

Back home, she gave Gavin a spoonful of Calpol, put him to bed and read to him till he fell asleep, then she stood by his bedroom window and thought. He was right, *she* was right, there was no feeling of the man, he had gone, and if Gavin was feeling off-colour it was natural that he should want whatever or whoever comforted him. Still, with any luck, when he wakened again the moment would have passed. Still, it was an odd feeling being without the man in the corner, she had never been without him herself in her entire life. So was he imaginary? she wondered. Was she now, with husband and son to care for, to consider herself an adult? Was that why he had gone? Yet Gavin had been aware of him, too, so how did that work, exactly? Some kind of ESP, something he had tuned in to via his mother? It was certainly possible, she imagined, they spent so much time together. She looked around the room. It had been her bedroom once, the bedroom from which she had seen Stuart all those years ago, so what was that all about? It *was* Stuart that day, she could hear the scrunching of his feet on the gravel driveway getting louder as he came nearer to the door. She had looked through the glass at him only a foot or so away, then she had turned her head to shout to her mother and, when she turned back, there was no Stuart. All the strange little things that had happened throughout her life, the feelings and sensations no one else seemed aware of, the dark clouds – whatever all that was she didn't want it for Gavin. Thinking of dark clouds she suddenly froze and thought of Gavin asleep behind her and of her mother in the flat below, then sighed. No, there were no clouds over them. As she closed the curtains she saw the trees swaying in the slight breeze outside and smiled. Even the trees were healthy, not a dim branch in sight.

Two days later, Gavin and Eileen were restored to full health and, Annie was happy to note, not another word had been uttered about the man in the corner. They were downstairs with Eileen having lunch, his favourite sausages and beans or, as Gavin called them, 'sosiboys and beans', when he looked at her suddenly and said, 'He still isn't there.'

'Who, Gavin?' Eileen asked, trying to slip some brown buttered bread onto his plate unnoticed.

'The man,' he said. He looked at his mother. 'You promised he'd come back,' he said accusingly, 'but he hasn't.' He pushed the brown bread off his plate.

'I didn't promise,' Annie replied, 'I only said he might.'

'Well he hasn't. Why hasn't he?'

Eileen looked from one to the other and back again. 'Who are we talking about?' she laughed.

'The man,' Gavin repeated.

Eileen looked at Annie, who shook her head slightly. 'His imaginary friend,' she whispered.

Eileen clapped her hands and laughed. 'Oh, your mummy had an imaginary friend, didn't you, Annie?'

'Yes,' Annie replied tersely. 'Lots of people have special friends that only they can see, Gavin, they go away when you grow up.' She felt like an assassin.

'I don't want him to go away,' Gavin protested.

'But it means you're a big boy now,' Eileen said encouragingly.

'I don't want to be a big boy!' he said, his voice rising. 'I want the man back!'

'Look, Gavin, can we talk about this later?' Annie said while thinking, 'Why are you speaking like this to a child of four?'

'You said we'd talk about him before, but we didn't,' he said accusingly.

'Well, that was because you weren't feeling well and went to bed for a sleep, wasn't it? We will this time, I promise. Now don't make a fuss, you know Granny Eileen's just home, be nice.'

Gavin stared at her till she felt her cheeks burn under his gaze, then he turned away abruptly and continued with his lunch, but he hadn't forgotten the conversation and when lunch was over he sat on the floor with his crayons and colouring-in books as Eileen and Annie chatted.

'That's what he looks like,' he said, getting up. He ripped a page out of one of his books and handed it to his mother while staring into her eyes, as though daring her to deny it.

'It's a very good drawing,' she said cheerfully, and her heart fell, because it was. 'Now draw something else.'

Gavin stood in front of her and as she tried to hand his drawing over he pushed it firmly back into her hands. 'He's got furry boots with big zips,' he said seriously, pointing to the figure in the drawing, 'and a furry jacket.'

'Yes, I see that,' Annie said brightly. 'How about a plane? You like drawing planes.' She could've bitten her tongue off.

'And he has this shiny hat thing with a strap, but he doesn't always wear it, and big gloves and a funny thing around his neck. Look.' He pointed at the picture. 'He's got a mask thing, like the ones Daddy uses at work. He's got a nice smile, and smiley eyes, too.' He looked into his mother's eyes. 'Like Mummy's,' he said, 'and very curly hair,' he said, his gaze moving upwards from Annie's eyes to her hair.

Eileen joined the discussion. 'What a lovely drawing!' she enthused in a grandmotherly voice.

'He used to sing to me,' Gavin said sadly, 'I used to hear him, it was nice, but he never talked and now he's gone away.'

'Oh, look, Gavin,' Eileen enthused, 'he's got hair like yours,' and she winked at Annie.

The child's hand holding the crayon went to his hair and he fiddled with a lock. 'And Mummy's,' he said.

'And those are very interesting clothes,' Eileen said, in the interested tone adults always use when pretending to treat children as equals. 'Now why do you think he's wearing those?'

'Because he flies planes,' Gavin replied calmly.

Annie felt as though invisible feet were marching towards the three of them, feet she couldn't stop because she couldn't see them. 'Well, what else would Gavin's friend do?' she said cheerfully to Eileen to hide the panic. 'You know how he loves planes.'

There was a silence. She looked sideways at her mother and saw Eileen still holding the drawing, her face suddenly frozen mid-smile, but it wasn't the childish, indistinct drawing she recognised, Annie sensed, it was the description. In that split second she knew her mother recognised the man, and yet somehow she wasn't as shocked as she thought she should be.

'Yes,' Eileen said slowly. 'Yes.'

'Tell you what,' Annie said, 'what if I help you to draw a plane like the one Granny Eileen brought you back from France?'

'It's not the one the man drives,' Gavin said uncertainly.

'Well, you know, I think your friend must be very clever, I'm sure he could drive any plane he wanted, don't you?'

Gavin nodded, half-convinced.

'I am a manipulative, deceitful mother!' Annie thought desperately, aware that her own mother was still staring silently into the distance behind them.

Annie started the new drawing, forcing the pace and increasing the detail, using every trick she knew to take her son's attention away from the man. When she looked up again, Eileen had taken the lunch things into the kitchen and was busy washing them and putting them away.

'I think I'll take him upstairs, Mum,' Annie said, leaning Gavin across to hug his grandmother. 'He still needs a nap in the afternoons.'

'Yes,' Eileen replied, 'of course,' both of them aware that Gavin usually slept in Eileen's bed after they had lunch together. It felt false, contrived, as though they were dancing around each other while trying to pretend that they weren't.

Upstairs, Annie put Gavin down for his sleep, still clutching his drawing, and sat thinking, or trying to. There had been an opportunity, she told herself, there was a chance there to say 'Actually, Mum . . .' but she hadn't taken it. Why? Why was she so afraid of her mother finding out about the man in the corner and all those odd things that had happened throughout her life? It was the stress in the house, she reasoned, instinct had told her that the situation between her parents had been, well, odd, and like all children, she wanted to keep life as it was because it was all she knew and what she didn't know could very well be considerably worse.

'Yes, very good, Annie,' she said to herself, 'very noble, but that wasn't all, was it?' There was a connection between her mother and the man, she didn't know how she knew that, but deep inside she had always known, even if she hadn't — still didn't — want to acknowledge it. Even when she had been a child she had felt a sadness about her mother, a feeling she couldn't put into words, a look in Eileen's blue eyes that suggested something; she'd thought of it many times, but she couldn't work out what she thought she saw there because it slipped away from her before she could isolate it. Was that what she had been doing all these years? Protecting her mother from the sadness she saw in her eyes? And even if it was, how did she bridge that now, a habit of thirty years, and who was to say her mother wanted it bridged? What if Eileen denied it all, blanked her, just thought Annie was slightly mad, what would that do to their relationship? Just then she heard a tap at the door and jumped; she knew who it was, that was why she was afraid.

'Come in, Mum!'

Eileen walked across the sitting-room floor and sat across from Annie. 'Is he asleep?' she asked, rubbing her hands together.

'Yes,' Annie smiled. 'You all right?'

Eileen nodded. There was a long, deep distance between them.

'What is it, Mum?' Annie asked kindly, leaning forward and taking her mother's hands. 'They're frozen!' she said, rubbing them between her own.

'I've just been washing up, remember?' Eileen smiled, but Annie saw that she was hunching her shoulders, pulling herself inwards as though feeling a chill.

They watched each other.

'Annie,' Eileen said, 'about France, I wasn't quite truthful. It wasn't just one of my trips, I was there for the burial of a friend.'

'Oh.'

'Someone I knew a long time ago, thirty-one years ago, in fact.' She looked away. 'This is very difficult, Annie,' she said, her voice full of tears. 'What I think I'm about to tell you may hurt you so badly and I don't want to do that, but I've been thinking and thinking and I feel I can't not tell you, so please forgive me for what I'm about to say.'

Annie felt terrified. 'You're OK, aren't you?' she asked. 'You're not ill or anything?'

Eileen shook her head. 'No,' she smiled tightly, 'it's nothing like that. It's about you and . . .'

'And the man in the corner?' Annie said in a small voice. 'Who is he, Mum?' she asked. 'I know you recognised who Gavin was talking about, so did I, he's been around me all my life.'

'*All* your life?'

Annie nodded.

'You never said.'

'No.'

'Why?'

'Because I didn't know what it was like not to have him there. I didn't know that other people couldn't see him, and even if they didn't I liked having him there, I didn't want anyone to do anything that would perhaps take him away.'

'You weren't afraid?'

'No!' Annie laughed quietly. 'I didn't know Gavin saw him till the day you were coming home, he wanted to know where the man was and why he'd gone. I'd like to know that, too. I know other people will think this is very peculiar, but for me and for Gavin it's perfectly natural.'

'He was your father,' Eileen said at last, not looking at her.

Annie nodded.

'You don't seem very shocked, I thought you'd be terribly upset.'

'I don't feel shocked or not shocked, I can't explain why, it's just a feeling I've always had about him, I felt he belonged, even if I didn't know how or why.'

'Your father,' Eileen said, 'Alex – he never knew, he adored you, you know that.'

'And I loved him, Mum, he was my father, but there were things that bothered me. I remember once hearing someone say I looked like him and I stood in front of a mirror and stared and stared, and I knew I didn't look like him at all.'

'It was the dark hair and eyes,' Eileen smiled.

'But they weren't his, I know,' Annie said. 'I think you'd better tell me everything.'

And so Eileen told Annie about her wartime experiences and the young Scots-Canadian pilot she had known for a short time, though long enough to know he was the love of her life, and about finding she was pregnant weeks after he had been shot down and killed over France.

'You'll think I'm a terrible person when you hear the next part,' she said, and then explained about how she had hoodwinked Alex into believing the child – Annie – was his, and how he had believed it because he had been too drunk to know they hadn't slept together.

'Even then it was possible to get rid of a baby,' she said. 'There have been ways, people who knew how to do these things, for as long as mankind has existed, but I wanted Calli's baby, I wanted you, and that was the only way I could manage to have you. In those days it was a great shame to be pregnant if you weren't married, I'd have been no better than a tramp, even in the eyes of my family, and you would have been second class all your life, if that, they wouldn't have wanted to know you, yet it wasn't your fault. Do you see?'

Annie nodded wordlessly.

'As it was, I don't think your father – Alex – could have children, there were no more after you, so I suppose I comforted myself by saying I at least gave him something precious that he wouldn't otherwise have had.'

'But things weren't right between you,' Annie said.

'How do you know that?'

'It was a feeling, I can't explain it, I always felt I had to be on my best behaviour in case something bad happened. There was a feeling of . . .' she stopped and thought, ' . . . of hurt, pain, I suppose. You didn't seem happy, either of you.'

Eileen, standing at the window with her arms wrapped around herself, lowered her head and wept. 'Dear God,' she cried, 'I thought I was giving you a happy family life, but that's not what it was, was it? I'm so sorry.'

Annie got up and hugged her. 'Stop it,' she said softly. 'It wasn't your fault, you did what we all do for our children, your best. And what was the alternative? You gave me Alex, he was a great dad, I just felt he wasn't as good a husband, and you gave Calli a child, you allowed something of him to carry on. You gave me that lovely man in the corner.'

They hugged each other for a long time. 'Do I look like him?' Annie asked.

'Very. So does Gavin. A few months ago they found his plane in Normandy with the remains of the crew inside. The RAF arranged the funerals, that's why I was in France. His family was there, his mother, brothers, the only real father he had ever known as well, and for the first time I understood the terrible thing I had done to them, not letting them know about you and Gavin, and to you, keeping the truth about your past from you.'

'Don't judge yourself so harshly,' Annie chided her gently. 'I think you did a magnificent job, I hope I'd have had the guts to do the same if I'd been in your position.'

'Really?'

'Of course, I think you were so brave, I'm sure Calli thought so, too.'

Eileen blew her nose. 'You know that lock of hair you and Gavin have? He had that, too. And that line between his eyes, and –' she started to cry again.

Annie took her to sit down.

'His family were Scots who'd settled in Nova Scotia, he said they had the Second Sight, though his mother would have none of it. It was so strange seeing them, talking to them, and I knew all about them, but they hadn't a clue. I felt so deceitful.'

'There you go again, it wasn't your fault,' Annie said. 'And you were a WAAF, now there's something, the tales you must have to tell!'

'Besides *that* one?' Eileen asked, trying to laugh.

'So what do we do now?' Annie asked.

'I don't know,' Eileen said wearily. 'I've been thinking of nothing else since I saw them in France.'

'I'd like to meet them. Do you think they'd like to meet me?'

'Oh, I'm sure of it! The difficulty is in knowing how to tell them, when, where, all of that.'

'Let's leave it at that for now, then,' Annie said. 'Let's see what happens, see what presents itself.'

'What about David?'

'Oh, David will be fine with it, Mum, he hardly knew Alex anyway. He'll probably be jealous of my exotic past, though! I've never even told him about the man in the corner, so I don't think I'll tell him about the other stuff yet, don't want to completely freak him out.'

'Other stuff?' Eileen asked. 'Like what?'

'Maybe you'd better sit down, Mum,' Annie smiled, then she told her about Stuart, the little old lady sitting in the house they had viewed and various other odd events in her life.

Eileen was shocked. 'You were seeing all these strange things yet you never once gave any indication to me. Weren't you afraid?'

Annie shook her head. 'It was natural and ordinary to me, so I wasn't afraid. Besides, it had always been there and by the time I understood that other people didn't see the things I saw I knew enough not to mention it. I thought they would treat me differently, think I was peculiar, maybe that was partly why I didn't tell you, that, and because I knew it would cause some sort of upset within the family, and I suppose I knew that if other people would treat me differently, you might, too.'

There was a long silence.

'And you really saw him?' Eileen asked at last. 'Calli was there all those years? You saw him?'

Annie nodded. 'He used to sing to me when I was a baby, too, and one night there was a Gaelic programme on the television and this woman came on singing a lullaby, and I found myself singing along with her, word for word, yet I had no reason to know a Gaelic song. He sang it to me, he sang it to Gavin, too.'

'You can actually see him!' Eileen repeated, incredulously, weeping again. 'What I'd have given to see him!'

'Well I don't see him now, neither does Gavin, that's what the tantrum was about before we picked you up the other day. Looking back he disappeared around the time he was buried in France. Isn't it strange, Mum, that he was there all those years till both sides of his family were brought together again? Isn't that kind of wonderful?'

31

In Canada, Calli's other family were still settling down to the new reality the discovery of the plane had brought about, and the fact that their grief was, inevitably, bringing memories and thoughts to the surface they had forgotten they had. They were having to come to terms with putting Calli in the past. Laid to rest with proper goodbyes was an entirely different story from missing in action, though perhaps only those who had gone through it would have understood. It was final, the end, closure, and though it brought a certain relief, it brought another wave of sorrow as well.

It was the second Monday in October, the traditional Canadian Thanksgiving Day. Over that all-important border to the south, America had their Thanksgiving Day every November to celebrate the safe arrival of the Pilgrims to the New World, but Canada had already been giving thanks forty years before the US, to mark the end of successful harvests. There were creeping influences from America of course, brought over by the loyalists who had fought on the British side during the War of Independence, and pumpkin pie and turkey had gradually been added to the usual waterfowl, goose, ham and venison. The family gathered as usual at Pine Edge, with two more grandchildren that year, as Ceitlin and Young Padraig's wife had both given birth to sons.

'You know,' Feargie said across the table, 'I've been thinking.'

'We've all been doing a lot of that,' Gil smiled quietly, exchanging a look with his wife.

'You remember the letter Calli sent during the war? The one old Dr MacDonald got to us? Well, he said there was no headstone on the graves of Annie and Old Ruairidh, he promised to put that right one day.'

'I remember,' Nancy said.

'What if I arrange to have one put up now?' Feargie asked.

'That would be a lovely gesture!' Nancy replied.

'Well, I can't take credit for it, Mom,' Feargie said quietly. 'It wasn't my idea, it was Calli's, he wanted to do it for Granny Martha, I would only be keeping his promise to her, wouldn't I? And he would've done it, too, if he hadn't, you know.' Despite being a surgeon and therefore not inexperienced in such matters, Feargie was still having a problem describing his brother as dead. 'I'll be going over to a cardiovascular conference in London next spring –'

'Another booze-up,' his mother said, to lighten the atmosphere.

'A meeting of wise men, the leaders in the world of cardiac surgery, Mom –'

'With the minimum of carefully matured Highland spirits being consumed,' Gil remarked seriously, 'and that for medicinal purposes only.'

'Exactly, Gil, precisely. I thought I might get the paperwork done now and travel up to Raasay to see the headstone being put up while I'm there. What do you think?'

'I think it's a splendid idea,' Nancy said thoughtfully. 'Will you be seeing Dr MacDonald's son while you're in Scotland?'

'Young Dr MacDonald will be at the conference as well, as it happens, I've already arranged to travel north and stay a couple of nights with him,' he said. 'I was telling him where that nice woman, Mrs MacLean, lived, and he said her house is only a few hundred yards from his own.'

'Isn't that incredible?' Gil mused. 'The world is a small place indeed.'

'So I thought I might call her, drop in for a chat. Do you think she would mind?'

'No,' said Nancy. 'I don't think she'd mind at all. She was such a nice woman, I think she'd be happy to see you.'

*   *   *

It was the end of April the following year when Feargie made it to Glasgow and called Eileen. He would be travelling to Raasay on family business, he said, and if it was all right with her he would pay her a visit before he went back to Canada.

When she put the phone down Eileen remembered what Annie had said the previous year. 'Let's see what happens,' she had said when they had discussed contacting Calli's family, 'see what presents itself,' and now something had.

She had no idea what would happen, how to tell Feargie – or even whether to tell him – about Annie, so she arranged to see him alone in her flat in the Kirklee house, and for Annie to join them later, then, as Annie had said, they would 'see what presents itself'.

A few days later Feargie arrived, he was staying with a friend, the son of the old Dr MacDonald he had mentioned in France.

'Does he live nearby?' Eileen asked.

'I think you can see the road from here,' Feargie laughed, 'Redlands Road? My brother stayed there over one Christmas and New Year.'

Eileen held her breath; to think that all those years she had been living yards from where Calli had stayed. He hadn't been sure of which part of Glasgow he had been in, it was a big, grey, wartime city when he had visited. The fact that old Dr MacDonald had lived within a short distance of the Western Infirmary wasn't in itself significant, most of the medical staff tended to stay nearby, but the thought of Calli having been there brought him that bit closer somehow.

'His son lives there with his family now,' Feargie said, 'and he does know your son-in-law. We seem to be connected in all sorts of ways, Eileen.'

Eileen didn't reply, she just sipped her coffee and raised her eyebrows slightly. Then there was a tap at the door. 'That'll be my daughter, Annie,' Eileen said, and Annie came in holding Gavin by the hand.

Feargie stood up, smiling, ready to shake hands, then the smile froze as his hand got no further than half-lifted, and he stared at Eileen's daughter and grandson.

Annie held her hand out, but Feargie was still staring at her, so she laughed uncertainly and looked at her mother, as Gavin returned Feargie's gaze, the toy plane from his grandmother in his hand.

Feargie sat down, looked away, then looked back at them again. 'I've just had the strangest feeling,' he said, in a distant voice, looking away again. 'In fact I'm still having it.'

'Is there something wrong?' Eileen asked, and out of the corner of her eye she saw Annie cover her mouth and laugh. 'What is it?' she whispered to her daughter. 'Why are you laughing?'

Annie shook her head, still laughing.

'I've got a plane,' Gavin said, walking over to where Feargie sat. 'I'll let you look at it, but I don't want you to break it, OK?'

'OK,' Feargie replied. 'Is it a special plane?'

'All of his planes are special planes,' Annie said, 'or to put it another way, all planes are special to Gavin.'

'I used to know a boy who thought exactly the same way,' Feargie said, staring at her again. 'Forgive me, but when you came in you reminded me so much of someone else.'

Eileen and Annie exchanged glances.

'You see, I was the younger of two brothers, and the first memories I have of my mother and my brother are of seeing them just as I saw you and your son just now. It was like *déjà vu*.'

Annie smiled, feeling shy at being under such searching scrutiny.

'You really are incredibly like my mother at your age,' he said, 'and Gavin is so like Calli,' he shook his head and turned away again, tears in his eyes; he seemed unable to stop looking at them, but the memories they brought back were so intense that he had to look away again.

'Feargie,' Eileen said gently, 'there's something I didn't tell you when we met in France last year, I wasn't sure if I should, and anyway, I had to tell Annie first. Annie is Calli's daughter. I didn't tell her that till I came home from France.'

'Why is the man crying?' Gavin asked, leaning in all directions to get a better view of Feargie. 'Is it because he can't play with my plane?'

'Something like that,' his mother said gently, scooping him up. 'Look, Granny Eileen has got your favourite cakes,' she said brightly, 'and juice, too!'

Gavin was still watching Feargie. 'OK,' he said resignedly, holding out the plane, 'you can hold it, but be careful.'

He put the toy into Feargie's hands before turning his attention to the cakes and juice.

Annie shook her head as he settled down on the floor. 'Tunnock's tea cakes,' she said, watching Gavin employ his favourite way of attacking the one in his hand: tongue straight through the chocolate into the marshmallow. 'They're a great delicacy here, Dr MacDonald, God knows what they do to his teeth, but grandmothers don't seem to mind these things, only mothers.'

'I think you'd better call me Feargie, don't you?' he said.

So Eileen told him the story, and she grew in Feargie's estimation as he listened.

'I'm not proud of letting my husband think Annie was his, but there was no way out, I had to provide her with a father after Calli was lost.'

'I've told her she did the right thing,' Annie sighed, 'the only thing. Don't you agree, Feargie?'

He nodded. 'I wish we had known sooner, though,' he said sadly.

'Well, I couldn't have told your family while my husband was still alive, and to be honest, I didn't fully understand what I'd done till I saw you all in France,' Eileen explained.

'Yes, I see that,' Feargie replied, 'and I'm not criticising you, Eileen, it's just one of those sadnesses.' He looked at Annie again.

'I'm sorry,' he said, 'I can't help it, I can't stop looking at you, and at Gavin.'

They all looked at Gavin, who in turn looked at them, his face now covered in chocolate, and they laughed together.

'I don't know if Calli told you,' Feargie said, 'but there's this thing called the Second Sight in the family.'

Eileen nodded. 'That your mother won't hear mentioned,' she laughed.

'Well, she wouldn't, but she's always said that she felt Calli wasn't entirely gone, it's something that's bothered her all these years. Something about the branch of a tree, or perhaps that was my grandmother's saying, she used to tell me and Calli these strange tales when we were young and make us promise not to tell our mom.'

Annie didn't reply. This event was enough, there would be time to compare notes about trees and to tell Calli's family about the man in the corner.

Eileen, Annie, Gavin and Feargie flew to Canada in mid-May. Pine Edge and the house on Calli's Hill could wait for now, the only place to be at that time of year was Cape Breton. The family were already at Mull River in Mabou, when Feargie called his mother and told her he had one or two surprises for her.

'Don't get your hopes up,' Young Padraig had teased Nancy, 'it's probably a haggis, or whatever the plural is.'

'If it is, you're eating it!' Nancy replied. 'I'm not your grand-mother, I don't think *everything* that comes from Scotland is golden!'

'Or maybe the surprise is just that he got on and off a plane without hyperventilating,' Young Padraig tried again, laughing at his brother's fear of flying.

'It's likely that he's brought photos of the headstone in Raasay,' Gil said reasonably, 'and maybe a little something from the Duty Free shop for an ageing relative as well.'

'Something medicinal, Pop,' his son suggested, nodding his head.

'Exactly,' Gil said seriously. 'That's what I was thinking of.'

As the car drew nearer to Mull River, Eileen asked Feargie to stop. The blossoms were everywhere in the place Calli regarded as home, it was just as he had described it. 'I'll take you to Cape Breton in May or June,' he had said all those years ago, 'when the blossoms from the fruit trees fall as heavily as the snow in winter, and as gently, too, and the breeze smells sweeter than any perfume.'

'I don't think I've ever seen anything so beautiful. Isn't that a wonderful smell?' Annie said. 'Gavin would pick now to sleep, he's missing it.'

'It'll still be here when he wakes,' Feargie replied. 'It lasts through June. But don't think it's always like this. The flies will be here in June, too.'

'Yes, I know,' Eileen replied, looking at him and smiling, 'but they'll be gone again by August.'

Then they climbed back into the car and started the last part of the journey towards Mull River, where Nancy was waiting for her surprises.

Acknowledgements

I always find acknowledgements difficult because in the course of writing a book there are few people I leave unquestioned. Mainly, though, I have to thank my son, Euan, for the unending patience with which he shared his knowledge of all things military, especially the RAF. It was his interest and enthusiasm that took the family to Normandy some years ago, where the seeds of this book first took root. Then there are easy ones are those like Jim St Clair, of Cape Breton. On the back of one of his books it says of him: 'James St Clair of Mull River, Mabou, resides on the MacFarlane property settled by his great-great grandparents in 1820. A genealogist and a freelance broadcaster with CBC, Jim is an architectural enthusiast and is the Nova Scotia member on the board of the Society for the Study of Architecture in Canada. A graduate of Harvard University, he is Assistant Professor in the School of Applied Arts and Development Studies, University College of Cape Breton.' More than that, though, he has proved to be a generous and enthusiastic friend throughout, giving his time and knowledge freely and allowing me to use his family's experiences as a loose pattern for the main family in the book, indeed the family home in the book and on the cover is his home. His knowledge of Cape Breton and its history are endless and I can honestly say that without Jim this book would never have been written. Likewise everyone at the Highland Village Museum in Nova Scotia, especially Director Rodney Chaisson and Genealogist Pauline MacLean, for their unstinting help in finding answers to various questions sprung on them out of the blue.

*   *   *

Gratitude, too, to my friends and fellow authors, Alanna Knight, for sharing her experiences of the second sight, and Angus Calder, who always allows his brains to be picked, even though he argues a lot; Lee Heide, a Vancouver boy who joined the RCAF and was awarded the DFC, and who showed possibly more bravery as well as generosity by allowing me to make any use I wanted of his early war years with Coastal Command, as recounted in his memoir *Whispering Death*. I also thank Patricia Grimshaw, Assistant Historian at the Canadian War Museum in Ottawa, for her help with the details of the Canadian Forces in WWI. Without her I wouldn't have been able to follow the movements of the Canadians or understood their massive contribution to both wars. I have had an affection for Canada long before visits there confirmed it, based solely on stories I heard from my mother, whose favourite uncle, George Johnstone, emigrated and became a Mountie. He came back to visit his family when my mother was a child, and as she recounted the tale I saw him in my mind wearing his red tunic and Smokey-the-Bear hat, riding a splendid steed through the streets and right up the stairs of a Glasgow tenement; it never occurred to me that a Mountie would arrive in any other fashion. So Canada has always had a special place in my affections, but it wasn't till I visited the Museum to Peace, in Caen, Normandy that I began to understand the Canadian contribution to both World Wars. Most UK history books barely mention the Canadians, an honourable exception being Lyn MacDonald's meticulous and moving collections of oral histories. Acknowledgement of their part is long overdue and the more I learned of what they had done the more respect was added to my affection for Canada.

Next up is my good friend Norma MacLeod, a genealogist on the Isle of Skye, who has written a book on the history of the Isle of Raasay which for some reason I decided to make my starting point. Norma's knowledge of Raasay is very detailed and she has kept me right throughout, as well as indulging in some mutually enjoyable gossip. Thanks, too, to Sarah Gerrish of the National Museum of Scotland for advising me on antique furniture restoration; Florence Mahoney and the women of the WAAF Association; the Air Historical Branch (RAF) of the Ministry of Defence, especially Sue Rattray, for explaining the details of her work; Frank Potts and the Campbellford Seymour Heritage Society; Frank Haslam and the Squadron 207 Association, and all the friends and relatives who were misguided enough to mention interesting anecdotes they had picked up and were sent forth to seek out the full story, even those who were ungracious enough to protest that they were being used as unpaid dogsbodies, and they all know who they are. Happily, though, they never learn.

Lastly I have to thank my husband, Rab, for once again enduring the obsession with good grace and boundless patience.

The details of the last mission of Lancaster Bomber Mark 1, serial number ED498 EM–O, which I've recreated in the book, are all true. The crew were:

155212 Pilot Officer Robert George Pearcey (23) – Pilot.

1212445 Sergeant John Charles Cunningham (21) – Flt Engineer

132802 Flying Officer George Blakeman – Navigator

1397951 Sergeant James Stanley White (21) – Air Bomber

1035586 Sergeant Jack Kirkman (21) – Wireless Op/Air Gunner

1586239 Sergeant Robert Wilcockson (23) – Mid Upper Gunner

R.172270 Sergeant Harry Clement RCAF (21) – Rear Gunner

The plane crashed at Beuzeval (Calvados), 1 km east of Houlgate in Normandy, France, on the night of 15/16 August 1943. F/O Blakeman was the only survivor and was taken, badly injured, to

Stalag Luft 3, in Sagan & Belaria, where his POW number was 2257. He remained there until the end of the war and, with the Russian guns sounding in the distance, the POWs were told by their German guards that they would soon be free. Hitler then intervened, ordering that they should be marched through snow three feet deep to keep them out of Russian hands. Evetually the Russians caught up, and instead of freedom the POWs were held captive for a further 6 weeks while their new captors negotiated the return of the Cossacks, who did not want to go. Eventually one set of POWs was put on a pontoon in the river Elba, the Cossacks on another and they were pulled in different directions. George stayed in the RAF after the war and was sent to Cyprus to sort out administrative chaos in Nicosia, for which he was awarded the OBE and retired as a Wing Commander. Thoughts of the crew of his Lanc, buried in Houlgate Communal Cemetery, have remained with him, and he confesses to 'feeling guilty every day of my life. Why did I survive? Why me?' The lack of recognition accorded to the boys – and they were boys – of Bomber Command, and to Bomber Harris, still saddens him. 'Even now they would rather we shut up,' he says.

Coming upon the graves of his crew mates some years ago was the start of this book. Everyone says, 'They were so young,' but it's not till you stand by their graves, especially with a son of a similar age, that you understand just how young. They deserve more than flowers, but it's all we can do, apart from remembering them and all the others with respect and gratitude. So though this book is dedicated to my son and his wife on their wedding day, I hope there's enough left over to pay tribute to Wing Commander George Blakeman OBE, his crew mates and all the boys in Bomber Command.

SOURCES

Raasay, the island and its people, Norma MacLeod. (Birlinn Ltd, 2002)

They Called it Passchendaele, Lyn MacDonald. (Michael Joseph, 1978, Penguin, 1993)

No Place Like Home, Mary K. MacLeod and James O. St Clair. (University College of Cape Breton Press, 1992)

Whispering Death, Lee Heide. (Trafford Publishing)

www.rafinfo.org.uk

Meg Henderson

The Holy City

'*The Holy City* is a novel about growing up in the close-knit blue-collar community of Clydeside from the Twenties through to the present day, as seen through the eyes of Marion Katie MacLeod. Meg Henderson has pieced together an enormous jigsaw of memories to create a vision reminiscent of a Stanley Spencer painting. The overall effect is of being at your auntie's, of listening to an enthusiastic storyteller, of the fascination of taking a microscope to seemingly ordinary lives, seemingly mundane situations and bringing them into dramatic focus.'   *Scotland on Sunday*

'An enchanting tale of a remarkable woman from Clydebank, whose sometimes heartbreaking, sometimes hilarious but always mesmerising memories of the wartime blitz on her beloved town stay sharp half a century later, giving her the strength and the courage to meet everything that life throws at her.'   *Scotsman*

'This marvellous debut is packed with characters whose grittiness and passion transcends poverty and tragedy.'   *Options*

'A hugely absorbing story. Henderson brings the horror and pain of these wartime experiences vividly to life with vigorous humour, common-sense wisdom and vitality.'   *Observer*